KILLERS AND VICTIMS

The albino—A powerful and vengeful man from the East who unleashes a high-tech nightmare across America.

The protector—He travels to the Amazon to help a tribe being inexplicably slaughtered. Now, mankind's most potent killers stalk him.

The Legion—Some will kill now, some will kill late, and when they are finished with America, it will be theirs. . . .

THE OMICRON LEGION

An explosive novel of international terror by the bestselling author of THE VALHALLA TESTAMENT, THE EIGHTH TRUMPET, THE ALPHA DECEPTION, and THE GAMMA OPTION.

THE
OMICRON
LEGION

Jon Land

FAWCETT GOLD MEDAL • NEW YORK

A Fawcett Gold Medal Book
Published by Ballantine Books
Copyright © 1991 by Jon Land

Library of Congress Catalog Card Number: 91-91823

ISBN 0-449-14635-9

Manufactured in the United States of America

First Edition: June 1991

ACKNOWLEDGMENTS

In many ways this is the most important page of the book, because the people mentioned upon it affect so many other pages. As always, a special thanks to those who have appeared here before. Also as always, any mistakes contained on the pages following are mine, not theirs.

First and foremost is Toni Mendez, whose genius as an agent is exceeded only by her brilliance as a human being in times both good and bad. Ann Maurer continues to amaze me with her knack for making my words better. If there's a better editor in the business than Daniel Zitin, I haven't met him. And the whole Fawcett family, especially Leona Nevler, Clare Ferraro, and Susan Petersen, have never stopped believing in me as a person as well as an author.

Emery Pineo continues his streak; he has never failed to solve a technological problem for me. Morty Korn, meanwhile, remains the only person to have read all my works in early drafts that I would never have shared with another soul. Tony Sheppard has also bravely struggled through my first drafts.

Special thanks to Walt Mattison, the real Blaine McCracken and newest member of the team that helps put all the pieces together. This will be the first of many appearances on this page for him.

Thanks again to Marc Levine for his help with Boston geography, to David Schecter for probing the manuscript for potential legal concerns, to Jim Bilopeau for help with Japanese terminology, to Richard Levy of Corporate Air Newport for assistance in all matters pertaining to aviation, and to Chuck Flanagan for introducing me to the world of firefighting. My appreciation also goes to Lee Ann Sink for her help with Newport News and to the warm staff of Colonial Williamsburg.

Finally, my most special acknowledgment to my guides Geldo Laffront and Luis Antonio Nunes Pereira for showing me the real Rio De Janeiro.

PROLOGUE

"Do you accept death?''

Escerbio gazed at the cup of liquid steaming beneath his nose and nodded.

"For those not worthy of manhood, this cup brings the bitterness of death,'' continued the tribal Gift Giver. "Do you still wish to taste?''

Escerbio nodded. Across from him, on the other side of the fire, another boy also nodded.

"Then let us hope the gods are with you,'' said the Gift Giver. He handed the wooden mug to Escerbio's friend first.

Escerbio watched Javerrera raise the mug to his lips and gulp down some of the liquid. The boy's face wrinkled and grew pale. Now the Gift Giver offered the cup to Escerbio. He was an ancient man who had somehow tricked the spirits into letting him see a third century of life. His face was creased and worn, like a battered hide barren of oil. The smell of his breath was rancid and bitter, not unlike the noxious liquid Escerbio now accepted from his hand.

Across the fire, Javerrera's head was rolling from side to side. His eye sockets had emptied. Escerbio drained the rest of the liquid, and the cup dropped from his hand. He gagged, and it was all he could do to force down the bile that rushed up into his throat. A fire blazed in his stomach. He seemed to have forgotten how to breathe.

Escerbio had always feared the darkness. As a younger boy,

he had trembled through many sleepless nights in his hut. But he did not fear this night. He welcomed it because tonight he would become a man. In the Tupi tribe, the fourteenth birthday marked the beginning of manhood, and midnight would bring that blessed time upon him. That moment would see all his boyish fears and uncertainties vanish in the haze of the mysterious ceremony conducted by the tribal Gift Giver.

Escerbio tried to open his eyes, then realized they were already open. The Gift Giver had tossed the wooden mug in the fire, where the flames accepted it with a burst of white that cast a youthful glow upon his ancient face. It looked to Escerbio as if the old man had received the fire into his being. The warmth had spread through Escerbio's body, and he realized he was trembling, though not from fear. He felt extraordinarily relaxed and full. Deep within him the strange liquid was burning away the last of his boyhood.

The Gift Giver was announcing that the time had come for the spirits to be summoned. They would decide if the boys were worthy. If not, the boys would die.

The Gift Giver was moving in a circle around the boys, his pace becoming more and more frantic. Escerbio grew dizzy trying to watch him. The old man was chanting in the language of the Forgotten Times, calling upon the spirits to rise and make their choice.

Across the fire, Javerrera's frame had gone totally limp. If not for the darting of his friend's eyes, Escerbio would have been sure he had failed the test and was dead.

"Assah matay toato," the Gift Giver chanted. *"Assah semblah oh santaytah. Oh santaytah tas!"*

The breeze shifted suddenly, blowing Escerbio's long hair wildly about his head. The fire surged toward him and he closed his eyes against the certainty that its fierce tongues would singe his flesh. He could smell his own fear and he willed it gone, along with the last of his boyhood.

Be gone . . . Be gone . . .

Escerbio opened his eyes.

The Gift Giver was standing behind Javerrera now and chanting. His age-ravaged hands circled about the boy's head.

"Assah matay toato. Assah semblah oh santaytah. Oh santaytah tas!"

Behind the Gift Giver and Javerrera, a figure rose from the shadows of the night. Escerbio could distinguish only its huge outline against the blackness of the trees, but that was enough.

The spirits have heard the Gift Giver and have come! he thought excitedly. *They have truly come!*

The spirit descended on the Gift Giver. Escerbio fought through the blurriness of his vision to watch.

He saw the Gift Giver's head swallowed by what looked like spade-claw hands.

He saw the old man's legs dangling in midair as he was hoisted upward.

He heard something rip.

Embers danced from the fire as something dropped into it. Escerbio gazed into the flames.

The Gift Giver's head gazed back.

Escerbio could see that Javerrera was now in the grip of the spirit. *Stop!* he wanted to scream out. *Stop!* But his breath caught in his throat. He could form no words. He realized Javerrera was screaming. There was a squishing sound and Escerbio was showered by his best friend's blood. It streamed over him, and in the next instant he was running.

He understood that he had failed both himself and his tribe. He was unworthy because of his fear, and this was his punishment.

Escerbio ran faster. The jungle was a single dark splotch before him. He did not look back. He simply charged through the night, vaguely aware of his flesh being scraped and torn by the tree branches. Whimpering, he stumbled and fell, then dragged himself over the underbrush until he came to a tree. Leaning on it, he regained his feet. Escerbio was sobbing now. The night owned him.

"Help me! Somebody help me!" he screamed as he rushed forward again. He ventured a glance over his shoulder to see if the vengeful spirit was chasing him, but there were only the tangled branches of the thick undergrowth and the blackness of the night. Escerbio hurtled forward.

He saw the spirit too late to turn. He started to scream when the spirit drove its spade-claw into him, shredding his abdomen. Strangely he felt no pain, even when the spirit lifted him upward. Escerbio knew his body was now far off the ground.

He could feel his legs twitching in the air. His bowels and bladder drained. He looked into the eyes of the spirit and the darkness that had betrayed him for the last time looked back.

Then there was nothing.

PART ONE

The Heart of Darkness

**Fairfax, Virginia:
Monday, November 18, 1991; 10:00 P.M.**

CHAPTER 1

BAILEY was waiting when the limousine slid around the circular drive in front of the large house in Fairfax, Virginia.

"Good evening, ma'am," he said as he opened its right rear door.

The woman slid out, high heels first, her long legs and hips clad in tight-fitting black pants. "My, you're a polite one now, aren't you?"

Bailey squinted at her. "I don't believe I've seen you here before."

"Special order, lover. What the general wants, the general gets."

Bailey stiffened. "You've been briefed, I assume."

"This one'll go in the *Guiness Book*."

"Come this way," Bailey said, not bothering to hide the reluctance in his voice. He hated these nocturnal binges the general insisted he needed to maintain his sanity. He hated them, but never breathed a word of his contempt to the general. God, he revered the man, *loved* him. After all the general had been through in Nam, and with the tremendous responsibility he bore today, he deserved to indulge whatever idiosyncrasies he might have, no matter what anyone else thought.

Bailey had been there when the general had walked out of the jungle after escaping from a Charlie POW camp. He had served the general as he became one of the most powerful men in the Pentagon. Bailey held the rank of major, but he wore his uniform very infrequently these days, as did the general.

Bailey led the woman through the foyer and up the staircase that circled toward the second floor. She walked behind him, but Bailey was careful to keep her in his peripheral vision. He'd been a Green Beret long before shedding his uniform, and some things stuck.

On the second floor he stopped at the third closed door they came to. "This room leads directly into the study. The door is on the left side."

The woman winked at him. "Like I told you, I've been briefed, lover."

"I'll be outside the whole time."

"That's up to you."

"When he's finished with you, you will leave straightaway."

"Just the way I like it," the woman said, and disappeared into the room adjoining the study.

Bailey assumed the stance of his silent vigil, regretting he could not move far enough from the study to obliterate the sounds that would soon be emanating from within.

Inside, General Berlin Hardesty sat eagerly in his leather chair, two yards away from a thirty-five-inch television. He heard the woman in the adjoining room and raised the remote control device that lay upon the chair's arm. He knew the placement of buttons by heart, and went through the proper sequence without even glancing down. The first button turned the room to black, the second lit it a dull gray from the blank picture on the television. A third sent an unseen VCR whirling and brought the screen to life.

For all the technical wizardry, the quality of the television picture was notably poor. Grainy and hollow, too much contrast. The picture focused on a young woman lying naked on a bed of crimson sheets masturbating feverishly. The camera drew shakily closer to her, locked on her face.

The woman was Vietnamese.

General Berlin Hardesty's fists clenched briefly, then he groped for the pair of small headphones perched upon the other chair arm and fitted them over his ears. The sounds of her moaning filled his ears. Hardesty smiled in anticipation of what was to come.

Seconds later a pair of masked figures strode into the shot. Surprise filled the woman's face. They dragged her from the bed, where the camera followed them to a chair. The men thrust her naked form into the chair and strapped her arms and legs to it. The woman was still struggling. Her protests filled the general's ears through his headphones. The camera zoomed in on one of the masked figures whipping forth a knife, then panned to the bulging eyes of the woman who suddenly froze. Her screams must have been too much for the microphone because they dissolved into static at their crescendo.

The general's thoughts burned with visions of the past, of being tortured by the Vietcong during his six months as a POW. When he had at last escaped and emerged from the jungle, the memories of the pain had proven to be as real as the pain itself. Psychiatrists said he had to put it out of his head, to displace it on to something else. How right they were. The pain of others proved the only way to vanquish his own. And the pain of a Vietnamese—well, that transformed relief into ecstasy.

On the screen, the masked man sliced off the woman's right nipple. The sounds of her agony drove Hardesty to moan with pleasure. As if on cue, the door from the room adjoining the study opened, and the nude form of the woman emerged. She glided toward him, her path illuminated by the dull haze of the television. She took her position in front of the general and crouched down. The picture's dull light splotched over her as she slid her fingers over Hardesty's crotch and found his zipper. His hands were working through her dark hair now. He could not say whether she was Vietnamese or not. Close enough, though.

On the big screen, the woman strained agonizingly against her bonds as her left nipple was severed.

Hardesty gasped as the woman took him in her mouth. On-screen the masked figure drew the girl's head back to expose her throat. Blood slid down from the right corner of her mouth. Terror and pain had silenced her rage, but her whimpers were delicious in the general's ears. The camera drew in to capture her pleading face, then pulled back to include the knife poised for its next thrust. Hardesty's hands dug into the head sliding back and forth over his groin.

Mira drew her hands upward, smiling to herself. Men were weak creatures, truly weak, so vulnerable to pleasure, so lost in it. This was the first of her allotted victims. How fitting that the kill would allow her to make use of the most special skills she had developed over the years.

And the special weapon.

She had gotten the idea watching a television commercial for artificial fingernails. A bit of glue, press on, and voila! Mira made her own, frosted the tips with melted steel, let them harden, and then filed them razor sharp. A glancing twitch to any major artery was all it would take.

Mira waited. She could follow the action on the screen from the general's responses. She knew his moment would mirror that of the blade being drawn across the throat of the Vietnamese girl.

It was all Mira could do to keep from laughing as her fingers of death crawled up his chest.

Hardesty watched the steel blade touch the throat of the woman on the screen. In his ears her final pleas emerged weakly, hopelessly, in that bastard language. Her breath would be rank with their awful food. Her skin and hair would smell of the oils of that filthy country.

Just like the guards. *Just like the guards!*

The general saw the knife begin its arc, saw the spurt of blood leap toward the camera. The woman's gasp filled his ears. His pleasure in that instant was so great that he felt only a slight twinge at his throat. In the next instant the screen was splattered with his blood, seeming to mix with the blood of the dying woman. Hardesty's last thought was to free the air bottlenecked in his throat. He realized the gurgle in his ears was his own, since the Vietnamese girl was silent. She stared blankly at him, just as he stared at her. Soon his corpse was lit only by the pulsing glow off the television screen, which had turned to static with the end of the tape.

Bailey didn't enter the study until he was sure he heard the sound of static. His key slid the deadbolt aside, and he opened the door and burst in. What he saw shocked and numbed him.

The general was sitting in his chair, blood pouring down his chest from the neat tear in his throat. His dead eyes bulged open. Bailey saw the open window. His soldier's mind took it all in, prioritized his actions. Using the phone on the general's desk was the first order of business. The woman was gone; she could only be found by marshaling forces that would lead to embarrassment and disgrace. The number he dialed had nothing to do with alerting them.

"Disposal unit required," he said. Coolly he provided the general's address.

"My God," he heard the voice mutter. "How many?"

"One."

"Stay on scene. Thirty-minute arrival time."

Click.

Bailey pressed the button only long enough to get a fresh dial tone. Things would get cleaned up; the general's good name and reputation would be preserved through it all. But the complications created by his passing could not be denied or ignored. Bailey knew what he had to do next. He calmly punched out another number.

"Section Twelve," a voice said.

"I need Baxter."

"One moment . . ."

"Baxter here."

"Do you know my voice?"

"Yes."

"I'm with the general. We're running at Code Seven."

"Oh . . . *Christ*!"

"Listen to me. You know what has to be done. Shred Omicron. Every file, every paper. It never existed. You hearing me?"

"Yes, sir."

"Then get to it, son . . . And don't fuck up!"

CHAPTER 2

CARLOS Salomao leaned across the table. His eyes darted around the restaurant as he spoke again in a hushed voice.

"You must understand, *Senhor* McCracken. They would kill me if they knew I was meeting with you."

Blaine McCracken leaned across the table also, his arms nearly resting against those of the Brazilian. "Just who *are* they, Carlos? You haven't told me that yet, either."

"*Nao sei, senhor.* I don't know . . . at least not for sure. It would be best if we start from the beginning."

"That means with Johnny. I want to know where the hell they've got him stashed."

"Please *senhor*. I must tell it my way."

Blaine shrugged and pulled back. "*Muito bem.* As long as you tell me first where I can find Johnny Wareagle."

Carlos Salomao's eyes continued to scan the nearly empty restaurant. Every time the door opened, his shoulders tensed and his spine arched. Meeting in downtown São Paulo had been his idea. McCracken had expected him to choose a spot where he felt more at ease. Unless there wasn't one.

"He is being held at a jail outside the city. We call it *Casa do Diabo.*"

"The house of the devil?"

"Many years ago prisoners were tortured within its walls. It is just a jail now, though fear of it still discourages crime."

"If anything bad's happened to Johnny, I'll teach the jailers plenty about fear."

McCracken had flown into Cumbica Airport some two hours before, after a flight lasting more than half a day. He had returned from London to Maine early Thursday. His Thanksgiving at home was uneasy, with Johnny Wareagle nowhere to be found. The call from Carlos had come yesterday evening, Friday, with a shadowy explanation as to why the Indian hadn't been around as planned. Blaine had been able to make a Varig flight out of Kennedy Airport with a single stop in Miami. But if one hadn't been available, he had been fully prepared to charter a jet to make the trip.

Carlos Salomao did his best to look Blaine in the eye, but his eyes kept drifting—first to the unsightly scar running through McCracken's left eyebrow, then back in the direction of the front door.

"*Senhor* McCracken, your friend is in jail because Brazilian customs officials denied him entry into the country. He lacked a visa. They had no choice, but he took exception to their denial."

"By exception, you mean . . . ?"

"Several of the police officers attempted to restrain him. He injured a number of them."

"Which doesn't tell me what he was doing down here in the first place."

"I sent for him, *senhor*, just like I sent for you."

"*You* sent for him? Just who the hell are you, Carlos?"

Salomao tried to smile and failed. "I am many things, much like you."

"What do you know about me?"

Salomao looked confident for the first time. "Before Vietnam or after?"

"Let's try after."

"Let's see . . . You spent the rest of 1972 in Japan and then joined the CIA. You led the covert U.S. assistance effort for Israel during the October Yom Kippur War of 1973, then remained in Israel until the early part of 1974. From there, you took part in activities in South America, Africa, Germany, and Italy. You were suspended from active duty following an incident of gross insubordination in London, 1980."

"Like to hear about it, Carlos? British feet dragging cost a plane load of people their lives. I decided to voice my displeasure by shooting the groin area of Churchill's Statue in Parliament Square. Won me the nickname 'McCrackonballs'."

"*Senhor*, I—"

"And yours are next on my hit list—unless you tell me how you happened to come by some supposedly classified information."

"I am in the information business, *senhor*. It is how I found your friend."

"Found him for who?"

"I am part Tupi Indian, *senhor*. I was born in the Amazon Basin. I left, but my roots remain strong." Salomao's lips quivered. "Just over a month ago, three members of my tribe vanished in the woods. Since then, the killings have continued. No matter what steps they take, no matter what defenses they erect, some nights one or two of my people disappear. Sometimes hunters go out during the day and never return. When they are found—what is left of them, that is—it is terrible, *senhor*. They believe a demon has risen from the underworld to punish them, a demon they call *Ananga Teide*, the Spirit of the Dead. They asked for help, but only a special person from outside the tribe would be trusted."

"Johnny Wareagle . . ."

Salomao nodded. "They accepted him as the living incarnation of Tupan, the Tupi god. He came down here to help, but he never got the chance to try. Now he is in *Casa do Diabo*—and there he will remain for a considerable time . . . without your help."

"And how do you expect me to bring this off?"

"With your influence perhaps. And if that falls short . . ." Salomao's shrug completed his thought.

"Yeah, bust him out so he can go up to the Amazon and finish what you called him down here to do. Thing is, I know he never would have told you or anyone else about me."

"*Nao*. I was able to get a look at his passport. Your name was listed as next of kin."

Blaine smiled in spite of himself. "Close enough."

"I am responsible for this, *senhor*. It is a wrong I must right."

"Bullshit, Carlos. If you knew Johnny Wareagle at all, you'd know that he's not about to walk away from an unfinished job. He'll head straight for your Tupi tribe even if he has to plow through the whole Brazilian militia en route. And since you're so up on my file, you know that I'll be with him."

Salomao didn't bother denying it. "What I don't know, *senhor*, is whether the two of you will be enough."

Sao Paulo is a thriving, bustling metropolis, the center of Brazil's banking and commerce. By far the largest and most modern city in South America, it seems a combination of the pace of New York and the expanse of Los Angeles. Skyscrapers dominate the horizon in jagged concrete clusters, while below, the din of screeching brakes and honking horns are common sounds within the ever-present snarl of traffic.

Because of this traffic, the drive from the airport had taken an interminable sixty-five minutes. But the traffic was lighter leaving the city; eventually giving way to a freshly paved four-lane divided highway leading north to Atibaia. As the miles sped by, the modern look of the city gave way to simpler and more rural forms of construction. Whitewashed stone and terra-cotta replaced steel and glass as the dominant building base.

The jail Johnny Wareagle was being held in, on the outskirts of Atibaia, was rectangular in structure and three stories high. The building had the look of an old fort, except for the chain-link fence topped with barbed wire that enclosed it and the blacktop parking lot within. Blaine's papers were found to be all in order and, after a casual frisk revealed him weaponless, he was escorted down a long corridor. The walls smelled of must, mold, and age. McCracken figured the mere running of his finger across them would cause the years to peel back, layer by layer. He felt his nostrils clog with the dust filling the air and noticed that the loose-grouted floor tiles were producing a rattling echo underfoot. His escort opened the door to a small windowless room and told Blaine to enter.

McCracken did as he was told, but elected not to take one of the two chairs at a thick wood table. Except for these, the claustrophobic cubicle was barren.

Christ, Johnny. What the hell happened?

It made no sense, none of it. Johnny Wareagle was the most rational man Blaine had ever known, and their friendship stretched back over twenty years. Always, though, it was Blaine coming to Johnny, his mystical Indian friend, for help.

Until today. The tables had turned now. It was Wareagle who needed help, and Blaine was here to provide it.

He heard the already familiar rattling echo and turned back toward the door. As the rattling grew closer, a second sound joined it—that of clanging metal. Its origin was obvious even before the door was thrust open to reveal Wareagle, his wrists and legs chained in irons. He had to duck his seven-foot frame to make it under the doorway. The pair of accompanying guards shoved the big Indian inside and closed the door behind him.

"Hello, Blainey."

"Hello, Indian. Nice digs you got here."

McCracken's humor seldom gained any reaction from Wareagle, and today was no exception.

"I'm sorry you were bothered," the Indian apologized as he bowed his coal-black ponytailed head. "It was not my choice."

"I'm here, Indian. Now tell me, what gives?"

"What did the little man tell you?"

"That he asked you to come down to Brazil to help out some Indians. That you landed here after busting up some Brazilian authorities who didn't welcome you into the country with open arms. Accurate?"

"More or less."

"Which?"

Wareagle gazed down at him, the stare unlike any Blaine had seen from him before.

"He should not have involved you, Blainey."

"Too late. I'm here." McCracken pulled back one of the wobbly chairs. "Let's sit down."

Wareagle obliged, settling himself uneasily in the chair that was much too small for him. Its legs creaked from the strain.

"You're in a hell of a mess, Indian. Two of the cops you put in the hospital are gonna be there for a while. Not like a man of your experience to lose control."

Wareagle hesitated. "I have never experienced anything like that which drew me down here."

"Carlos drew you down here—and the biggest mistake you made was not calling me before you left."

"You were in England. I did not think it fair to disturb you."

"My holiday could have been postponed."

Johnny looked at him somberly. "I needed to come alone."

"I missed you Thanksgiving, Indian. I'm not much good in the kitchen," Blaine said, instantly aware that his attempt at humor had failed again.

"Please, Blainey. Do not look for that which is too far out of your line of sight. I am a warrior. In my veins flows the blood of others who shed it fighting for who they were. The spirits counsel that we only die when we fail to live true to the legacy of that life force. After the hellfire, I died and the blood ran cold in me. But then you breathed new life into me that winter night and reminded me of my true heritage. There was so much I had to make up for. Years, Blainey. Years where I forsook the very creed that made me. This is my chance to atone, to push the blood of my ancestors through veins that beg for it. For them. For me."

"You're speaking about now, Indian?"

"My work is not nearly finished."

"Not a lot you can get done behind bars."

"I will find my way out in time."

"Not without help, you won't."

"This is not your fight, Blainey."

"Sure, and the dozen or so I've involved you in weren't yours, either. Look, Johnny. I might not be able to hear those spirits of yours yet, but I've got a pretty good sense of how they talk. If you're down here for a reason, then I must be, too."

Wareagle could do nothing but shrug.

"Look, Indian. All the pull in the world's not gonna get you out of here anytime soon. So first off we've got to come up with our own version of early release. Then we head up the Amazon to find whatever the hell it is that's killing these Tupis. See, I'm signing on, Johnny. For once, your war becomes mine."

The Indian smiled faintly. "Blainey, our fates are connected at the level where only the spirits roam. I knew it from the first time we met in the hellfire, where we fought the Black Hearts. But the enemy we face this time has no heart at all.''

''Monsters, Indian?''

''As close as can be, Blainey.''

CHAPTER 3

JERRY Dean Taylor left the homeless shelter just after midnight. The unseasonably cold temperatures had brought more people in off the streets than the staff was prepared for, and the result was a frantic rush to create enough bed space and come up with sufficient hot food. Volunteers didn't show up in volume until the real Philadelphia cold kicked in, so Jerry Dean found himself dishing out soup for the better part of the evening.

The funds that allowed for the center's existence and upkeep came from his foundation, but Jerry Dean was not—had never been—the hands-off type. He threw himself headlong into a problem he saw as the scourge of America. What kind of country was it that couldn't ensure adequate homes for all its people? Obviously the public sector was failing, leaving it up to the private sector to pick up the slack. The program Jerry Dean was piping millions into was being used as a pilot all across the country.

Jerry Dean had parked his car two blocks from the shelter, but it might have been miles, his knees making him pay for every step. Seven years of high school and college football had ruined both of them, and spending the night on his feet wasn't exactly aspirin. They'd been better since he'd lost the thirty pounds to get back to his college weight of two-fifty, but there weren't enough working parts left in either of them to make any weight loss vanquish the pain.

No jogging tomorrow, coach. . . .

Jerry Dean's car was in sight when he realized he was being followed. The steps were just muted enough to tell him the walker was trying to disguise them. He tensed. People knew him around here, knew what he was about. And he knew the gangs and the junkies, some on a first-name basis. Most people left him alone, and those that didn't know him should have been warned off by a frame that was still six-four off the ground, though a bit softer around the edges.

Jerry Dean spun as the muted footsteps continued to clack on the concrete behind him. Nothing was there. Just the night and the splotchy glares of shattered streetlights. But there *had* been someone.

Jerry Dean turned his attention to his car. Twenty feet away was all. Couldn't run, though. Worst thing he could do under the circumstances was show his fear.

But there's no one here.

Jerry Dean was scared, all two hundred and fifty pounds of him scared stiff as a frozen cheesesteak. He reached the car, relaxing a bit since the steps had not returned. His hand probed a key forward toward the lock, was just inserting it when the flash came. He flinched reflexively, but his hand stayed where it was. He heard the crackling thud just before the pain exploded in his wrist. Then he saw the glinting steel.

Jerry Dean howled in pain as a dark shape whirled in a blur beside him. The steel flashed briefly again, and he felt the side of his head give under the force of another impact. Jerry Dean felt himself reeling. He was dizzy and nauseated, but something kept him on his feet. The shape swirled at him again, and this time he managed to raise an arm into the flash's path. He felt his forearm give, and again pain flooded his insides.

But somehow he didn't feel scared anymore. He didn't even hurt.

All he felt was rage.

"Come on, you fucker!" he challenged, swinging alternately with both of his damaged limbs.

The blows, though, landed only on air. The shape was there, always ahead of him, dancing at the outskirts of his range. Jerry Dean had hauled back for a roundhouse punch when the worst of his two knees, the right one, got slammed and forced him hard to the pavement.

He screamed in agony as the shape loomed over him. In that moment, frozen in the landscape of pain, he thought quite rationally that his attacker was at least as big as he. The man was Oriental, cloaked in black, only a thick, round face exposed. Jerry Dean tried to block the attacker's downward blow with upraised arms. But the glinting steel split the distance between them and smashed his face.

For Jerry Dean the pain stopped there, but he was somehow still aware of the trio of blows that followed before life and consciousness were stripped from him at the same time.

Not even breathing hard, Khan stood over the pulp that had been a man. The screams he'd evoked caused lights to snap on and faces to peer out from behind the safety of windows. But before the first eyes looked down, Khan had melted into the night once more, his blessed steel killing sticks back in their sheaths.

The yacht fought its way through the sea, pounded at every turn by the crushing swells. The storm had ended hours before, but its residue was a harsh wind that kept the waves mean. Water splashed freely across the big boat's decks, lashing her windows like an unwanted guest determined to gain entry.

It was only a short distance from the radio room to the library, but Tiguro Nagami struggled for every step, forced to grasp the rail firmly to pull himself along.

"Come in." The voice came from inside before Nagami could knock. He entered.

Oddly, the yacht's sprawling library seemed to be spared the sea's vicious onslaught. Its semidarkness revealed a safe and steady setting, undaunted by the sway.

"Khan has reported in, *Kami-san*," Nagami reported to the figure huddled behind the huge desk. "Taylor has been eliminated. That brings Khan's list to three."

The figure behind the desk switched on his computer and pressed the latest data into the keyboard. The dim glow from the monitor caught the ghastly whiteness of his skin and hair and shimmered off his pinkish eyes. Any more light would have hurt those eyes. They had been the scourge of Takedo Takahashi's life since the very beginning, and the affliction was growing worse. It was now impossible for him to tolerate the sun. He spent each day behind drawn blinds, venturing out only at night.

"That makes twelve so far in all," Takahashi announced. "Exactly one-eighth of our list has been dispatched in barely six days. That's ahead of schedule, isn't it?"

"Slightly, *Kami-san*," replied Nagami.

Kami-san, translated as *Ghost man*, was the label Takahashi had been branded with for the better part of his life. He did not run from this reality; in fact, he mocked his own disfigurement by only wearing suits that matched his skin's pallor.

"And thus far no complications have arisen," said Takahashi. "We chose our people well, Tiguro, exceptionally well."

Exactly ten days had passed now since the meeting that had taken place in this very room. The lights had been turned up that night, but Takahashi still declined the sunglasses he normally would have worn, because he wanted the group of six assembled before him to see his resolve clearly at all times. They did not know his real name, nor did they want to.

But Takedo Takahashi knew them; if there were any more proficient killers in the world they would have been in the room instead. Six assassins of unparalleled prowess, chosen after months of scrutiny. Assassins who had not a single failure to their names. The room had quivered with the coldness they brought to it. Takahashi inspected each of the killers closely, focusing on features or mannerisms. The Mongol had the largest hands he had ever seen, yet was making a quarter dance nimbly from finger to finger. The bald-headed black wouldn't let go of a smile that flashed whiter than Takahashi's suit. The woman's beauty attracted even his stare. The Israeli and the Arab were seated next to each other as if to affirm their lack of political opposition. The American assassin had moved his chair back a bit from the circle.

". . . The time has come to explain why I have summoned all of you here this evening, to make clear what it is you are being hired to do. There are ninety-six Americans who must die within the next six weeks. Two of these are United States senators. Three more are congressmen. Four hold Cabinet-level positions. Five are associated in varying respects with the military. The remainder are business people: industrialists, financiers, manufacturers. In short, all individuals who have reached significant levels of power and influence.''

Takahashi paused to let his words sink in. He closed his pink, crystalline eyes briefly to rest them. They watered when he opened them again to view the response of the group gathered in chairs about him. The killers seemed flabbergasted. The huge Mongol had stopped twirling his quarter. The bald black was no longer smiling. Takahashi had continued speaking before any of them could interrupt.

''The ninety-six targets have been divided into approximately equal portions each of you will be allotted. Complete dossiers on all have been prepared and will be distributed to you in packets as soon as our business tonight is concluded. As indicated, you will receive one hundred thousand per killing, with the balance of the agreed upon twenty million paid on completion of the entire contract. . . .

''It will, of course, be necessary to take measures to avoid any connection being uncovered until it is too late. You are all professionals, so I need not offer counsel on how to go about this. Accidents, disappearances, a variety of means are at your disposal. You should not consider the targets' families to be sacrosanct if it aids you in your work. They are expendable. You need make no accounts or explanations for your actions. Travel arrangements and contact procedures are outlined in your dossier packets, along with the means through which you will obtain compensation. Reports following each of your successful eliminations are, of course, mandated, so I can stay updated on your progress. Now, if there are no questions . . .''

There hadn't been, and the six assassins were sent on their way. Now, ten days later, Takahashi reflected on the success encountered already. Twelve kills, imagine it! His plan had dared to account for an acceptable margin of error, but as of this point there had been no margin at all. Even he could barely believe it.

Takahashi gazed up from his desk, a rare smile etched across his face.

"You will keep me informed, Tiguro."

"Of course, *Kami-san*."

Takahashi's eyes had already returned to his computer, the milk-white glow off the monitor seeming one with his flesh. "Eighty-four more, Tiguro. Eight-four more."

"Then you're suggesting our competitors knew what to bid because they knew what our bid was."

"More than suggesting, Miss Eisely."

Patrick O'Malley was sole proprietor of the Devlin Group, one of the largest consulting firms in the world. Loyal to his Irish roots, O'Malley had given his business his mother's maiden name. The Devlin Group had created blueprints for hundreds of successful businesses spanning the globe. These blueprints were often imitated but never equaled, making Devlin the most sought-after firm of its kind anywhere. But in the last several months, other firms were coming up with virtually identical proposals for significantly less money. It wasn't the money that bothered O'Malley so much as the violation. Security was everything to him, and had been for years. Seeing it breached made his flesh crawl.

His offices and home were guarded twenty-four hours a day by trained bodyguards. They ran advance for him for all in and out of the country business trips. O'Malley never entered a restaurant until they had checked it. He never left one until the outside had been cleared. All guests entering the Devlin Building passed unknowingly through a metal detector. No bells chimed if a register was made. Instead, two of the guards would be waiting for the visitor when he or she stepped out of the elevator.

"Now then," Patrick O'Malley continued, reaching for his glass of Perrier, which he always drank with plenty of ice and a twist of lime, "if you'd be so kind as to turn to page five of the report, we can begin discussing the new security measures I trust all of you will enact and cooperate with."

The sounds of pages ruffling filled the conference room. O'Malley took a hefty sip from his Perrier and felt the ice cubes brush against his lips.

"First off," he began in the instant before his eyes went glassy. "First off . . ."

Patrick O'Malley tried to grab the conference table for support; when that failed, he groped for the arms of the chair behind him. He managed to find them, but crumpled before his purchase was firm. He hit the floor, kicking and twitching, before the horrified eyes of his executive staff.

"Call 911!"

"He's having a heart attack!"

"CPR! Now! Fast!"

O'Malley was dead before they could even get started, dead before the conference room doors burst open to allow a pair of security guards to rush through. Heart attack was indeed the initial diagnosis by the medical examiner, one later confirmed under autopsy.

Jonathan Weetz did not learn of the death until the following morning's *New York Times*. He had injected an incredibly potent and quick-dissolving form of taxine poison into the six limes present in O'Malley's office refrigerator. No way to tell how long it would be before he used a slice. The specifics, though, didn't matter.

O'Malley's death meant three down and thirteen to go, and thirteen was his lucky number.

CHAPTER 4

"**W**ELL, look what we have here. . . ."

McCracken had seen the burly figure in the Caesar Park

Hotel lobby an instant before the voice assaulted him. Now it was too late to turn away.

"Hello, Ben."

"Always said you meet people in the strangest places."

Colonel Ben Norseman was wearing the ugliest Hawaiian shirt Blaine had ever seen, a pair of monstrous forearms sticking out from the baggy sleeves.

"I'd like to say you were a sight for sore eyes, Ben, but mine didn't hurt until they saw you. Who's handling your wardrobe these days?"

Norseman plucked at the awful red floral pattern. "Hey, when in Rome . . ."

"I doubt you're down here as a tourist."

"Nope. Business. Usual stuff. Right up your alley, if you're available."

Blaine shook his head. "Sorry."

"Hey, what are the odds, the two of us meeting in the same place after so long? Call it coincidence."

"Call it unfortunate."

"Hey, fuck you, McCrackenballs. I was trying to be sociable."

"Hardly your style, Ben."

The two men regarded each other distantly from a yard apart. Norseman had changed as little in appearance over the years as McCracken. A few inches taller than Blaine at six-four, Norseman's neck was still creased with knobby muscle that pulsed with each breath. His mustache showed its share of gray, and his dome was now completely bald. It gave a harder edge to the colonel's face, as if he needed it.

Ben Norseman had been part of the Phoenix Project in Vietnam as well, a Green Beret who'd already put in five years in the jungle when Blaine arrived in 1969. Norseman stayed because he liked it, liked everything about it. He fed off the killing. When the war ended, interested parties in the government made sure it was still there for him. Last McCracken had heard, he and a small elite troop he was running were handling deep cover, strictly top drawer stuff. They were little more than hired killers, but they did their job exceptionally well.

So what was Ben Norseman doing down here? What "usual stuff" had brought him down to Brazil?

"Hey, asshole, our styles are more alike than different. I've been keeping up with ya. Heard about what you pulled off in Tehran. Damn good work. You get a mind to it, you know there's always a place in my bunch."

"Sorry, Ben. Kicking kittens and steering old ladies into moving traffic was never my cup of tea."

Norseman's lips puckered and the veins bulged in his knobby neck. "Anytime you want to settle what we've got between us, just let me know."

"Now would suit me fine. I'd ask you to step outside, but I'm afraid you might use a couple of kids for a shield."

The bigger man backed off a bit. "I'm on business, like I said. I wasn't, the two of us could dance right now." Norseman came close enough for Blaine to smell the spearmint gum on his breath. "Our day's coming, McCrackenballs. High time somebody gave yours a squeeze. Show you what it feels like."

"Your hands aren't big enough, Ben," Blaine said, and backed slightly away. He waited to see if Norseman was going to move on him. When he didn't, McCracken slid toward the front desk. "Be seeing ya."

"I'll be looking forward to it."

McCracken watched Norseman move through the hotel doors and approach a white van parked directly outside. Only the driver was visible, but Blaine knew there would be another five of Ben Norseman's men in the back. Killing machines born too late for Nam and making up for it now, all trained and hardened in the image of their fearless leader. Blaine was thankful for the fact that whatever they were down here for had nothing to do with him. If it had, Norseman never would have initiated the conversation. He was too dumb to play stupid, but he was as fearsome a soldier as Blaine had ever known.

McCracken had other things on his mind now in any event. Johnny Wareagle had supplied the precise location of his cell, along with all the information he had been able to gather about the jail complex itself. Blaine wasn't worried. This wasn't a prison, after all, it was a regular jail. Though well fortified, people came and went regularly, and there wasn't a lot of perimeter security.

He would still require explosives to get the job done, but elaborate charges were a luxury he would have to do without, which left him with no choice other than to utilize those of a homemade variety. A brief discussion in English with the hotel concierge provided him with the locations of area stores where the required supplies might be obtained. After a quick shower and lunch, he was off with shopping list in hand.

It took all of two hours to obtain the goods he needed. Purchases from a pair of markets, a hardware store, and the toy section of a large department store filled his needs admirably. Just before four o'clock, he and his four shopping bags returned to the Caesar Park for the more difficult task of assembling the charges.

Blaine emptied the contents of his shopping bags onto the large single bed and separated them into four piles. His first task was to combine all of the packages of children's clay he had bought into a single lump and then work the heavy steel roofing nails into the mass by pushing, sliding, and squeezing. The single irregular bulk then had to be separated into the proper shapes, as equally symmetrical as he could manage with only his eyes to guide him. Next he combined his store-bought chemicals and cleaners in the proper proportions, using three standard hotel ice buckets as pots. When this was completed, he poured the contents of all three into the plugged sink. Then he began easing the steel-laiden clay shapes in under the surface, one at a time.

It took nearly two minutes for each to absorb the proper amount of liquid. Blaine set the finished products to dry on towels laid over the double bed and turned his attention to the timing devices. He much preferred working with transmitter detonated charges in such cases, but no such luck—or technology—here. He'd have to rely on the guts of simple travel clocks, all wired to the same moment. The alarm activator would serve as the trigger, set with intervals of just seconds between each blast to maximize confusion.

The only remaining problem was how to gain swift access to *Casa do Diabo* with minimal risk of drawing attention to himself once the charges were set. And the answer occurred to him as he gazed over his balcony at the homeless drunks being carted away by the São Paulo police.

* * *

"Come on now! Get a move on!"

The parade of drunks flowed toward the jail door in a wavering stream. In the back, inevitably, a single laggard needed to be prodded on by one of the São Paulo policemen. In the front, just as inevitably, one would stagger and force those behind him to smack together like bumper cars in an amusement park.

"You there, where do you think you're going?"

Blaine McCracken was lumbering about at the periphery of the small mass, the illusion created that he had once been a part of it and was seeking to separate himself. He felt a pair of angry hands grasp him at the shoulders and shove him sideways, to be absorbed by the group.

"Bastard!" exclaimed the officer.

The pace and surface of São Paulo cannot hide the truth of the awesome poverty and unemployment that fills the city. Many of Brazil's poor have flocked there in search of what the countryside failed to give them, only to find that the city offers them no better. Accordingly, the drinking problem in the poorer sections of São Paulo and its outskirts is extreme. When confined, the problem is generally ignored. But every night, drunkards venture into the more respectable downtown sectors and are hauled away en masse to sleep off their troubles in the nearest jail.

Casa do Diabo.

The roundups started midevening and continued through the night, providing Blaine with the simplest means to enter the building unnoticed. He had pulled his stolen Ford off the road a quarter-mile from the jail and abandoned it. By a stroke of fortune, he discovered a main power junction on top of a pole halfway to the jail, and planted his first charge there before pressing on. He reached the fence that enclosed the complex and chose the darkest spot to make his climb. He used wire cutters to strip away the barbed wire at the top, then dropped effortlessly to the ground, his sack fastened tight to his back.

He stayed low and crept to the asphalt parking lot at the building's front. With uncharacteristic deliberateness he approached various cars in the lot and worked into place the remaining dozen homemade explosives he had fashioned that day. The best place to plant them was not near the fuel tank or engine, but beneath the fuel line itself. That way, when detonation came, the fumes would ignite and spread the fury throughout the engine.

Starting at midnight. Show time.

McCracken spread his work throughout the lot instead of focusing in a single sector. Unlike the plastic explosives he was more used to dealing with, his children's clay facsimiles did not readily adhere to the vehicles' steel undersides. A roll of duct tape was necessary, and he was careful to make sure the timing mechanism was wedged home tight and set before pressing on.

When midnight came, the explosive clay would spew its roofing nail contents outward and puncture the steel about it. The sheer force would then join the fumes and available gas in the line to create a fireball where a car had been just seconds before. Lots of noise and light. Those inside the jail would think they were under attack.

The parade of drunks was mounting the steps now. Blaine let himself be swept up in the flow, eyes kept low and shoulders hunched. He had covered his clothes with dirt and cheap rum for the desired effect. His thick hair was disheveled and pulled down over his forehead. He had disarranged his beard back at the hotel to give it an equally unkempt look. But he kept his head down on the chance one of the policemen might notice his piercing black eyes. A dead giveaway to a man with experience, a reason for suspicion for a man without.

Once inside the building, the mass did not pause at the front desk for booking. In fact, that station was bypassed altogether in favor of a door leading to the basement section of *Casa do Diabo*. The officer at the front jammed a key into the lock and then swung it open. A second officer led the way; when all the arrested drunks were through it, the first rebolted the door and brought up the rear.

Just two to overcome. Blaine couldn't have asked for any better luck.

The staircase was dank and cold, lit only by a single bulb dangling on a wire from the ceiling. The mass walked pressed against the side wall for balance. The descent leveled into a wide hall that was more hard-packed dirt than surface stone.

Blaine could hear the whimpers and wails of those already incarcerated up ahead. The smell of urine and sweat grew stronger by the step. The raw night dampness down in the jail's bowels was bone-chilling, the walls shiny with accumulated moisture and layered with patches of green mildew.

When he could see the cells flickering in the dim light ahead, McCracken began to ease his way forward through the drunks. Just six to pass by before reaching the lead officer. He moved gently, unnoticeably, quickened his pace at the last to bring the officer into range. Cells were clearly in view now, hands stretched between the bars, angry or desperate pleas shouted outward in Portuguese.

Blaine threw himself into a lunging stagger that engulfed the lead officer's legs and took him down. The whole throng reeled backward in a whiplash effect, some tumbling.

The officer was in the process of shouting out when McCracken's iron fingers found his throat to silence him. With no time to be subtle, he slammed the man's head against the hard floor to knock him out. The officer at the rear was storming forward by this point. He struck a meaty hand downward to yank McCracken up. Blaine let him, went with the motion, and came up with fists flying. The first blow to the solar plexus doubled the officer over with a violent expulsion of breath. The man was still slumping when Blaine slammed a knee under his chin. Impact lifted the officer off his feet; he slumped down against steel bars infested with curious hands forcing their way out toward him.

The drunks still awake in the cells had gone quiet for the brief duration of Blaine's work, but now were shouting and cheering as if they expected to be freed. The new lot that had shielded him had begun to back their way down the rank corridor when McCracken showed the gun he'd lifted off the first guard. In his other hand was a wad of keys.

The drunks slowed, then halted, disappointment obvious on their features. Blaine opened the less crowded of the two cells and herded them in. His original plan had been to throw the downed officers in here as well, but the mad eyes of the occupants dictated otherwise. There was a third cell, unoccupied for the moment, and he quickly dragged them into it after locating the proper key.

Stripping the clothes off the larger of the two officers and donning them in place of his own was next on the list. The drunks had bunched close together in both cells to capture angles that let them watch. Those with the best view cheered Blaine when he stripped off his clothes and booed him when he put the guard's on instead. By far the loudest reaction he got came when he exited the third cell tightening his gun belt and moved back down the corridor. The drunks shouted their anger at his not releasing them, then busied themselves with seeing if they could probe through the bars of the third cell to find purchase on the downed policemen.

McCracken reached the staircase at 11:49. Timing was of the utmost importance now if he was to reach Johnny Wareagle ahead of the explosions, and a significant obstacle remained to be overcome: gaining entry to the second-floor area of the jail where Johnny was being held meant retracing his steps up the staircase and passing right through the building's front area.

He mounted the steps quickly and used his keys to unlock the door. He fixed his cap lower over his forehead and slid outward. Not hesitating, he turned right and walked past the wall-less main room, which was busy with activity. Another stairway that would take him to the second level, where Johnny was being kept, lay straight ahead. The building's ancient design did not allow for monitoring stations on every floor. There were just lines of claustrophobic cells with heavy wooden, windowless doors. Patrolling guards, yes, but no central station to bypass.

11:51 . . .

McCracken rushed up the stairs and waited briefly at the top to see if a guard was patrolling the floor. The rattling *clip-clop* of boot heels alerted him to the presence of one before his eyes recorded the steady pace of the man heading his way on his pass. Blaine pressed his shoulders against the alcove wall and waited. When the guard had turned to go back the other way, he pounced. The man felt only a slight twinge in his neck before consciousness was stripped from him. Blaine headed on past the small room he had met Johnny in that afternoon to the cell where Wareagle was being held.

"This is your wake-up call, Indian," he said, turning the key in the lock. "Time to rise and shine."

McCracken pushed the heavy door open.

"Let's get a move—"

But the cell was empty.

Johnny was gone.

Blaine fought against panic. The unexpected was nothing new to him. The problem in this case continued to be time.

11:53 . . .

His fiery distraction would begin in seven minutes; if he didn't have Wareagle in tow by that time, it would be for naught. Obviously Blaine's presence here that afternoon had raised eyebrows among the jail's officials. They would have moved Wareagle to a more secure location, probably under personal guard on the third floor, because that would create the greatest distance to cover in the event escape was attempted. With time his enemy, and his explosive distraction no longer enough to ensure success, Blaine needed something else, something more.

The cell doors around him held the answer. Blaine started at the cell next to Johnny's old one and unlocked it with the keys lifted from the guard in the basement. He pounded on the door before thrusting it open, then moved onto the next one across the hall. He was working on the fifth door when the first of those inmates he'd freed emerged tentatively into the corridor. They regarded each other with confusion and took their first steps cautiously, as if still bound imperceptibly to their cells. But the bonds were quick to come off.

McCracken had opened over a dozen doors when the first complement of those he had freed surged by him. They kept their distance, unsure and skeptical of his motives. One stopped and smiled at him. Blaine smiled back and made his own way down the hall toward the group waiting.

11:57 . . .

"*Vamos,*" he told them, followed by, "*Adeus.*"

"*Muito obrigado,*" one of them said.

Blaine flew up the stairs to the third floor and pressed himself against the side wall. He peered around the doorway to find a trio of guards standing rigid before a single cell at the very end of the corridor. He gazed at his watch.

11:58 . . .

The waiting was interminable, seconds passing like hours before his eyes.

Come on, he urged the freed prisoners on the level beneath him. *Come on!*

He heard the shouts and screams first, pouring up the stairwell from ground level. The wailing, old-fashioned bell alarm came next. He made himself wait a few seconds more, wanting to seize the moment when indecision and fear on the part of Johnny's guards was at its peak.

Blaine moved an instant before his watch showed 11:59. He moved down the corridor—not charging but backpedaling fearfully—trembling gun aimed at nothing. Johnny's guards, who had already been looking that way, drew their guns as well.

"This way!" Blaine screamed at them. "Hurry! They're coming! We're under attack!"

McCracken had stopped his surge twenty feet from the door, pressed up against the wall as if for cover. The alarm's bells burned his ears, shouts and screams occasionally rising above them.

"Now!" Blaine yelled behind him.

Johnny's guards came forward, slow at first but then in an all-out rush. Blaine lunged into the hall in front of their charge and leveled his pistol, combat-style, back toward the stairway. The guards accepted him in that instant, and an instant was all he needed.

Two charged to his left, and he went for those first, a forearm launched into the face of one while a kick found the groin of the other. The men crumpled as they stood, the final guard turning in time to see them hit the floor, but not in time to swing his gun toward the figure whirling at him in a blur. McCracken separated the three guards from their weapons—in case they came to faster than expected—and rushed toward the cell they'd been guarding.

Only thirty seconds remained until midnight when he pounded on the door.

"Guess who, Indian?" Blaine asked, already trying to work the first of his keys into the lock.

"Hello, Blainey."

"Damn," McCracken muttered when the final key failed to do the job. "Hold tight, Johnny."

The door was too heavy and the lock too solid to shoot out. His only hope was that one of the guards he'd felled had the right key on his person. Blaine rushed back to the center of the corridor. The man he had kicked in the groin was twisting on the floor, only semiconscious. A single key dangled from his belt. McCracken reached down and snatched it.

Boom! . . . Boom! . . . Boom!

The first explosions sounded just as he jammed the key into the lock on Johnny's cell. The very structure of the building seemed to tremble, walls shedding dust. Blaine shoved the door open; Wareagle was standing in wait, his wrist and leg irons lying in pools on the floor behind him.

"I always figured Houdini was an Indian," McCracken said over the shrilling alarm bell.

Boom! . . . Boom! . . . Boom!

The next series in the parking lot sounded just as they started down the corridor.

"The hellfire, Blainey."

"Literally tonight, Indian. Gonna be plenty of pissed-off cops when the time comes to drive home."

Between the explosions and alarm came the sounds of sporadic gunfire. A stand was being made by police against the scourge of escaping prisoners. Blaine signaled Johnny to stop when they reached the staircase. His eyes were glued to his watch.

"More, Blainey?"

"Just a little. Right about . . . *now*!"

On cue there was a final *Boom!* that was muffled like distant thunder. The lights around them flickered and died.

"Figured we could use a little bit of insurance," Blaine explained, "so I wired the pole running the lines of juice into the building."

In the darkness he could feel Johnny smile. "Take their eyes and you take their guns."

"That's the idea."

They sped down the staircase and then descended the last stretch of the way toward the main floor. A dull haze of emergency lighting shone through the black. The loss of power had cut the alarm, and the only sounds were the shouts and screams coming from police struggling to regain control.

"Close your eyes, Indian."

"Blainey?"

"One final surprise . . ."

McCracken's hand emerged from his pocket with a phosphorus flare he had constructed that afternoon, plastic pipe tubing filled with three separate kinds of powder. He touched his lighter to the rawhide strip fuse and tossed it ahead, near the midway point between them and the door. The tubing struck the floor and rolled briefly before igniting in hot, lingering flashbulb-bright intensity. Men rubbed their eyes, opened them again to sight echoes of dazzling white.

Blaine and Johnny used the temporary freeze to rush through the main door. Outside, the parking lot was a shambles. Fragments of the cars Blaine had wired littered a pavement dominated by the flaming wrecks. The flames carved into the night and stole the cover of darkness away. Everywhere freed prisoners rushed for the fence.

"Time to get ourselves a taxi," Blaine said as they lunged down the stairs leading from the entryway.

As if on cue, a series of police cars sped through the gate with sirens wailing. They slammed to a halt while Johnny and Blaine sought cover behind one of the vehicles untouched by the explosions. The idea occurred to them at the same time, and, without exchanging a single word or gesture, they moved for the car parked at the end of the new row once it was abandoned. By the time its previous occupants reached the jail, their car was screeching its way back out the gate.

"Next stop the Amazon, Indian," Blaine said.

CHAPTER 5

PATTY Hunsecker awoke with the wind. The vertical blinds drawn over her open windows flapped wildly, rattling together like change shaken inside a piggy bank. It was a hot wind, but throwing back the covers Patty found that she was freezing. Cold sweat matted her blouse to her flesh. The cuffs of her jeans had crept up her ankles and now cut tightly into her calves. She was shivering. The nightmare had come again, the bulk of it already lost to memory, with only the residue left behind:

> *A dark sedan crashing through the guardrail and plunging over the cliff. In the front seat the Hunsecker's female Japanese house servant and her father's business assistant, Shimada, flailing frantically with the wheel. In the back her father's face glued against the window. Her father was waving at Patty.*
>
> *Waving good-bye.*

Patty climbed out of bed and nearly tripped on the boots discarded at its foot. She did not remember taking them off, did not remember giving herself up to sleep, either. She had been in the study earlier—her father's study—lost in the pile of press clippings that littered the desk. Clippings accumulated over the past day and a half that had turned her grief to terror since the funeral on Friday, the day after a Thanksgiving that left her nothing to give thanks for.

"Thank you for seeing me on a Sunday," she had told Captain Harold Banyan of the Los Angeles Police Department that afternoon.

"You said it was urgent, Miss Hunsecker. I knew your father. For what's it worth, I thought he was a great man."

"It may be worth a lot, Captain."

It was then that Banyan noticed the manila envelope Patty was clutching beneath her arm. He had seen pictures of her in the stories that cluttered the news about Phillip Hunsecker's tragic passing, but they did not do her justice. Her body was athletic and shapely, her skin bronzed, and her blond hair cut stylishly short.

"I'd like you to take a look at these," Patty said as she unclasped the envelope and handed a small stack of photocopied press clippings across the desk to Banyan. "I've got more, but these are the most clear-cut."

Banyan had begun fingering through them. "Clear-cut what, Miss Hunsecker?"

"Examples, Captain Banyan. My father isn't the only one, Captain. In the past five days, nine men like him have been killed; three others have disappeared. Five of the nine perished in 'accidents,' as well."

Banyan looked up from skimming the tear sheets. "By 'like him,' you mean . . ."

"Rich, powerful, influential. I spent most of yesterday in the library, going through out-of-town newspapers. I didn't get through them all. There could be more."

"More victims, you mean?"

Patty nodded.

"Then you're suggesting . . ."

"That my father and the others were murdered, Captain Banyan. That the deaths are connected, part of a pattern, some sort of conspiracy."

"I see."

"Do you?"

"Miss Hunsecker?"

"You haven't read the tear sheets. You just skimmed them. I made those copies for you. I've got another set. You can read them in detail and call me back when you're finished. If you want, I can wait out in—''

"Miss Hun—Can I call you Patty?"

"I've been calling you captain," she answered, trying for a smile.

"Patty, what led you to the library on this . . . search?"

"A feeling."

"That's all?"

Patty swallowed hard. "The skid marks at the scene of the accident. Something about them was all wrong. Something suggested that . . ."

"Go on."

"Suggested that my father's car was forced off the road."

"Our forensics unit spent half a day on the scene and disagrees with that conclusion."

"I'm well aware of that, Captain."

Banyan smiled curtly at her. "Your specialty is the sea—the ocean—is it not?"

"It was."

"Then I would say you were stepping out of line to make conclusions better reached—or not reached—by the police."

"If I hadn't found out about the others, I would accept that judgement."

Again Banyan fingered through the tear sheets. "Yes. And was your father acquainted with any of these others?"

"I'm sure he met a few of them."

"Any business dealings, political contacts?"

"Not that I know of."

"And do you have any reason to believe that these same men bear any direct connection to one another?"

"Besides the obvious, no."

"And just what is the obvious?"

"Their stature. The kind of influence they wielded."

"That's not a connection, Miss Hunsecker, it's a fact. You're trying to suggest to me that your father was a victim of some mammoth conspiracy. But there's no evidence to support that conclusion."

Banyan extended the tear sheets back across the desk. Patty's hands stayed on her lap.

"Just read them, Captain, in detail. Call the investigating

officers in some of the other cities. See if they have any suspicions. That's all I ask.''

Banyan pulled the tear sheets back toward him and let them flop to his desk. ''I'll call you, Patty. Give me a few days.''

''Thank you, Captain.''

But Patty knew a few days weren't going to make any difference, nor would a few weeks, or even a few months. Banyan wasn't buying into the story; he probably wouldn't make a single phone call. She walked out of the building feeling even more alone than she had while she stood with her younger brothers on either side of her at the funeral seventy-two hours before. She was responsible for them now; they were hers to raise and no one else's.

Your specialty is the sea—the ocean—is it not?

It was, indeed, and, God, how she missed it now, as she closed the windows and locked them. She had come back one year before to bury her mother—who'd succumbed after a long battle with cancer Patty didn't even know she was waging. The news of her mother's death had reached Patty in the Biminis, where she had started work on a new project with a new boat, the *Runaway II*. The ocean was her one great love; she had foresaken all else for it. She had left her family, left college, left the family's three Southern California houses to pursue a love that had been all-consuming.

She was so isolated that her family hadn't even known how to reach her. If she hadn't come back to port to resupply, Patty never would have known until her mother was long buried. She remembered the funeral, the sight of her two younger brothers, virtual strangers to her, held under either of her father's arms, gazing at her with unquestioning love, in search of reassurance she could not give them. She resolved then to forsake her life on the sea and stay with them, be the sister they never really had now that their mother was gone. The ocean could go on without her, and maybe her brothers could, too. But the issue was one of need.

Her mother's funeral had brought back sharp memories of how close she had once come to death herself. She had nearly perished with the first *Runaway* after she and it had been commandeered by a man Patty hadn't been able to stop thinking about since. Standing there at her mother's funeral, she had let herself imagine that Blaine McCracken was there by her side, offering comfort.

Of course, he wasn't; they hadn't even spoken since he had left her in a naval hospital on Guam six months before her mother's funeral. Patty had not called her parents during her own two-week-long hospital stay. McCracken did, though, and they flew out, insisting she let them help pay to reoutfit her. Patty stubbornly argued she would rely on grants; only when the folly of this became obvious did she accept what she insisted had to be a loan.

It had been her father who convinced her to return to the sea after her mother's funeral. They both had to get on with their lives, he told her, and she wouldn't be doing herself any good lingering where she wouldn't be happy. Her younger brothers were disappointed, but they understood. Besides, Shimada was there, and she was infinitely more capable of managing the household—as she had effectively done since Patty had been a child.

Shimada.

She had been born during World War II, in one of the Japanese internment camps in California. Touched by her story, Phillip Hunsecker had hired her as housekeeper and governess in 1970, when Patty was six. The relationship between the two of them had been strong from the very start. Shimada immediately christened Patty *Hana-shan*, which meant *Flower*. As Patty grew older, Shimada was drawn increasingly into Phillip Hunsecker's business affairs, eventually becoming his administrative assistant in addition to her continuing duties in the household. When Patty's mother had died, Shimada had been typically humble, willing even to miss the funeral so she could get the house in order for the many guests who would be coming after it was over.

Patty was in port when news of the accident had reached her, barely a week before. Details were sketchy at that point, and she found a glimmer of hope in that sketchiness. The glimmer was extinguished the instant she reached home. Both her father and Shimada had been killed instantly, their bodies burned beyond recognition. Her brothers were staying with friends. Patty realized how sad it was they were now orphans. With a chill she realized, she was, too.

She brought them back to her favorite of the family's houses in Laurel Canyon, insisting that was the best way to help them get on with their lives. She was done with the sea. The boys needed her, and here she would stay. Custody problems were inevitable and still forthcoming. The cushion of shock was still delaying matters, and Patty was grateful for that much.

Her arms wrapped about her body, she walked out of her room and into the hallway. Her bare feet rebelled against the coldness of the bare wood floor, and she moved quickly onto the Oriental runner that covered its center. She peered into the rooms of both her brothers and then decided to go down to the kitchen to make some coffee. But the downstairs was cold and dark, and to get there she had to pass her father's study.

Inside it a single desk lamp burned over her mounting collection of tear sheets and photocopies. She did not remember leaving the lamp on. She did not remember leaving the study in favor of plunging into bed without undressing.

Intending only to switch off the light, she entered the study and walked to the desk. The reading material spread over it clutched at her again, she sank into the chair and began paging through the clutter of papers once more.

What was the connection between these men?

Something had to hold her father and the other victims together. They were being killed for a reason—and at least some hint of that reason had to lie here, in these papers. She had filled half the pages of a yellow legal pad with notes based on her reading. Tonight she would make notes on the notes.

It was like sailing into a head wind. She wasn't getting anywhere.

What would Blaine McCracken have done?

Her eyes fell on the phone. She'd considered dialing the number he had given her so often these past few days that she could see it embossed on her eyelids every time she tried to sleep. But what was she going to tell him if he answered? What made her think his response would be any different from Banyan's?

I've got to find something to tell him, something that will make him—make all of them—believe, she thought now.

Patty flipped her second pad open to a chart she had been making with the victims' vital statistics. Nothing there that

even suggested a connection. Different hometowns, different
birth places, different colleges, different ways each had made
his fortune, different birthdays as well, she quipped to herself.

Then something made her go back to that final column.
Birth dates . . . Birth dates . . .

A chill shook her before she was even halfway down the list,
an icy chill just like the one that had awakened her earlier.

Well, I'll be damned, she thought. *I'll be damned*!

"A minor problem has arisen, *Kami-san*."

Takahashi looked up from his desk to see Tiguro Nagami
standing before him. He hadn't even heard his subordinate
enter the study.

"Speak, Tiguro."

"The daughter of one of the victims has been to the police.
She has apparently caught on to the pattern of deaths."

"She couldn't have."

"The police said as much."

"Then why must I know this?"

"The possibility that she will make inquiries in other arenas
is very real, *Kami-san*. One of these might provide a more
willing ear."

"Can you monitor the situation?"

Nagami nodded.

"If she persists, Tiguro, order her elimination. But don't
use one of our six specialists." The vaguest hint of a smile
crossed Takahashi's lips. "No sense throwing off their timetable, is there?"

CHAPTER 6

McCRACKEN mopped his brow yet again as the black waters of the Amazon slid by beneath him.

"Next year, Indian, remind me to choose Club Med."

Wareagle was hefting a long, thick log to help steer their boat clear of the shallows. Their pilot, Luis, had warned of the shallows just before finishing his last bottle of whiskey. That had been two hours back, after they had turned down the frighteningly calm trunk river that appeared on no map.

"You sure this is the right way, Johnny?" Blaine had asked.

"According to the directions passed on to me, yes."

"Wouldn't happen to have a map, would you?"

"The Tupis speak in terms of landmarks."

"What happens when we hit the jungle?"

"We follow the signs of the land."

"What about the spirits? Where are they this time? Somewhere air-conditioned, I'd bet."

Wareagle was not amused. "The words they speak filter through the light. The heart of darkness we are entering makes it difficult to hear."

Now only Johnny's massive strength pushing off of the bottom allowed the drunken Luis to steer the rickety ship that had been their home for over a day. After escaping from *Casa do Diabo*, Johnny and Blaine had driven straight to a small airfield outside of Sao Paulo. From there, unregistered flights were available to virtually anywhere in the country if the price was right. Fortunately Blaine had enough money left to make sure it was. Most of the men he usually dealt with weren't fond of credit cards, so Blaine always traveled with large reserves of cash stored within secret compartments of his carry-on bag.

The plane took them to Manaus, a sprawling river port with a population of almost a million that rose from the densest part of the Amazon jungle. A combination of high-rise buildings and older stucco structures dwarfed in their midst, Manaus attracts a huge tourist population, primarily because it is a free port. Bargains in electronic merchandise abound, televisions and stereos sold out of warehouse lots from piles of boxes stacked to the ceiling. The port section is cluttered with hucksters and fishermen selling their wares from the docks, boasting of incredible bargains and trading barbs about freshness.

Upon arriving early Sunday morning, Blaine and Johnny filtered among the streams of humanity in no mood to linger too long. The need for a boat brought them to the port section, but few were available. They opted for Luis's because he was lying drunk in a hammock and asked not a single question after being stirred. He didn't even inquire where they were going until they were a mile out in the Amazon. Then his questions were answered by the money Blaine flashed before him.

The early hours of the voyage were almost pleasant. The waters of the Amazon are black due to the dissolving of humic acid, which repels insects and mosquitos. But as morning grew into afternoon, a stifling humidity took over. McCracken sat on the deck dripping in hot sweat that drenched even his hair and beard.

The boat motored easily as Johnny's course took them into a maze of uncharted connecting waterways that ran green with the lifeblood of the countryside. With the coming of night came the onset of distinct unease on Blaine's part. They could not have risked carrying weapons through Manaus, and none were available at any of the markets, except for ancient hunting rifles and shotguns. McCracken opted for the best he could find of the latter, a pump-action job that had seen better days. That and a box of ammunition were all they had on their side against the Spirit of the Dead.

"We are close now, Blaffey," Wareagle assured him, joining Blaine in the bow, where he was keeping a careful watch on the bottom for sudden rocks. The morning had dawned friendly, but already the dripping humidity was starting to choke the air.

"You going on strike, Indian?"

"Our boatman says the shallows have ended."

Luis, behind the wheel, burped.

"And you trust him?"

"He has lived his life on the river, just as the Tupis have lived theirs in the jungle. He knows the waters as well as they know the land. Another twenty minutes and we will anchor."

The resolve on Johnny's face was sharp and keen. Mc-Cracken had seen it before, in other jungles, as other battles were looming.

They dropped anchor on schedule, and Luis helped them unload their packs; then Blaine instructed him to wait for their return. Luis gazed about him, not looking happy.

"*Quando volta?*"

Blaine gave him his best guess. "*Amanha.*"

"*Nao sei,*" the boatman said, resisting Blaine's orders.

"*Vehna ca, por favor,*" Blaine told him. And then, in English, "Come on. I've got something here for you."

Luis's eyes gleamed when Blaine produced the contents of a sack not yet unloaded: three bottles of decent whiskey he'd purchased at the port market before they'd set out.

"*Mueto bem,*" Luis thanked him. "*Muito obrigado!*"

"Then you'll be here when we get back?"

"Oh, absolutely," the boatman replied, cuddling up to the whiskey as if it were a long-lost friend.

The brush of the Amazon Basin was like nothing Blaine had ever experienced before. It was wholly unique, a world unto itself. There was no path to follow, just trees to slide between and bushes to shove back. The feeling that he might well be the first person ever to step where he was stepping was new and fresh to him. The entire jungle was alive, even more steaming than the water, with no breeze to cool the drenching sweat that poured off him.

Wareagle led the way, at first clearing their path with a machete. The deeper they plunged into the jungle, however, the shorter his swipes became, as if he were reluctant to disturb nature's delicate balance. Vines and broad leaves scraped at Blaine's face with the tenacity of iron. More than once he felt some reptilian creature slithering about his feet and feared that it might be a deadly bushmaster snake ready to inject its lethal venom into him.

The jungle about him was alive with constant animal sounds, some high-pitched and loud, others barely more than a chirp. Above, only slight rays of direct light were able to penetrate the thick canopy of trees that formed a shroud over the jungle. This part of the Amazon had thus far been spared the ruinous mining and senseless stripping of the land for profit by *bandeirantes*, the Brazilian backwoodsmen.

The jungle smelled fresh, too, in spite of the humidity; not rank like Southeast Asia. You hated Nam before you even knew you were there because the air stank. Here the woods smelled like a fresh salad and were blessed with an incredible diversity of plant and animal species that breathed vitality into the scene. Blaine dared ask himself if war might have been the difference in Nam. Perhaps it was the smell of hate more than anything that sickened him even in memory. Here there was no hate, only life; this land supplied one-third of the world's oxygen.

Wareagle followed the trail that was invisible to Blaine until they reached a large clearing that contained stray piles of wood and thick leaves.

"A tribe slept here last night," Johnny said. "Most of them set out at dawn, the rest followed closely behind to provide cover against pursuit. They were restless. Something happened that frightened them."

"You didn't tell me the Tupis were nomadic."

"Because they never were before."

They came upon the encampment two hours before sunset. Wareagle pointed out perimeter guards so well camouflaged that Blaine could barely discern them even when staring directly at their positions. The Indian then showed him where to silently wait until he returned with safe passage assured. Under the circumstances, the sight of a "white-face" might scare the Tupi guards. Their arrows and blow darts might not be as formidable as machine-gun fire, but death didn't know the difference.

Blaine watched Johnny disappear into the jungle and did as he was told. One minute dragged into another and he began to ask himself how much longer he would wait before impatience led him to make his own move. The next moments passed as slowly as any he could ever recall; he had very nearly made up his mind to follow in Johnny's steps when Wareagle's frame emerged from the brush, followed by a pair of Tupi warriors.

"We were expected, Blainey," Wareagle announced, bidding him to rise. "They knew I would be coming."

"What'd you tell them about me?"

"That you are a great white warrior who rescued me so I might rescue them. I called you *cheinama*, which in their language means a stranger who is a friend."

"Thanks for the recommendation," Blaine said.

The Tupis had been fortunate enough to find a rare valley in the Amazon Basin. As McCracken hiked down the slope to the hub of activity, he noted it was a uniquely defensible area. By the size of the branches the Tupi braves were hefting, and the way they were being stacked, he also noted that the tribe was not actually building a settlement.

They were building a fortress.

The bulk of the living quarters were being erected a story or more in the air upon sturdy tree branches linked together with tied-down logs. The construction was lean-to style and, once completed, would be accessible only by dangling vines easily pulled up to deny entry. The building of similar structures was underway closer to the rim of the valley, although these were clearly guard towers. The Tupis were developing their own early warning system.

"Looks like they're digging in," Blaine commented.

"With good reason. The chief is waiting for us."

The chief was seated cross-legged in the center of the valley, a vantage point from which he would survey all ongoing work. He was an ancient man, with white hair tied in a ponytail and a mask of wrinkles covering the coppery flesh of his face. He might have been a hundred or seventy, but Blaine could see that the muscles of his wrists and hands were those of a younger man, at least one who had never stopped using them. They protruded from a tribal shawl colored in a simple pattern with a dominant shade of wheat.

The chief spoke to Wareagle without looking at McCracken.

"He bids you welcome," Johnny translated, "and says he can tell he is in the presence of a great manitou."

"Tell him the pleasure is all mine."

Before Johnny could do so, the chief spoke again.

"O Memeka bu?"

"He wishes to know what tribe you belong to," Johnny translated.

"Tell him my own."

"Omei," Johnny repeated to the old man.

The chief laughed and said something softly to Johnny.

"He says he knew that, Blainey."

"Iti omoi reima."

"He says you are a strong man."

"Tell him thanks—and ask him what the hell is going on here!"

"Nefoteo nia?"

Wareagle waited patiently for the chief to finish before translating.

"He says they are digging in here to make a stand. He says there is no sense in running because the Spirit of the Dead will find them . . . like it found them last night."

Johnny waited for the chief to complete his thought before continuing his translation.

"Blainey, he says two boys were found missing from that clearing we came upon at dawn this morning. He says there were no tracks to indicate they wandered off and no tracks to indicate anyone had come for them. They simply disappeared."

"Thanks to this Spirit of the Dead?"

Wareagle nodded grimly. "The chief believes it to be a demon capable of appearing and disappearing as it desires. He says it was drawn up from the underworld one full moon ago by a Gift Giver still in touch with the Forgotten Times."

"In which case the defenses being erected here will prove woefully inadequate."

"They must make a stand, Blainey. Whatever is killing their people must be made to show itself where their warriors will at least have a chance."

"Ask him if any of his people have seen the Spirit of the Dead."

Wareagle obliged, and the chief shook his head methodically before responding.

"He says all that has been seen is the shape of the hatred the enemy leaves," Wareagle translated. "The enemy sucks the life out of the land, out of the world, and the result is a hollow spot, an empty spot. It is into this hollow spot that the Spirit of the Dead disappears after its work is finished."

The old man spoke again as soon as Johnny had finished speaking.

"There is more, Blainey. He says signs of the Green Coats were found in their search for the missing boys."

"Meaning soldiers?"

"Seven of them, their steps orderly and precise."

"Ben Norseman," Blaine replied, recalling his meeting with the Green Beret colonel in the lobby of the Caesar Park.

"They do not seem interested in his tribe, but they are out there, too."

Just then a panting brave rushed up to the chief and sat next to him, whispering. The old man listened calmly, then turned to look up at Wareagle and spoke softly.

"He says the missing boys have been found," Wareagle translated. "He wants us to come."

The boys' bodies swayed in the breeze, suspended from the tree by vines tied around their throats. The instrument of death, though, had been something much worse.

They had been disemboweled while still alive.

Large, jagged holes had been sliced in their abdomens, the contents drained a bit at a time. The pain would have been enormous, and much of it was still frozen on their faces. Blood from their mouths and noses had dripped down to their chests like paint running down a wall. Blaine kept his eyes on it to distract himself from the holes ripped where their stomachs had been. He kept to a distance where the smell was less intense.

"What did this, Johnny? What the hell did this?"

Wareagle had ventured closer, eyes cold as marbles. He stared at the corpses and swiped at the flies that had clustered about. The boys' toes dangled two feet off the ground, so Johnny was looking directly into their dead eyes.

"The vines are knotted in a way that would not bring on suffocation," he said, eyes lowering. "The initial stomach cuts were made with a sharp object, a knife perhaps, so the skin could be parted and stripped back. The contents could then be pulled out." He turned to McCracken. "By hand."

"Jesus Christ. . . ."

Wareagle had leaned over the stinking pile of the corpses' insides. Blaine drew up even with him, while the chief and Tupi warriors kept their distance.

"What about tracks?"

Wareagle was on his knees now, sliding his callused palms across the ground. "Nothing from the time of these killings. Much from after."

"I'm listening."

"Seven men wearing U.S. combat boots."

"Norseman," Blaine muttered. "Ben and his goons must have come in to hunt something down." He looked at Wareagle. "Our Spirit of the Dead maybe."

Wareagle looked up. "The Green Coats came in from the northeast. I can follow their tracks. They may bring us closer to what we have come to find."

McCracken gazed up at the last of the day's light. "Not without sun. We'll spend the night with the Tupis, help them make their stand, and leave come morning."

"Something might come before that."

"Save us a trip, Indian."

CHAPTER 7

THE Tupi warriors patrolled the valley's perimeter in positions shown them by Wareagle. Blaine hung back through it all; not yet fully accepted by the Tupis, he focused his energies in other directions. Perimeter guards out of contact with one another were too vulnerable to attack, too easy to eliminate one at a time, so Wareagle's plan had them patrolling in concentric circles that meant one brave would pass another every hundred yards. Still, this left too many easily breached holes in the perimeter. Hell, just the night before the Spirit of the Dead, as the Tupis called it, had made off with two boys without leaving any trace. Couldn't dare leave it any opening at all in view of that.

What the braves needed was a good set of walkie-talkies. Lacking that, Blaine would have to make do with what was available. He glanced at the tribal chief, still seated in the center of the valley, a small fire burning before him. McCracken smiled.

Thirty minutes later fourteen fires were going around the rim of the valley. Every three minutes the braves tending them would drop a special ash made from tree bark into the flames to produce a noxious white smoke. The white smoke would serve as the all's-well signal to the spotters in the valley. A missed interval would spell trouble, and the tribe would know where to concentrate their forces.

Wareagle paced into the black hours of the morning. The

51

jungle was louder then; animal and bird sounds seemed to travel farther in the darkness. Blaine approached him with the pump action propped on his shoulder. Johnny regarded the weapon with apparent disdain.

"Come on, Indian, whatever this Spirit of the Dead turns out to be, it's not bulletproof."

"But neither does it fear that bullets can stop it."

McCracken sniffed the air. Maybe, just maybe, a new scent sifted through. The beginnings of something rancid and spoiled. He shook his imagination away.

"We've been through this before."

"Not the hellfire, Blainey."

"Why not? Guns didn't always work against Charlie, either. Waving that big M-16 made you feel invincible until you stepped on a mine or a trap or got hit when one of them popped out of a tunnel."

"The Black Hearts did what they had to. What we are facing here does what it likes."

McCracken had to bring up what had forced its way into his mind. "You felt something else back where we found those boys, Indian. You didn't say anything about it, but I could tell."

Wareagle smiled. "Perhaps it is you the spirits have chosen to speak through this time."

"I'd welcome anything that helps get us out of here alive, including the whole truth of what you know."

"Feel, Blainey."

"Same thing, Indian."

Bursts of white smoke filled the air along the rim of the valley as another three-minute interval passed.

"The Spirit of the Dead enjoys what it does," Wareagle told him softly. "It is propelled by a need to kill like an animal that will starve if it doesn't hunt. The pain and suffering of its victims are its food."

"Then we'd better find it before it finds us."

"The daytime belongs to us."

"So long as we make it through the night."

McCracken half expected Wareagle to return from a sweep of the perimeter at dawn with a report that all the Tupi braves had been killed during the final three-minute interval. But the look on the big Indian's face told him all was well.

"The night passed without incident," he reported. "No sign of the Spirit of the Dead, Blainey, but evidence of the Green Coats was found to the south of us."

"Norseman?"

"Still seven men, heavily weighed down by equipment and gear. They could have entered the valley at anytime, but chose not to, almost as if, as if . . ."

"As if what?"

"They saw the valley as a trap."

"To catch what, Indian? Seems pretty obvious now they're after the same thing we are. The question is why."

"The answer may lie only in following the trail they have left us."

For the better part of the morning, Johnny followed the trail the soldiers had taken from the north through the jungle. The sticky heat of the afternoon sun was just beginning to make itself felt when Johnny stopped and stood pole straight. Blaine could feel the Indian's energy emanating outward like a strobe light, pins and needles dancing about his flesh and turning into daggers as they took to the air.

"What's wrong, Johnny?"

No reply.

"Johnny?"

Silence.

"Johnny . . ."

Wareagle turned. "We're close, Blainey. There's something up there, beyond those trees."

They started on again, Johnny moving like a big jungle cat. Where he walked, Blaine figured, there would be no trail, either. Johnny parted a huge thicket of overbrush and waited for Blaine to draw even. McCracken looked where Johnny was pointing and found himself gazing at the impossible.

There, in the thick of the jungle, was a massive building!

Just as quickly as his eyes had focused on the structure, it fluttered from his vision like a mirage in the desert, thanks to its sloping construction and shading. The lines and colors flowed perfectly with the jungle, as if construction had been carried out without disturbing a single tree or bush. Johnny led the way closer; a tall steel-link fence came into focus, camouflaged with brush that virtually swallowed it. None of this belonged here, yet here, undeniably, it was. Perhaps it held the answer to whatever was happening in the jungle.

McCracken looked at Wareagle. "What is this place, Indian?"

"I feel death, Blainey—more terrible than even you and I have experienced. We lived in the hellfire, and it lived in us. The land retained its life in spite of the death we brought to it. But what lies before us is nothing but black, a charred symbol on the crest of man."

"You're saying this is some kind of scientific installation?"

Wareagle looked at him. "The birthplace of the Spirit of the Dead."

Blaine could feel Wareagle's tension growing. "What's wrong, Johnny?"

"No one is watching for us. There should be guards, but there are none anywhere."

"If Norseman's down here, he's in charge. We'll ask him about the oversight when we get the chance."

Johnny stepped through the parted overbrush. "Walk lightly, Blainey. Follow my every step."

McCracken did just that. They reached the steel fence; Johnny followed until he came to a gate. The lock was missing. The gate shifted slightly in the breeze. McCracken steadied his Remington pump.

They slid into a courtyard. On the uphill grade that led to the building, McCracken expected guards to lunge out at every turn. But Johnny's stoic stance ahead of him proved no one was on patrol in the area.

The courtyard ended at a set of rock steps chiseled into the hillside. The structure itself had been painted a bland shade of olive and was totally absorbed by the tangle of flora growing about and partially enveloping it. Finding such a perfect spot must have been difficult.

At the installation's main entrance, Blaine's eyes were drawn immediately to the dual cameras mounted over the door. The cameras did not move as they should have to follow their progress. The big Indian worked the latch. It gave, but the door resisted opening. A hefty shove forced it in far enough for them to enter.

Halfway inside it became clear what had been blocking their way. A guard's body had been propped against the door. His dead hand still gripped a machine gun. Blood drenched his midsection and the floor beneath him.

"Dead about eighteen hours," Blaine said after inspecting the body. "A day at the outside."

"He died barring the door, Blainey."

Blaine observed the trail of blood that ran down a dimly lit corridor. "But he was killed inside."

"Let's head on," Johnny said.

They walked side by side. The first door they came to was a monitoring station that served as the broadcast point for the many video cameras placed inside and out. Beneath the darkened monitors lay the bodies of three men in the same olive uniforms as the guard. They weren't armed, but had been killed in a similarly messy fashion. McCracken had the same feeling here that had struck him the day before when he and Johnny had come upon the bodies of the two Tupi boys. He backed out of the monitoring room ahead of Wareagle.

In silence the two of them continued on their way. The narrow corridor gave way to a wider one. Four bodies in bloodied white lab coats lay crumpled at irregular intervals. Wareagle hesitated over the first; his face showed revulsion. Blaine could see it was a woman and got close enough to see something else.

Her face had been torn apart.

"Mother of God, Johnny! What the hell did this?"

Wareagle gave no answer. He continued on to an open door from which a burning smell emanated. McCracken followed him inside what had been a conference room. Its chairs had been upended to clear a space in the middle of a floor now covered with embers and ruined tile. Against one wall a series of file cabinets lay tipped over and emptied. Obviously their former contents had fueled the flames. McCracken noticed the blackened edge of a page fragment wedged beneath one of the fallen chairs and retrieved it while Johnny surveyed the rest of the damage.

"Anything, Blainey?" he asked.

Blaine held the page up to the room's single emergency light.
"Too badly damaged to lift anything off. Except . . . Wait a
minute . . . There *is* something. Not much, but . . ."

He was able to trace four bolder letters at the edge of the
page, all that had not been lost to the fire. O-M-I-C.

"Mean anything to you, Blainey?" Wareagle asked from
behind him.

"Not a fucking thing, Indian."

They checked the room thoroughly, but could find no further
fragments. Whoever had hit the complex had been thorough.
Since the hit had come from the inside, though, the victims
had quite obviously known their killers. He thought of Ben
Norseman, wondering if for some reason this had been his
work. This might not have been even Ben's style, but there
was no other logical explanation.

"I can't believe Ben Norseman and his men would do something like this, Indian."

"I don't believe they did, Blainey. Outside the installation,
their tracks indicated they returned here *after* the massacre,
and they went out again."

McCracken put it together in his mind. "After whatever was
responsible, a trail that took them to the area of the Tupi camp
before we made our appearance yesterday."

"The camp was the Green Coats' trap, Blainey, just as we
suspected."

"Only whatever was behind this massacre didn't go for it."

Wareagle's stare grew distant. "The people here were killed
from within," he said.

"By *what*, Johnny?"

"Perhaps the installation can still tell us."

They proceeded on in their investigation of the facility, but
everywhere the results were the same. Equipment smashed.
Hallways, rooms, and labs littered with bodies. The killing
had been carried out with brutal efficiency, no one spared, no
mercy given.

Wareagle looked to the walls as if they might provide some
explanation. "The dead feeling present in the forest is strong-
est in the steps we have followed. It started here and spread
outward."

"Then there's something we can be sure of, Johnny. To take all these people out so quickly and systematically, there had to be more than one of these Spirits of the Dead, whatever they turn out to be." His eyes bulged in realization. "Meanwhile, Norseman must still be after them. Seven Green Berets armed to the teeth who eat nails for breakfast." McCracken looked at his Remington. "Better shape than we're in."

"This complex would have been in better shape, too."

Close scrutiny of a rear wall revealed to McCracken a hidden door behind which were stairs descending into the bowels of the complex. The air instantly felt chillier, and Blaine imagined a breeze sifting by him as he and Wareagle headed down. The lighting here was brighter, and the first door on the right was open. It led into an office of some kind. The remnants of a paper shredder's work had overflowed from a trash can. Filing cabinet drawers were open down here as well. They had been yanked out and completely rifled.

"Looks like somebody was busy on this level, too, Indian. Destroying everything, by the looks of it."

"Not everything, Blainey," Wareagle said as one of his massive hands emerged from the depths of the shredder bin with a partially mangled leather report cover.

He showed it to Blaine so the title was clearly visible: THE OMICRON PROJECT.

McCracken recalled the letters O-M-I-C from the fragment on the floor above. Omicron, the fifteenth letter of the Greek alphabet. Slightly distracted now, he followed Wareagle onward. The next series of rooms all housed medical laboratories that still smelled faintly of alcohol. It was almost a refreshing scent, considering what they had been exposed to in the complex thus far. Lab bottles and test tubes lay in pieces everywhere, and they found another five corpses covered with debris. The glass doors of locked cabinets had been smashed, and their contents coated the floor with a carpet of slivers. The remains of needles could be seen, along with shards of thicker containers.

The final door on the hall led into what appeared to be a surgical unit. Much of the equipment in here had proved too bulky to destroy; what remained was a collection of machines of a sort Blaine had never seen before.

"Imagers, I think," he said, fingering one. "Used during microsurgery and for diagnosis."

There were standard X-ray and CAT scan equipment as well, along with an operating table that was bolted to the floor. Dangling from all four of its sides were leather straps used to tie a patient down.

"Looks like the Omicron Project involved some pretty heavy medical R and D," said McCracken. "Using human subjects."

"Or what used to be human."

"The only thing we know for sure about them is they're gone. Let's check out the next floor."

They found the door at the end of this corridor to be different than the others: ten-inch slab steel with an electronic locking mechanism. The door had been opened and the mechanism shorted out to keep it that way. The air grew still colder as they descended to the complex's second underground level. The corridor here was slightly shorter, and six doors thinly spaced apart opened on either side, with an equal number closed.

Blaine and Johnny's inspection found them to be identical in every way: windowless cubicles complete with bed, chair, desk, and bureau. Joined to the near wall of each was a closet-sized bathroom. The door was of six-inch steel, with triple-thick hinges and an electronic locking mechanism. At ceiling level on the far wall was the protruding tip of a video surveillance lens.

"Not a great place to bring a date, under the circumstances," said Blaine.

At the other end of the corridor rose another steel security door, this one featuring a thick glass slab at eye level.

"One-way glass," Blaine said when he got there.

He pressed his eyes against the cold surface and peered through. It was a room much like the others, except it was bigger. The mattress had been shredded, the bed frame pulled apart at the joints, and the chest of drawers smashed into splinters. Blaine backed away so Johnny could get a better look, but even without the Indian's spirits there to tell him, Blaine had the feeling that what had happened in the complex had started right here, behind this final door.

McCracken felt a tremor of fear pass through him. It wasn't

an unfamiliar sensation and sometimes was even welcome. But this time it lingered long enough to become distressing. He had the urge to find a radio and call for help, even though he knew the communications equipment would surely have been trashed.

"Forget the Spirit of the Dead," he said to Johnny. "Looks like your friends the Tupis were up against a *tribe* of spirits."

"*Wakinyan* is the Sioux word for them, Blainey."

"Meaning?"

"Thunder beings, as savage as the storm itself. Merciless and indestructible."

"Let's hope not."

CHAPTER 8

TUESDAY's dusk was barely three hours away when Blaine and Johnny emerged from the death-filled complex. In all they had found twenty-eight bodies, and even McCracken found himself shaking slightly.

"We must go, Blainey," Wareagle announced, gazing ahead as if to sniff the air.

"Are you on their trail, Indian?"

"Yes and no."

"No riddles. Please."

"The only trail I can find is Norseman's. Following it will take us to what we seek."

Two miles back into the jungle, Wareagle crouched down and began working his fingers in the dirt.

"Norseman?" Blaine asked.

"There's more. Now part of another trail separate from his team's. Fresher."

"You're saying he's being followed?"

"Doubled back on is more like it."

"How many?" McCracken asked, thinking of the dozen empty beds plus one they had found at the complex.

"I cannot tell. The evidence is slight, a slip, or perhaps one of them leaning over to do just what I'm doing now."

"What you're telling me is that you can't find a single track belonging to whatever doubled back on Norseman?"

"For a creature in harmony with the land, walking without any trace is quite possible."

"How far are they behind Norseman?"

"An hour, maybe two."

"And us?"

"At least that much behind them."

The jungle turned harsh and brutal from there, more humid and steaming than ever. The animal and bird sounds lost their harmonious ring. The heavy green foliage became tangled and more difficult to part. The route was hilly, irregular. Sudden drops occurred without notice. Branches scratched at McCracken's flesh, and he flailed at them in frustration. Blaine couldn't have said if fatigue and foreboding were to blame, or if the *Wakinyan*, as Johnny called them, had led Norseman's team into these treacherous parts for a reason. In any case, this direction also led to the trunk river, where Luis would be waiting with their boat.

Night's dark fingers were starting to spread across the sky when Johnny went rigid in his tracks.

"What's wrong, Indian?"

"I heard something, Blainey."

"Where?"

"Ahead of us . . . As much as a mile."

"Any idea what?"

"I'm . . . not sure."

Wareagle's gait changed from there; now he moved like a great predator approaching prey that had its back turned. Mc-Cracken followed—and stopped abruptly behind Johnny when the big Indian froze, his arms flexed by his sides.

"Sniff the air, Blainey."

McCracken did. "I don't—Wait a minute . . . Holy shit, you're right!"

There was an unmistakable scent of gunpowder and sulphur-based explosives sifting through the wind.

"How far, Indian?"

"A half mile, at most."

They covered that distance with little regard for the fact that the *Wakinyan* might be retracing their steps directly for them. Somehow Blaine felt even if the enemy knew they were here, it was not in their plans to do anything about it. That enemy had other priorities, which it would pursue with all haste.

The gunpowder smell grew into a full-fledged assault on their nostrils in the last dozen yards before they stepped into the clearing. They stopped dead still.

"Norseman," Blaine muttered.

Or what was left of him. The seven ravaged corpses had been arranged in a trio of yard-deep chasms in the ground. Crosses made of branches had been jammed through the center of their chests, and the bodies had been left so that the crosses flowed in one precise row, so precise that only by changing his perspective could Blaine actually tell there was more than one.

Wareagle had moved further into the clearing, and bent to pick up discharged shells and empty clips on the ground. A bit deeper in he came upon discarded grenade pins and the tripod for an M-60 that lay nearby.

"How did this happen, Johnny?"

"Norseman's men didn't know they were being ambushed until it was too late. They responded with fire in all directions."

"Then whatever they killed must have been hauled away."

"I don't believe they killed anything, or even *hit* anything. Their shots were wild. It is clear they had no targets, only sounds they were supposed to hear."

"And then our friends from the complex rushed in and opened fire when they were facing in the wrong direction?"

Wareagle shook his head. "No, Blainey. All the shells here belong to Norseman's men. Their bodies have no bullet wounds."

"Wait a minute! You're telling me seven Green Berets armed to the teeth couldn't protect themselves from an *unarmed* attack?"

"I said no guns. I did not say unarmed."

"How could they let the *Wakinyan* get so close? How could Ben Norseman's men let those things parade right into the middle of a firefight and not take a single one out with them?"

"I can't say, Blainey. There are no tracks leading in or out except for Norseman's. Everything stops here."

"Except us, Indian. The one good thing is that the *Wakinyan* left all the weapons behind. Virtually confirms the fact that they still don't know we're in the neighborhood."

"Or suggests they want to give us a chance. More sport."

"No, they want out. They hit the installation because they had somewhere else they wanted to be. Norseman was in their way. We're not."

"Not yet."

McCracken moved to Ben Norseman's corpse and stripped the pack from his back. Inside was a thick, oblong metallic cylinder about eighteen inches in length. As Johnny brought the cylinder closer to him, it seemed to tremble in his hands.

"Blainey?"

"It's a fuel air explosive, Indian. Once activated it spreads a highly volatile gas over a wide radius for a predetermined period of time and then detonates. The gas ignites, and what you end up with is a huge air blast that leaves nothing behind."

"Perhaps Norseman was out to set a trap of his own."

"And then he never even got the explosive out of his pack. He would have tried, you know. When what was happening to him became clear, he would have used it."

"Which means the *Wakinyan* didn't give him the time."

"Wouldn't have taken much, so they must not have given him any," Blaine said, and started away.

Stepping through the clearing, Blaine's foot bumped something solid concealed beneath a bed of leaves. He pushed them aside and grasped a black electronic device. He found the On button and the screen jumped to life, showing a square grid dominated by a circle sweeping over it and then starting again, like a miniature radar screen.

"A range finder, Blainey?"

McCracken nodded. "Five-hundred-yard radius, by the look of it. Norseman wasn't taking any chances with his pursuit. High tech all the way. Doesn't look like it helped much."

"They knew he was coming. They knew where."

"What are you saying?"

"I'm not sure. The men were killed at close range—when they should have had plenty of warning as well as time. They had neither."

McCracken's eyes fell to the range finder. Its sweep continued, programmed, he assumed, to the specifications of what Norseman had been told he was hunting. The circle closed and started again, nothing showing in the grid.

"Coast looks clear, Indian."

"Like it did to the Green Coats, Blainey."

"How far to the boat?"

"Two hours in the dark. Easy level ground."

McCracken was strapping the M-60 to his shoulder. "No reason to travel light then."

The moon would have made for plenty of light, if its rays had been strong enough to push themselves through the dense cover of the jungle. In some places it might as well have been a darkened cave they were walking through. Occasionally slivers of moonbeams briefly illuminated a path that seemed unchanging.

In the darkest parts, the range finder's sweeping red grid made for a grim luminescence. McCracken had been carrying it since they'd left the clearing and the corpses of Ben Norseman's team. The thing made a slight beeping sound with each circular pass. Blaine figured they were still thirty minutes from the river. There were no guarantees Luis would have waited the extra time with the boat. Their best chance there lay in the hope that the whiskey had lasted longer than expected. If not—

Beep, beep, beep, beep, beep, beep . . .

McCracken heard the range finder come alive in his hand. Suddenly its circular sweep was lined with red flashing dots clustered along a narrow sphere in the bottom left-hand grid.

Wareagle had already gone rigid.

"We've got company, Indian."

"Where, Blainey?"

"Behind us to the south. Five hundred yards back, if I'm reading this right."

McCracken stripped the M-60 machine gun from his shoulder. Damn thing weighed a ton. He'd handled a 7.62-mm Vulcan in the streets of Tehran, but not dead tired and in darkness so profound it was sure to confound his aim.

"No, Blainey," said Wareagle.

"What?"

"Norseman and his men would have seen the same thing. They reached the clearing and made their stand because that is what the *Wakinyan* wanted. The Green Coats saw only what they were supposed to see."

On the range finder, the blips had moved into the next grid.

"What are you saying?"

"The graves, Blainey. I realize now the graves are the key. They did not dig them to bury Norseman and his men. The holes were already there when the Green Coats arrived. The *Wakinyan* dug them so they could hide and then lunge upon the Green Coats from within their midst. It explains everything. By the time Norseman and the others opened fire, it was too late."

Beep, beep, beep . . .

"Then . . ."

"They're ahead of us as well as behind. Planted somewhere, camouflaged, waiting in the very spot they know we will make *our* stand."

McCracken's eyes darted back and forth from the range finder to Wareagle. "But they knew Norseman was trailing them. We're a different story."

"The night has betrayed us. They must have circled back. Or . . ."

"Four hundred yards, Indian. Or what?"

"They knew about our presence from the start."

"And left Norseman's weapons out in the open?"

"Giving us what we wanted, what we needed to play their game."

"Three hundred and fifty yards . . . What now?"

"They timed their move perfectly. All routes north and south are impassable."

The range finder seemed to be getting louder.

"Leaving us with only east and west. Terrific."

"There is a third option, Blainey."

"Three hundred yards, Indian."

"They know even before we do where we will choose to make our stand ahead. Their greatest weapon is this very understanding. It was no different in the hellfire with the Black Hearts. Remember, Blainey?"

McCracken's mind drifted back and wanted to stay there. "We became the Black Hearts, and that's how we beat them. That's how we stayed alive."

"As we must do again, Blainey."

Beep, beep, beep . . .

CHAPTER 9

THE ditches they dug in the ground were just deep enough to conceal them under a layer of dirt and brush. Blaine had switched the range finder off when the blips were less than one hundred yards away. Then Johnny helped him cover himself. How the big Indian could manage the same task all by himself, Blaine would never know. But there was plenty about Johnny he couldn't fathom and never would.

Blaine silently counted out the steps of their pursuers, trying to anticipate the second those steps would be upon their position. If Wareagle's ploy didn't work, death would come with no chance for resistance. But Johnny's words had their usual ring of confidence. The best strategy makes use of something the enemy uses himself, something so personal that the idea of another using it is inconceivable.

Blaine recognized that the means by which the *Wakinyan* had dispatched Norseman's team had changed Johnny's view of them. Their use of such a brilliant stratagem revealed them to be clever tacticians as well as murderous monsters.

A faint rustling reached Blaine in his self-made crypt. Not a sound so much as a disturbance in the ground he had become a part of. It was no more than the here-and-gone ruffle a small creature would make as it went its way in the underbrush. And yet it belonged to creatures powerful enough to savagely murder seven Green Berets.

He could feel the ground stir directly above him.

One of them's right above me . . .

Gone, though, before he could even complete the thought. Somehow that slowed Blaine's heart. The test had been passed. Johnny's plan, this part anyway, was going to work.

But a fresh fear washed over him like cold water down the back on a hot summer day. He had made the world of the enemy his own world in Vietnam, in Israel, in a dozen other countries. He had felt his heart lurching for his throat and his guts twisted into bag ties to hold in his breath. The feeling that had just passed over him now was not the black cold he remembered. It was more like a frigid void, a white noise darkening in the night, as if a vacuum were walking above.

Blaine hardened his resolve to keep from trembling. He almost retched, and his sense of time deserted him. With his other senses already stifled, the vise of panic tightened around him.

Fight it, dammit! Fight it!

Forming that resolve coherently was enough to do the job. The shallow breathing he allowed himself steadied. Blaine flexed his fingers to regain physical control.

Then a hand drove down into his hollow. McCracken kicked for freedom as it pushed for his face.

Blaine recognized the hand as Johnny's just in time to still himself.

"We must move quickly, Blainey. They will be back before long."

Wareagle helped McCracken to his feet and watched him stretch the life back into his limbs. Then Blaine leaned back over and retrieved the range finder from his hollow.

Beep, beep, beep . . .

"Moving away from us, Indian."

"Not for long."

The red blips continued to move farther from the center of the grid.

"So, what now?"

"We use more of their medicine against them. We set a trap, Blainey. With us as bait."

"Because Ben Norseman was kind enough to leave us with the snare we needed," McCracken said as he pulled the fuel air explosive cylinder from his pack.

"The *Wakinyan* who walked upon our graves will meet up with the rest soon," said Wareagle. "When they backtrack our way, our own personal hellfire will greet them."

"Gonna piss off a lot of conservationists, Indian."

"The land will understand, Blainey. Something must die if the balance of nature is to be preserved." Wareagle gazed through the dark jungle in the same direction the range finder was aimed. "They're coming."

"Pretty decent breeze. What do you make for direction?"

"At our backs now; blowing west to east."

"And say two to three minutes for the *Wakinyan* to cover the five hundred yards the range finder gives us." He turned the cylinder over to work the timer. "I'll set the timer for a minute and a half. Catch them dead in the center that way."

"Not right here, Blainey."

"Why?"

"The shock wave could still catch us. We're in a valley right now, but we can make that work for us by climbing out after setting the charge near the rim."

"I like your thinking, Indian."

Heading west, they soon reached the point where the valley began to slope upward. Blaine's eyes darted furiously from the trail to the range finder, which so far had shown nothing.

"Get ready, Blainey."

McCracken handed the range finder to Johnny and pulled the explosive cylinder from his pack. It was heavier than it looked, and he lowered it to the ground to set the timing and release mechanism. The whole process was incredibly simple.

"Just tell me when."

The sweep of the range finder's arrow found a small splotch coming in from the east and the wind that blew toward it.

"Now, Blainey."

McCracken had already set the timer on the 1:30 mark. He flipped a switch; a small light next to it glowed dull dusty red.

"Let's move, Indian!"

They sped up the slope and out of the valley, never looking back. McCracken's eyes darted constantly to his watch. Wareagle counted the seconds in his mind. At a minute twenty-five, Blaine started to shout a warning that was lost in the blast that followed.

It came like a sonic boom, a hammer blow striking the earth itself. The night was instantly alight with a blinding orange flash that turned white as heat poured from it. A hot gush of air caught Blaine and Johnny from behind and pitched them airborne. Branches, stones, fragments of boulders and trees rained down on them as they instinctively covered their heads. A fire that was too hot to burn very long continued to light up the night. The air crackled and popped. McCracken's face was singed, and his breath was hot.

"The *Wakinyan* are burning in hell, Indian," he said finally.

"Only if hell will have them, Blainey."

They moved over tough terrain, up a steep grade. The flames died before long, but a whitish glow continued to emanate from the area of the blast. A huge, gaping scar would be left in the body of the jungle, but its soul was unmarred. Johnny assured Blaine of this.

The two men walked until the terrain became too treacherous and they were forced to stop until the next morning. Though both were exhausted, they maintained alternate watches all night. Neither wanted to admit their fear that the *Wakinyan* might have survived the massive blast, but they felt it nonetheless, and Blaine spent his watch with his eye on the range finder.

The arrow swept monotonously and found nothing.

At dawn they started out for where they had left Luis and

their boat. It was a two-hour journey, much of it downhill. The last stretch was accompanied by the quiet sounds of the trunk river, which had delivered them to the jungle in the first place. At last Wareagle led the way down the first path that looked familiar. It was all McCracken could do to restrain himself from bursting out of the jungle in glee. Everything considered, it wouldn't bother him terribly if he never saw the Amazon Basin again.

Up ahead, Wareagle had stopped on the trunk river's bank, shoulders stiffening in familiar fashion.

"Son of a bitch," Blaine muttered when his eyes followed Johnny's toward the water.

The boat was missing. Luis was gone.

"Looks like I didn't give the bastard enough whiskey."

"No, Blainey," said Wareagle.

And that was when McCracken realized Johnny was looking upward to the right, toward a shape swaying in the breeze. Luis, more accurately what remained of him, had been hung from a tree branch twenty feet off the ground. His eyes bulged, and his tongue protruded grotesquely. Hanging had not been the worst that had happened to him.

His hands and feet had been sliced off. The blood that had dropped from the stumps had pooled in the brush and leaves, scarlet red against dark green.

Blaine and Johnny barely had time to glance at each other before the pair of Blackhawk helicopters swooped down over the river and hovered with machine guns clearly leveled at them.

"Raise your hands in the air and hold your positions!" a voice blared over a loudspeaker. "Repeat: Raise your hands in the air and stay where you are!"

McCracken found himself doing just as he was told, though his gaze was fixed on the course of the empty river. The descending Blackhawk pushed its stiff back wind into him, and he closed his eyes against the sudden onslaught of debris. He couldn't see anything now, but there was nothing to see. Their boat was long gone by now, and the blackest part of this heart of darkness was surely on board.

PART TWO

Omicron

Laurel Canyon:
Thursday, November 28, 1991; 8:00 P.M.

CHAPTER 10

" . . . **P**LEASE wait for the tone to speak."

Patty Hunsecker left the same message yet again, this one perhaps a bit more harried and frantic, because she felt something was dreadfully wrong.

Of course, she had felt that way for some time now, but this was different. She found herself lingering by the upstairs study window that overlooked the front of the family's Laurel Canyon home, seeing nothing but the dark.

Nothing.

That was what Captain Banyan of the Los Angeles Police Department had thought of the story she had brought to him, passing it off as sheer fabrication. The FBI and the Justice Department had agreed. Most recently her collected tear sheets, now a bit ragged around the edges, accompanied her to the office of her congressional representative. The man's chief aide promised to get right back to her.

He hadn't.

There was only one place left to turn, the place she probably should have gone to in the first place: Blaine McCracken. Why not? He owed her, didn't he? Hadn't he said as much in Guam eighteen months before? Maybe he had forgotten. In any case, he hadn't returned the emergency calls she had been leaving on his private answering machine.

Call back, McCracken, goddamn you! Call me back!

She looked away from the window toward the phone. It didn't ring.

Her mind drifted to the time in her life when she had first met McCracken. She'd left Stanford after her junior year and used the trust fund left to her by her grandmother to purchase and outfit the *Runaway*, a research vessel crammed with scientific equipment. She was going to spend her life at sea, dedicating herself to studying the oceans and preserving their ecological balance. It was a good dream. But her parents had resisted even discussion of the issue, so she hadn't included them in the decision. Strange people, her parents. They'd married young, and had had her barely a year later. Around the time she turned thirteen, they decided to have more children. Her first brother was born later that year, her second brother two and a half years after. The boys were not even of school age when she left the house for college; they were still strangers when she took off for the Pacific.

But now her parents were both dead, and the boys were fully in her charge. There was so much to consider, so much to do. She had inherited not only her brothers, but also her family's great wealth.

Phillip Hunsecker had been one of the original makers of the Silicon Valley complex that later made him. His business interests were wholly diversified now and all successful. The same could be said for the others who had perished as he had. And now, at last, she had found a link between them. Tenuous, yes, perhaps even a bizarre coincidence. Nonetheless, it was there, and still, no one would listen. But Blaine McCracken would, once he called, if he called. . . .

Patty could do nothing now but wait for that call. Standing by the window in the isolated two-and-a-half-story Laurel Canyon house, she could see the winding canyon road at the end of the driveway. Patty realized that since she'd been away the trees had grown so thick that a clear view of the street was now all but impossible. Only when an occasional stiff breeze parted them could she see the road beyond.

During one of these sharp breezes, she saw the car for the first time. Normally *nobody* parked on this street. They parked in driveways if they had any business being in the neighborhood at all.

Her brothers were doing their homework. There were no guard dogs, no servants, just a security service that did regular drive-bys. Their car maybe? No. The security company drove metallic silver sedans with light assemblies on top. The one she had glimpsed outside was black. Patty stayed by the window waiting for the wind to part the trees. Each time it did, the black car was still there. She heard her thirteen-year-old brother, David, playing the latest from Guns and Roses; the eleven-year-old, Tyler, yelling to turn it louder so he could hear, too.

The black car was still outside. Probably nothing.

Fuck that.

If you didn't trust your feelings, what good were they to you? A feeling had assured her there was far more to her father's death, and now the same uneasiness in her stomach returned about the car. She'd call the police and make something up to draw them here. Maybe just call the security company direct. For what the family paid monthly, they'd better send a car around. Let their imitation cops play it for real. Patty moved to the Queen Anne desk in the library and picked up the phone.

No dial tone.

It was dead.

Enough of this shit. There was a panic button rigged into the security system, and she rushed to the keypad and hit it, ears braced for the high-pitched wailing.

Nothing.

She barely had time to consider fear, let alone feel it, when the lights died—and the big house was plunged into darkness.

"Must be the circuit breakers," Patty's brother said as he reached the halfway point of the circular stairway.

Patty bounded upward and stopped him there. Tyler was standing still in the dark at the top.

"Hold it," she told David.

"Hold what?"

"It's not the circuit breakers."

"How do you know?"

"I do, that's all."

Just then Tyler screamed, and Patty raced up the rest of the stairs.

"Outside!" the boy wailed, gesturing fearfully toward the huge bay window in the front. "I saw someone moving outside!"

"Get back in your room!" Patty ordered.

"No!"

"David!" she shouted. "Take your brother and get into his room."

The elder of her two brothers, incredibly, didn't look scared. "Dad had a gun," was all he said.

"Where?"

"I don't know. I don't know where he kept it. Somewhere in his room. That's where it's gotta be."

Patty weighed her options. The phone and alarm were useless to her. To escape on the ground would be impossible with her brothers in tow. There were two family cars parked in the garage, but the garage was detached, and it would take a dash from the house to get there. Even if they made it, they would have confined themselves to an unacceptably small space, and for what? If the parties beyond had the resources to knock out the best security system California money could buy, it was a cinch they'd like nothing better than to trap their prey in the garage.

"Want me to look?" David was asking.

"No," Patty said. She wasn't much good with guns anyway.

Blaine McCracken was, damn him. Why hadn't he returned her calls? All that stuff about owing her after Guam, and this was what it came down to. He hadn't listened; no one had listened.

As David began to protest her decision, Patty saw with horror that Tyler had edged closer to the huge glass window.

"No!"

Even as she screamed, Patty had hurled herself into motion. Two quick steps and then a lunge. She engulfed Tyler with her body and took him down just as segments of the window shattered into spiderweb patterns.

"Get down!" she yelled at David.

"Those were bullets!" he screeched back from the floor.

"Stay down!"

Dragging Tyler with her, she moved toward David, reaching him just as more glass popped inward with soft *pfffffft* sounds. The bastards outside had made it difficult for themselves by killing the lights. She continued pulling her brothers to the nearest doorway as glass continued to spray over them. At least they'll know I'm telling the truth now, she reasoned. Banyan and the rest of them. She could see it on her gravestone now: HERE LIES PATTY. NOBODY GAVE A FUCK UNTIL SHE WAS DEAD.

But there were her brothers to think about here, as well. If she couldn't be there for her mother or father, at least she could be here for them now.

As soon as she closed the door to her father's upstairs study, she realized what a lousy place it was to make a stand. Feeling cornered, Patty tried to think of something, anything . . .

Her eyes fell on the brick chimney above the fireplace on the near wall. What she saw there determined her next series of moves.

"Dad's gun," she said to David.

"I can go find it."

She grabbed his shoulder. "Can you fire it?"

"He took me to the range. Twice."

"Find it and come back here to your brother. Anyone comes up the stairs besides me, shoot them."

David swallowed air, "What about *you*?"

"They gotta get in to hurt us, pal," she said as her eyes returned to the crossed Civil War swords hanging over the mantle. "I'm gonna be waiting when they do."

The sword was heavier than it looked. Patty tested its tip with a finger; a tiny drop of blood proved its sharpness. Moving back into the corridor with it, she felt quite absurd. The closest she had ever come to wielding a sword had been an underwater knife, and that wasn't very close at all. She crept down the circular stairway with her body tensed to spring, the sword gripped too tightly in her right hand.

She felt certain the house had not yet been penetrated. The outside doors showed wood veneer exteriors, but boasted a heavy steel core. The windows were triple-paned, easily penetrable by a bullet, but not at all easily by a man. There would be noise when penetration was attempted, and when she heard it, her best hope was that she and her sword would be close enough by to act.

At the foot of the stairs, she crawled toward the main entrance. Barely two minutes had passed since the gunmen had shot out the upstairs window. Time was on their side. Patty and her brothers weren't going anywhere, and no help was in the offing. A waiting game, then.

For all of them.

She had almost reached the front door when the faint scent of cigar smoke reached her nostrils. She passed it off initially to a stale odor from her father's most unfortunate habit. But the scent was nothing like his Havanas. Patty took a deep breath, grasped the sword in both hands, and raised it over her head. Then she leaped into the doorway of the library.

A man was sitting there in one of the burgundy leather chairs, a cigar stub smoldering in his mouth.

"There were three of them," he said. "There aren't any-more."

Patty stood rigid, sword still held high. The man was wearing a black suit and his nose looked mashed.

"Name's Sal Belamo," the man said. "Blaine McCracken sent me."

"You can put the sword down now," Sal said.

"I think I'll just keep it like this for a while."

"You'll end up with a pair of sore shoulders, lady." The ashes from Belamo's cigar stub fluttered to the hardwood floor. "Say, you wouldn't happen to have an ashtray anywhere around? Not much holdin' these damn Parodies together."

"How do I know you're not one of them?"

"I told you, lady. They're gone, finito. I tried not to make a mess. McCracken wouldn't've had to kill the fucks, but that's why he's McCracken."

The sword came down a little. "What'd you say your name was?"

"Sal Belamo."

"How'd you get in?"

"I'm good with locks."

"And he sent you? Blaine sent you?"

"Well, not exactly. See, lady, one of your messages reached my desk, and when I couldn't reach McCracken, I figured I'd better come out here and check up on ya. Been outside since sunset."

Patty remembered the car parked precariously on the canyon road. At last the sword came down all the way.

"Saw the fucks lurking about just before your lights went bye-bye. Sorry 'bout your upstairs windows. Guess I don't move as fast as I used to. I was a boxer, you know. Fought Carlos Monzon twice, and he busted my nose both times. Can't tell shit from lilacs out of the right nostril, and the left's not much better."

"You came here just to guard me?"

"Your message sounded like you were pretty spooked."

"But I was only trying to reach McCracken."

"Yeah, well, his friends are my friends, and he doesn't like to see his friends in trouble."

"Which makes you his friend."

"You ask me, everything's relative. You get offed when I coulda done something about it and I got McCrackenballs to answer to."

"Not a warm prospect."

"Let me put it this way, lady: Given the choice of facing a pissed-off McCracken or climbing into a meat oven, I'd get the tenderizer ready every time."

CHAPTER 11

THE Blackhawk helicopter sped McCracken and Wareagle north out of the jungle and Brazil. They crossed the border into Venezuela and landed at a small airfield, where a twin-engine plane was waiting. This brought them to a larger military airport just south of Caracas, where they were locked in a steaming, windowless room for nearly eight hours before being escorted back to the tarmac. Resting there was an unmarked 707, which had obviously been dispatched to pick them up.

"Where we headed, soldier?" Blaine asked a lieutenant who seemed to be in charge.

"I'm not at liberty to say, sir."

"Classified info, is it?"

The lieutenant shrugged. He had been supervising the eight-man team that had attached themselves to Blaine and Johnny from the time they'd been lifted out of the jungle. On the plane the soldiers kept their guns at the ready. The men were keeping their distance, too, which told Blaine they had been briefed on exactly whom they were dealing with.

He didn't bother contemplating the details of what had brought the Blackhawks into the jungle. There could have been any number of causes, including the ravaging of the complex and the loss of contact with Ben Norseman's team.

Blaine asked the lieutenant no further questions, and the flight passed in silence, which gave him the chance to get much-needed rest. When the beginning of the jet's descent jolted him awake, he could see the Washington skyline ahead in the early morning light. It was Friday, according to Blaine's watch, 6:30 A.M.. It wasn't much of a surprise that they were going to Washington. Word had obviously reached the capital that McCracken had interfered in the operations of a foreign government. A diplomatic nightmare, reparations certain to be demanded. The Brazilian authorities needed to be somehow appeased.

Through it all, when Blaine and Johnny's eyes met the message was clear: The *Wakinyan* had fled the jungle ahead of them. They had somehow survived the fuel air explosive that had torn away a patch of the Amazon Basin. They had stolen Luis's boat and escaped. Above everything else, whoever was waiting for Blaine in Washington had to be made to understand the ramifications of that. The Omicron Project had to be fully investigated. Somebody's problem was running free now, and, if what Blaine had seen was any indication at all, the mayhem was just beginning.

The 707 came in for a landing at Dulles Airport and pulled up to the diplomatic terminal situated off by itself to the south of the main complex. Again Blaine and Johnny glanced at each other and nodded.

Blaine looked out his window and saw a black stretch limousine parked just off the tarmac. He could see nothing through its blacked-out windows. The lieutenant came down the aisle and beckoned him to rise.

"Let's go, Mr. McCracken."

"I still hold my rank, soldier. It's captain to you."

"Yes, *sir*."

Blaine realized a congestion of soldiers had taken up positions enclosing Wareagle.

"He goes or neither of us does, soldier."

"I have my orders, sir."

"They come from that limo out there?"

"I wouldn't know, sir."

"Wanna go out and check?"

"Negative, sir."

"Look, son. The Indian and I have been nice to you fellas. Didn't embarrass you all by escaping, and didn't give you any trouble at all. Now there's eight of you and two of us, and you got guns, sure. But either you let the Indian walk off with us, or he and I will end up walking out of here together and alone. *Capisce*, Lieutenant?''

The soldiers stood there like mirror images of each other, thoughts straying to the guns they would still have to raise or draw to make use of. McCracken looked at Wareagle and watched him tighten just a little.

The lieutenant relented with the slightest of smiles, his own way of saving face. ''I can take the two of you as far as the limousine, Captain. From there on, you'll have to deal with whoever's inside.''

''For sure.''

One of the limo's rear windows slid down as they approached.

''I should have known better than to expect a private conference,'' came a woman's voice from within.

''Maxie,'' said Blaine, ''what a pleasant surprise.''

''Save it, Blaine, dear, and just get in here with your Indian friend.'' And then, to the soldiers, ''They're in my charge now. You've done well to all still be in one piece.''

Virginia Maxwell opened the door herself so Blaine and Johnny could step inside the limo. Maxwell was an elegantly dressed and coifed woman in her mid-forties, her glamour evidently better suited for a different post. Barely six years before she had taken over the directorship of the most secret of the country's secret organizations. Several years prior to that, when the CIA had come under increasing scrutiny and the methods of the NSA under fire, a gap resulted in what the intelligence community needed to accomplish and what it could effectively get away with. The new organization created to handle the stickiest matters worked between traditional three-letter organizations in order to fill the gap. Hence its name: the Gap.

Virginia Maxwell was only its second director, and she had proved to be an effective one. Her most important contribution had been to pull the Gap even further out of the mainstream, away from jurisdictional squabbles and congressional scrutiny. She held no meetings with presidents or their advisors unless she was the only person in attendance. If the Gap was to deal with what slipped into the crevices, then it had to be treated as a crevice itself.

Of course, this did not mean Virginia Maxwell had any desire to reside in a crevice herself. Her hair was perfectly styled, perfectly blond. Not a wrinkle showed anywhere on her face, including the soft skin around her eyes. Her teeth were actress bright, the same shade, it seemed, as the pearl necklace around her neck. She wore a mink coat and the biggest diamond McCracken had ever seen. One wrist showed a sapphire bracelet, the other a diamond-studded Rolex watch.

Wareagle followed McCracken inside and had trouble positioning his head comfortably under the big car's roof.

"I only wanted him to wait in the jet for his own comfort," said Virginia Maxwell.

"Whatever you say, Maxie," Blaine followed.

"But as long as he's here . . ."

"Just why *are* we here?"

"Patience, my dear. Look at you, Blaine. All that time in gorgeous Brazil and not a bit of tan to show for it."

"The jungle makes for a great sunscreen."

"There's less of it to make for anything now, I'm told."

"The Indian and I got careless roasting marshmallows."

"Not the only thing that got roasted I've heard."

"Just what have you heard, Maxie?"

"Let's take a drive, shall we?"

"Whatever you say."

The limo left Dulles and headed for Washington. Traffic was just beginning to thicken, and they made decent time.

"Awful the things we get that no one else wants to touch, my dear," Virginia Maxwell told him.

"I know the feeling."

"Ben Norseman—I think you know him?"

"Not anymore."

"Of course. In any case, he sent out a distress signal that reached several of our South American strongholds. Had the big brass scrambling, let me tell you, dear. But that doesn't mean they knew how to handle it, or that they wanted to. They woke me out of a sound sleep, and I wasn't too happy about it."

"The troops in the Blackhawks . . ."

"Gap men, dear. Finding you was quite a surprise to them. That gorgeous young lieutenant opted to ferry you out in one of his birds, while the other went to survey Norseman's last known position. Actually it's quite a coincidence, because I've been trying to track you down for days." Virginia Maxwell reached into her Gucci briefcase and came out with a handful of file folders. "Do you play Trivial Pursuit, Blaine, my dear?"

McCracken shook his head. "I wasn't around for too much of the trivia."

"Then let's play our own version, shall we? I'll hand you a file, and you tell me what you know about the subject, starting with this one. . . ."

McCracken accepted the first folder and opened it. A thick Oriental face looked back at him. The photo was grainy, obviously pulled from another source and enhanced by computer.

"Hired killer named Khan," Blaine said, without checking the nameplate. "A Mongolian. Especially brutal. Big man. Bigger than me. Not as big as Johnny."

"One for one, my dear. Now number two." Virginia Maxwell handed him the second folder.

"Israeli named Moshe Berg. Killed lots of Arabs illegally and then disappeared before he could be brought to trial. Has been a free-lancer ever since and does quite well."

"Two for two," the head of the Gap said, and handed him a third folder.

McCracken opened it. "Here's a good one. Female killer known only as Mira. Lots of aliases. Specialist in political assassinations. Equally legendary in bed."

"Let's move on to number four, Blaine."

"This is Nelson Fox, the size of a whole offensive line. Big-time mercenary and now an equally big-time assassin. Maxie, what the hell is going on here?"

"Still two to go, my dear, and you're batting a thousand."

Blaine accepted number five. "Shahim Tafir. Learned his trade under Abu Nidal and graduated to the international contract arena. Money is most dear to him. He's even worked for Israel on a few occasions. Maxie—"

"Just one more, dear."

"Jonathan Weetz. Got his start in the mob before he had hair on his balls. Killed his first man at the age of fourteen. This guy's an anachronism, built for the days when the five families would hit the mattresses and war it out with one another. He likes to kill, and if the price is right, he'll kill anyone."

Virginia Maxwell slapped her well-creamed hands together. "You made a perfect score."

"What gives, Maxie?"

"What would you say if I told you all six were in this country at the same time?"

"I'd say maybe Disneyland appeals to them as a vacation spot."

"And if it didn't?"

"I'd say, given their backgrounds, that it was impossible."

"Almost. Odds of roughly a million and a half to one against it happening. Except it did. Each of these killers has been positively identified sometime in the past ten days."

"On business, you think?"

"That's what I need you to find out. Just how good are they, my dear?"

"Six of the ten best in the world maybe, and you're looking at two of the others right here."

"My, my, my . . . Eight of the top ten in my jurisdiction as we speak. Two working for me . . . and the other six for someone else."

"That's jumping to conclusions, Maxie."

"Not really. They couldn't all be in America if the circumstances were any different. The odds, remember?"

"I meant about Johnny and me working for you."

"You're the only ones capable of finding out what they're doing here. You're the only ones who can stop them."

"Running short of field men at the Gap?"

"None of them are fortunate enough to be in the top ten, Blaine, dear."

"Love to help, Maxie, but the Indian and I've got some other concerns on our mind."

"Brazil?"

"Not anymore."

"Pray tell. I'm dying to hear."

"Lots of people are going to be dying, Maxie. Lots more than already have. . . ."

McCracken proceeded to outline everything that had happened. He started with receiving Carlos Salomao's phone call, springing Wareagle from jail, and then their trek into the Amazon. He became more specific when it came to the ravaged complex and their cat-and-mouse game with the *Wakinyan*.

"They escaped the jungle because they had somewhere else to go," Blaine said at last.

"Interesting conclusion, dear."

"And obvious."

"Thirteen of them, you say?"

"That's how many cubicles there were."

"Twelve along the corridor and one behind a door at the end of it."

"You're a good listener, Maxie."

"Apparently not good enough. I lost you somewhere around the time you claimed these—what did you call them?"

"Wakinyan." Blaine nodded toward Johnny. "Indian word that means Thunder Beings."

"So you claim these Thunder Beings lived at a secret American research station they later destroyed."

"And it's part of something called the Omicron Project."

Virginia Maxwell seemed to lose the slightest bit of her legendary composure. "As in the Greek letter?"

"For sure. Believe me, I've had experience with Greek letters before." And he produced the leathery report cover recovered from the complex's shredder.

"The Omicron Project," read Virginia Maxwell, both bemused and mystified.

"Ever hear of it?"

"Absolutely, my dear. The Gap, and thus the humble I, was in charge of security for the project."

"Not up to your usual standards, Maxie."

"You didn't let me finish. I spoke in the past tense for good reason. The Omicron Project was abandoned three years ago."

"Then what did Johnny and I come across in the jungle?"

"Haven't the foggiest, but let me check something. . . ."

She shifted over to the center of the limo, where a seat faced a CRT screen and computer. She pressed a few keys, selected the proper menu entry, and waited for her selection to appear.

"Pentagon liaison for the Omicron Project was General Berlin Hardesty."

"Is that supposed to mean something to me?" McCracken asked her.

"It will. General Hardesty was murdered in his home ten days ago by a woman believed to be Mira."

"So Hardesty gets whacked, then a week later the installation under his jurisdiction gets wiped out."

"*Omicron* was under his jurisdiction, my dear, not this installation."

"Use your imagination."

"Why should I bother when you've used it for me by drawing a connection between my pursuits and yours? One of these killers we learned was in the country was behind the death of the military liaison for the secret project you stumbled on in the Amazon . . . Or I more accurately should say the *remnants* of the project. Do I have it straight, dear?"

McCracken chose to ignore her sarcasm. "Could he have kept it going on his own?"

"You know how Washington works. It's certainly possible."

"It'd be helpful if you told me exactly what the original Omicron Project was all about."

Virginia Maxwell slid back to where she had been sitting. "I'll give you the short version, my dear. I don't have to tell you about the shocking events that have occurred in what used to be the Communist Bloc over the last two years. I do have to tell you that to plenty of the true policymakers of this nation it didn't come as any great surprise. They predicted it almost to the month a number of years ago. With that in mind, a new approach to national security and deployment seemed to be required. For the first time in our history, the United States would be without a standing enemy. The future lay not in prolonged entanglements but in minor squabbles of the kind we were woefully ill-equipped to deal with."

"Terrorism," Blaine interjected.

"And its many cousins, my dear. That, of course, would include warfare in arenas that posed strategic dilemmas."

"Like the desert?"

"For one, yes. The Omicron Project was funded with an open checkbook to pursue alternative means to deal with these kinds of engagements, new strategies for combating what would become this nation's collective, if you will, standing enemy. It was dropped three years ago with nothing much accomplished—with the exception of some work by a Professor Reston Ainsley."

"The name rings a bell."

"His specialty was robotics, and that was the line he was pursuing when the funds got yanked."

"Or misdirected."

"Possibly."

"Not possibly. I was down there, Maxie. I saw a different line Omicron had proceeded on, and I saw its results. Jesus Christ, don't you get the point? The Indian and I met up with something in the woods that isn't in the woods anymore. I don't think the members of this Omicron legion are waiting down in Rio for the festival season to start, either. They're here in America, because someone wants them here."

"For what, pray tell?"

"Too bad we can't ask Hardesty."

"We can ask your Indian friend—who up to now has yielded the floor to you."

Johnny Wareagle hesitated before speaking. "They live for what they have been created to do," he said finally.

"And for what were they created, Mr. Wareagle?"

"To perform the tasks demanded of them. The process stripped them of their manitous and replaced them with something else."

"You're conceding they're just men."

"In appearance maybe, but not within, where the truth of the being resides. Within they are as different from man as the tiger and the jackal."

"Predators, Mr. Wareagle?"

It was Blaine who took up the task from there. "You weren't down there to witness their handiwork, Maxie. Believe me, predators is a good word for them. A few minutes ago you showed me pictures of six of the most successful paid killers in the world. Well, none of them can even hold a candle to the thirteen members of our Omicron legion.''

"And can the members of this legion hold one to you?''

Blaine glanced at Wareagle before responding. "They managed to somehow survive a blast just short of a tactical nuke. I'd say that qualifies them.''

"And just what do you propose we do about them now?''

"Find who dispatched Norseman and we learn who's really running things.''

"I'd already checked, my dear. His routing orders couldn't be traced back to their original source. Too many shields and screens in place. Not terribly unusual, under the circumstances. Where does that leave us?''

"Back to the connection with Hardesty. Since Mira was one of *six* killers, we can count on the fact that there have been other violent deaths. Have you been able to lock on to any pattern?''

"There have been several other isolated incidents involving government officials, but no link among them we can find. A congressman was beaten to death, an undersecretary of state was run off the road and crushed in his car. But the three incidents had nothing in common that we can find.''

"Then we start with Omicron—and that professor you mentioned.''

"Reston Ainsley.''

"Right. How soon can I get to see him?''

"Immediately. He lives right here in Washington, though he's become somewhat of a recluse. I can get you a file on him if—''

"Don't bother. An appointment will suffice. Besides, you've got more important matters to attend to. Since the first you heard of that research lab in the jungle was from us, I assume your team missed it. Better send them back in, Maxie, with a vengeance.''

"What am I telling them to look for, pray tell?''

"Anything that might tell us what the hell went on in there . . . and who in Washington might have been responsible. This whole thing smells like someone's power play all the way. The proverbial fine-tooth comb might be in order. Send only the best.''

"I only use the best, my dear. Why else would I have called on you?"

CHAPTER 12

T HE yacht swayed easily in the calm waters of the Atlantic. Takedo Takahashi sat in his study with the lights dim enough to soothe his eyes. He had grown up hating the sun and embracing the night. Somewhere, buried deep, was a memory of a blinding flash and a rush of heat crumbling everything in its path.

Of course, Takahashi couldn't possibly have remembered; he was barely a fetus that dark day that had so violently altered the rest of his life. But his mind's eye made it a memory and, who's to say that consciousness does not begin early enough to allow for the dim recall of such a trauma.

The milk-white skin and snowy crop of hair were constant reminders—even if the mind's eye had been dim. So, too, the pinkish eyes that detested light of every kind, the sun most of all. As much as possible, he slept through the day. It was a vampire's life.

Every moment of his life had been lived with the White Flash in mind. It had made him the freak that he was—had ultimately determined the path his life would take. He was on this yacht now because of it. The six killers had been dispatched because of it. The ninety-six Americans had to die because of it.

Once again he heard the familiar shuffling of Tiguro Nagami's feet as his associate approached the door.

"Come in, Tiguro," he called even as Nagami was raising his hand to knock.

Nagami entered, dressed as impeccably as always. He was slight but broad-shouldered, and had all his suits custom-made in London. Unlike Takahashi, he had lived among the Americans for the better part of his life, and therefore his English was perfect.

"You have brought word of more successes for me to punch into my computer, no doubt," Takahashi said. "Who has called in?"

"It is not that, *Kami-san*."

"Weetz, then. Has Weetz arrived?"

"He is waiting on deck, *Kami-san*. But I have come with unfortunate news."

Takahashi's pinkish eyes bore into him. "What is this unfortunate news?"

"The people we dispatched failed to eliminate the Hunsecker woman."

"You're telling me she was too much for them?"

"She had help. That much we know. From whom, we don't."

"You assured me no one had placed any credence in her story."

"No one we were aware of," Nagami said, and swallowed hard.

"This is not good, Tiguro."

"Our sources are searching for her even now. She has dropped out of sight."

"What of her brothers? Perhaps we could use them. . . ."

Nagami shook his head. "Also no trace."

Takahashi's face crinkled in disgust. "You will keep me abreast of your progress in this matter, Tiguro."

Nagami bowed slightly. "Yes, *Kami-san*."

"Do not disgrace me."

His head was still lowered. "Of course not, *Kami-san*."

"Now send the American down to see me immediately."

Nagami bowed again and was gone.

* * *

Weetz strutted in with the grace of a cat. His suit was a dark gray Italian, perfectly tailored. He was a tall man with eyes like razors. He was chomping, as always, on a piece of chewing gum, when he sat down facing the albino's desk.

"Your work goes well, I understand," Takahashi said to him.

"You called me here to compliment me?"

"Hardly. You recall I said there were ninety-six targets?"

"Sure."

"There are ninety-seven. I left one out—one that requires special attention."

Takahashi slid a file folder toward the killer. Weetz took it, eyes never leaving the Japanese until the folder was open on his lap. Takahashi watched those razor-sharp eyes narrow.

"I see what you mean," said Weetz.

"Yes."

"So why me?"

"This is your specialty, I believe."

"It also entails more risk than the other sixteen kills combined."

"Can it be done?"

Weetz smirked. "Look, mister, hide a man down in a mine shaft and I'll shoot him through the air hole. We're talking levels here."

"This level requires your expertise."

"Won't come cheap, boss."

"Name your price."

"Five million."

"Make it seven point five. That's what I was prepared to offer."

"When?"

"You'll have forty-eight hours notice. You will not act until given the word."

Weetz gazed back down at the folder in his lap. "Hits like this take time to set up."

"You'll have to make do," said Takahashi.

"Seven point five on completion, right?"

"You're well worth it, Mr. Weetz."

CHAPTER 13

PROFESSOR Reston Ainsley lived in a brick house enclosed by a narrow yard on the outskirts of Georgetown. Virginia Maxwell had arranged a car for McCracken, and he squeezed it into a space just beyond a tow zone. The Ainsley residence seemed well kept, if undistinguished. The first of the fall leaves had already been swept off the walkway and stacked in piles, waiting to be bagged. Blaine climbed to the porch and rang the doorbell.

"Ainsley residence," a mechanical voice responded through a speaker. "Good afternoon. What can I do for you?"

"I'm here to see the professor. He's expecting me."

"State your name."

"Blaine McCracken."

"Yes, he is expecting you."

There was a click, then the solid wood door swung mechanically inward. Blaine stepped through and heard a soft *whirr*-ing sound an instant before a hulking mass of steel and wires approached from the right. He tensed as the robot drew directly up to him.

"Professor Ainsley is waiting for you in the study. Please follow me."

The robot's head was an opaque oblong attached to a flexible steel neck. The words emerged from a plate just above a host of flashing diode lights in its chest. Its midsection was chiseled into the form of a man's, and its arms were lifelike as well, albeit connected by visible wires and fittings instead of sinew and tendons. Its hands ended in steel pincers. Its torso and legs were covered with wires and what looked like Kevlar tubing. The thing actually walked like a man, right down to a slight flex in its metallic knees. Its feet pads were rimmed by steel pods that flattened out as it lowered its weight. The thing could look Blaine in the eye at six-two, and it seemed incredibly nimble for a machine.

"Mr. McCracken to see you, Professor."

"Show him in, Obie One," responded a nasal human voice, and the robot extended its hand outward to bid Blaine on.

"Thank you," he found himself saying.

"You're welcome, sir."

Blaine eased past the robot through a pair of double doors that led into a den cluttered with machines. It had the feel, strangely, of a child's playroom, where the toys had been left out long after the boy or girl was finished with them.

"Drat," came the nasal voice again, and McCracken watched as a man seated near the window dumped the contents of his lap onto the floor. Professor Reston Ainsley spun his wheelchair around and rolled toward McCracken, crunching bits of previously discarded materials beneath his wheels. "I see you've met Obie One, Mr. McCracken."

Blaine remained fascinated by the robot. It was advanced far beyond anything he thought science had achieved.

"Actually, we haven't been formally introduced."

"Then, allow me," offered the man in the wheelchair. Ainsley's wild white hair made him look like a first cousin to Einstein. His right ear was totally concealed by jagged curls, the left uncovered. "Blaine McCracken, this is Obie One, short for Operational Ballistic Droid."

On cue, the robot extended its right hand and opened its steel fingers all the way.

"Right." Blaine met the robot's grasp with his own. "Likewise, Obie One."

The robot gave him enough of a squeeze for McCracken to feel its incredible power. It could have crunched his bones had it wanted to.

"Would you like me to remain, Professor?"

"That won't be necessary, Obie One. But please inform

Obie Three Mr. McCracken and I will require some refreshments." The old man turned his wild eyes to Blaine. "Some lunch, perhaps?"

"Just a soft drink will be fine."

Ainsley looked back at Obie One. "And I will have my usual, Obie One."

"Yes, sir."

McCracken watched the robot swing around on its heels and stride away noisily.

"Now, Mr. McCracken, what can I do for you?"

"Incredible . . ."

"Excuse me?"

"I was just admiring your work. Obie One, I mean."

Ainsley accepted the compliment with a faint smile. "At one point I envisioned an army of them; resilient, indestructible. Not subject to the effects of nuclear fallout or chemical warfare. Impervious to pain. Capable of sight, hearing, even smell a thousand times more sensitive than a man."

"Developed as part of the Omicron Project."

Ainsley's shoulders flinched as if he'd been shocked by a thousand volts. His features tensed. "Developed *as* the Omicron Project, Mr. McCracken."

"Blaine, Professor."

"Please, why don't you sit down?"

McCracken searched around for a spot. Every chair or sofa was covered with manuals, computer printouts, and fragments of things waiting to be built. Tools littered the floor; computer floppy disks covered a desk built into the farthest wall. Seeing Blaine's problem, Ainsley spun his wheelchair around again and motored toward a leather armchair. A single sweep of his arms brushed its contents onto the Oriental rug.

"There," pronounced Ainsley, and he backed up his wheelchair in order to face Blaine from a comfortable distance.

McCracken took the chair. "Am I wrong or does modern science say a robot like Obie One won't exist for another generation?"

The professor smiled boyishly. "No, you're quite right, Blaine. In fact, so far as the scientific community knows, Obie One and his brothers don't exist yet."

"Brothers?"

"Six, to be exact, though only three are currently functional. All prototypes for what I foresaw would become an extended family. Alas, though, the family extends only as far as this house. No more were ever produced. Omicron stands today where it stood three years ago."

"Why was the project scrapped?"

"Lots of reasons . . . Mostly lack of vision on the part of the check writers. They are creatures of extremes. Well over two billion dollars went into my work during the initial four years that produced the Family. But there were problems in the testing end. Nothing I couldn't have handled, you understand, but they had lost their patience. Suddenly it was over. No more checks. No more production facilities. The problem in the end, I suppose, was money. They looked at what Omicron was supposed to do, and less nimble minds realized they could operate fifty thousand men for that price. Only problem was a corps couldn't pull off what the Family could."

"The Family," Blaine echoed.

"Obie and his brothers, of course. You understand the basic concepts of Omicron, I'm assuming."

"Limited entanglements in a confined arena. Maybe the first attack wave in less than desirable arenas. The counterinsurgency of the future."

"Yes, as opposed to past war-zone strategies. The global arena has been reduced to minor microscopic grids, and that is where the battles of the future will be fought. Israel's West Bank, the center of Beirut, the Kuwaiti desert, a terrorist seizing of a school or an oil field. Rapid deployment forces aren't really that rapid at all—and once they get where they're going, they're really too bulky to do much about most things."

"Hence the perfect rationale for the Family."

Reston Ainsley looked appreciative. "Very good, my boy, you're catching on. All of the droids I developed under Omicron had a specialty, a key part of a greater whole. Strategies could be developed along any number of scenarios, relying on these specialties to a greater or lesser degree."

Just then McCracken felt something graze his leg. He looked down, expecting to see a cat, and froze when what emerged from beneath the chair was what looked like a huge steel snake.

"There you are," said Ainsley, beckoning the thing toward him. "Come right over here now, you scoundrel."

The snakelike thing continued to emerge. It was as long as a boa constrictor and at least as wide. It was silver in color, and McCracken could not see how it propelled itself.

"Another of the Operational Ballistic Droid series, obviously," he concluded.

"Obie Four, to be precise, Blaine."

The thing reached Ainsley's wheelchair and nudged his leg. Then what McCracken had perceived to be an eyeless head rose like a cobra's and looked the old man in the eye.

Ainsley stroked its head as if it were an affectionate pet. "Obie Four's specialty is reconnaissance. He can burrow under any surface and disable mines en route to his target area. His antennae can pick up conversations while buried a good ten feet underground, and he's also equipped with a camera that can transmit video signals when appropriate.

"And he likes to wander."

"You noticed."

"I hope he's housebroken."

Ainsley laughed at that. "How much do you know about artificial intelligence, Blaine?"

"About as much as you just told me."

"Let me give it to you in a nutshell. Artificial intelligence is simply programming machines to learn from their mistakes and make logical choices when presented with a series of options."

"Nothing simple about that, Professor."

"Depends on your perspective. For the Obie series to have any chance of succeeding in the kind of encounters it was designed for, the droids had to be able to make their own decisions. Their instinctive decision-making had to be on a par with that of seasoned troops. All input had to be weighed in the blink of an eye, the correct alternative selected."

"Like I said, nothing simple."

"Let me finish. The options a man is confronted with in a situation of crisis are exceedingly small in number. You of all people should understand that."

"Me?" responded McCracken.

Ainsley smiled. "Obie One," he called out, in a conversational tone. Seconds later the humanlike droid was standing in the doorway. "Tell Mr. McCracken what we learned about him before he dropped by for a visit."

The robot's voice emerged in a droll, electronic monotone, as if it had no interest at all in the information it was relating. "Blaine McCracken. Following graduation from high school, started basic training in September of 1967 at Fort Knox, Kentucky. Transferred from there to Fort Polk, Louisiana, for Advanced Individual Training and infantry training. Volunteered for Jump School at Fort Benning, Georgia, where he was accepted into Special Forces training with highest GT score ever recorded. Remained at Benning for Pathfinder and Ranger schools. Upon completion, subject was sent to Camp Mackall at Fort Bragg for Special Forces Qualification course, followed by graduation with honors from Recondo training. Assigned then to Fifth Special Forces Group and sent to JOTC at Fort Sherman Canal Zone. Entered Vietnam in 1969 at Lang Vei, where subject was recruited by CIA for the Phoenix Project. After five months in field, received field promotion to captain following death of—"

"Very good, Professor," Blaine interrupted.

"Thank you, Obie One." The robot turned and took his leave. "I do believe he's jealous, Mr. McCracken."

"Tell him the feeling's mutual."

Reston Ainsley seemed ready to bounce out of his chair. "You're getting the idea, I can tell! You reached the level you did—and survived at it—because you chose the correct options when confronted by crises."

"Sometimes I got lucky."

"But the point is you responded without thinking. Well, technically machines can't think, either. But teach them to recognize and choose options, and basically you take the guesswork out."

"So you just drop your Obies into a given entanglement and let them do their thing."

"We're talking about two billion dollars worth of machinery here, Blaine, not simple robots."

Before McCracken could respond, a new *whirr*ing sound drew his attention to the door of the study. Passing over the threshold was yet another of the professor's OBD series, this one a boxlike, waist-high contraption with multiple arm and pincer extremities emerging from slots in its top. It was carrying a plate containing some sort of sandwich and a pair of soft drinks. The sandwich was perfectly layered and cut. The soft drinks were still fizzing over four ice cubes.

"Meet Obie Three, Blaine."

"An excellent delivery boy. If Domino's had a few of these, they'd be able to guarantee delivery in fifteen minutes."

"He didn't just deliver my lunch and the drinks. He also prepared them."

Blaine was astonished.

"His pincers and hand extremities are a hundred times more agile and precise than our paltry fingers, Blaine. Imagine him wiring explosives . . . or *dewiring* them."

"Then this is your explosives droid."

Ainsley nodded. "His hull is composed of titanium steel alloy with Kevlar coating on the outside and an inside layer of copper to reduce heat. His shell allows for the storage of sixteen cubic feet of explosives, supplies, anything." The old man removed his sandwich from the droid and placed it on his lap. "Now take Mr. McCracken his drink, Obie Three."

With no hesitation at all, the droid rolled six feet forward and spun so the soft drink was conveniently within Blaine's reach.

"Thank you," said McCracken.

"I'm afraid this one doesn't talk."

"Each one's a specialist, kind of like a George Lucas version of *The Magnificent Seven*. If one of them looks like Yul Brenner, I'm leaving."

"No, you won't, because clearly something important has drawn you here. It's been two years since anyone in the government's come to see me for any reason other than to check if I've finally gone round the bend. They're not crazy about me keeping the droids, but they know it's the only thing that keeps me happy . . . and quiet. So when a man like you shows up on my doorstep with two hours notice, I can only conclude that somewhere something has gone very much awry."

"In a word, yes."

"I'm not a violent man, Blaine. But I understand violence, and I understand the need for it. I lost the use of my legs in a car accident when I was twenty. Maybe the creation of these droids is my subconscious way of working out the physical limitations thrust on me by fate.'' Ainsley pointed at Obie Three and then Obie Four. ''Each represents a different device my handicap has torn from me. They each carry a part of me in them, you see.'' He smiled. ''I know you, Blaine, better than you think. God made man in his own image, while I made my droids in images I cannot touch. But you are as close to one of them as I ever could have envisioned.''

''Obie One?'' Blaine asked.

''Not quite,'' Ainsley responded.

He pressed a button and a set of bookshelves built into the right-hand wall parted to reveal a darkened compartment. The old man hit another button and the compartment was instantly alight. Blaine's eyes bulged at the steel-gray shape revealed within.

''Obie Seven,'' the professor said.

The final entry in the OBD line was nearly as tall as the eight-and-a-half-foot ceiling. Its head was a globe dominated by a pair of red glowing lights. Its midsection was rectangular, a pair of arms extended forward, ending with open holes. Its bottom was a pod that widened into a housing for wheels or treads. Maybe both.

''*Klatu barata nikto*,'' was all Blaine could think of saying, struck by the robot's likeness to Gort in the science-fiction film, *The Day the Earth Stood Still*.

Professor Ainsley was gazing forward with intense pride. ''You are looking at a simple killing machine. Perhaps not as fancy or elaborate as some of the other Family members, but equally effective in its own right. Those arm assemblies are fitted for Vulcan 7.62-mm miniguns—''

''I know Vulcans,'' broke in Blaine, ''but comparing me to this guy is a bit disconcerting.''

''I was talking in terms of effectiveness, and I meant it as a compliment. You'll have to forgive me. I don't have guests often, Blaine. What I'm trying to say is how much I enjoy meeting with someone who can appreciate what I've done.'' The old man took another bite of his sandwich and spoke between chews. "And now that you know what Omicron was, you can tell me what it has to do with your coming here."

McCracken's eyes lingered briefly on Obie Seven before turning back to Ainsley. "What if Omicron wasn't abandoned? What if the project was started up again after your work was squashed?"

"Under whose auspices?"

"Good question. I'm going to tell you a story about a different legion, Professor. Finish your sandwich . . . Maybe even have Obie Three make you another. This may take a while."

In the end it took just over an hour, McCracken leaving nothing out and becoming especially explicit in his retelling of what happened after he and Wareagle had reached the Amazon. Ainsley's reaction evolved from trepidation to befuddlement to a fear that set his hands trembling with Blaine's depiction of their encounter with the *Wakinyan*.

"What do you think, Professor?" he asked finally, after allowing a few minutes for the story to sink in.

"Well, you've given me a wealth of information. I need time to think."

"You've already got some notions. I can tell."

"I'm a scientist, Blaine, and a scientist never speaks until he's certain what he postulates has some merit."

"A lot of people have died already. Plenty more may be about to."

"I understand."

"I hope so. What was going on down there wasn't called Omicron for nothing. Whoever was behind it could only have had the same concerns in mind as you did when you created the OBDs, at least originally."

Ainsley looked hurt. "My concerns never included murder, Blaine."

"I'm sorry. I didn't mean it that way. But I need to know what was going on down there, Professor, and right now you're my best bet. I'll have a shorter version of my story transcribed and sent over."

Ainsley smiled. "Don't bother." He stroked the neck of the

snakelike reconnaissance droid affectionately. "I believe Obie Four got it all."

CHAPTER 14

"**I**s that all you've got to say, Indian?"

Wareagle faced McCracken from the window. "This professor spoke words of science that have no bearing on what must be done."

"He gave us our first insight into what this Omicron legion might be about."

"The legion is about many things, Blainey—none of which he has any insight into."

They were speaking in the living room of the suite Virginia Maxwell had provided for their use in a safe house used exclusively by members of the intelligence community. Blaine had heard from Sal Belamo that morning and accommodations had been arranged for Patty Hunsecker as well, something Mc-Cracken saw as an unwelcome distraction at this point. She was clearly in trouble, though, and Blaine wasn't about to forget the debt he owed her. Sal had already stashed her brothers under guard back in California, but Patty had steadfastly refused to stay with them, insisting she had to see Blaine.

"You've lost me, Indian."

"It is not for you to understand, Blainey, not this time. The system needs you—and to accomplish what you desire, you must work within it."

"Which indicates you plan to do otherwise."

"I went to Brazil in search of something that is now in this country. My search must continue."

"Sounds personal. And you're the one always telling me to detach myself, to let my will be directed by the spirits."

Wareagle twirled a finger through his ponytail and walked to the window. He gazed out as he spoke.

"Blainey, the hellfire was a beginning. It revealed to us the blackness of men's souls. But a beginning requires an end. I waited all those years for you to come back into my life because I knew your lot was to lead me to the truth of my existence. Our journeys together have confronted us with Black Hearts in many forms. But this time we face the enemy I was reunited with you to face. Everything the spirits have shown and made me—everything I have done—has built to this. The *Wakinyan* are out there, and I must find them."

"Not alone, Indian."

Wareagle swung slowly back to McCracken. His massive shoulders blocked the sun from the window.

"My people have a test for all braves seeking to become warriors. It is called *Hanbelachia*—vision quest—a series of rituals through which the brave must pass to enter manhood." The big Indian's eyes bored deeply into McCracken's. "Blainey, facing the *Wakinyan* is part of my vision quest."

"Aren't you a little old to be entering manhood, Indian?"

"It is a difficult path and never truly complete."

"Where will you start?"

"Wherever the spirits direct me."

They stood there staring across the room at each other, even after a repeated knocking came on the door. At last McCracken walked over and opened it.

"Jesus H. Christ, McCrackenballs," said Sal Belamo. "What I gotta do, scrape my knuckles raw to get your attention?"

Patty Hunsecker followed Belamo into the room and wrapped her arms around McCracken.

"Good to see you up and around again," Blaine said, easing her away.

"I've been up and around for a year and a half now."

"But the last time I saw you, you were lying in that hospital bed in Guam."

"Thanks to you," Patty said only half jokingly.

In point of fact, McCracken *had* saved Patty's life, but only after he had nearly lost it for her. He had procured use of her original *Runaway* because it was the only ship on the island with deep-salvage equipment. A battle with a twin-engine Cessna had sunk it—and nearly sunk them—Blaine managing to keep both of them afloat until help arrived.

"Yeah," Blaine said, "but apparently you didn't learn from my mistakes. Almost getting yourself killed is getting to be a habit."

Patty's stare hardened. "On the ocean you told me you were doing things for individuals these days. For people in trouble."

"Mostly."

"I need your help. My . . . father died a week ago."

"Oh, Jesus. I'm sorry. Really."

"He was killed, Blaine. He was murdered."

McCracken could see her struggling to hold back the tears. Eyes glistening, she looked toward Sal.

"My brothers and I would be dead, too, if it wasn't for him. You've got to help me. I'm all they've got. My mother died, too. Before. A year ago."

Patty broke down, collapsing into Blaine's arms. He held her tight and spoke softly.

"I didn't know. You should have called me. I wish you had called me."

Patty eased herself away from him, looking embarrassed. "Recent experience shows you're not an easy man to get hold of."

"You're here, aren't you?"

"And I've got something to show you. . . ."

Patty pulled the crinkled manila envelope from the inside pocket of her leather jacket. She held it tight, as if to let go was to relinquish something much more important than paper.

"They wanted me dead because I was stirring up trouble, talking to the wrong people. No one listened, but I guess that didn't stop them."

"Listen to what?"

"Something's going on. My father's not the only one. There've been others, lots. Men killed, made to disappear. Important men, powerful men, influential men."

McCracken stole a glance at Wareagle. His nod affirmed he was thinking just what Blaine was: Virginia Maxwell had mentioned a pattern as well. Six assassins who had killed General Berlin Hardesty and others. He pried the envelope from Patty's grasp and opened it.

"You scared me in Guam, McCracken. Scared me because of what you were, what you could do. I'd never seen so much rage. It was repressed, yeah, but always there, right below the surface."

Blaine lifted his eyes from the envelope's contents to meet hers.

"I understand now. They killed my father. And when I went after them, they didn't just go after me, McCracken. They would have killed my brothers, too. A couple of kids. *Kids!*"

"You're right, Patty. You do understand."

"This proves I'm onto something, doesn't it?" she asked as he began to scan her tattered tear sheets. "This proves I'm not crazy!"

"Jesus Christ," Blaine said as he flipped through them.

"I know that look, McCracken. I've seen it before. You know I'm right!"

Blaine looked at Johnny. "All these incidents have occurred in the past ten or eleven days."

"Since the entry of the six killers, Blainey."

"What killers?" demanded Sal Belamo. "You ask me, there's a party goin' on here old Sal ain't been invited to."

Blaine finished skimming the tear sheets and handed them to Wareagle, who started looking them over quickly.

"This must be the Indian friend you told me about," Patty remarked. "You should introduce us."

"Johnny, meet Patty. Patty, meet Johnny."

Wareagle's huge hand swallowed Hunsecker's. "You must excuse Blainey's insolence."

"I'm used to it, believe me."

"Let's get back to these tear sheets," McCracken broke in. "Did your father know any of the other victims?"

"Not that I can find any evidence of. But there is something

I realized a few days ago. Nobody else thought it meant anything, which—"

"What is it?"

"Age. All the victims were between forty-two and forty-five."

McCracken looked at Wareagle. "Berlin Hardesty was forty-four, Indian."

"What the fuck's going on here?" Belamo asked, a whine creeping into his voice.

"Plenty, Sal. We'll tell you all about it in good time."

"You ask me, good time ended when I stepped through the door."

"Who's Berlin Hardesty?" demanded Patty. "You know something. What is it, McCracken?"

"Simply this, Hunsecker. We know six killers who rival Johnny and me for downright meanness are at large in this country. It looked like the victims were limited to government types, but you've opened up a whole new door."

"I tried to go through it, but—"

"You had it slammed in your face. Don't worry, you've come to the right place."

"I want a computer," Patty said suddenly, after a pause.

"Come again?"

"I want a computer with access to a data bank that can help me find more links between the victims. Maybe I can find more victims . . . and potential future ones."

"U.S. taxpayers pay good money for pros to do that."

"The pros don't have a stake in this. I do." When Blaine started to protest, she talked right through it. "This is my trail, McCracken, in case you've forgotten. My father's the one who's dead. My brothers were almost killed."

Blaine turned to Belamo. "Sal?"

"I can make the arrangements no sweat. Maxie'll be pissed, though."

"Be good for her complexion. Okay, Hunsecker. You're in."

Patty looked relieved, and a new sense of determination replaced the sadness on her face. "I wouldn't have it any other way."

The phone rang, and McCracken answered it.

"Such a dear man," said Virginia Maxwell, "making me wait for only two rings."

"I had an enlightening meeting with Reston Ainsley, Maxie."

"So he told me . . . . after you failed to. Oh, well, now that you're working for us again, I suppose I can forgive a few such lapses."

"With, Maxie, not for."

"Either way, my dear, your best interests would be served by getting yourself to Gap headquarters on the double."

"We going to have torrid sex, Ms. Maxwell?"

"Better. The report from my team in the Amazon just came in."

Takahashi gazed closer at the face displayed on the computer monitor. It looked fierce and hard even through the graininess of the reproduction, the beard a dark splotch the same black color as the eyes.

"This man's name again?" he asked Tiguro Nagami, who stood just to his right.

"Blaine McCracken."

"I have read about him, haven't I? When we were selecting our team, his name surfaced."

"Rejected immediately, *Kami-san*. He does not do this kind of work."

Takahashi scrolled through the classified file. "Apparently, he does."

"Only by his own choosing. He could be a dangerous foe."

Takahashi stopped scrolling and read in detail the selection on the screen. "I see he spent a year in our country."

"He studied under Hiroshi."

The albino's skin seemed to pale even more. "That explains much."

"McCracken is many things, *Kami-san,* but mostly he is a warrior. Those who failed to recognize that have paid dearly."

"You're telling me this is the man who rescued the Hunsecker woman?"

"An associate of his did. Our sources indicate that the associate has now delivered her to his protection. Our report indicates he owes the woman from the past. He is a man who pays his debts.''

Takahashi's pink stare turned distant. ''Aren't we all? She has told him everything, I presume.''

''And he will probably pay attention. I have also learned that McCracken met with Virginia Maxwell. Therefore, he is probably aware of our six killers. That places their missions in great peril.''

''We can send word out. They can be warned.''

Nagami took a deep breath. ''May I speak frankly, *Kami-san*?''

''You may, Tiguro.''

''*Kami-san*, there is too much going on here beyond our control. Blaine McCracken is onto the pattern of our killings.''

''There is no pattern!''

''There is . . . enough.''

''What would you have me do, Nagami? What would you have me do?''

''Recall the killers. Suspend their work until we are able to deal with McCracken.''

Takahashi gazed again at the face wavering on his computer monitor. ''Do you truly think we can?''

''I think we must try.''

Takahashi rose from behind his desk and walked methodically to the centrally placed portal in the yacht's large study. Beyond him, there was only the sea.

''I do not have the right to do as you suggest, Nagami. This is not just my battle; it is the battle of our people. Since the war . . . I should not belabor the details. You know what suspending our work would mean.''

''I know what continuing it now can mean.''

''There is only one certainty, Nagami, and that certainty gave birth to something forty-six years ago. Are we to ignore that fact? Are we to forget the truth?''

''Recent events have changed that truth.''

''No,'' Takahashi said staunchly as he swung from the portal. ''They have only redefined it. We are all that is left, my friend. We are alone in a battle we must see completed.''

''There is still McCracken, *Kami-san*.''

Takahashi's pink eyes flamed red. ''Our work will go forth

until I have punched all ninety-six of the names into my computer. Not a single one can be spared. Do you hear me? *Not a single one!*''

CHAPTER 15

As head of the Gap, Virginia Maxwell had moved its headquarters from downtown Washington to the Oyster Point district of Newport News, Virginia. The Gap's secret, unchartered existence had made its Washington location an impediment. Too much scrutiny threatened to make politics a concern where it was never supposed to be.

The Oyster Point office was situated amid banks and business and professional offices in the center of the Newport News peninsula. Most of the buildings were modest, modern structures, two to four stories high. The Gap, on the other hand, was located in a spanking new office high rise on Thimbal Shoals. Two nearly completed smaller high rises flanked it on either side.

At twenty-four stories, the Gap building was the tallest in the city. Floors fourteen to eighteen, where the Gap actually had its offices, were serviced by a different elevator bank from the rest of the building. They also had an internal elevator system and stairways that linked the floors together, totally isolating them from the rest of the building.

McCracken drove to Newport News through the last of the early evening traffic. He had left Belamo to arrange a computer

for Patty; Johnny Wareagle pursued his own agenda. Blaine
followed Virginia Maxwell's instructions for gaining access
and found her waiting at the elevator when he stepped out on
the eighteenth floor.

"Right this way, my dear."

She led him down the sparsely traveled hall, high heels
*clip-clop*ing softly on the imitation marble flooring. Somewhere in the maze of Gap budgeting, Maxie had found the
funds to gradually transform her headquarters into an Italian
art deco showplace. Desks curved and sloped. Everything
was thin and shiny, ageless, like Virginia Maxwell herself.
Even though night had fallen, workers remained at computer terminals sorting through information. They sat on
soft leather chairs.

Maxie was dressed in brown tweed tonight, and her brace-
lets clanged lightly together as if in rhythm with her heels. She
said nothing until they had entered a screening room where
they took chairs in the front row. Each chair had a remote
control device built into its arm. Video had become a prime
component of the kind of work the Gap was often called on to
do. Much better for reconnaissance than stills and computer-
enhanced satellite overviews. Sign of a whole new age in the
intelligence business.

"The base was wiped clean, just as you suspected," Virginia Maxwell reported as she closed the door behind them.

"I wouldn't be here if you hadn't found something,
Maxie."

She nodded. "They should have torched the place. Don't
ask me why they didn't. Anyway, your description of the physical layout was accurate as always, except this time you missed
something: two additional floors to be exact."

"Didn't see an entrance."

"With good reason. The elevator compartment was built
into the wall. My people almost missed it, too. Let's make
ourselves comfortable."

They settled into seats that felt airline stiff. Blaine found
himself fingering the controls on his armrest, but he left it to
Maxie to punch in the proper commands.

"I've fastforwarded ahead of the floors you've already seen.
I'd like to hear what you make of this."

Virginia Maxwell touched a button on her armrest that gave the screen a black sort of life. The next button filled it with the jittery motions of the cameraman proceeding down the corridor of the second underlevel, past the dormitorylike cubicles. At the very end of the corridor, where a segment of the wall had been, the team members had managed to locate the elevator the Gap head had spoken of. The camera jiggled once more during the descent, but steadied again as the doors slid open. Its lens became Blaine's eyes as it surveyed what was revealed.

McCracken leaned forward. The base's third underlevel was nothing more than an elaborate, high-tech gymnasium. He recognized some of the machines from health clubs he had worked out in, others from drawing-board sketches he did not know were in production. In addition to the machines, there was an assortment of punching bags, treadmills, and Lifecycle exercise bikes. The camera panned to the right rear corner, and McCracken fumbled at his armrest for the Stop button.

"Freeze it there," he told Virginia Maxwell.

The picture on the screen locked in place.

"What do you see?"

"The way those mats are laid out there on the floor. It's got to be martial arts. And there, furthest to the right, zoom in."

Virginia Maxwell obliged.

"*Markiwara,*" said Blaine. "Pad-covered boards for striking practice used in hand-conditioning. They've been pretty much beat to hell."

"Hand-to-hand combat, my dear?"

"At a very advanced level."

"Let's fastforward, shall we?"

Fresh thoughts formed in Blaine's head as the pictures whizzed by on the screen.

"I assume your people found nothing more in writing."

"You assume correctly. Ah, here we are. . . ."

Virginia Maxwell changed the tape speed back to normal, and Blaine recognized the elevator compartment once more. Almost immediately the doors slid open on what must have been the fourth sublevel. A brief walk followed, taking the recon team into a room bathed in darkness. The searching beam of a flashlight could be seen, then the slow blooming of fluorescent ceiling lights.

"Look familiar?" asked the head of the Gap when the picture was fully illuminated.

"I'll say. It's a target range. For small arms and rifle fire." He looked at Maxwell. "Any shell casings?"

"Not so much as a smidgeon of powder, my dear. Did you expect any less?"

"Just lost my mind for a minute."

What he had gained, though, was, at last, a clearer understanding of what the secret base had been designed to create.

Not monsters at all, but the next best thing.

Somebody was training killers, an elite group on a par with any Blaine had faced before. In itself that was not unusual. What *was* unique was what had preceded the training. His mind strayed back to the pictures Virginia Maxwell had skipped over of the first two underground levels. The ultra high-tech laboratories and examination rooms. Broken glass, remnants of syringes and specimen bottles. The link between those two levels and the two he was seeing today was undeniable.

"What do you make of these?" Virginia Maxwell was asking.

On the screen was a progression of normal-sized rooms, each containing only a single chair. A few of the rooms had window slats high up on the walls, either for observation of the subject or perhaps projection of a video display inside. The camera zoomed in on one of the chairs.

Leather straps dangled from every part of it. Blaine could see some were cracked and broken, evidence of severe stretching.

"Sensory deprivation?" he suggested. "Some sort of mind control or brainwashing?"

"Your guess is as good as mine, my dear."

Virginia Maxwell continued the tape, but McCracken's mind had locked on those thirteen cubicles he and Johnny had found on sublevel two. His image of the prisoners they had held was beginning to gain substance.

"That about does it," Maxwell said. She switched the video off and turned to look at him. "There's more, but I've given you the highlights."

"What about the bodies Johnny and I found?"

"Fasten your seat belt, darling. They were all on the government's payroll. They all had top security clearance."

"Specialties?"

"This is where it gets interesting. Eliminate nine whom we've IDed as members of the Marine Corps or the Special Forces. They were there to provide security."

"Alas, not very successfully."

"That leaves nineteen, and at least half of those came straight out of the upper echelons of the bio-tech sector. Strictly top drawer. Best in their field. Plenty of chemical engineers, too, along with a trio who specialized in computer microcircuitry."

"And the rest?"

"Brain surgeons and specialists."

"Specialists as in shrinks, Maxie?"

"Anything but, my dear. Specialists in brain function—what specific part of the brain controls which attributes and emotions, and how those parts combine to form a magical whole."

"Interesting group to have gathered in the Amazon."

"And one name kept surfacing at the top of their routing orders."

"Don't tell me," interrupted Blaine. "The late General Berlin Hardesty." He paused. "There're still thirteen residents of the installation unaccounted for."

"There's no evidence suggesting anyone else was even there. We did microscans for fingerprints and came up with only twenty-nine sets."

The anomaly struck Blaine suddenly. "But Johnny and I only counted twenty-eight bodies."

"Very observant, my dear. One escaped death, obviously, because he was not present at the installation when your Thunder Beings struck. His name is Jonas Parker. I've got his file right here."

"And if he's still alive . . ."

"We'll have someone who can tell us exactly what was going on down there."

"Very good, Maxie."

"Finding him would be better, my dear."

"Leave that to me."

CHAPTER 16

"PROFESSOR Ainsley is expecting you, sir," Obie One said, as it opened the front door for McCracken.

"Obie One," a voice bellowed from the study, "bring him in here now!"

"Yes, sir."

The edge in the old man's voice was unmistakable. When Blaine had spoken to Ainsley earlier in the day, he had been smooth and calm. Something had obviously changed. As Blaine moved toward the professor's study, he noticed that Obie One was staying put by the door. At McCracken's urging, Virginia Maxwell had sent over a copy of the videotape taken at the installation in the jungle. Ainsley had called to demand his presence three hours later.

Ainsley was waiting for him inside his study, now even more littered than before with papers, gadgets, and fragments of abandoned droids. Blaine noticed instantly that the gargantuan Obie Seven had been moved into the open against the far wall. Its square eyes glowed red. McCracken could see Vulcan 7.62-mm miniguns had been fitted into its extremities.

"What gives, Professor?"

"They're not going to take me without a fight."

"Who's not?"

"You're in danger, too, Blaine. I should have expected this as soon as you told me your story."

"Expected what?"

"You knew about them and you told me. They'll be coming for us before long, both of us. We're threats to them."

"Them?" McCracken echoed.

Ainsley regarded him anxiously. "You really don't know what it is you've stumbled onto here, do you?"

"Not yet."

"Suppose I can't fault you for it, Blaine. After all, this isn't your field. You couldn't know."

"I'm a quick study."

"Omicron! The key is Omicron! When I began developing it, do you remember the purpose, the goal?"

"Devising the perfect solution for limited, specific entanglements."

"Hence the Obie series. But it was canceled because of costs. And because of something else: an alternative."

Blaine just looked at him.

"I should have suspected as much from what you told me this morning. All the clues were there. It couldn't have been anything else, but I held to the hope it would be. Then, when the information came from the Gap . . ."

The old man's voice trailed off. His eyes were fixed on the monstrous shape of Obie Seven.

"I called my work Omicron because it represented the fifteenth attempt at achieving the project's goals. I wondered at first why the force you uncovered in Brazil hadn't changed the title. Now I realize it's quite fitting they left it as is. We were both going about things the same way, you see. Creating machines to do what previously only men had done."

"There were no Operational Ballistic Droids found in the jungle, Professor."

"No, Blaine, there weren't . . . Because they escaped on your boat. Thirteen of them."

"Machines?"

"What is a machine, Blaine? How shall we define it? In terms of mechanical parts formed of steel and diodes like my Obies, no. But in terms of being brought into existence and programmed toward a specific end, yes. A machine exists merely to perform a task that it will perform tirelessly until told to stop."

The old man's head bobbed madly as he spoke, wild white hair tossed about as if it were a mop.

"The purpose of the Obie series, the purpose of Omicron, was to imbue machines with more of the qualities of men—to better enable them to perform certain tasks. What if, instead, men were imbued with more of the qualities of machines?"

McCracken shuddered. He didn't reply.

"What you discovered in the Amazon, Blaine, was a twisted version of my project. Thirteen men, created in whatever image some perverse man-god determined."

"Created?"

"Poor choice of words on my part. Refined would be closer to the point."

"Robots?"

"In a figurative sense, yes, but not a literal one. No hardware was involved, at least nothing beyond—"

"Beyond what?"

"I can't account for the presence of the microprocessing experts. But they were there for a reason; that much is for sure."

"Get back to the *Wakinyan*, Professor."

"I'm speculating here, so bear with me. Say the primary purpose of what you're creating—refining—is to kill. You would start with a thousand or so possible subjects and eventually narrow them down to a couple dozen before beginning."

"You mean a single dozen."

"Not at all. A dozen of the cubicles you found were unoccupied, remember? But that wouldn't have always been the case."

"Then what happened to—"

"I'll get to that in good time, Blaine. You move your two dozen subjects to one of the most secluded spots on the face of the earth to avoid detection. Money is no object. Your complex is fitted with whatever it requires."

"And there you train them to be perfect killing machines," Blaine concluded. "The gymnasiums, the firing range."

"But you'd be limited, wouldn't you? You've known this kind of man, Blaine. Good Lord, you've killed plenty of them. Something more was needed than just training and conditioning."

With that, Ainsley spun his wheelchair around rapidly and screeched toward his wall-length worktable. The wheels bounced over debris several times, and the chair itself rocked right and left. The old man took something from a large open drawer and spun back toward McCracken.

"This is the brain, Blaine," he announced, motoring back. "A plastic model of it, anyway."

Ainsley held the mass of yellow-gray sectional pieces together. It looked real enough for Blaine to wonder whose skull it had been lifted from.

"The list Ms. Maxwell provided me with, of logged researchers at the complex—together with your story and my own analysis of the videotape—can only mean they were working on brain manipulation down there. Neurosurgeons, chemical engineers, biotechnicians, DNA experts—it all fits. With the exception of those microchip people, of course." Ainsley pulled several of the top sections of his model brain off and tossed them to the floor with the rest of the debris. "Truly a wonder of nature, Blaine. *The* wonder of nature. No one knows what percentage of the brain's capacity has yet to be tapped. Estimates range from fifty to as high as *ninety-five* percent. The point is that the final frontier lies not in outer space. It lies quite literally within our own heads.

"The frontal lobe, the parietal lobe, the occipital lobe, the temporal lobe," Ainsley said, pointing in turn to each of the sections of the brain. "I could go on naming sections and subsections for hours. But all you need to know is that research these last several years has concentrated on identifying the specific parts of the brain that control specific functions, emotions, and abilities. How does a professional athlete's brain, for example, differ from that of an overweight man with a sedentary life-style? A murderer's from a priest's? A musician's from a laborer's? And if that specific determining region can be identified, then perhaps it can be manipulated, *stimulated,* to refine or enhance skills already possessed by the subject.''

''Sounds farfetched.''

''In a sense it is. The sedentary man could not duplicate the actions of the professional athlete because he has not been properly trained to carry them out. But add training to an artificially altered brain pattern and credibility becomes quite within reach.''

''Training,'' Blaine murmured.

''Exactly. Tell me the features of an ideal killer, Blaine.''

''I could go on naming them for hours.''

''Start with the physical.''

Blaine seemed reluctant. ''It's hard to say. Of the best I've run into, I've never run into two who were alike.''

''But there must be certain common factors.''

''I guess,'' Blaine said. ''Reflexes . . . A kind of instinctive quickness that eliminates lag time.''

''Lag time?''

''The gap between realizing what you have to do and doing it. Killers who stay out there the longest have the shortest lag times. They can almost be in two places at one time. You can't move faster than a bullet, but you can move faster than the man firing it.''

''I understand. Proceed.''

''Awareness. Great reflexes don't help unless you stay in tune with what's around you. The attack can come from anywhere. Recognizing it in time to respond determines your life expectancy.''

''Ah, so if an attacker can move faster than you can respond, he wins.''

''Or she. In a nutshell, yes. Like . . .''

"Like what?"

"An animal. They don't think, so the lag between determining an action and undertaking it is nonexistent."

"And if that same lag could be eliminated in a man? If there was a way to somehow stimulate and alter the area of our brain controlling response and reaction time?"

McCracken looked down at the plastic model in Ainsley's lap. "You're saying that's what they created down there?"

"That and more, Blaine."

"Yes, physical skills. The strength and quickness of the *Wakinyan* have been enhanced, too."

"Enhanced to a hyperdegree, I should suspect, in subjects selected for already possessing large degrees of both," Ainsley confirmed. "But there's even more. The new makers of Omicron wanted to create machines, remember? You saw the handiwork of the *Wakinyan*. What comes to mind about it first?"

"They enjoyed it," Blaine said, without thinking.

"You're quite certain of that?"

"Oh, yeah." McCracken's thoughts drifted back to finding the Tupi boys' bodies, then the ravaged corpses at the complex, and finally the corpses of Ben Norseman's men. "No question about it. They loved every minute of their work."

"Interesting," commented Ainsley. The fear in his face had been replaced by contemplation. The darkened room seemed to lighten ever so slightly.

"Why?"

"Killing for pleasure, my boy, is not something well documented in the animal kingdom—and certainly not in the world of the machine. We have come to our first anomaly in the equation."

"Meaning? . . ."

"Meaning a rule the makers of this Omicron legion had to write themselves to accomplish their task. It wasn't enough to refine and expand the skills of their subjects. To achieve total success, the subjects had to be conditioned to *enjoy* killing. Don't you see?"

"See what?"

"The deaths of all those Tupi Indians that brought your friend to the Amazon. The Omicron subjects stalked their prey not just to practice their skills, but also to provide positive reenforcement. A reward, if you will."

"I've known plenty of individuals who enjoy killing, Professor, thrive on it even—and there was no biochemical engineering behind it."

Reston Ainsley shrugged. "Perhaps not. Then again, if my theories are correct, it was their brain chemistry that was behind it. Granted, there was no engineering involved, but that doesn't mean there couldn't be."

"No," Blaine argued, glancing briefly at the cold black finish of Obie Seven, "there's got to be more, something beyond enjoyment."

"I believe you might be quite right, my boy. The conditioning chambers on the fourth sublevel bothered me. I can account for virtually everything else, but not this."

"Brainwashing," Blaine proposed.

"More like mind-conditioning. Different terms, same effect. And in this case, the results are what matter. What if killing was made an addiction for this legion? What if they actually needed to kill to survive? Think of drug addicts. They may love their chosen poison, but their addiction is more a question of hating the consequences of being without it." Ainsley raised his plastic-and-rubber model of the brain to catch the light. "So now we have our two dozen subjects, carefully selected for already possessing an overriding capacity for violence, whose brains have been fine-tuned, so to speak, and skills refined to a great extent."

"*Two* dozen."

"Only for a time. To truly create a perfect legion of killers, an element of uncertainty would have to be factored in. The twenty-four subjects would know only twelve were to be chosen, thus only twelve could survive."

"You're saying the dozen that came up short were executed?"

"I'm saying that one dozen were killed by the surviving dozen. The Amazon Basin was not chosen at random. The final field tests might have involved matched competition in the jungle. The twelve survivors became the legion."

"Except you're forgetting about that extra cubicle Johnny and I found at the end of the hall. What lived in there, Professor? Why was it kept separate from the rest?"

Reston Ainsley had no answer.

PART THREE

The Legion

New York:
Saturday, November 30, 1991; 3:00 A.M.

CHAPTER 17

The woman had died much too quickly. She gave up her life to him as easily as passing a quarter to a beggar, and he had packed it away in his pocket with a painful awareness of how little it weighed.

He sat on the edge of the bed, feeling that he owned the darkness. He liked the night, for it made him feel more superior than the day. When it was light he could be seen as well as see. But his eyes could pierce the darkness while his prey had no hope of seeing him. Since leaving Home Base, he had done most of his sleeping in the day.

Of course, he did not sleep much. Sleep meant hours lost to inactivity, and this he did not tolerate very well. Sleep also meant dreams, and these he hated most of all—because they were the one thing he could not control. From the first time he had ventured into the woods and killed the three Indians that night, his dreams had been twisted and difficult to comprehend. He wanted to comprehend; he *had* to. Control was something he relied on. He had learned anyone, anything, could be controlled. There were always ways.

The name they had given him at Home Base was Abraham. The others had been named after the twelve disciples of Christ. Of course, they were different from him.

He was alone.

Abraham could not have explained why he was different from the others. He could say only that he was better. He had seldom worked with them, and, even more seldom, interacted. Interaction was kept to a minimum, in any case, since it could actually prove counterproductive. Only alone can a man confront that part of himself that must be bettered and better it.

And Abraham was better.

He still had memories of the person he had been before coming to Home Base, but they mostly came only in his dreams. This was another reason to loathe the sleep that brought them. Thoughts themselves made for comparisons, and comparisons made him uneasy. He recalled the time he'd been part of a secret military action against a drug lord in Thailand. A shrapnel blast had torn up his face. Plastic surgeons had had plenty of sewing to do, and, for days after the bandages came off, Abraham had refused to look in the mirror. He was afraid of not recognizing the person he saw.

And now that person was gone. Today he was, simply, what he could do. A man must be defined in terms of his capabilities. More than anything else, it seemed, Home Base had changed his methods of looking at others. They had not had time to prepare him and the twelve disciples for life outside the jungle and it showed. Much of what had impressed him previously, impressed him no more. Money was nothing besides something to help make preparations for what he must do. People lived behind facades that must be meaningless even to themselves. Weakness, everywhere weakness. Could it be this was the same world he had left all those months ago?

How many months?

Abraham tried to pin the answer down, then gave up when it didn't seem to matter. The hotel's flickering neon light penetrated the torn slivers of the window curtain. It made the blood on the woman's naked corpse look shiny. Abraham put his hand in the blood that had pooled on the sheet beneath her. He brought the hand to his nose, expecting it to smell of more than salty copper. Its scent was everywhere, but the scent was meaningless and insignificant.

Insignificant, and yet this was the scent of life itself, freed of its paltriness only in death. How ironic. So much Abraham saw now that had been denied him before Home Base. Once, long ago, in the memories forced upon him by his dreams, he had seen pleasure in life. Now there could be pleasure only in

death. Vast pleasure beyond anything he thought possible. He
wanted the pleasure as much as he needed it.

Abraham had hoped the woman would last longer. He had
found her down on the crowded street. She had arranged for
the room while he had hovered out of the desk clerk's line of
vision. If the man ever noticed him, Abraham would simply
kill him. He might choose to kill him anyway.

He wiped his fingers on the soiled sheet. The woman continued to regard him with bulging glazed eyes. When Abraham
had killed for the first time he thought that the death stare
looked strangely familiar, but he couldn't place it until he
looked in the mirror. His own steel-blue eyes held the same
emptiness, the same dark vacuum. He wondered what it felt
like to be dead, then realized he knew already.

When you were dead, you couldn't be hurt. The fears and
pains of life were at last vanquished. Abraham had no fear.
Abraham couldn't be hurt.

He stared into the woman's dead eyes. He tried to straighten
her head to line up with his, but it wobbled on her neck. He
had snapped it like a twig and then, with the woman spasming,
had driven his hardened fingers straight into her stomach. Made
them rigid and bent them slightly back. Felt the blood soak
thick as he probed for a souvenir to take out with him. He
locked on something sinewy that resisted at first, but then
came free. Abraham had left it there, somewhere in the pool
of gore beneath her.

Turning from the corpse, he rose from the bed and moved
toward the bathroom. The single light did not work; Abraham
regarded himself in the cracked mirror through the darkness.
He had to stoop down to get any view at all, since the mirror
was positioned for someone considerably shorter than his six
foot six. As always, he did not recognize his face. It was not
an altogether unpleasant face. It was rather soft, except for the
scars that had outlived his several surgeries. A few dribbles of
sweat slid down his forehead from his straw-colored hair.
Abraham kept it cropped short, brushed straight back.

Only cold water came from the tap, and Abraham washed
the blood from his hands as best he could. Even that slight
exertion forced the muscles of his arms and shoulders to pulse
and ripple. He looked up into the mirror from his bent-over

stance and saw his face with the cracks in the mirror down the center of it. The result was a carnivallike impression that should have disturbed him, but didn't. Abraham felt only then that he was gazing at his true self, and it was a picture he quite liked.

There was a shuffling sound from the corridor, and he spun quickly and tensed. The sound evaporated as quickly as it came, and Abraham found himself facing the door of the dingy room. It was time to leave, anyway. His work for the night was finished. Soon his real work, the work he had been created for, would begin. Abraham looked forward to that with an excitement akin to what he knew in the days before Home Base.

Yes, he reckoned, closing the door behind him in the hallway. Very soon . . .

The cabin lay in the heart of the woods, blind and isolated. It was simple in design, a two-story structure built against a hillside at the edge of the Rocky Mountains.

A tall man turned from looking out a second-floor window that faced the driveway.

"I can't see the guards," he told the others.

"It's all right," replied a stout man who was seated on a couch covered in plaid fabric. "They would have called us on the walkie-talkie if there was trouble."

"What if they didn't have time?" the tall man demanded. "We could be alone in here, dammit. We could be in danger!" He turned to look out the window again.

"The trip wires would have sent us a signal," replied the third man in the room, the only one of the three who wore his hair long.

"Trip wires wouldn't mean anything to them if they got this far. You know that."

Just then, one of the patrolling guards emerged from the woods and stopped to light a cigarette. The tall man turned away from the window, but did not breathe easier.

"See," said the stout man on the couch.

"They won't be able to find us, Benjamin," said the long-haired man, joining the taller one by the window.

"And what if you're wrong, what then, Pierce? And don't

try to tell me your security will keep them out if they discovered our location.''

"We'll be gone from here before they get that chance.''

"Your reassurances no longer hold much weight with me, Pierce,'' the fat man said. "Your plan was enacted to guard precisely against this eventuality!''

"And the plan succeeded. To a point.''

"Not a great enough one in my mind. We should strike out at them while we have the opportunity.''

"In time, Benjamin.''

"If we have it, you mean.'' The tall man swung toward the stout one seated on the couch. "What do you say to this, Nathan?''

"We have lost track of our pursuers, Benjamin. They could be anywhere now.''

"Stalking us? Searching for us?''

"They have no reason to. You know that as well as I do.''

"All I know is that this hasn't gone as we expected it to. I refuse to accept anything at face value.''

"Stop whining,'' roared Nathan. "You stand there worrying about our lives when there is so much more at stake.'' He looked toward Pierce. "We must face the fact that we may have to rethink our entire strategy.''

"All is proceeding as planned, in spite of the setbacks we have suffered,'' Pierce responded.

"No,'' Benjamin said vehemently. "The final phase has been enacted without proper safeguards, without the very precautions that have dominated our lives.''

"And what choice did we have?'' Pierce shot back at him. "I thought we had gotten them all.''

"We all did,'' acknowledged Nathan. "But Benjamin is right on that point. The fact is, we didn't.''

"Could we find him now?'' Benjamin asked.

"Eliminating him would not keep the killers from finishing their work. Besides, we have used that very strategy to our own benefit.''

"And how long do you think it is before they realize the truth?''

"Long enough.''

"And in the meantime we stay here. Waiting." Benjamin looked furtively out the window again.

"We move to our final destination tomorrow."

"That is supposed to reassure me?"

"I don't really care whether it does or not."

Benjamin stormed back from the window. "And what about the door left open back down in Brazil? Are we to feel safe in spite of that, too?"

"On the contrary, we have enlisted the services of a most reliable ally to help us close it."

"Really?"

"Blaine McCracken."

Benjamin stood very still and waited for Pierce to explain.

Johnny Wareagle knelt barechested in the cold late autumn air. There may have been a time long past when the chill would have raised goose bumps on his flesh. He actually thought he remembered the last instance. It was a night in the hellfire, when the cold and rain were so bad that the team had to camp for the night. Wareagle took the first guard duty with his water-logged poncho for company. The cold wetness had brought the gooseflesh.

Then the Black Hearts had come, and the gooseflesh had vanished.

He had never felt it again, he supposed, because his mind associated its rising with the coming of the ambush party that night. Johnny had killed them all himself, before the rest of the unit awoke. Whenever the gooseflesh should have come, his mind retreated into the heat of the battle, and the chill vanished.

The muscles of Wareagle's massive upper body tensed and relaxed in the breeze. He sought comfort from the trees and brush, from nature, but nature refused him. This was his land, his home, where he came to ground, where the spirits could hold the demons of the past out so he could sample a peace he knew didn't belong to him. Today, though, the spirits had deserted him, just as they had in Brazil.

Why? Johnny wondered.

The question did not frustrate or perturb him. Their absence implied a lesson he needed to learn. A host of birds landed at the edge of the clearing, and Johnny reached into his pouch for the feed he carried with him whenever he ventured into the woods. He filled his palm and extended it outward, waiting for them to approach and eat from his hand as they always did.

The birds waddled a bit nearer, testing the air, then stopped as if struck by an invisible barrier. They came no closer. Still Johnny held the feed out in his usual way, waiting patiently.

They're afraid of me.

The realization struck him like a burst from a jackhammer. He was no longer the person the birds knew and trusted. The essence of his manitou had changed.

First the spirits had stopped speaking to him. And now this.

The connection was inarguable. Yet the spirits had not deserted him. Their silence was counsel in itself. They had helped him reconcile himself to the past. But the future they would leave to him. Johnny could see it in all its obscurity, had seen it since first setting foot in Brazil.

Somewhere there was an enemy he had to face, an enemy who would test the very foundations on which he had built his life. All else, from the hellfire on, had been merely the proving ground leading up to this final rite of passage. The guidance of the spirits had taken him this far, but now he must face his *Hanbelachia*, his vision quest, alone.

He was changing and evolving. Soon he would face an enemy who would determine whether the rest of his days would be spent as a true warrior or with his ancestors. The enemy was vast and powerful, as black as the heart of a moonless night with an ice storm for a soul.

Out there now waiting.

Waiting for him.

Sal Belamo got Patty set up in her own personal office. She had always loved computers. She had never set out to sea without a portable along. This computer was simple enough to use, but it was powerful enough to analyze data coming in from an incredible number of government sources. Sal knew all the right access codes and passed them along.

Patty had started by calling up every bit of information available on the list of victims she already had. There were fifteen now with the names McCracken had added. She read every-

thing on them she could find, much of the information classified.

The first part of the answer came to her quite by surprise.
She was simply staring dreamily at the frozen screen when an
item caught her eye. A simple fact and nothing more that made
her think of her father. But it reminded her of something else,
and she scanned fast to another entry.

A chill moved up her spine.

She spent the next hour rechecking seven more of the victims. Here was a connection.

Incredible. But what did it mean?

She resisted the urge to call Sal right now. She was on a roll
and she knew it. This clue would lead her to others. The truth
was within her grasp.

CHAPTER 18

"Y OU ask me, chief, be a good idea if you let me ride
shotgun with you back to the jungle," Sal Belamo offered
stubbornly.

They had stopped outside Dulles Airport in the predawn
hours of Saturday, where a government jet was waiting to fly
Blaine McCracken to Rio de Janeiro.

"I don't want Patty left alone, Sal. It's as simple as that."

"You don't trust Maxie's people to do the job?"

"I don't trust anyone right now besides you and Johnny.
Something about this whole business smells wrong to me, but

I can't pin down where it's coming from. You and I go to Rio together, there's no one up here to pick up the pieces."

"How 'bout the Indian?"

"Johnny's got his own stake in this."

"You guys seem to read each other clear as the morning paper."

"I carried him through a mine field once, and he's been carrying me ever since."

When Sal frowned, his twisted nose pointed to the right. He reached into his pocket and came out with a pair of clips for Blaine's Heckler and Koch 9-mm pistol.

"Well, if you don't want me tagging along, how about I give you a little going away present?"

"I've got plenty of bullets."

"Not like these, you don't. Got a friend who makes 'em up special. Puts a glass capsule inside each with a mixture of ground glass and picric acid."

"Potent stuff."

"Extremely shock sensitive, he would say. Anyway, mixing it with the ground glass makes it less sensitive and allows it to be fired from a gun. Once it goes bang, the bullet distorts, which breaks the glass capsule and allows the acid to mix with lead."

"Forming lead picric," Blaine concluded.

"Big boom when it hits its target. I call 'em Splats, since that's what happens to whatever they hit."

McCracken accepted the clips, noticing they were stored in clear plastic, which was carefully molded over their contours.

"Oh, yeah," Sal added. "Thing is, you don't want to get them wet. My friend says it undermines the explosives' stability. Point is, you don't load Splats until you're near sure you're gonna need them."

Blaine ran his fingers over the plastic. "What kind of firepower we talking about?"

Belamo winked. "Fire one of these into a watermelon and you won't even have any seeds left to plant."

"I'm not hunting fruit, Sal."

"Splats don't discriminate, chief. They'll turn anything into paste."

They parted right after that, and Blaine's thoughts turned to tracking down the only man he knew of who could shed light on what had gone on at the installation in the Amazon: Jonas Parker. For some reason, Parker had been absent during the time of the massacre. After it, he would have known he was a marked man in grave need of protection. Assuming he had been successful in that quest, he would still be in hiding now. The trick would be finding him.

Toward that end, McCracken called Carlos Salomao, the man who had drawn both him and Johnny Wareagle to Brazil in the first place.

"If you were in Brazil and needed to disappear fast, who would you go to, Carlos?"

"That is simple, amigo. Fernando Da Sa. Ever hear of him?"

"Can't say that I have."

Fernando Da Sa, Carlos explained, was the most powerful crime lord in Rio—and thus the entire country. As head of the *Commando Vermelho*, or Red Command, he controlled narcotics, weapons, gambling, prostitution, even the lotteries in the Rio mountainside slums. The Brazilian police were far more corruptible than their American counterparts and, as a result, Da Sa operated virtually untouched.

"Can you set up a meeting for me?" McCracken asked.

He could feel Salomao's reluctance over the phone. "Da Sa is not fond of foreigners, amigo."

"We'll get along just fine."

So McCracken flew to Rio determined to reach Da Sa himself if Carlos' efforts failed. From Galeao Airport, a thirty-minute taxi ride brought him to the Sao Conrado district, where he would await the call from Carlos at the Rio Sheraton. Blaine chose to stay in American-style hotels wherever possible when he traveled. Ease and comfort were important to him, when danger was always right around the corner.

He checked in at two on Saturday afternoon, and fifteen minutes later he was drinking a virgin guaraná on his room's terrace. His fourth-floor room offered a magnificent view of the private Vigidal Beach below. It was almost summer, and the temperature in the upper eighties was made pleasant by the breeze off the sea. With his feet propped up on the plastic terrace table, Blaine felt himself starting to slip off to sleep when the phone jarred him. He answered it, expecting to hear Carlos Salomao on the other end.

"I trust your trip went well, Mr. McCracken." It was a heavily accented voice.

"Fernando Da Sa," Blaine said.

"I am honored that you have graced my humble surroundings. You require a meeting, no doubt."

"It won't take much time."

"It will take what it must. Come to the Copacabana Beach directly in front of the Hotel Meridien in exactly one hour. My guards will be waiting."

"How will I know them?"

"They will know you."

Da Sa hung up without saying any more. He didn't have to. His people had been watching McCracken since the moment he emerged from the jetway, and they would watch him all the way to the meeting.

Blaine changed into shorts and a loose-fitting shirt, then took a hotel cab the fifteen-minute stretch to the Meridien Hotel at Copacabana Beach. Cars were parked diagonally across the stone walkway separating the street from the sand, and the cab pulled into an open slot. Blaine paid the fee in the Brazilian cruzeiros he had obtained at the Sheraton and stepped out. The beach before him was enormous and, since it was Saturday, crammed with people fighting for every inch of sand. Some boys battled for soccer balls in the sand; others played volleyball.

Blaine strode toward the beach between two of the many thatch-roofed stands along the street. Native fruits and foods were available, as well as Coca-Cola. Nearby a marimba band played. McCracken was about to step out onto the beach as instructed when a pair of strikingly beautiful Brazilian women in bikinis closed in on him from either side. One was black, the other looked more Latin.

"This way," the black woman said, and moved forward to take the lead. The other woman brought up the rear. He had expected to be met by the typical muscle-bound thugs and found the surprise quite pleasant indeed.

The women escorted him onto the fine sand of the beach. They walked carefully to avoid the cluttered patches of blankets and towels and to avoid soccer balls in flight. Blaine watched as a kicked ball rolled to a stop in front of the first guard. The young players froze. No one made a move or said a word until she had kicked it back at them.

"Obrigado," one muttered.

"De nada," she answered.

Close to the sea, they swung left toward a section of the beach that appeared strangely vacant. There seemed to be only a single cluster of beach chairs under a canopy. Four tall, beautiful women were going through patterned dance steps in two pairs. The moves possessed a balletlike grace, but the daring near-misses with hands and feet, along with lightning responses, suggested martial arts *kata*. As he got closer, Blaine could see the women's bodies were layered with well-defined muscles. Sweat glistened off their washboard abdominals and bulging bronzed shoulders. In addition to these four, he now noticed three more sunbathing off to the right of the canopy.

A single clap of hands brought the quartet of female practitioners to rigid attention, chests heaving from their exertion under the hot Rio sun. Beyond them Blaine glimpsed a single figure beneath the canopy. He was seated in a half-lounge chair that seemed buried in the sand, and he made no effort to rise as Blaine drew closer.

"Step into my office, McCrackenballs," Fernando Da Sa said.

He stretched out his long legs and clasped his hands comfortably behind his head. He wore a white shirt unbuttoned to reveal a firm midsection that protruded slightly over his bathing trunks. The flesh was the same dark bronze color as his face, accentuated further by his jet-black hair, which showed gray only at the temples. A thin, shiny mustache graced his upper lip.

McCracken stopped at the entrance to the crime lord's canopy. A nod from Da Sa, and one of his female guards placed a beach chair directly facing his.

"Please, make yourself comfortable."

The chair had been placed so Blaine's shoulders remained in the sun, but the front of his body was shaded by the canopy.

"You like my girls, eh, McCrackenballs?"

"Most men with eyes would, Mr. Da Sa."

"The routine you saw them performing is called *Capuela*. It was developed by slaves who were forbidden to practice self-defense. Because of its dancelike appearance, the masters paid no attention to it, but it is actually a deadly fighting art."

Blaine stole a glance at two of the participants who still lingered just beyond the canopy. "I don't doubt it."

Da Sa smiled with pride. "My girls are the best fighters in all of Brazil."

"Tough to conceal a gun in those outfits, though."

"You did not check beneath the towels, my friend."

"Perhaps I shall."

Da Sa laughed gently. "I am glad to see you came unarmed. It is a gesture of good faith on your part and is much appreciated."

Da Sa bowed his head slightly at that, and McCracken returned the gesture. Obviously the two women who had escorted him here knew he wasn't carrying without needing to pat him down. That implied a high level of proficiency.

McCracken struggled to get his beach chair settled evenly in the sand.

"Can I offer you a drink, McCrackenballs?" Da Sa asked.

"Absolutely. Something from one of those coconuts. Unleaded."

Da Sa gave the appropriate signal. "I understand you don't drink alcohol."

"Afraid I might get to like it too much." Blaine glanced around him. "Especially in a place like this."

"I can understand what you mean." The crime lord hesitated. "It seems strange to you, doesn't it?"

"What?"

"That I can conduct business here without any worry."

"Your counterparts elsewhere in the world couldn't work this openly."

"My manner of conducting business is not like the others in my field. I am not a criminal, Mr. McCracken, I am a purveyor, an entrepreneur. To the people I am a hero, but I am at home among them. I am just one of them who has reached a different station.''

"A station that requires nine bodyguards.''

"One has certain enemies, Mr. McCracken.''

"The Red Phalange, for example, Mr. Da Sa?''

Da Sa nodded. "I see you have done your homework, Mr. McCracken. My enemies in the phalange are not welcome here and they know it. Would you care to hear why?''

"Of course.''

"The people. They do not have the support of the people. They have done nothing for them except take their money. You have heard of *Esquaderao da Morte*?''

"Death squadrons.'' Blaine translated.

"With the tolerance—even the support—of the police, these roving bands murder homeless children and dump their bodies in the sewers. They claim the purpose is to reduce street crime. They claim these children have no families. But I am their family, Mr. McCracken. I am family with all of Rio.''

Blaine's drink came and he accepted it gratefully. It was cold coconut milk, and he drained half of it in the first two gulps. He licked off his upper lip and dabbed with his arm what he had missed.

"You fund orphanages, halfway houses for released convicts, and food banks for the poor.''

"There are a great many in my country.''

"There were a great many more before your war with the Red Phalange.''

"I centralized power, McCrackenballs, and the results speak for themselves. I give back a huge percentage of what I take in from the city. It is good business. I am a good businessman.''

"And it's important that I know that?''

"It's important that you know how I function, my friend, in the event I am not able to grant your request.''

"I think it will be in your best interests—as well as the best interests of the party I am seeking.''

"Really?''

"This is beyond your usual sphere of influence, Mr. Da Sa.''

"This is Rio, McCrackenballs."

"The roots are elsewhere."

The crime lord shoved his chair closer to McCracken's. "The roots of what?"

"Sometime within the last week a man came to you, an American. He asked for new identity papers, perhaps for protection."

"Was this man in trouble?"

"Not necessarily," Blaine said, the drink cooling his palms. "He was simply part of something that didn't exist anymore. Maybe if he had walked into the U.S. Embassy, everything would have been all right. But he didn't."

"What is this man to you?"

"He has answers I need, answers no one else has. That makes him a valuable commodity, Mr. Da Sa. For both sides."

"And which side am I on, McCrackenballs?"

"Neither. This time you're in the middle."

Without warning Da Sa bounded out of his chair and strode quickly to the water. McCracken drained the rest of his drink and followed close behind, as did the guards, too, at a discreet distance. Blaine stopped next to the crime lord and water lapped over their feet as Da Sa spoke again.

"This is Rio, my friend. I am both sides *and* the middle."

"Not this time, Mr. Da Sa."

"Assuming this man, this American you speak of, is under my protection, I would not force him to meet with you. What do you offer that may encourage him?"

"You can tell him what you know about me. Tell him I'm the one who can get him what he wants."

"And just what is this?"

"If he's still in the country, as I suspect, it's because you learned he was too hot to move. But what the man wants is to get out and go home. That's where I come in. He cooperates . . . the arrangements get made tomorrow."

Da Sa laughed. "My sources were right about you, my friend. You think with your balls."

"Cuts down on the headaches."

"And you believe you can succeed in this where I have seen difficulties?"

"I have the advantage of knowing exactly what we're facing."

"That might not provide sufficient impetus for the American to accept a meeting."

"Then tell him the Omicron legion is still at large. Tell him thirteen is my lucky number."

"That means nothing to me."

"It will to him."

Sal Belamo gazed from the screen to Patty Hunsecker and back again.

"In-fucking-credible," was all he could say. "You sure about this?"

"Absolutely," she said. "Every one of the victims on the list with my father was adopted, all within a three-year period."

"Beginning forty-five years ago and ending forty-two? . . ."

Patty nodded. "For whatever it's worth, yes."

"It's worth more than a kick in the ass, lady, and that's what it feels like. Damned if I can make any sense of it, though."

"Wait until you try to make sense of what else my nimble fingers uncovered: All the businessmen, my father included, had extensive dealings with the Japanese."

"Come again?"

"They brokered deals. They ran interference for buyouts and mergers. Some made a fortune. Some didn't. The Japanese ended up the biggest winners."

Belamo hesitated, trying to take it all in. "How many additional victims you say you came up with?"

"Another five at least."

"You ask me, lady, the thing to do is use your pattern and find out who else might be on the list."

"I already have, Sal, and one of them is sure to interest you. Here," she said, sliding back from the monitor screen, "have a look."

Belamo squinted to read the name clearly, and then his eyes bulged.

"Holy fucking shit," he muttered.

CHAPTER 19

McCracken agreed to meet under any conditions Jonas Parker requested.

"The thing is," he said to Fernando Da Sa, "I won't be the only one in Rio looking for him."

"And these others, you think my participation in such matters simply slipped by them? Why would they have not come to me as you have?"

"Because they knew you would have seen through their motives."

Da Sa grasped his shoulder tenderly. "You need not worry about these others, my friend. This man is under my protection, and that means very much in Rio. In addition, I will dispatch a dozen of my ladies to provide security, assuming, of course, he agrees to meet you."

Blaine was told to go back to his hotel and wait by the pool. He would be contacted there with the details for the meeting.

It was cool in the late Rio afternoon, the sun having disappeared behind the Sheraton, and Blaine had been lying by the pool for only twenty minutes, when a tall, dark woman lay down casually on the chaise longue next to his.

"Eight o'clock tonight at the Jardim Botanico."

"The what?"

"Botanical Garden. Enter from the Avenue of the Royal Palms. The gate will be left open for you. Walk until you reach the bronze fountain. The man you seek will appear only if you come alone, make no phone calls, and speak to no one before leaving. If you're late, the meeting is off.''

She rose and walked away.

"Nice talking to you," said Blaine.

McCracken reached the Jardim Botanico right on time and found the security gate to the Avenue of the Royal Palms open, just as promised. His path led beneath palm trees of every variety that had been among the seedlings planted by Prince Regent Dom Jaoa in 1808. Since then, samples collected and nurtured over the course of the years included water lilies measuring twenty-one feet in diameter and a spectacular collection of carnivorous and poisonous plants.

With just the moon for illumination, McCracken could only make out the shapes of trees and plants imported from a hundred countries. The wide path that ran between the spreading palms was formed of hard-packed dirt inlaid with rock. Other narrower paths, some enclosed by vine-wrapped steel overhangs, joined the main one to create a serpentine maze of intersecting passageways through the various flora. Blaine could make out a large lake off to his right.

Despite the calm and beautiful scene, McCracken was nervous and wary. Da Sa's guarantees of protection seemed meaningless because the crime lord's guards had no conception of what they were up against.

With that in mind, McCracken carried his Heckler and Koch along with Sal Belamo's twin clips of plastic-covered Splats. He wore baggy, full-fitting trousers for comfort as well as to hide his pistol in an ankle holster. He had asked Da Sa for permission to carry the gun. The crime lord believed the weapon would be superfluous, but Blaine told him he liked playing things safe.

He strolled down the Avenue of the Royal Palms with eight o'clock still several minutes away. He knew he was getting close to the fountain when he heard its dripping sounds. It was nestled in a small open grove, surrounded by many statues and stone benches.

Blaine checked his watch. It was eight o'clock. Perhaps

Parker had decided not to show after all. Perhaps something had stopped him en route.

Blaine caught the faint sound of footsteps on the soft ground of the narrow walk to his left. A shape emerged, motions tense and jittery. Blaine stiffened, but he didn't rise. The figure passed into a patch of moonlight and Blaine recognized the face he had seen in Virginia Maxwell's file. The man quickly approached and stopped a few yards before the bench where Blaine sat.

"Mr. Parker? Or is it Doctor Parker?"

Parker stood rigid. "Mister will do fine." A pause, then, "Da Sa says you can help me."

"You have to help me first."

"Anything. Everything. I just want this to be over."

"Then sit down."

"It won't make me more comfortable."

"It will make you a smaller target."

Each motion long and deliberate, Parker joined McCracken on the bench.

"Of course, we might be safe with Da Sa's guards posted all around us," Blaine continued, "but I don't think so. And I've got the feeling you don't, either."

Parker's eyes widened in the moonlight. "How much do you know about *them*?"

"I know there are thirteen. I know they escaped after killing the rest of the personnel at that installation in the Amazon. I also know you went into hiding because you knew sooner or later someone would realize they missed you. Probably sooner."

"On my Christ . . ."

"What made you so lucky, Mr. Parker? Why did you survive?"

"I was project liaison with General Hardesty. My job was to perpetuate the illusion that the project was government funded. It was called Omicron."

"I know."

"How much *do* you know?"

"Not who was above Hardesty."

"I don't, either."

"Bullshit."

"No! My involvement began and ended with the general.
When he died and the shred order came down, I made myself
vanish."

"What shred order?"

"The general's staff was following S.O.P. With Hardesty
dead, his files had to be closed."

"Ben Norseman . . ."

"I heard he was coming, and I knew why. *They* wouldn't
have been his only targets. I knew that, so I ran."

"But Norseman got down there he didn't have any
targets at all. Base personnel had already been slaughtered,
and the *Wakinyan* were gone."

"The *what*?"

"Indian word for Thunder Being. Close enough."

Parker swallowed hard.

"Somehow they got wind of what was going down. Something tipped them off; they took matters into their own hands
before Norseman showed up. Then Norseman went after them
and got himself butchered. I found the bodies. It wasn't
pretty."

"But how? How could they know?"

"Tell me what I'm dealing with and maybe I can give you
an answer."

Parker looked puzzled. "You must know. You just said—"

"I don't know shit, really. I know you were in the warrior
business, transforming man into superman. I've got a rough
idea that it has something to do with biochemical brain alteration and conditioning."

"The *Wakinyan*, as you call them, are . . . disciples."

"As in the Bible?"

A nod. "There were twelve in the initial stage, and they
were given the names of the disciples. But names didn't matter
much to them—not the names they used to have, and not the
ones we gave them." His eyes glinted in the darkness. "You
called them supermen before. Well, you're not far off. The
basis of Omicron was the creation of the perfect human fighting machine, men conditioned to behave and respond like machines."

"More than conditioned," Blaine said.

"Yes. Processed, reordered, remade. Choose any word

you like. We broke down most of what they were and made them into what we wanted them to be. The selection process was as long as any of the phases. Certain predispositions and qualities were required from the outset.''

''A shell from which to build . . .''

''In a sense, you're right. Omicron never could have succeeded if the proper preconditions weren't met. We searched for subjects who fit the profile: soldiers who had already displayed the proper levels of brutality, who, in short, thrived on violence. The project was centered around the chemical stimulation and alteration of existing brain patterns. Back in the States, this theory is being put to use in the treatment of epilepsy. Today the technology exists to implant a computer chip the size of a rice grain into the cerebral cortex to maintain proper chemical balance and prevent seizures.''

''That explains the microcircuitry experts at the base.''

Parker nodded. ''The theory was that if such an implant could maintain a balance, it could also change a balance. We were dealing with the very core of the central nervous system, refining and remaking subjects with the proper propensities instead of wiping the slate clean and starting from scratch. Someday maybe, but not yet.''

''You sound proud of it, Parker.''

Resolve replaced fear in his eyes. ''Because we succeeded, McCracken. Years of research and testing, of failure and frustration, for once paid off. We had a hundred subjects at the outset. A number died during the early stage of the procedure, their brains short-circuited. Still more were not sufficiently affected by the process. Others, in spite of apparent success, proved untrainable in the mode envisioned for disciples. We ended up with eighteen, of which six were gradually weeded out, bringing our total to twelve.''

''Thirteen,'' Blaine said. ''Thirteen are known to have walked out of your installation.''

''Abraham.''

''What?''

''Number thirteen was called Abraham. He was the first success of the second phase of Omicron and the prototype for all future disciples. Infinitely more skilled and . . . changed by the implant and subsequent procedures.''

"The leader?''

"On the contrary. He was the ultimate loner. All the disciples are loners unless instructed to be otherwise. The nature of their tasks demands it.''

Blaine thought back to his final night in the jungle. "They seemed to be getting along just fine when the Indian and me almost ran into them in the jungle.''

"Because it suited their purpose.''

"Which was escape. Because somebody needed them for something somewhere else. They were created for a purpose, Parker, which brings us once again to the people above Hardesty. They knew his death would place the project in jeopardy. So maybe you weren't the only plant at the base, and the other one learned of the shred order, too.''

"And let them out? *Helped* them?''

"Only to be killed with the others for his efforts.'' Blaine gritted his teeth. "I saw the handiwork of these disciples, Parker. I saw what they did to the Tupis and to Norseman's team. Next time you want to play God, do it by His rules.''

"That was just the point!'' Parker exclaimed excitedly. "Eliminate conscience, inhibitions, all traces of guilt. Replace them with a need to kill, a self-perpetuating love for the act equaled only by the capacity to carry it out. No hesitation. No remorse. Physical abilities tapped and developed to a new degree. Think, McCracken! You of all people . . .''

"Me, what?''

"I just thought . . .''

"Thought *what*, Parker? Go ahead. You won't hurt my feelings.''

"The way you function, the way you think and operate. The causes you fight for. Tell me you're not ruthless. Tell me you let anything get in your way.'' He lowered his voice. "Tell me you haven't killed.''

"Only when I have to, and I never enjoy it.''

"A slim distinction.''

"Between me and your disciples?''

"We made them what you made yourself.''

"Bullshit! You let them out into the jungle to kill helpless Indians. I saw a pair of boys with their intestines piled on the ground. Is that what you made?"

"No skill can be trusted until it is practiced."

"You think all their victims will be unarmed kids?"

Parker hesitated ever so slightly. "Norseman and his men weren't unarmed."

"You're defending these monsters, goddammit!"

"Not defending, just explaining. You wouldn't be talking like this if you'd seen them work."

McCracken bounced to his feet, needing to separate himself from Parker. "You're as crazy as the things you helped create."

Parker jumped up after him. "And what about you? Look at yourself . . . who you are, the way you live. Day to day. Always alone. Defining yourself in terms of the task before you. When there is no task, there is no definition."

"What makes you such an expert on me?"

"You really don't get it, do you? The profile that was developed for the Omicron legion wasn't arrived at by accident. Studies were made, features identified and ranked in order of necessary development. Examples were studied, scrutinized." Parker stopped and looked at him. "You, McCracken."

The statement sent a tremor up McCracken's spine. He felt his emotions boiling over, tried to contain them in order to keep his focus on the matter at hand.

"You made your monsters in my image?"

"Partially, yes."

Blaine thought of Sal Belamo's exploding bullets. "Guess I'll have to shed a tear when I blow each of the fucks away."

Parker shook his head. "Not even you could."

"I still have a few tricks I reserve for myself."

"It's not a question of tricks. The disciples are advanced as much beyond you as you are beyond a thirteen-year-old boy. And it won't stop there. We learned from the original twelve. Abraham is the prototype now."

The sudden twist in Parker's train of thought chilled Blaine. "Prototype for what?"

"Don't be naive, McCracken. Our work in the Amazon was just beginning. The original disciples were ready to be dispatched, yes, but a second phase soon would have taken their place."

"It's a shame the installation's been lost."

"Only this one. My understanding is that there are a dozen more bases scattered about the world. Whoever Hardesty was fronting for was building an army."

CHAPTER 20

HIS name was Matthew. What his name had been before he probably could have discovered if he dug down deep enough into his brain. But the person with that name was as much a stranger to him as someone he might pass on the street. The slate had been wiped clean. Nothing that mattered remained beneath the new person that he was.

He crouched in a thick nest of bushes in the western quadrant of the Jardim Botanico. He did not know exactly where his twelve targets were; he knew he would find them when the time was right.

Matthew slid in amid the bushes. He was not a large man. He had to look up to see six feet, and before his experiences in the jungle, had not been overly muscular. The training had changed all that. Matthew grew strong beyond his wildest expectations; that is, while he still had expectations. Somewhere along the line he had lost them, too. There were only tasks to perform. All other considerations were superfluous.

At times, Matthew wondered whether the person he had been before had existed at all. The only thing that preserved the memory was the echo of feelings churning in his head. He would see or hear things that would bring him back to another time, and for an instant, he would feel as he had felt before. A fleeting flutter. By the time he thought to grasp for it, it was gone.

Suddenly Matthew emerged from the bushes. He did not know what had told him the time was right. When he moved, the night did not give him up. His motions came like the cat who stalks its prey unseen in the open. There was always cover; the air was cover. The trick was to use it.

He found the first woman fifty yards ahead, behind a massive tree, her body concealed under its umbrella of branches. He smelled her before he saw her, as he moved carefully to avoid being caught in the moonlight that snuck through tree branches. Matthew felt his breathing slow, his heartbeat a mere flutter in his chest. He had his usual weapons, yes, but he would use his hands here. Hands were the best.

Matthew came right up behind the woman and clamped his hands on opposite sides of her head. A single twist was all it took. There was a crack and he kept on twisting. In his mind he could see the cartilage stretched and torn. Muscle and sinew shredded. Matthew had the woman's face turned all the way around so he was staring at thin rivulets of blood running from her nostrils and lips. Her eyes were bulging. The sight made him smile; he just held her there away from him until her head flopped over between her shoulder blades and stayed kinked at a downward angle.

Matthew let her crumple at his feet and moved onto the next one.

"Where are these other bases?" McCracken asked Parker.

"I don't know. And if I did, I wouldn't tell you until I was safely in the States."

"You better give me reason to believe you can help lead me

to who's behind the Omicron legion, if you expect me to get you there.''

"You know as much as I do on that subject."

"All I know is that Omicron was abandoned three years ago by legitimate authorities before it got reborn down here in another form. That means resources sufficient to make possible technology that plenty of experts had already dismissed as impossible.''

"What are you saying?''

"I'm not sure exactly. But it was backed by an enormous supply of funds, and by someone who knew exactly what they wanted; that much is clear. What's missing is the frame of reference from which it emerged.''

"I don't understand.''

"I'm still putting the pieces together for myself, Parker. For one thing, they had a running start. There was nothing hit-or-miss about Omicron, was there?''

Parker considered the question briefly before responding. "Not in the jungle, anyway.''

"Nor anywhere else is my guess. Whoever's out to kill you knew exactly what they were doing—which meant they or someone else had done it before.''

"How could I tell? I wasn't a scientist.''

"Right, but the men and women who *were* scientists weren't operating blind. Everything was precise. Someone was directing their every move. Someone who knew.''

"What's it mean?''

"I don't know. But I will, you can count on that.'' Blaine paused. "I'll need you to repeat this.''

"Just get me safely back to the States and I'll repeat it to anyone you sit me down in front of.'' He watched McCracken swing around suddenly. "What's wrong?''

"Keep quiet!''

"You heard something!''

Blaine drew the Heckler and Koch from his ankle holster.

"Stay behind me. We're getting out of here.''

"Da Sa's women . . .''

"Just do what I tell you!''

* * *

Matthew knew the final snap had been too loud, considering that this was the closest guard to his targets. He had dispatched the first eleven women without a bother: six with his bare hands and five with the knife now pressed back into the sheath wrapped around his ankle. What he wanted to do was break a spine, snap one like a twig, using enough force to double a body over upon itself. He had used the knife to give his hands a rest, but the knife gave him little satisfaction. The hard swish of blade parting flesh was too transitory. The victim spasmed, writhed, and the whole process was much too messy.

The final woman, lying prone in the brook, had looked up an instant before he was about take her. Before she could cry out, Matthew had slapped a hand across her mouth with such strength her front teeth broke from her gums. She struggled, and he jerked her head back. Her neck cracked, then her vertebrae crunched, one after another. At the end, she was bent almost perfectly in two. Matthew discarded her that way and moved on at a faster pace, the sound of the first crack still loud in his ears and, he feared, in someone else's.

"I don't think we should leave," Parker protested. "We should stay until the women—"

"They're dead," McCracken interrupted.

"What?"

Blaine swung around to face him. "It's just you and me."

"How do you know? How *could* you know?"

A faint smile crossed McCracken's lips. "I'm no different than your disciples, remember?"

"But if one of them—"

"Just do what I tell you," Blaine said. "Just—"

He heard the soft *pop* an instant before Parker's left eye exploded in a cascade of blood. Blaine hit the ground and watched as Parker's right eye was shot in similar fashion; a third bullet caught the man in the center of his forehead before he fell. Blaine spun onto his stomach and fired a rapid burst just beyond the Avenue of the Royal Palms, where the shots seemed to have originated.

Nothing. No sound. No return fire.

McCracken's mind worked frantically. What he was up

against here was clear now. He started to reach into his pocket
to exchange the rest of his dwindling clip for Sal Belamo's
exploding Splat shells.

A rustling sounded to his right, and Blaine twisted around.
A kick lashed upward and pounded his wrist. The Heckler and
Kock went flying. Another foot came toward his face. Blaine
ducked and twisted away, saw the foot that missed him ram
into the base of a tree and carve a chasm from the bark. Blaine
was still rolling when another kick grazed his temple. He managed to get an arm out to block the next blow, which was aimed
at his ribs.

"Get up," instructed a voice that seemed to belong to the
looming figure somewhere over him.

McCracken bounded to his feet, facing in the figure's
direction.

"Very good. You knew where I was."

The figure was five or so inches shorter than he, but incredibly broad, stretching the confines of his black suit and turtle-
neck. His clothes were not mussed. He wasn't even breathing
hard.

*Not even breathing hard, and he had just offed a dozen of
Da Sa's killer guards!*

"I was supposed to kill you, too," the disciple told him.
"But I wanted to talk to you."

Feigning dizziness, Blaine stumbled around on his feet, his
back to the tree near where his gun had been lost.

"I could not kill you from a distance. I respect you too
much."

Blaine lunged. His fingers had barely touched the figure
when he felt himself being lifted up and thrown. He crashed
into the row of bushes that rimmed the fountain pool. As he
started to spring upright, a savage kick to his back drove him
forward again. A fist slammed his head from the rear, and
stars exploded before him. Then, dazed, he felt a pair of iron-
strong hands grasp his shoulders.

"Talk to me, McCracken."

The speaker waited a few seconds for a reply; when none
came, Blaine was hurled headlong over the bushes and into
the fountain pool. McCracken felt his insides mashed together.

"You're very disappointing. I expected so much more. I

suppose I should have shot you the same way I shot the traitor.''

And then Blaine was being pitched back, through the bushes this time. He landed halfway between the fountain and the tree. Blaine willed his eyes to focus and saw a slight glimmer of steel near the tree, illuminated by the meager moonlight. Blaine blinked, opened his eyes again. The Heckler and Koch sharpened before him. He fingered the clips of Splats in his pocket.

The disciple emerged through the bushes, and Blaine forced himself not to move, bracing for the kick that shook his ribs and spun him onto his back. He pretended to cower there until the enemy's powerful hand hoisted him upward and jammed his shoulder against the tree.

''Time to die,'' said the figure, rock hard fist pulled back directly in front of his face.

The fist jumped forward. Blaine shifted his head sideways just before impact, timing it close enough to feel the *whoosh* of power thundering by. The blow crunched into the tree as McCracken kicked into the figure's knee, then dropped and rolled away. He retrieved his pistol, twisted, and fired all in the same motion, finger never leaving the trigger. Three bullets missed the figure that, incredibly, had remained in motion. Blaine couldn't get a fix until the final shot, which grazed the disciple's shoulder and spun him around briefly before he disappeared into the darkness.

McCracken ejected the spent clip, popped off the plastic coating of a fresh one, and locked Sal Belamo's Splats home fast.

He listened for a hint of sound that might betray the disciple's position, but there was nothing. Even if there had been, he couldn't take a chance until he was certain. Fire a Splat without a sure target and he would give away the true potency of his weapon. He had to outthink this adversary.

A *predator*, he thought, *so comfortable in the role of the hunter*. . . .

Why not give it to him, then? McCracken was in motion before completing the plan. He darted from the clearing, down a narrow path enclosed by a massive steel planter covered with vines. He knew the disciple would give chase, so at the

first opportunity McCracken would swing around and fire a
Splat.

Blaine realized he was running toward the sound of the
brook. He charged up a set of stone steps built alongside a
thicker patch of woods that promised cover.

When the soft rustling reached his ears, he was not surprised. The disciple was coming fast, closing the gap. When
the final stone step was past him, Blaine spun and fired in the
same motion, the Heckler and Koch kicking a bit more than
usual behind the powerful bullet's exit.

Twenty yards in front of him a tree exploded with a thun-
derous jolt. McCracken gazed down and saw a rubber ball;
the disciple had used it to create the rustling sound. It rolled
to a halt at the foot of the stone steps.

Damn!

A fresh sound came from his right, and he aimed that way.
The Splat found a stone bench this time and blew a portion of
it apart. The pistol felt heavy in his hand. The wind howled
and sounded like laughter.

Just to his left and up a little rise was an ivy-wrapped stone
gazebo that overlooked much of the Botanical Garden. Blaine
dashed inside and dived low, beneath the waist-high wall. He
could see and hear anything from this vantage point, and the
position was strongly defensible. The disciple could not possibly approach without him knowing.

Or could he? McCracken couldn't help thinking he had
played straight into this monster's hands. Maybe he was out
there laughing even now, waiting only to compose himself
before he struck.

Blaine wasn't waiting. He threw himself out of the gazebo
and down a steep hill that led to another dirt path in the serpentine garden. He slipped and fell, sliding the last measure
of the way. He regained his feet with pistol sweeping his pe-
rimeters. He backed off, then started to run, looking for the
first exit he could find.

The path widened; it was formed of hard dirt and rock,
which was why the anomalous soft depression struck him so
quickly. He knew the sensation all too well from Nam, and
experience sent him into a headlong dive for his life.

The spikes embedded themselves in a tree at just the spot

his head would have been. The disciple had attached them to a thick, pliable branch and had bent the thing tautly backward, waiting to be triggered.

Did he know I would come this way?

No, but the disciple had certainly planned for a fight and a chase. In all probability, similar traps would be set all over the garden. That thought drew Blaine's gaze downward, which was when he saw the wire suspended over the path, affixed to a tree on either side. McCracken hurdled himself over it, then reached back and yanked it with his foot while still lying prone on the ground.

Blaine pawed his way ahead as a net mired with sharp thorns and prickers dropped down from the trees, covering the spot he had occupied just seconds before. Then he did what he knew the disciple eagerly awaited.

He screamed, a bellow of terrible agony, backpedaling on the ground at the same time. Sure enough, a shape was slinking down the path, keeping to one side. Blaine propped himself slightly upward and fired at the disciple.

But the muzzle flash encompassed the entire pistol in the same instant the roar reached his ears. The hot flames singed McCracken's wrist and palm and he cried out in agony. His dip in the fountain must have soaked through the clip's plastic coating just enough. He let go of the pistol and struggled back to his feet. It was clear he would have to make a stand somewhere in this garden . . . Somewhere without a gun.

Fighting to remember the garden's layout, Blaine regained his feet and charged on. The disciple was no longer in sight, and there was no sense in Blaine looking until he had some weapon to fight him. Their exchange back at the fountain taught McCracken he had no hope of winning a hand-to-hand struggle, though he felt certain that was what his adversary still wanted. It was something he had going for him, perhaps the last thing he had to make use of.

His flight took him around to the north and back to the Avenue of the Royal Palms. Making a dash for it seemed his best chance . . . until he reached the glass hothouse containing the carnivorous and poisonous plants. Most of them grew in simple pots, looking harmless and innocent in the night. One stood out. Standing upright in the center was a smaller version of a tree Blaine recalled all too well from Africa. It looked like a massive rosebush, its thorns the size of thin fingers. But McCracken knew the thorns were actually deadly spines loaded with a curarelike poison.

McCracken knew he had his weapon now. Making it work was another matter. The substance of the plan still forming in his mind, he kept kicking at the glass until a hole big enough to accommodate his bulk had been formed.

The sound of breaking glass drew Matthew to the hothouse. He had sensed from the beginning it would end here. Too bad, really. Unfortunate.

"I'm not holding my gun, McCracken," Matthew said calmly, as he approached the hothouse. "I don't have my knife out, either. I was supposed to kill you back there, but I didn't. You're more like us than them. Join us. Tell me you'll join us, and I won't kill you."

Matthew reached the jagged hole in the glass and started through.

"We knew it was you in the jungle. You and that Indian. Only you could have eluded us in the manner you did . . . The Indian's idea, no doubt."

Glass crackled beneath him as Matthew drew further into the small hothouse. There were just a few places to hide.

"Norseman went easy. He was just a soldier, a killer. But you're different. You understand what we are, what we're capable of. Join us, McCracken. It's your only hope. If I don't kill you, you'll die anyway—when all of the United States dies. We're going to kill it, McCracken, and inherit what's left. Join us and you can be spared."

Matthew realized that all of the potential hiding places were vacant just as the rest of the glass in the section behind him shattered in the vague outline of the shape hurtling itself forward.

McCracken had the thick shard of glass squeezed into his right hand, held high where the moonlight might catch it.

And the disciple would be sure to notice.

He saw the disciple's empty eyes sweep toward it and his arm come up instantly in defense. Blaine kept the force of the blow coming, true intention not betrayed as his arm was stopped and twisted over as the disciple went for the break.

Just as McCracken would have done.

Anticipating the move perfectly, Blaine bent his knees and dropped his free shoulder against the disciple's side. The disciple responded by reaching back for more purchase. That one instant cost him his balance, and McCracken drove him forward. The disciple seemed to flow with the move briefly, then he realized its deadly intent, the truth reflected in his bulging eyes as Blaine rammed him into the bushy tree poised in the hothouse's center.

The tree's spines pierced the disciple's flesh in four separate places. The pain from this alone would not have been enough to even make him waver, but a breath later the poison was flooding his veins, sabotaging his blood and short-circuiting his system. He pounded McCracken twice before the first spasm shook him. His body locked upright as Blaine backed off. His mouth gaped. He gasped just before his throat swelled from the poison and closed. His face turned purple. He tried to free himself from the tree, but succeeded only in flapping his arms before they dropped helplessly to his sides and he slumped.

The disciple was still twitching when he hit the floor, eyes locked open and no more dead, Blaine thought, than when he had been alive.

McCracken backed away, pain racking his body, his eyes on the disciple. When he didn't stir, Blaine at last backed out of the hothouse.

One battle won meant only another lay out there to be fought. Parker had said an army of them were being created. The process could be infinite, the number of perfect killing machines expanded. Someone had arranged for their escape—not only because of Hardesty's death, but because their services were needed.

The disciple's words rang in his ears. *"If I don't kill you, you'll die anyway—when all of the United States dies. We're going to kill it."* If the words were true, whoever was responsible for the Omicron legion was also planning something much worse. And what it was had to be somehow connected to the six killers who were systematically eliminating the people on Patty Hunsecker's list.

McCracken retraced his steps out of the Jardim Botanico, staying in the shadows on the chance the Rio authorities had been alerted by the commotion. None appeared, but he reached the street still wary of every step. He knew his most pressing goal after escaping from the Jardim was to flee Rio before the power controlling the remaining disciples could marshall its forces again.

Fernando Da Sa seemed his best bet for assistance. The crime lord would certainly have his own reasons for joining the fight now; a dozen of his best women guards had been killed in the garden tonight.

It took a few minutes, but Blaine finally managed to hail a cab. He told the driver to take him to the Bali Bar in São Conrado, Da Sa's current headquarters and the place he had directed McCracken to come to in the event of trouble. Tonight's adventures certainly qualified. . . .

He considered his plight in the cab's cramped quarters. Whoever was behind the Omicron legion had known he was coming back to Rio. The disciple he had killed must have been following him all along, waiting for his rendezvous with Parker before making his move. Blaine had played right into the enemy's hands. They had used him to hunt down the only living person who formed a direct link to the legion, played him for a fool, but he had fooled them in the end by staying alive.

The Bali Bar, as it turned out, was located in the fashionable Itanhanea shopping park. Blaine saw it set off by itself to the far left. Saturday night made for a jam-packed parking lot, and the cab deposited him on the edge of the clutter of would-be patrons milling about trying to determine if and when to enter. The building itself was decorated in a South Pacific island motif. It had the look of a massive bamboo hut wrapped freely with enormous vines. A palm tree grew out of an inner courtyard complete with outdoor bar to handle the overspill of patrons from within. The letters announcing the bar's name were cleverly slanted and painted in bold, vibrant colors that glowed in the night.

As Blaine headed for the entrance, he noticed that the patrons were exceedingly young, some no more than fifteen. Except for a large bouncer posted near the turnstile permitting entry, there wasn't a single adult to be seen. McCracken felt the young people staring at him—more for his age, he gathered, than his look of disarray. His clothes were still not dry from his plunge into the fountain, and his crash through the hothouse glass had made neat tears through his jacket. His face was bruised, and he was favoring his right side. His wrist was singed and blackened, but not swollen.

McCracken moved through the turnstile and up into the crowded bar area. Blisteringly loud music smacked his ears. Most of the room's light sprang from four television screens playing the same music video. Everything was dark and brown, the lamps attached to the wooden support beams shedding only candlelight illumination. More young teenagers were milling about, nursing drinks, and Blaine walked over to a set of empty tables in the back of the room.

He chose a table against the wall and sank into a chair. When a waitress finally came over, Blaine asked to borrow her pen and grabbed a napkin from her tray. He wrote quickly.

DA SA—
    I'M DOWNSTAIRS. NEED TO SEE YOU.
                       MCCRACKEN

"Give this to the manager, please," he said in Portuguese, handing it to the waitress along with a generous tip.

Two minutes later, a curly-haired young man in his mid-twenties approached the table.

"He told me you might be coming," he said in English. "I was to send you up as soon as you arrived."

"I've arrived."

The young man pointed to a set of stairs on the left. "His office is on the third floor. To reach it, go up to the second landing and cross the dance floor. The guards will be expecting you."

"Dance floor?" Blaine asked. He couldn't wait to ask Fernando Da Sa why he had chosen the Bali Bar as his base.

Making it up the stairs was like fighting traffic on the L.A. freeway. The dance floor was packed with bodies twisting and churning beneath flashing multicolored lights. A large man stood guard near a door across the floor, and Blaine found himself dodging bodies as he made his way there.

"McCracken," Blaine announced to the guard over the din.

The man gestured toward the stairway just behind him with his eyes, the outline of a pistol obvious beneath his sports jacket. Blaine slid by him and climbed the steps. At the top of the stairs, another man directed him to an open door on the right side of the corridor. McCracken headed toward it.

The anomaly actually struck him as he passed inside.

Male guards instead of female guards. Why?

But a half-dozen steps inside the office and the why was made clear.

"Mr. Da Sa?"

The crime lord was seated in a high-backed leather chair behind his desk, immobile because of the neat slice in his throat that had spilled blood down the center of his suit and splattered it over his desk blotter. In the same instant that Blaine put everything together, his ears registered steps pounding his way. A window directly before him was open to the Rio night, and he lunged toward it, a step ahead of the machine-gun fire suddenly struggling for a bead on him.

Rat-tat-tat . . .

The sound peppered his ears as he hit a narrow strip of the second-floor roof. He tried for balance, but the slippery metal tripped him and he fell, thumping hard to the cobblestone drive below. Wobbly he regained his feet just as machine-gun fire from down the hill came his way. Blaine swung and retreated up the cobblestone driveway. Swinging right at the top, at the Bali Bar's rear, he crossed into an alleyway that ran between the bar and an athletic club. He was running, but his feet felt heavy. He felt dizzy from the fall and started to crumple, just as he realized the alley came to a dead end.

He was trapped, the guards starting down the alley after him. He fought to get back on his feet, but his strength was gone. The alley swam before him. He reached instinctively into his jacket for the gun he'd lost at the Jardim Botanico. He was too groggy to notice that just behind him the round cover of a telephone-line tunnel had popped open.

Blaine was clawing to hold on to his last bit of consciousness when a pair of hands pulled him down into a dank darkness his mind at last surrendered to.

PART FOUR

Children of the Black Rain

Washington:
Sunday, December 1, 1991; 6:00 A.M.

CHAPTER 21

THE nightmare began for Patty Hunsecker when the phone jarred her from sleep at the first light of dawn.

"Whatever you're selling, I don't want any," she said, knowing full well it could only have been Sal Belamo.

"Wake up, lady," came Belamo's rapid voice. "Wake up quick."

Patty was upright in the next instant. "What's wrong, Sal?"

"We got us some problems, lady. Do what I say and you'll be all right. You hearing this?"

"Yes."

"Okay. I'm calling you from one of these goddamn car phones. The safe house isn't safe. *You're* not safe. Clear?"

"Crystal," Patty said, not as bravely as she had hoped.

"I'm on my way there now. Chances are someone's gonna beat me to the building, so here's how we're gonna play it. You gotta get out, and you gotta do it now. Back stairs. Rear exit . . . No, they could be watching that . . ."

"Who, Sal?"

"Good question, lady. Not a good answer. Give you the shitty details when I pick you up. Suffice it to say everything makes sense now, most of it anyway. Old Blaine'd be proud of me . . . and you."

"What's going on?"

"You're leaving, and I'm picking you up. Go up to the roof. Do you hear me? Go up to the roof. You'll find some heavy

165

twenty-foot planks up there. There's an apartment building next to the safe house that's the same height.''

"I know it.''

"What you gotta do, you gotta slide those planks across and walk on over. Then head down through the unlocked door on the building roof to the alley on the western side. I'll be there.''

Patty was fully awake now, and so was her fear. "What about security? Can't we call—''

"Fuck security. If they're not dead, they're useless. Just do what I tell you.''

Patty dressed quickly in jeans and a sweater. She moved cautiously into the corridor, holding her breath in fear that a gun barrel would greet her. There was nothing, no sounds, no shapes. She slipped silently to the stairwell and started to open the door when she heard the echo of steps ascending. Hard to tell how many. A single man, perhaps two.

Patty felt panic swell within her. She had to reach the roof, but obviously this approach was out. Something had spooked Sal Belamo—and whatever it was was coming up the stairs for her. She bolted back toward her room, trying to frame the building's structure in her mind.

The fire escape! That was her only chance! She reentered her room and locked the door behind her. Then she rushed to the window and lifted it open. The fire escape lay before her, rusty and providing no reason for confidence. Nonetheless, she pulled herself outside onto it. Her boots clanged noisily on the metal tubing. Rising to a crouch, she slid the window back down and began her climb up the ladder.

The cold Washington morning bit into her lightly clothed body, and her breath misted before her face. There were four flights to cover, the steps were cold and slippery, wet with morning dew. A few times she had to stop just to wipe her palms on her jeans. As she neared the top, her heart thundered with the fear of being caught, but she managed to swing her legs off the ladder's top rung and onto the roof without anyone stopping her.

Scanning the rooftop, she spotted the planks Sal had mentioned and ran over to examine them. To her dismay, only one was usable, the other too rotten to be trusted to carry her.

This meant she'd have to get to the neighboring building with only ten inches of cushion.

Patty hoisted the plank and slid it over to the adjacent roof with the utmost care, aware a mistake now could ruin her only viable escape route. No sooner was it in place on the opposite roof, its middle section sagging noticeably, then fresh sounds of pursuit reached her from the stairwell door. She was actually thankful for the sounds; they gave her the burst of adrenaline she needed to step out on the plank and begin her walk.

It was much easier than she had expected. She kept her eyes focused on her goal—the roof of the adjacent building— forcing herself not to look down. Even though her stomach was twisted in knots, the fear of the men in the stairwell proved greater than her fear of falling. She reached the other building with a final leap, remembering to pull the plank after her so whoever was following couldn't use it to get to her.

The door to the roof of the building she had just escaped from crashed open just as she reached the one Sal Belamo had directed her to.

Please let it be open . . .

It was. Patty was through it in a flash, hoping her pursuers hadn't caught a glimpse of her. She thundered down the steps and swung left when she reached the building's lobby. She bolted through the door to the street just in time to hear a car screech down the alley at the end of the block.

"Hop in!" Sal Belamo ordered from behind the wheel of an ancient Pontiac GTO.

To reenforce his command, bullets pounded their way from the head of the street, shouts and screams behind them. Sal grabbed Patty and yanked her in from the driver's side. Her feet pushed off the windshield to help her reach the passenger seat as Sal tore away, leaving a burned rubber smell behind him. Patty found the seat at last and felt some exposed springs dig into her buttocks.

"I ain't exactly finished with her renovations," Sal apologized as bullets peppered the rust.

The rear window was one of the few parts of the car that was whole—until a burst of fire shattered it and sprayed pieces of glass on both of them.

"Uh-oh," Sal muttered.

Patty caught a glimpse of a dark sedan sliding to a halt at the other end of the alley. The car's doors whipped open.

"Hold on," Sal said, and the GTO surged forward with a blitzing roar.

The gunmen managed to lunge out of the way as the GTO smashed their car broadside, shoving its collapsed frame into the center of the street, where a morning delivery truck finished the job. Belamo spun the wheel madly one way and then the other, righting the GTO, which, except for an extra crinkle across the rusted hood, seemed undamaged.

"They don't make 'em like they used to," Sal said, with a grin.

"I'll say."

"Titanium steel bumper," he explained. "Part of my own option package when I decided to rebuild this baby."

Belamo gave the big engine some gas and screeched around a corner. Patty unhunched herself in the seat and brushed off the glass stuck to her clothes.

"Stay down!" Sal barked. "Don't know if we lost them yet."

"Doesn't this come with a rear oil spray?"

"Nope. And no bulletproof shields or machine guns, either. I was workin' on the ejector seat, though."

"I can tell," Patty groaned, shifting to avoid the exposed springs still scraping at her buttocks.

"There's gonna be hell to pay for this," Sal said, heading toward the first of the morning traffic.

"You mean what they did to your car?"

"The fuck-up that brought it on, first class all the way, let me tell ya. You ask me, the world's gone to hell, and a few of us just don't know it yet."

"What happened, Sal?"

"Shit hit the fan, lady. And guess who was standing in front of the blades. Here," he said, and flipped her a wrinkled envelope.

"What's this?"

"Some cash, an airline ticket, and a passport. You're on your way to Rio."

"I'm what?"

"We gotta get a message to old Blaine, lady, and I'm too

hot to play delivery boy. All you gotta know now is that it's you, me, McCrackenballs, and the Indian. Nobody else. Dig?''

"The Gap? Virginia Maxwell? . . .''

Belamo took a corner hard, and Patty slammed against the right-hand side of the car.

"Listen to me, lady, we had it all wrong. Only reason I know now is 'cause of you.''

"*Me?* What are you talking about?''

"Better fasten your seat belt to hear this, 'cause it's gonna jolt you more than my driving. . . .''

Patty reached Rio early Monday morning, nearly a day after Sal's desperate phone call had awakened her. She started looking for McCracken at the Sheraton Hotel, as Sal had advised. Her call from the airport told her that he had never checked in. Nonetheless, he would have left information about his actual whereabouts at the Sheraton, available to anyone who knew how to ask.

At the hotel, her cab driver had to squeeze by a procession of tour buses lined up around the Sheraton's circular drive. Patty squeezed through the arriving hordes and entered the hotel through one of the twin revolving doors. The Sheraton lobby was a sprawling affair. A comfortable seating area and escalators dominated the right, while the lobby-level jewelry shop took up most of the left. She headed for the reception desk directly across the way.

"Excuse me," she greeted the clerk.

"Checking in, miss?''

"I think one of your guests left a package for me.''

"Your name?''

Patty provided the one Sal had given her. "Smithers.''

The clerk punched some keys on his computer terminal, waited for the response to show up on the screen.

"I'm sorry, miss. I have nothing here under that name.'' He looked up at her. "What was the man's name who was supposed to leave it?''

I didn't say it was a man.

That realization struck her before she had a chance to respond to the clerk's question. She backed away from the counter as he scrutinized her.

"Miss?" he called softly. "Miss?"

Patty didn't stop. She had learned everything she was going to at the hotel. She wasn't the only one looking for Mc-Cracken. And whoever else there was would now be looking for her.

She swung away from the clerk, finally, and found herself face-to-face with a pair of Japanese men who were standing on either side of a large plant in the center of the lobby. Their eyes locked unblinkingly on her. They remained motionless.

All the victims showed prominent connections with the Japanese. . . .

That bit of her own research echoed in her mind as she swung to her left, toward the elevator bank, only to find another pair of Japanese there. Trying to act as naturally as possible, she moved past the Japanese in the center of the lobby. Their eyes followed her every step. She moved toward the escalators; two more Japanese were standing in front of them, their expensive suits almost a perfect match. She looked over at the entrance; three more men were hovering amid the wave of arriving guests. She was surrounded, boxed in. What could she do? What would *McCracken* do?

A baggage cart overflowing with suitcases squeaked toward her. Making an instant decision, she closed her eyes and stepped out into its path. The collision rocked her, and Patty made sure to use her shoulders to jostle the bags. The results were perfect. The cart wobbled, and suitcases spilled everywhere. Patty went down harder than she had meant to, then lay still as a crowd began to gather.

"So sorry, miss, so sorry," the Brazilian bellhop was saying in a mixture of English and Portuguese, reaching down to assist her.

Patty accepted his help, saying, "I was just on my way out, actually."

"Then let me help you to the door."

"I'm fine, really."

"Can I get you a cab? I'm so sorry."

"It was my fault. I wasn't looking. I'm fine."

Patty's eyes swept the area around her and saw four of the Japanese men mixed among the crowd. They seemed unsure as to what their next move should be. Clearly she had complicated their task, hopefully buying the time she needed to get safely out of the hotel.

She backed her way out of the open hotel doors, colliding with a group of arriving guests. At least four of the Japanese were coming her way. There was a long line of guests waiting for taxis. She would have to get away on foot.

But the Sheraton's isolated location left her with little maneuverability. There was just the Vidigal slum rising up the nearby mountain, and that was no answer.

She turned toward the lobby again to search out the Japanese and ended up colliding with an arriving guest. They knocked into each other with such force she almost fell.

"Easy does it, ma'am," he said in English. He was big! And he was American!

"It's about time," Patty snapped, reaching down to pick up the cane the man had dropped when they'd collided.

"Time?" he echoed, stupified.

"Where the Christ have you been?" she demanded.

Patty grasped his arm on the pretext of regaining her balance, which allowed her to draw close enough to him to speak softly.

"Help me," she whispered, and for just an instant their eyes met—the same instant the Japanese men came out of the hotel doors.

"I'm sick and tired of all this," she continued, her loud ranting beginning to draw the crowd she sought.

"I'm . . . sorry," the man forced himself to say.

"Let's just get out of here. Now!" she demanded.

He seemed to notice the Japanese then. "Listen, it couldn't be helped. It—"

"Now!"

"Fine. All right."

He took her arm with his free hand and aimed her toward a jeep an attendant had been about to park. She climbed in ahead of him, and he pulled himself inside, grimacing with the effort it took. He pulled his cane in after him and closed the door.

"Thank you," Patty said, with a sigh.

It was then she saw the pistol the man held low by his hip.

"Give me one reason not to shoot you," he said.

CHAPTER 22

"You'd be doing their job for them."

"*Whose* job?"

Patty turned to look back toward the entrance. The Japanese were gone. The rest of the crowd had dissipated.

"Just drive. *Please*."

"That bad?"

"Worse."

The man stowed the gun beneath the seat and extended his hand. "Name's John Lynnford."

Patty accepted it gratefully. "Patty Hunsecker."

He gunned the engine and looked back in the same direction her eyes had taken. "What's this all about?"

"You're rescuing a damsel in distress."

John Lynnford's stiff leg worked the accelerator as he pulled the jeep into traffic. "Distress from what?"

"Not what—whom. Did you see those Japanese back there?"

"Can't say that I did."

"They were after me."

"What'd you do, buy an American car back home?"

"No, I'm Emperor Hirohito's illegitimate daughter."

Lynnford regarded her briefly. He was a heavyset, thick-boned man with unevenly styled blond hair, and blue eyes that made him look younger than he probably was. She instinc-

172

tively trusted him, even though she had no good reason for doing so.

"The Japanese were waiting in the lobby," she explained.

"For you?"

"For anyone who approached the front desk and asked the right question."

"Which was?"

"Has to do with a friend of mine that I've got to find."

The jeep glided to a halt at a red light, and John Lynnford looked at her again. "You want to get out?"

"Not really. You want me to?"

"That depends."

"On what?"

"Your willingness to work my show."

"Your *what*?"

"Show. You're looking at the sole owner of the Orlando Orfei Traveling Circus and Carnival. We're setting up for a run in Barra da Tijuca."

"Always wanted to join the circus," said Patty.

The Orlando Orfei Circus was setting up shop in a muddy field in Rio's most modern shopping district. Located amid the Casa shopping complex and Carrefour Mall in Barra da Tijuca, the location could not have been better when it came to drawing crowds.

John Lynnford took the roads like he knew them, and they exchanged few words during the ride. As they approached the area, Patty heard the eerie whine of a calliope, along with the constant thud of stakes and studs being pounded into the ground. A number of men seemed to be issuing orders. To her right was the shell of a soon-to-be Ferris wheel. Just beyond it was a merry-go-round, and beyond that the midway was taking shape.

John Lynnford climbed out of the jeep ahead of her, easing his boots gingerly to the muddy ground, then retrieving his cane from the cab. Patty joined him.

"This way," he said, and started off. "You can wait in my trailer while I send someone back into the city to apologize for my missing the meeting I had scheduled at the hotel."

"Sorry."

"If we end up opening a day late, you'll have to do better than that."

"I'll make it up to you."

"How?"

"Tell me how much you'll lose, and I'll make sure you're reimbursed."

John Lynnford leaned on his cane and regarded her sardonically. "Yeah, right."

"I'm serious."

"You were serious about a bunch of Japanese trying to kidnap you, too."

"You don't believe me?"

"Look, ma'am—"

"Patty. Please call me Patty."

"Look, Patty. I've heard these kinds of stories before, but you really don't fit the type."

"What type?"

"Someone on the run, looking to hide. Look around you. That's how plenty of these people got started. That's how plenty of them will finish."

"And you?"

"Uh-uh. You first."

"Then let's go to your trailer," Patty said, taking him up on his suggestion. "This is gonna take a while. You'll be more comfortable sitting down."

John Lynnford didn't question her during the tale, not even once. The only break in Patty's monologue came when, without the use of the cane, he limped to a small refrigerator and took out a bottle of beer. He drained it in a single gulp and started on another without offering any to Patty.

"Wow," was all John Lynnford could say before he swallowed the rest of his second beer. She had just finished her story. "Jeeze, forgive my manners," he said, eyeing the bottle and beginning to pull himself up from the chair.

"Nothing to forgive. I'm not thirsty."

"Go on, then."

"There's nothing more to tell."

"Where's this McCracken fellow?"

"I don't know, and I haven't got the slightest idea how to find out."

"They could have gotten to him, you know. You mighta come all this way for nothing."

"No," Patty said. "You don't know McCracken."

"You're right about that, and I'm thankful for it."

"You'd like him, John."

Lynnford rolled his eyes. "That's what they told me about the last city controller who jacked up my show's tariff."

"You and McCracken would get along just fine."

"What makes you say that?"

"Mavericks always get along."

"Interesting analysis."

"You denying it?"

"Let's stick to the subject at hand, Patty."

"Can I have that beer first?"

This time Lynnford used the cane to reach the refrigerator; he came back with a third bottle for himself as well.

"You need a glass?" he asked.

"Nope."

"I always like a woman who drinks her beer straight up."

"Men don't have a monopoly on lips." She took a hefty gulp of the beer. It was cold and wet and that was all that mattered. "You believe me now, don't you?"

He sighed. "Everyone here has a story, Patty. When you've been with the circus long enough, you learn to tell the ones that are true from the ones that are made up." He sipped his beer. "The difference is most of the stories I hear come from people who wanna stay here and hole up for a while. Not the case with you."

"No."

"So here you are, up the creek with a toothpick for a paddle, and it's only a matter of time before somebody follows the current."

"Meaning? . . ."

"Meaning the hounds chasing you probably won't be paying customers—and having them nosing around the Orlando Orfei won't do either of us any good."

"I really don't want to endanger anyone. If you want, I'll—"

"Shut up, Patty. I said I wanted to help you, and I meant it. Lots of people who've moved to the midway've left skills behind. A few of those skills just might be what you need."

"Part of their stories?"

"Almost surely."

"Speaking of which," Patty said, straightening up, "I haven't heard yours yet."

John started to raise the beer toward his lips, then stopped. "Not much to tell," he said softly. "Not compared to you, anyway."

"So bore me. I'm not going anywhere for a while."

Lynnford looked out the window at the work going on outside. "You're looking at my life, Patty. And it's been my life for as long as I can remember. Some of the family was into the business end of circuses and carnivals, others like me were performers. Three cousins, my brother, and I formed a trapeze act when all of us were barely out of puberty. Became a big attraction, a lead one even. It lasted six years, until I was twenty-two—'bout fifteen years ago. My cousin forgot to catch me on a routine swing, and the net did the same. Shattered my leg on impact. Not a bone left whole to this day. More steel than marrow, Pat. Guess I shouldn't complain, though. I'm alive, right?"

"Alive here."

"Ever so true. The family bought out the Orlando Orfei chain, and I saw myself as the perfect person to manage it."

"I understand."

"Not until you've been here awhile, you won't. Nobody asks any questions. They accept you for what you are and leave it at that. Your life can begin fresh the day you walk in. You're not the first person to come to us the way you did, and you won't be the last."

"Except I'm not staying."

"But you're not about to find your friend McCracken without a hint of where to start looking, either."

"I have to try."

"And I understand that. What you gotta understand is you've got to be ready to move fast if things take a turn for the worst. That's where we come in."

Patty rolled the beer bottle between her palms. "We? As in the people here who are going to help me?"

Lynnford rose and tapped his cane toward the window. "They're all working now. We'll get the ball rolling as soon as they break for lunch."

"Are you happy now, Benjamin?" asked Pierce, standing in the doorway of the room that would be the tall man's home for the foreseeable future.

Benjamin stared at him for a time. "I won't be happy until we're all together, until all this is finished."

"Which will be very soon," said Nathan, who had come up behind Pierce. "He wants to see us."

"Now?" Benjamin asked fearfully.

"He called us here for a reason," Nathan answered. "It's time. Or damn close to it."

"Let's go," Pierce suggested.

"Yes," Nathan agreed. "Let's."

And they waited for Benjamin who, shrugging his shoulders, joined them in the corridor. The bunker was located some ten stories beneath ground level, constructed at a cost of nearly a billion dollars over the course of the past decade. All the work had been overseen by the man who had at last summoned them here. As far as they knew, this bunker was one of several scattered strategically across the United States, safe and insulated from anything that occurs on the surface above.

As a result, the air in the bunker had a sterile, antiseptic scent to it. Overdry, it played hell with the sinuses, but the slightly larger oxygen content kept the men from noticing. The worst feature of all, each would have probably said, was the lack of windows. With no world beyond to relate to, there was nothing to provide life with scale. Nothing, that is, other than the plan that had brought them all down here.

Nathan led Pierce and Benjamin to an elevator, which they rode to the very bottom floor of the complex. It was lit in a dull red haze and was colder than all the others. The lack of light, coupled with the absence of windows, was maddening. Stomachs clenched, they passed through an archway and into an even darker conference hall. The hall's ceiling lights were encased by drop-off coverings that spread the light sideways instead of down. Everything else in the room was pure, pristine white. Untouched, virginal. Pierce thought it looked a little like snow.

Three places had been set at the huge conference table.

"Sit," came a command spoken from the darkened slab that was the front of the room. "Please, my children, sit."

The voice echoed through the hall's sprawling limits, emerging in a slightly garbled, watery tone. Only the outline of its bearer was visible; a shadow hunched in a chair. What little life there was in his voice came from the echo. Pierce, Nathan, and Benjamin did as they were told.

"My children," the voice started, "I am happy to report that all is proceeding on schedule."

With that the hall's light dimmed even more and a map of the entire continental United States was projected on the wall behind the shadow's voice. The map's glow cast his frame in an eerie translucence, outline bathed in a spill of light that might have come from the heavens themselves. Slivers of the light glowed red when the next instant brought twelve red splotches to the map, scattered irregularly over the United States and focused amid the nation's largest centers of population. Accordingly, by far the heaviest concentration was along the Eastern seaboard. Six red lights dotted New York through Miami, while the West Coast and Midwest showed only three each.

"Everything is going as planned," the voice explained emotionlessly. "No adjustments have had to be made in our timetable as a result of the complications."

"Than the matter has been settled?" Pierce asked.

"Not quite," answered the voice as the intensified glow from the red lights bathed the wall like blood. "I regret that it has now become necessary to alter our strategy to a very minor degree. One of the disciples must be replaced."

"It was McCracken, wasn't it?" Benjamin asked the question tentatively.

"Our efforts to eliminate him in Brazil failed, yes."

"You're saying you sent one of the *disciples* in and he *failed*?" Nathan asked incredulously.

"That's exactly what I'm saying."

"Is McCracken that good?"

"We knew he was from the beginning. In reality, we have learned much from the encounter. The details are sketchy, but they provide a lesson, nonetheless. We won't make the same mistake again."

"But this mistake has cost us, hasn't it?" challenged Pierce.

"Do not take that tone of voice with me, child."

"Your precautions to deal with McCracken were inadequate. He's faced similar battles before and won them all."

"Not against the likes of our legion."

"What happened to the disciple in Brazil?"

"Misjudgement, by all accounts."

"No. As long as McCracken is still at large, our operation is in jeopardy."

The shape took a deep breath. "We will watch him smolder in the ruins of his world. When we rise to claim the ruins, we will crush him like an ant. He represents everything you were conceived to destroy, the type of American who crushes everything in his path in the same way his nation once tried to destroy us by every means available. Your existences came about in response to this, and for nearly fifty years we have waited for the day that is soon to come. You three have helped chart everything. You three above all should know."

"We want to be sure," said Benjamin in conciliatory fashion. "That's all."

"McCracken has disappeared," reported the shape. "But we have effectively isolated him. When he surfaces, we'll know it. He is alone. No one in Rio would dare befriend him. He has become a pariah."

"Why?"

The shape laughed a laugh that sounded more like the shrill wind ahead of a thunderstorm. "Apparently witnesses have placed him at the Bali Bar. He's been blamed for the murder of Fernando Da Sa."

"The news is bad, *Kami-san.*"

Tiguro Nagami had found Takahashi outside in the garden of the estate in Kyoto. The day had given itself up to twilight, the only time Takahashi's pained eyes allowed him to drink in the rich sights, however much of their beauty might have been lost without the sun.

"I felt as much," he replied.

"The woman escaped us, and we are no closer to finding McCracken."

"There is more. The tone of your voice speaks of it."

"I have collated the reports of what occurred in the Botanical Garden. Twelve additional bodies were found, *Kamisan* . . . All savagely killed."

Takahashi turned to face him. "Then it begins."

"You don't sound surprised."

"Why should I be?"

"Because up to now we could never be totally sure the enemy had succeeded."

"Children of the Black Rain," Takahashi muttered.

"I didn't hear you."

"Nothing. I trust we still have a chance of locating the woman and McCracken."

"In any event, we have hope."

"But it is dwindling, isn't it, Tiguro?" Takahashi turned and gazed off into the garden for a long moment before shifting back toward Nagami. "Weetz will be in Philadelphia tomorrow."

"His report confirms all is ready."

"Then our battle continues. The death of the vice president will set them back, Tiguro. That is something, anyway."

Johnny Wareagle stood in the center of the Delta Airlines terminal in Boston's Logan Airport. He had parked his jeep close to the first terminal he came to and had spent the last several hours wandering about from one concourse to another. In his mind was the feeling that there was somewhere else he needed to be. A destination was calling out to him with a purpose all its own. The Delta terminal was no different in most respects from the others, but for some reason Johnny stopped in the center of its concourse.

In that moment the existence of the enemy was very real to him. In that moment, between breaths and heartbeats, he felt himself enter the mind of his greatest adversary. The concourse went black, and Johnny felt chaos and cool processed rage. He felt a soul cold enough to be frozen solid and a manitou that was formed of purpose and nothing more. Animals had more soul, more spirit than this. He felt he was glimpsing a machine, albeit one that gave off a foul odor of sulphur and rotten eggs.

Something lay dead in the blackness, and Johnny conjured memories of the jungle place he had walked through with Blainey. It was there that some part of his foe had been killed and replaced with another. The dead part might have reached out occasionally, but his foe never reached back. In the last instant before he slipped back, Johnny felt his adversary's incredible power, an enjoyment of death equaled only by the capacity to bring it on.

Johnny opened his eyes, realized he was sweating. He had reached into a *Wakinyan's* head for the first time, and a portion of his mind had come away scorched and seared. The night before, the spirits had brought his ancestors to him while he knelt by the fire. He could not see their faces, but their voices were clear. They told him the time for his *Hanbelachia*, his vision quest, had come at last. Everything he was, everything he had tried to be, was merely a prelude to the task before him. There would be only success or death, and nothing in the middle.

Johnny wanted to ask them about the hellfire, wanted to ask them about the obstacles he had overcome then, only to be faced with others. Was there no end? Would this test give way similarly to another? But his ancestors were gone, and there was only the breeze.

Johnny had smiled then. Life was a circle, after all, and a circle has no definable end or beginning. Strangely, McCracken seemed to have realized this ahead of him. He did not search for meanings or purpose; he merely acted. They shared the same circle, but seldom the same space in it.

Johnny started walking, his seven-foot, three-hundred-pound frame moving with the grace of a jungle cat even along the concourse. Many gawked, but few paid him a second glance. Or maybe by the time they tried to, he was gone. He gazed up at a screen listing departures, his eyes locking on the second one from the bottom: a Delta flight leaving in two hours.

For Philadelphia.

CHAPTER 23

McCRACKEN came awake slowly, clawing past his eyelids for the light he felt beyond him.

"He's coming around, Reverend," he heard a young voice call from above him.

"Let me have a look, then. Let me have a look."

Blaine's eyes opened to an eerie half-light and the sound of water dripping somewhere nearby. A rank odor filled his nostrils, a putrid stench mellowed enough by an anomalous cold breeze to be tolerable. Suddenly a face attached to a shock of raggedy, long hair was peering down at him, twisting to get a better view.

"How you be then, governor?" asked the man, with a shadow of a British accent.

"If I'm dead, this better not be heaven."

"Hell be more like it—and even that might be giving it too much credit," said the man, and Blaine saw a pair of medium blue eyes set in a face layered with month-old beard stubble. "You're in *Harocimha*, largest *favela* of them all. Home for me and my boys."

Blaine was aware of feet shuffling toward him, the sound like rats lunging for a meal. It made him bolt upright, and a thunderclap erupted in his head.

"Easy does it, governor," the man said, easing him back down to what Blaine realized was a straw mattress placed on top of a rickety set of bedsprings.

In the next instant, the two of them were engulfed by a sea of young faces and eyes, smaller ones pushing their way forward to have a look and being shoved backward for their efforts. Gazing about, Blaine saw he was in some sort of shanty. Poorly layered brick and clapboard formed the interior of the structure, cutouts for windows, but no windows present, allowing the only light in. The interior was multileveled and steep. Only the remnants of a floor were visible, the rest being hard-packed dirt and rock. McCracken turned toward the sound of dripping water and saw a deep ravine running from outside the shanty down through it, carrying what could only be raw sewage based on the scent.

"Toto, I've got a feeling we're not in Kansas anymore," was all Blaine could think to say.

This time he succeeded in propping himself up a little. The young eyes and soiled faces backed off a bit. Blaine smelled unwashed hair and bodies mixing with the other scents sifting through the cavernous mustiness. He recalled now a similar scent as he was dragged down into a tunnel from the alley behind the Bali Bar. It was all coming back to him, and little of it was pleasant. Splotches of memory were missing, but he did recall an agonizing walk up a labyrinth of stone steps, his arms propped upon young shoulders and the pain everywhere. The steps had undoubtedly led here to the *Harocimha favela*, Rio's most infamous slum.

"Be glad it ain't anywhere but here, governor," the raggedy-haired adult told him. "Here no one can find you no matter how hard they try. Here nobody can find anyone. Great thing about the *favela*."

McCracken was finally clear on where he was, but not on how he had gotten there. He knew more than a million natives called the *favelas* of Rio their home. Little more than shacks hammered out of wood, stone, and abandoned brick, many of the structures would be washed down the mountain come the rainy season. Others were more sturdily built and even boasted running water and electricity. But the sewage system was no more than a series of channels like the one running through his hideout, draining down the mountain and into the sea.

"How long have I been here?" he asked.

"You been in and out for damn near a day and a half now."

"That makes today . . ."

"Monday, governor," the man said, and extended a boney hand covered to the lower knuckles by what had once been a glove. "Name's Reverend Jim Hope. Pleased to make your acquaintance."

Blaine took it reluctantly. At the same time his eyes swept through the boys gathered about him. He counted twenty, ranging in age from seven to maybe sixteen. Their skin colors seemed as disparate as their ages. There were blacks, mulattos, well-tanned Portuguese who could have passed for Americans, and various levels in-between. "For a man of God, you been awful busy procreating."

The comment took a while to sink in. "This flock's mine in the spiritual sense, not the biblical." He slapped his arms around two of the boys' shoulders. "They ain't the product of my loins much as the product of my conscience. Homeless till I gathered them here. I educates them, too, in the ways of man and machine."

McCracken noticed the bed cots and straw mattresses laid about in no discernible pattern over the crusty floor. Propped up on and against the wall were a number of battery-powered lanterns. There were tables and chairs, an ancient refrigerator with a whining motor, and a working gas stove rimmed with squat steel cannisters containing fuel. He saw cupboards and chests, along with a sink overflowing with dirty dishes that might have been there forever. McCracken turned his attention to himself and checked the tightly wrapped tape enclosing his ribs, then touched the sutures and bandages dotting his face.

"Teach one of them to be a doctor, Reverend?"

"No, governor. But the *favela* meets all needs. For a price, of course."

"And just how did you pay it?"

Jim Hope removed his gaunt arms from the shoulders of the two boys and stuck his hands inside his great coat. They emerged fingering a host of wallets, billfolds, and jewelry.

"In cash, governor," he said, smirking.

"I see what you mean by educating them," said Blaine.

"Lucky for you it was, too. If my boys ain't've been in the Bali Bar when they was, you'd be a dead man now, I reckon."

"To pick a pocket or two, right?"

"No, we stick to the tourists to earn our keep. Don't we, Edson?"

A boy who could have passed for American tossed an arm upon Reverend Jim's shoulder.

"Please, sir. I haven't eaten in three days," Edson said mournfully.

"Well, then," said Reverend Jim, mocking the motion of extracting a bill from one of his many wallets. In the next instant a second boy had snatched the wallet from his hand and mocked escape.

"This was the streets, governor, he'd be two blocks away by now." Reverend Jim accepted the wallet back. "Good job, Marcello. You, too, Edson."

Both were smiling triumphantly.

McCracken sat all the way upright, and this time Reverend Hope's young charges didn't shrink away.

"They like you, governor. Said you handled yourself pretty damn well. Man like you'd fit in just fine with this bunch."

"Sure, and we can tell prison stories by the firelight."

"You'd be better off not making fun, governor."

"I'm sorry," he said. "The truth is, I've really got to be on my way."

"No easy task in itself, I'm afraid," Reverend Hope said. He pointed to the ceiling. "Men back in the city seem pretty intent on finding ya since two nights back."

McCracken started to swing his legs off the cot. "I've still got to get out of here."

Young hands immediately surged forward, doing their best to restrain him. A few of the older boys showed knives.

"Reverend, tell them to put the blades away before someone gets hurt."

"That would be them, of course."

"Yup."

"Do as he says, boys." Then, to McCracken as the knives disappeared, "I've met men like you before. Most of the time I was running from 'em."

"If they were like me, you wouldn't have got away."

"But we all need help from time to time, now don't we?"

"Apparently."

''And me and my boys are willing to keep helpin' ya, but you gotta wait a bit.''

''I may not have a bit.''

''You may not have a choice. Got a few of my lot out now checkin' the streets for scuttlebutt, governor. They come back, we'll know more.''

''In the meantime, Reverend, I'd like to meet the boys that saved me.''

''Wanna thank them personal like, right?''

''Not exactly.'' Blaine glared in feigned anger at a young mulatto who was still holding him down. ''I think one of them stole my wallet.''

By lunchtime the Orlando Orfei Circus had been magically brought to life. Patty had managed a brief nap on the couch in John Lynnford's trailer until his gentle, calloused hand roused her. He led her outside, and she saw the rides were all assembled; a few had even started into their test spins. The finishing touches were being placed on the booths and stands that formed a makeshift midway. The big top for the animal and clown acts was halfway erected, as were the much smaller tent-topped auditoriums for entertainment in the form of exotic dancers and the freak show.

One of the first things John tried to do after taking over the Orlando Orfei was to put an end to the freak show, but it was the arguments of the freaks themselves that persuaded him against it. This was their world, they insisted, the only one where they felt truly comfortable. People were going to laugh at them anyway. Let them do it for a fee and then leave the freaks alone to be with their accepting fellows.

Using his cane to aid him across the uneven ground, John Lynnford led Patty beyond the midway and into the cafeteria tent. They approached a table whose lone inhabitant was a dwarf who was reading a newspaper with the aid of a magnifying glass.

''Good afternoon, Professor,'' John said.

''Quiet,'' the dwarf snapped. ''Can't you see I'm reading?''

He turned the page gingerly, and Patty saw its edges were creased and yellowed, the paper so brittle it seemed ready to break off in his hand.

"Okay. That'll do," he said as he folded the paper fondly into quarters. He looked Patty over. "I guess you'll want the sports page."

"No, I—"

"A challenge, then! You've come with a challenge."

Patty was turning toward John when he began to explain. "The professor here is the world's foremost authority on facts."

"All facts," the little man broke in, and tapped his head proudly. "Photographic memory."

"His booth is my personal favorite. People challenge him with a day in history, and he can always name a noteworthy event that occurred on that day."

"Or they name the event," the little man elaborated, "and I name the day. Doesn't matter either way. I never lose. What have you for me? Perhaps you'll be the first to stump me."

"He reads newspapers," John continued. "Day and night. How many languages, Professor?"

"How many are there?" He looked back at Patty and leaned farther over the table. "A challenge, girl! Try me!"

"The first Superbowl," Patty managed.

"January fifteenth, 1967. Green Bay versus Kansas City. Final score 33–14 in favor of Green Bay. Try again! A date this time."

"April twelfth, 1861," she asked after thinking for a moment.

"Category?"

"History."

"History! Of course!" The little man barely needed to think. "Southern artillery opens fire on Fort Sumter. The American Civil War begins. More?"

"That's enough."

"Another date, then!" The little man drummed the table in eager anticipation.

"October tenth, 1980," John chimed in.

The professor regarded him playfully. "A dirty trick, my friend. The day I joined the circus."

"He was a forger," Lynnford explained. "The best in the business."

"The best ever!" the little man boasted, but then his expression grew sad. "Until my eyes started to go. They're still going. A little harder to read my papers every day, it is. I made a mistake with some counterfeit money. Cost a few gentlemen millions and left them most unhappy. Some went to jail. I came here."

"Passports, Professor," John coaxed him.

"Simple work. Beneath my degree of expertise."

"For my pretty friend here."

"Hmmmmmmmm . . . You either match her face to a picture or match a picture to her face. The latter means starting from scratch."

"Can you do it?"

"Check my files. Let you know." He studied Patty's face. "Strong features. Difficult to match. Means starting from scratch. Leave me her measurements and specs. But no picture until she's finished with Teresa. Go now. I've got my paper to finish."

"Who's Teresa?" Patty wanted to know after they had left the tent.

John just looked at her. "You'll see."

John pushed himself up the four steps leading to a rusted metal trailer.

"It's me, Teresa," he called after knocking.

The door opened, and Patty caught a glimpse of a woman in a clown suit; no, not a suit, just flour-white facial makeup with red highlighting her cheeks, eyes, and mouth. Her hair was tied in a bun, ready to be swallowed by the clown's typical dome and wig. She was wearing baggy jeans and a black shirt. Her hands showed traces of white makeup.

"Can we come in, Teresa?"

The woman gazed down the steps toward Patty. The warmth disappeared from her expression. She looked suspicious.

"It's all right," John said soothingly. "She's with me."

Teresa nodded reluctantly and let John enter, backing away as Patty climbed the steps in his wake.

"The professor's working on a passport for her. She needs a new appearance. Can you do something?"

The clown regarded Patty closely for the first time. She shrugged, then nodded again.

"She's a friend, Teresa," John said softly. "You can trust her."

But far from looking convinced, the clown moved into another section of the trailer.

"Teresa was already here when I took over," John explained. "No one knows her true story because she hasn't spoken a word since her arrival. There's also not a soul on my payroll here who admits to having seen her without her makeup."

"My God . . ."

"She just represents the extreme of what all of us are going through. We're all hiding; Teresa just manifests it more blatantly. But the beautiful thing is that nobody ever pesters her about it, and she's the best clown we've got."

"But don't you wonder what happened to make her withdraw like this?"

"Of course I do, except it's none of my business." John Lynnford paused. "At any rate, you've got to change your appearance before you leave here. The professor will provide you with the means, and Teresa will take care of the face."

With that Teresa returned, she was carrying a vanity case. She backed a chair against the kitchen sink and signaled Patty to take it. The clown eased her neck gently backward, drenched her blond hair in water, and combed it straight back. She massaged what might have been shampoo into it, rinsed it, then went through the whole process again.

"You'll be here for a while," John said. "I've got to see how things are going. We open at sundown."

In all, the transformation process took over two hours. Patty's hair emerged jet black and tightly curled from the perm process. Makeup gave her face an entirely different hue and tint. Contact lenses made her eyes dark brown. But there was more, enough so that when at last Teresa allowed her to look in the mirror, she didn't recognize the face that looked back.

She looked ten years older, at least, harder and meaner, with furrows accentuated on the forehead, brow, and under her eyes.

John Lynnford was coming up the steps when Patty stepped through the doorway.

"Do I know you?" he asked.

"I'm the new attraction for the spook house. Let me loose inside to scare the little kiddies."

"It was time you grew up, anyway."

"Fifteen years in two hours is pushing it a little."

"Added to how many years in the past month or so?"

"I get the point."

"I really wasn't meaning to make one."

He led her to the professor's trailer. The little man had no idea who she was until he put on a different pair of glasses.

"Get her some clothes, boss," he said to John. "Have her picture taken and get it over to me. The passport's almost finished."

Back outside, Patty stopped and touched Lynnford's hand.

"How am I ever going to thank you for all this?"

"Some ticket sales would help. Come back when you've got more money."

"I'm serious."

"So am I. Look around you. We're a community here, a family. We've all been down, and we all know what it's like not to have anyone there to pick you back up again. It's a lousy feeling, and the best way to forget it is to pick up someone else. That's what we do."

Patty looked into his eyes. "I wish I could do the same for you."

"Sorry. Lost cause."

John started to move away. Patty closed the gap and grasped his arm gently.

"You weren't the only one injured in that fall," she said, with sudden understanding. "Your cousin didn't miss the catch, did he?"

Lynnford's lips trembled. His cane burrowed its way into the ground. "It was our grand finale. The five-person pyramid swing we were known worldwide for. I was the top rung. Everything depended on me. I tried to be fancy, and I slipped. The bar wobbled, and that was that. The net wasn't built to handle five people tumbling into it at once. It gave way, and no one came out of it whole. Two broke their necks, another his spine. I got out of it best of all because there were other bodies to cushion my fall. That's why I've never asked Teresa why she doesn't speak. I figure she's got her reasons and she deserves them. We've all got our reasons and they've got to be respected. You've got your reason to leave, so we help you. If you had chosen to stay, we would have helped you there, too.''

Just then the circus strongman, Zandor, rushed up to John Lynnford's side. His rippling muscles glistened with sweat that seemed to pour like a fountain from his bald dome. He gestured with a pair of massive arms toward the shopping mall and parking lot on the left as he whispered his report.

''You're sure?'' Lynnford asked him.

''Yes.'' Zandor nodded.

With the strongman still standing rigid at his side, Lynnford turned back to Patty.

''I'm afraid we've got company.''

''More of the Japanese.''

Lynnford shook his head. ''Locals, by the sound of it, and not the most honorable sorts, either. Maybe sent by the Japanese.''

''Then you've got to get me out of here. You've got—''

''No way,'' Lynnford interrupted. ''We don't know if they're still around the area or not, so this remains the safest place for you. This may even work to our benefit. We can make it work.''

''How?''

''We know they'll be coming, and we know when.'' John Lynnford paused. ''Tonight, at the Orlando Orfei's opening.''

McCracken's immediate goal was to get some strength back into his weary, battered body. The effects both from his desperate fight with the disciple and his ill-fated fall from the roof of the Bali Bar had taken their toll. A half hour of painstaking exercise brought him a good portion of the way back, though not all. He knew the rest would be there when he needed it, and he might need it soon, because the news Reverend Jim Hope's boys brought back from the streets wasn't good. Not surprisingly, the murder of Fernando Da Sa had been pinned on him by the true perpetrators, and the crime lord's soldiers were scouring the streets for him.

''And there's more,'' Reverend Jim reported.

''Can't wait to hear it.''

''The same men are looking for a woman who showed up at your hotel.''

Blaine looked up from the plate of brown rice and fish the boys had cooked for him. "A woman?"

"As luck would have it, one of my boys was in the area at the time." Hope winked.

"I'm sure. Just go on."

"Something spooked her and she ran off, but then word got passed that she was working with you, and Da Sa's people got interested."

"Describe her!"

"Cute, athletic, blond hair."

"Patty!"

"You know her, then."

"What I don't know is what the hell she's doing down here!"

Thoughts raced through Blaine's head. Patty Hunsecker must have come to Rio to find him, alerted to the procedure by Sal Belamo. This could only mean something had gone dreadfully wrong back in the States. Sal would never have risked sending Patty down here if her life wasn't equally endangered back home.

McCracken placed his plate down on the stool in front of him. "Do you know where she is?" he demanded.

"We might be able to find out."

"How?"

"Da Sa's men. If they latch onto her, it won't stay secret from my boys."

"It's good to hear they steal more than money."

"Lots of times information's more valuable. Plenty of my lot used to run with the younger ones in Da Sa's bunch; when they grow up they'll probably join them." A frown crossed Jim Hope's face. "Course the problem we got now is plenty of Da Sa's soldiers come from the *favelas*. So once they learn you're here, we can't rely on protection from within, governor. Quite the opposite, if you know what I mean."

"I do. Just find the woman."

"What happens when we do?"

"I go in and get her."

Hope smiled. "Had a feeling you were gonna say that, governor. Course you know that'll probably put you up against Da Sa's boys . . . who are out to get you anyway."

"I'll let them bring in plenty of reinforcements to even out the odds."

The boys drifted in and out of the shanty they called home throughout the afternoon. One pair arrived brimming with pride. Reverend Jim Hope let them accompany him over to Blaine.

"These got a present for ya, governor."

Blaine took a thick travel wallet from the reverend's extended hand. Inside was a passport belonging to a man of his approximate size and likeness: thick hair, dark features, and a beard. No scar through the left eyebrow, but it was doubtful any customs official would notice the oversight.

"We figured the papers you got with you might not get you outta the country."

"You figured right."

"Somebody you work for turn the tables, governor?"

"I'm not sure yet, Reverend."

"This woman might be able to tell ya, though."

"That's what I'm hoping."

To pass the time while he waited for some word on Patty to be brought back, Blaine listened to the story of what had brought Reverend Jim Hope to Rio—and what had kept him here for over a decade now. A bank job had gone bad outside of London, a guard shot by one of his cohorts. Jim was only the driver, but he'd still have to pay the same price as the shooter, so he took off. Rio wasn't chosen for logic; it was the first international flight he could book passage on. A single stop in his apartment to pick up a tote bag and off he went to Heathrow.

He met the first of his boys, ironically, when a pair of them tried to pick his pocket his first night in. Jim was drunk, and instead of giving them a licking, he gave them a wink.

"Now, you wanna see how to do it right, chaps?"

The boys couldn't speak English, but they seemed to get the point. Teaching them English was the second order of business. After all, a great percentage of their targets would be Americans, so speaking the language would help. He took the name Reverend Jim Hope and took in as many boys as he could handle without losing control. When they got old enough they left. There were always new ones waiting to replace them.

"Thing is," Jim Hope said, "this city's a mess, governor. Sure, tourists come down here for the beaches and the sun, but they don't see the poverty 'cept when they look up the mountain and see the *favelas* rising up the side. And the poverty feeds off itself. You know why there are so many babies born in Brazil? 'Cause the government pays all the costs. Don't pay for no abortion or birth control, though. So more kids keep gettin' added to the picture. Them that has 'em don't want 'em, so they end up in the streets."

"Adding to the surplus population."

"What?"

"Nothing."

Jim Hope gazed about him proudly. "Anyway, these boys'd have nothing without me. I keeps them safe, clean, and alive."

"You don't owe me any explanations."

"Done some bad turns in your time, governor?"

"A few."

"I met men like you in prison. Didn't talk much about what they did that got them there. People pretty much left them alone. Never did anything to prove themselves, but I suppose some don't have to."

"And some do."

"And what is it that you do, governor? What is it that got you down here? I ain't asked that yet."

"Let's keep it that way."

Reverend Jim Hope wasn't about to. "Something busted you up pretty bad. Doc patched you up, but the way I see it, there's smarter things to do than going out to ask for more."

"Believe me, I don't have a choice."

"Like me with the boys?"

"Sort of."

Hope's eyes swept through the shanty again and came to focus on the stinking sewer stream running down the channel in its side. "Ain't much, but the boys think they're livin' like kings. Compared to most around here, they are, too. Given a choice not a one of 'em would leave, neither. This is all they know, and none sees a reason to know any more."

Just then, the sound of feet pounding quickly up the steps

leading to the shanty made both Blaine and Reverend Jim turn toward the doorway. Hope met the trio just inside, and the lead boy whispered something in his ear.

"They found the woman, governor," he reported, turning back toward Blaine.

Blaine rose rigidly to his feet. "Where?"

More whispering. "It ain't good, governor."

"Where!"

"She's holed up at a circus in Barra da Tijuca, and Da Sa's men are gonna move on her come the opening tonight."

Blaine came forward. "Da Sa's men? Why?"

"I reckon whoever turned them against you, turned them against her, too."

"Just tell me where, and if one of your boys can get me a gun . . ."

The much smaller Reverend Jim stopped him with a hand pressed flat against his chest. "Need yourself an atom bomb to go against these odds, and one of those ain't easy to pick out of a pocket."

"You got a better idea?"

Hope's wide smile revealed the brownish edges of his teeth. He spoke as the complement of boys present in the shanty came forward to enclose him.

"When going up against an army, governor, it's best to bring one of your own."

CHAPTER 24

"HIDING would seem a safer bet," Patty suggested as she walked alongside John Lynnford toward the Ferris wheel, her post for the evening.

"Meaning a concealed place where you have limited range of motion. They find you and it's over."

"True."

"And if they aren't supposed to see you, neither can we. We wouldn't be able to help you. . . . Patty, have some faith in Teresa's work. All these people have to go on is a description you don't fit anymore. Now do you want to hear the rest of the plan or not?" John asked her.

"I'm in your hands, right?"

"You'll be taking tickets right in front of the platform. Someone else will run the ride, so you won't have to worry about pushing any buttons or controls. You'll be on ground level and not in plain view."

"Why the Ferris wheel?"

"Central location on the midway in a relatively dark spot." John pointed with his cane to the shopping mall parking lot on the circus's right. "We'll plant a car there this evening. When we close tonight at twelve o'clock, I'll have one of our roadies escort you to it—just a couple melting into the crowd—and drive you to the airport. The professor's working out the airline schedules."

"What about tickets?"

"I'll give you some cash to buy them out of tonight's receipts."

"That's the problem," Patty said, with a sigh.

"What is?"

"Where exactly do I go? I came down here to find the only man I could trust. I've *got* to get that message to him. If I don't, he's dead, and so am I. Eventually. Soon."

"You want to stay with us, that's fine, too."

"Thanks for the offer, but no can do. What I know now goes way beyond me."

"This a vendetta?"

"It used to be. Now I don't know what it is."

The yellow truck rumbled toward Barra da Tijuca, the boys filling its open back clutching the rails for handholds.

"Makes me feel like Bill Sykes," Blaine said to Reverend Jim, who was squeezed next to him in the front seat.

"Bill *who*, governor?"

"Never mind."

Originally the plan was to take buses to the site of the circus, but seeing the yellow truck hauling fresh gas cannisters for the stoves of the *favela* gave Hope another idea. He knew the driver, and a quick exchange of words convinced him it would be in his best interest to drive the group to Barra da Tijuca. Blaine, dressed in native garb, could pass well enough for a local. The biggest problem was his muscular chest and arms, which made him stand out. The Brazilians were built lean and sinewy and the people of the slum seemed most impressed with such a well-developed stranger.

The *favela's* construction boasted no overall plan. Layers piled atop layers, shanties tucked in wherever space permitted, created the serpentine structure of the steep, narrow walkways squeezed between them. Privacy was nonexistent, and ownership often changed as quickly as it took a pair of fast hands to pull clothes from a makeshift line.

Which was how McCracken's tattered outfit had been obtained.

The sun was down by the time the truck dropped them off in the field adjacent to the Orlando Orfei Traveling Circus. Before entering the grounds, Reverend Jim gathered the boys around him, then gave each of them money for enjoying the attractions. Hope had also brought a pocketful of firecrackers with him; setting them off would be the signal that there was trouble. Beyond this, they had no plan. All Blaine could be sure of was that, according to Da Sa's people, Patty was here, and that they were going to move on her tonight.

"Wait a minute," Blaine said to Hope before the boys were dismissed to run amok. "Can they spot Da Sa's men? I mean, can they tell them apart from the rest of the patrons?"

The boys' collective smirk provided their answer as Reverend Jim nodded proudly.

"Interesting."

"Got yourself an idea, governor?"

Blaine nodded. "Gather round, boys," he said, "and pay attention. . . ."

The crowds had begun arriving an hour before sunset, somewhat before the scheduled opening. The midway was already fully functional, although there were still some finishing touches to be added to the big top. The first show was scheduled for eight o'clock; succeeding shows would continue every hour on the hour throughout the evening. It was not an elaborate or lavish setup so far as such things went, but especially for the economically depressed people of the region, the circus was a not-to-be-missed highlight.

Patty quickly fell into the flow of taking tickets from the people forming an eager line in front of the Ferris wheel. The creaky apparatus whined into motion at the start of each ride, a speaker pounding out the same tune in rhythm with every turn.

She surveyed the strollers and ticket holders alike as inconspicuously as she could. She felt safe even in the spill of the thin light, even though she knew that, in all likelihood, the people who were after her had to be somewhere in the crowd. But they would be looking for the woman they got a glimpse of at the hotel, not the person Teresa had created. That, more than anything, gave her reason for hope and security.

Still, she had never felt more alone, and thinking of that made her think of Blaine McCracken. He lived in a world apart, alienated from the rest of a civilization that needed him to maintain its balance. He once told her how much he envied Johnny Wareagle's reclusive existence in the forest, not realizing how much his own life had come to resemble it. You don't have to pull out to pull away. McCracken had helped teach her that much back in the Pacific.

The Ferris wheel spun into the start of another ride, and Patty stuffed the tickets through the slit in the box in front of her. By sunset the ride was running at full capacity, seeming to strain under the weight. The entire midway was jammed now, no game or ride spared the inevitable line. Even the professor's booth boasted a few skeptical patrons eager to test his knowledge.

Before her, the huge, muscle-bound Zandor was strutting proudly down the midway. He obliged children by letting them feel his muscles in the hope their parents would come to the entertainment tent, where he performed his act. Patty knew the steel bars the strongman bent were the real thing.

She concentrated on taking tickets, but once the ride started, she let her eyes roam. So far she hadn't spotted anyone who looked suspicious. She took a deep breath. The chances of her being spotted had been reduced significantly now that it was getting dark.

A *pop!* sounded suddenly; behind her the Ferris wheel ground squeakily to a halt. A few of the people caught near the top screamed. Patty shuddered. Talk about bad timing! The damn thing had broken down, and now practically everyone at the carnival was looking in her direction.

"A cable broke loose down below," the man running the ride told her. "I can see it. I'll try to fix it."

The man grabbed his tool belt and moved off toward the wheel itself, dropping down below it to get to the works and the faulty cable. The racket made by the stranded riders continued to attract bystanders. Although the true villain was the broken cable, accusations were hurled at her—in Portuguese, to boot—which she barely spoke at all.

She saw John's face in the crowd. He was coming toward her, to rescue her from this mess! Then she noticed he was walking without his cane. Two men on either side of him were supporting him. The men were smiling. John wasn't.

They've got me, she realized, actually more worried about John than herself. *They've got me.* . . .

Blaine had been walking about for twenty minutes when he first noticed the ticket taker at the Ferris wheel. He looked away, but something made him gaze back her way. The hair was the wrong color, the age, too, but something, *something* . . .

Could *this* be Patty?

He wasn't sure until he saw the two men moving the woman's way, dragging a third between them. Da Sa's soldiers had one captive in hand and were now heading for the woman.

"Now!" McCracken ordered, rushing up to Reverend Jim. "Now!"

Hope's hands jammed into his pockets and emerged with some fireworks and a lighter.

"Come on!" Blaine urged, just ahead of the first hiss, as flame met fuse, and Reverend Jim tossed the initial trio forward.

Pop! Pop! Pop!

McCracken shoved him aside. "Keep your eyes on the boys, Reverend. Keep them safe."

"Where are you going?"

Blaine looked back one last time before sprinting for the Ferris wheel and the men approaching Patty Hunsecker.

"To work," he said.

The popping sounds cost Patty a heartbeat, as John and the two men holding him captive neared the platform. The Ferris wheel had started to spin again, and behind her customers were piling out. She stood frozen, unable to move.

Turn myself in and maybe they won't hurt him. What choice do I have?

That thought had been barely formed when she saw the shape whirling toward the platform, just to the rear of the trio approaching her. The night was dark, and he was darker, but Patty saw the beard, recognized him as his hands shot out in the direction of the men holding John Lynnford.

* * *

The goons holding the man with the limp never even turned. Blaine's approach angled slightly from the left. He grabbed the one on that side by the scruff of his collar and heaved backward. When the man resisted, Blaine went with the motion and smashed him facefirst against the steel railing meant to keep eager patrons back. The one on the right had turned by then, the gun that had been pressed against Lynnford's side coming up but not getting there before Blaine smashed the whiskey bottle against his face. It shattered against bone and flesh and the man reeled backward, crumpling, his cheeks and nose a spiderweb of blood.

"Come on!" he yelled to Patty.

Instead she leaned over to help John, who had been thrown down in the struggle.

"There are others!" she screamed at Blaine.

"I know," Blaine said, ducking the gunfire that pulsed their way, bodies toppling in the path ahead of them. "The kids didn't have enough time!" he shouted. "They didn't have enough time!"

The plan McCracken had outlined to the boys was risky at best. Once they heard the sound of the firecrackers, they were to move in pairs on targets chosen by themselves. Not to lift wallets from pockets, though, not tonight. Tonight their targets were the pistols the enemy force undoubtedly wore beneath their jackets or clipped to their belts. Blaine had hoped to give them plenty of leeway. To pick and choose the time after he spotted Patty. As it turned out, he'd given them a minute at most, which meant few if any had completed their assigned task.

As he grabbed for Patty and Lynnford, he would have been surprised to learn that six of the fourteen additional gunmen had already been stripped of their pistols. Others either were equipped with minimachine guns or wore their pistols too well secured to make off with. But for these, the boys had an answer as well.

McCracken had expressly forbidden them to use the guns they had pilfered; nothing could have seemed worse to him than turning children into killers. But they had brought an assortment of other weapons that worked just fine. When a number of the still-armed gunmen drew their weapons, the boys were all over them with spray-paint cans, distorting their vision and confounding their aim. This much was accomplished ahead of the initial bursts of fire. At the sound of the gunshots, the boys scattered among the rest of the patrons along the midway, which had been turned into chaos.

A stray bullet caught John Lynnford in the shoulder as Blaine and Patty helped him backward. McCracken heard him gasp; he shielded the man with his own body as they dragged him into the cover provided by the guts of the Ferris wheel.

In the process, McCracken realized angrily that some of the boys had totally disregarded his orders and were in the process of firing back at the gunmen. For a time they held their own, but now those of Da Sa's soldiers who had been stopped temporarily by the spray paint were joining the battle, shots firing wildly in all directions. Bodies surged down and through the midway, changing directions from one burst of fire into another. Booths toppled as patrons sought refuge. McCracken watched as a bald strongman lifted a gunman brandishing an Uzi up overhead and tossed him effortlessly into a neon sign advertising the TEST YOUR STRENGTH booth. Bulbs popped and crackled. The bell at the top chimed as the gunman crashed into the apparatus and tumbled it with him.

"Zandor!" Patty cried happily.

"Stay here!" Blaine ordered.

"Where are you going?"

"Out there to do what I do best, lady. And do it fast."

McCracken had just slid out from the makeshift hiding place when five trucks roared onto the scene with gunfire marking their path.

He should have figured the opposition would have left some reinforcements back a bit—to be used only if needed, like now. The trucks roared onto the scene. The gunfire surging from them was indiscriminate, and bodies fell everywhere, some hit, some trying to find cover.

Blaine's first order of business was to get a gun. He had scarcely left the cover of the Ferris wheel when he spotted the dark figure of Reverend Jim waving to him with pistol in hand. In a crouch, he rushed toward Hope, only to be caught in the spill of a truck's headlights, making him an easy target for the gunmen on board. At the last possible instant, a shape lunged between the truck and him. The angle allowed Blaine to see the young American-looking boy named Edson, who had been part of that morning's demonstration back at the slum, firing straight at the truck. It veered and crashed into the Ferris wheel, tearing away some of its supports and forcing it into a dangerous list.

Edson was turning proudly toward McCracken when a bullet smacked him in the stomach and blew him backward.

"Shit!" Blaine shouted, reaching the boy just ahead of Reverend Jim.

He grabbed for the boy's pistol and rolled, bringing it up to fire on the gunman who had done the shooting. The three remaining bullets excavated the man's chest, and he fell over backward. Blaine moved on toward Edson, who was twisting on the ground and screaming, greenish-blue eyes filled with fear. Reverend Jim got there ahead of him and was holding the boy still as best he could. He raised one hand long enough to give Blaine the pistol he had been waving.

"Get him to safety," McCracken ordered. "Stay with him." Blaine looked at the writhing boy. "When you get him quieted down and more comfortable, round up as many of the others as you can. I'll join you later."

"Sure about that, governor?"

McCracken looked at the four trucks still barreling through the midway spitting death.

"You can bet on it."

The members of the circus had responded as well as could be expected, not fleeing but choosing to defend their patch instead. John had obviously prepared them for this kind of battle—Blaine could see men and women—every kind of crude rifle hidden behind the cover of what had been booths and stands—firing resolutely at the gunmen and the trucks. Their bullets kept the enemy at bay, allowing at least a portion of the crowd to dash to safety.

For his part, Zandor was hurling shards of steel rail used to fasten down the big top at the trucks as they passed by his position. Blaine saw one of his tosses strike a driver square in the face. The truck crashed into the refreshment stand and spun onto its side.

He felt he could handle the three trucks that now remained. The problem was how to stop the enemy still patrolling the grounds, shooting at anything that moved.

The answer occurred to Blaine when his eyes found the big top. He and Reverend Jim had taken stock of its contents when they had done a fast walkabout through the circus grounds earlier.

He dashed toward the big tent against the tide of people streaming out from it. Those inside were late finding out what was happening outside, but now they were joining the flow of the escaping mass. McCracken held fast to his two pistols, ready to use them at an instant's notice if necessary. For now, though, even if he had been able to pick out the gunmen, it would be all but impossible to hit them without risking the lives of innocent people. Well, he was about to make what was already chaotic worse, though to his own advantage.

Dropping to all fours, he lifted a flap of the big top and crawled under, then made his way beneath the steel layers of platform seating. The show featured the circus's fifteen trained lions, perhaps the attraction it was best known for. All the lions were still in the large performance cage, left there when the shooting started. They prowled anxiously about, roaring and bellowing. Blaine reached the door to the cage; it was locked. He fired one of his pistols at an angle certain to keep any ricocheting bullets away from the great beasts. Two shots were all it took. The lock lay in pieces. McCracken climbed up onto the heavy steel of the cage and swung open the gate. The lions emerged and padded silently toward freedom.

"Go to it, fellas," he said as they began to roar.

CHAPTER 25

THE sudden appearance of the lions outdoors changed everything. Blaine emerged from the big top and saw two of the remaining trucks crash head-on, the drivers' attention diverted by the sight of the great beasts loping across the fair grounds. The gunmen, trying to protect themselves against the lions, would stand out now, and Blaine had plenty of bullets left for them, even if the circus people didn't.

Gunfire pouring from the final truck winged one of the galloping beasts and another leaped for its cab, terrifying the driver. The truck careened wildly and smacked straight into the Ferris wheel, tumbling it to the ground in a shower of sparks. Blaine had already switched his attention back to the gunmen on foot. They were easily identifiable since they were trying to buck the crowds, not flow with them, and his two pistols clacked alternately at easy targets.

One of Da Sa's men managed to creep up unseen behind him, only to be smothered by a rush from the boys Reverend Jim had managed to gather together. Another two seeking cover were found and dispatched in quick fashion by Zandor. Blaine was flashing him the okay sign when his eyes fell on the tumbled remnants of the Ferris wheel.

"Patty," he muttered to himself. "Patty . . ."

And then he was running toward the pile of ruined steel, where he had last seen her.

* * *

Patty had crawled out from under the corpse of the Ferris wheel when she saw the gunmen approaching. Dashing across the midway, she leaped on top of the merry-go-round, which had somehow continued to spin throughout the entire battle. As she dived behind a wooden horse for cover, gun-fire aimed for her splintered the wood and tore its painted head off. The merry-go-round picked up speed, and Patty stayed low, eyes searching for her hunters. She could see figures approaching through the rampaging crowd. The fun house would make for the best cover according to John. It was the next building over, set back a bit.

The merry-go-round circled again, and the approaching gunmen opened fire on the position where they had last seen Patty. Another horse blew apart as she scampered toward the edge, ready to make a run for the fun house. The ride was moving at its fastest clip, and the maneuver was not as easy as she would have thought. But she couldn't risk another pass that would put her directly in front of the approaching gunmen, so it had to be now.

Patty leaped and hit the ground hard, rolling to absorb a measure of the shock. The fast-spinning merry-go-round pro-vided the cover she needed. Patty ran up the ramp leading into the fun house and plunged into its dark confines.

She could tell from the murky lighting and eerie sounds that it, too, had remained operational throughout the chaos. She walked on, able to see barely a yard in front of her through the fake fog that was the first effect to greet patrons.

Suddenly a pair of red eyes flashed before her, accompanied by a shrill howling. Patty lurched back as the spring-driven ape-man recoiled upward, returning to its slot. The quickness with which the thing had struck gave her an idea. She reached in her pocket for the screwdriver she'd used to fasten the ticket box at the Ferris wheel into place. Looking around she found a crate and, after positioning it properly, stepped up on it and went to work.

Seconds later, she was finished, frame pinned against the wall, as the gunmen pounded up the ramp leading into the fun house. The two men entered the fake mist just a yard apart, confused by the darkness and the swirling fog.

Just a little farther, she urged the lead gunman. *Just a little farther . . .*

The first man reached the spot where Patty had been greeted by the recoiling ape-man and, once again, the mass of rubber, wood, and fur dropped downward. Only this time, there was no spring mechanism to stop its fall and send it back upward, because Patty had removed it. The thing simply crashed into the man, knocking him down.

Patty, meanwhile, put the rest of her plan into action. She plowed into the second man with as much force as she could muster. The man was quick; he started to pull back on his trigger almost at once. But Patty had made his gun hand her first target; as she jammed it upward, the barrel spit orange heat.

"Arrrrrrrrgggggghhhhh!"

For an instant, Patty wasn't sure who was screaming; then she realized the ape-man's tape was caught in a loop and was playing the same ugly cry over and over again. She held fast to the man's gun hand with her left hand, while with her right hand she went for his eyes with her finger nails. She felt the nails part flesh, then tear sickeningly into his sockets. His screams were worse than the ape-man's.

Patty spun away from the man, who was now groping blindly around, and grabbed the gun from his limp hand. She turned back in the ape-man's direction just as the first man was shoving it off him, his gun coming up.

Patty shot first. Once, twice, as many times as she could pull the trigger until the distinctive *click* sounded, and then she kept on pulling in her panic. Ten feet before her the gunman let the pistol slide from his grasp. He looked more confused than anything else, as a pool of blood gushed from his upper chest. His head collapsed suddenly, but his eyes stayed open. The second man was still wailing, clutching desperately at his ruined eyes.

Patty pulled herself together again. These two weren't the only ones left. More would be following them into the fun house, and she had to make use of this darkened labyrinth of a hiding place.

She crossed through the manufactured swamp area, complete with its eerie night sounds and moist, fetid walls, and realized she was still holding the spent pistol in her hand. She dropped it and felt strangely naked. Listening intently for sounds of pursuit, she kept walking, but the fun house's taped sound effects made it almost impossible for her to hear anything.

Patty approached the chamber of horrors and crossed a threshold that triggered the monsters into motion. The mummy lunged from an upright crate. Frankenstein's monster walked an unvarying path—forward and back—thanks to a spring connecting him mechanically to the wall. Dracula rose from a coffin that opened with a squeal and a whine.

The coffin! Maybe, just maybe . . .

Patty dashed over to it and stripped off the spring mechanism that opened it mechanically at regular intervals. The coffin top began to drop down suddenly, nearly crushing her hand. Chewing down her pain, Patty pushed herself into the coffin and squeezed the waxen vampire figure to the side. Then she closed the lid back down, the darkness swallowing her.

Zandor reached the Ferris wheel just after Blaine. Together they threw pieces of the shattered wooden platform and steel housing away to clear a path into the debris.

"Patty!" Blaine yelled as he dug through the mess. "Patty!"

At last he could see into the ruins of the chamber containing the Ferris wheel's works. A single shape lay there, partially entombed by ruptured and splintered parts.

John Lynnford coughed out dust and dirt when Blaine reached him. His face was mined with cuts and lacerations.

"Where's Patty?" Blaine demanded.

"They saw us under here," Lynnford muttered, "so she left. To save me."

"When, dammit?"

"Four minutes ago, maybe five. She went in the direction of the fun house."

Patty regretted her strategy instantly. It wasn't just dark in the coffin, it was black—and the figure's poorly kept wax smelled like death itself. The coffin trembled slightly. Footsteps, lots of them, were thundering into the chamber. There were voices, too, rising in muffled fashion over the chamber's sound effects. There would be no chance of escape at all, if the enemy lifted the coffin's lid.

Frantically Patty began to feel about in the blackness for a weapon, but all she could come up with was the screwdriver she had used before. She took it from her pocket and held it tight with a sweat-soaked hand.

The footsteps were coming closer. The coffin trembled a bit more. She willed the lid not to open, but the lid began to rise, slivers of half-light puncturing the blackness of her tomb. She froze for a moment, then plunged the screwdriver outward at the blurring figure. A steellike hand grabbed her wrist in midair as the coffin opened all the way.

"Hope you don't mind if I wake you up, Countess," said Blaine McCracken, Zandor the strongman was peering over his shoulder.

Blaine helped a trembling Patty from the coffin, who then embraced him.

"I liked you better as a blonde," he said, easing her away. "Tell me, what brings you to Rio?"

"Information, McCracken, and none of it pleasant. I found out what the victims all had in common. They were all adopted, each and every one. And many had extensive dealings with the Japanese."

"Including your father?"

"Most certainly. But that's not all. I asked the system to generate a list of potential victims based on the profile. I remembered that's what you asked for."

"Why is it I think you found some names I'm not going to like hearing?"

"Because I did, McCracken. One, anyway: Virginia Maxwell."

CHAPTER 26

"HEAD of the Gap," Blaine muttered, all the levity gone from his expression.

"I told Sal, and he tried to warn her. Next thing I know he's calling me at sunrise to tell me someone tried to kill him and I'm next on the list. I just made it out."

"I should have known, dammit. I should have caught on . . ."

"Caught on to what?"

"Later. Once we're out of here."

McCracken's face was grimly set as he led Patty through the fun house.

"Sal sent me down here to tell you. He said you'd know what to do."

"I've got a few ideas."

"What's it all mean, Blaine? What's going on?"

They emerged into the night air, and Patty saw John Lynnford being carried across the midway on a stretcher. She rushed over to him.

"You've looked better," she told him, taking his hand.

Lynnford grimaced. Bandages soaked with blood were wrapped tightly around his shoulder.

"Keeps me from thinking about my leg, anyway," he joked, managing a weak smile. "That's a first in quite a while."

McCracken caught up with them and checked Lynnford's

wound. "Bullet passed straight through. Minimal bone damage, by the look of it. You're lucky."

"And you're Blaine McCracken."

"Ah, once again my reputation precedes me!"

Lynnford's eyes swept the midway. "All of it deserved, apparently."

"I'm sorry."

Lynnford propped himself up on his good arm. "For what? You saved my circus. You saved her life."

"All in a day's work."

"You'll still need help getting out of the country. Even more so now."

"Suggestions will be entertained."

"I've got a few." Lynnford winced in pain. "Just let me get patched up a little."

"No sweat," said McCracken, his eyes falling on Reverend Jim. "I've got someone else I've got to see."

Reverend Jim met him halfway. They both looked at the cluster of his boys gathered around a pair who lay still in the night.

"We lost two," Hope said sadly. "Edson and one of the older ones."

Blaine's stomach sank. "Both dead, thanks to me."

"It wasn't your fault. If they had done what you said—"

"It *was* my fault, all of it. They were doing fine in your world. They weren't ready for mine."

"Can't say I ever met another sort who was."

"But that didn't stop me from using them, did it?"

"It was what they wanted, governor."

Blaine started toward the boys, but Reverend Jim cut him off. "You could help them better by makin' off with yourself and the lady, so this won't be for nothing. Time's a wastin', governor. You read me on that?"

"I've got to do something."

"Getting the people behind the bullets'll do just fine."

"Not for me, it won't. Oh, I'll do that all right—But I've got something else in mind."

"Save it, governor."

"Yes, Reverend, save. I'm going to leave you a contact code

so you can reach me. Start using it in a week and then every day after. When my business here is finished, we can talk about paybacks.'' Again Blaine's eyes drifted to the children. ''I want to send you some money to help set this straight—to set *them* straight.''

''Nobody's asking you to.''

''Nobody had to. Believe me, I have to do this. I'll send you a hundred thousand dollars to begin with. That should be enough to get them out of the *favela*. After that, I'll send you as much as you need to keep them from ever going back.''

Reverend Jim's eyes were bulging. ''Where'd a man like you get that much cash?''

''Friends in the right places, Reverend,'' Blaine replied, staring into the distance. ''All over the world.''

''What happens now?'' Patty asked him as he started the engine of the car John Lynnford had left in the mall parking lot.

''We follow John's plan and hope it works,'' Blaine answered, stowing the directions to the airport Lynnford had had written out for them in his lap.

The route would make as much use as possible of back roads, steering clear of major arteries, where more of Da Sa's men might be concentrated. Of course, this also meant that traditional means of escape couldn't be used. A letter signed by Lynnford would hopefully provide the alternative here. The Orlando Orfei Circus frequently required the use of cargo services to bring animals and equipment into the country. Sometimes the proper papers were nonexistent, and cash was exchanged in their place. The letter presented to the carrier Lynnford most trusted should guarantee Blaine and Patty passage on the next cargo flight out of the country. The destination didn't matter. The general direction of the United States would suit Blaine just fine.

''Finish what you started to say back at the carnival. I want to know what's going on,'' Patty said as the circus disappeared behind them. ''I want to know what's really going on.''

''I was hoodwinked.'' He looked at her. ''You were, too.''

''Make sense!''

''I can't. Not yet. Virginia Maxwell solicits my services and then turns out to be a potential victim of what I'm supposed to stop. But when Sal warns her, she tries to have him killed. What does that say to you?''

"I don't know. If I did, I wouldn't have asked."

McCracken squeezed the wheel. "Okay, we've got these successful Americans, all adopted and all suddenly on a hit list."

"And the Japanese link—don't forget about that. Which reminds me about the men . . .''

"What men?"

"The ones waiting for me at your hotel. All Japanese. They knew I was coming. Do you think Maxwell sent them?''

"No way. She'd never have dispatched any group that stood out that much.''

"Who, then?''

"Good question. Wish I had an answer. The thing is, there've been two groups operating in this all along. Your father and Virginia Maxwell are part of one. Whoever sent out the six killers is part of another. But where does that leave the disciples? . . .''

"The *what*?"

"Sorry. Just thinking out loud.''

Patty thought for a few moments as the car drove on through the night. "Who was it that was after us at the circus?''

"A crime lord named Da Sa got himself killed, and I got blamed. Whoever really killed him made sure of that . . . and then made sure to link you with me.''

"The Japanese?"

Blaine shook his head. "No, I don't think so." He hesitated. "The thing is . . .''

"I'm listening.''

"No, it's too crazy.''

"Nothing's too crazy at this point.''

"Okay, try this out. What if one of our forces was behind the placing of all these adopted babies? Your father, Virginia Maxwell, every last one of them.''

"Toward what end?''

"They grew up to be rich and powerful, didn't they?''

"What are you saying, McCracken?''

"I'm not sure yet, Hunsecker.''

Patty turned away and gazed out the window into the night. "What about my father? Maxwell tried to kill me, and you've drawn a link between—"

"I haven't drawn a link between anything. I'm just playing with the facts, seeing how they fit together. Anyway, Virginia Maxwell is still alive."

Patty shifted in the passenger seat and pressed herself against the door, staring at her dim reflection in the window.

"I killed a man tonight," she said, with strange matter-of-factness.

"Who would have killed you if you hadn't."

"Save the dime-store philosophy for somebody else, okay? In that moment I think I understood you better than I ever have, McCracken. I understood what it's like to be cornered and have no choice but to fight back. I understood what it's like to kill someone and not feel anything about it."

"Because you had no choice."

"That's what I'm talking about. I look back and I want to be sick, feel sick, but I can't. All I feel is . . . nothing. That man doesn't have any meaning, like he wasn't real."

"He was real only in the sense of trying to kill you, Patty. That's what Johnny Wareagle would say, and he's right. You saw him in the context of what he was, and that context is the only meaning he had to you."

"You don't understand. The context is the problem. I could shoot a man, I could do everything I've done these past couple weeks, because of my father. Except now I find out maybe my father wasn't the innocent victim I thought he was. Maybe he was part of something I didn't know about that got him killed, and maybe, too, he wasn't such a nice guy after all. You see, McCracken, if his life was a lie, then so is mine. None of it means anything anymore."

"Wrong. The meaning's just changed. John Lynnford could have kept you safe and hidden at the circus, but you insisted on coming with me instead because it still means plenty."

"I can't wait to find out what!" she said, half sarcastically.

"Exactly. That's what keeps you going. That's what keeps me going, and Johnny, too. Like *Hanbelachia*."

"What's that?"

"A vision quest, an Indian rite of passage ceremony. Johnny

told me he was still waiting for his, and I'm beginning to think mine's gonna come at the same time."

Patty's eyes lost some of their sadness. "You're really starting to sound like him."

"Mostly because I'm starting to really listen to him. He makes sense, Hunsecker. And when all is said and done, he's probably the only man I know who does."

Patty shifted again and sighed. "Well, from my perspective, it's—"

A quick *pop!* ended her words an instant before the car swerved violently out of control. Blaine struggled to right the wheel. He was turning into a skid when a second *pop!* sent it whirling into a wild spin.

"They've shot out the tires!" McCracken shouted.

Blaine twisted around, trying to unfasten his seat belt and go for his pistol at the same time. Incredibly he managed both before the car came to a complete stop. He started to shove the door open when the bright lights blinded both of them. A number of figures stormed forward, guns marking their paths.

"Drop your weapon!" a voice ordered, and when Blaine didn't, gunshots peppered Patty's side of the car.

"All right!" Blaine let his pistol slide to the soft ground off the road.

"Now step out of the car with your hands in the air!" the voice continued. "Both of you!"

Blaine looked at Patty and nodded. He kept his hands in view while he kicked the door open the rest of the way in order to climb out. Patty followed him out the driver's side, and saw his shoulders stiffen just before she saw the faces of their attackers in the spill of light.

They were Japanese, each and every one of them!

CHAPTER 27

"**W**HERE to?" the cabby wanted to know.

"The city," replied Johnny Wareagle.

"Sure, but where in the city? Uptown? Midtown? Downtown?"

"Downtown," said Wareagle, his massive frame scrunched in the backseat.

Johnny had reached Philadelphia unsure of what awaited him there. He got into the taxi because he knew it was the city itself where he was needed, where he would meet the foe who had visited him in his dreams. Beyond that, Johnny knew nothing. He was relying on the spirits to guide him—and on his ancestors to ensure that they did. He did not question the mysticism that so dominated his life. It had been a part of him for as long as he could remember, but not clarified until he had passed into his teenage years.

Johnny had grown up on a Sioux reservation in Oklahoma, where the old ways had been miraculously preserved. On the eve of his *Hanbelachia*, the tribal shaman took him aside.

"Do you understand what you are, *Wanblee-Isnala*?" the old man had asked him.

"I am a Sioux, greatest warrior tribe of the plains."

"Not what *we* are, what *you* are. You don't, do you?"

Johnny shook his head.

"You feel strange at times."

Johnny searched for the right word. "Different."

"From your peers, from your friends. It is time you knew why. There is different blood in your family. Every other generation of your grandfathers have been shaman for their tribes. I replaced your father's grandfather, who died when you were an infant. He and the others were gifted in ways that have been lost over the years, lost but not forgotten. Know this, *Wanblee-Isnala*: You have great powers, but not in the same way as your grandfathers. Your fate is that of a warrior. You will face many enemies." The shaman saw the young Johnny Wareagle's face set in determination, his thoughts easy to read even for one not blessed with the gift. "Know this, though. Your *Hanbelachia* will not take place with the others of your year."

Johnny had known not to challenge the words of the shaman, but he could not help posing the questions that rushed through his mind.

"When? Where?"

"You will know the time . . . and the place. Your ancestors will guide you, and the spirits will bring you their words. You have the gift of listening, *Wanblee-Isnala*. Only those who listen can hear."

Johnny listened now from the back of the cab, but no words reached him. He knew everything he was and had been was constructed toward a rapidly approaching moment. The foe that would test him was in this city, and Johnny would follow the spirit's words.

When? Where?

The old questions were raised once more. But the spirits did not answer questions. They simply provided guidance. The communication was one-sided, as it always had been.

"Traffic's a mess," the driver said, sighing.

"Yes."

"Wish the fucking veep could have picked some other city to visit."

"Veep," repeated Johnny.

"Yeah, the vice president's in town. Giving some kinda speech at Independence Hall. They closed off Walnut and Chestnut streets for his motorcade. Goddamn people are lined up everywhere. We got that to thank for this."

A chill spread through Johnny, and he felt a smile come to his lips.

The spirts often did not speak to him directly. Sometimes they passed their message through other parties.

"That is where you must take me."

"Where?"

"Independence Hall."

The driver suddenly swerved into the right lane. "Get you as close as I can."

"Pit Crew Leader, this is Pit Crew One."

Arnold Triesman raised the walkie-talkie to his lips. "Read you, Pit Crew One."

"We are inbound on the expressway. Racer is secure and comfortable. Ten-minute ETA to city limits."

"Roger that, Pit Crew One."

Arnold Triesman began another circuit along Chestnut Street in the historical section of downtown Philadelphia. He was in charge of the Secret Service security detail for the vice president's appearance here, and he wasn't the least bit happy with the logistics. Ever since Kennedy and Dallas, motorcades scared the shit out of all men in his position. You couldn't watch every corner of every rooftop; it just wasn't possible. Add to that maybe a hundred thousand people crowded into the street and you were holding a ball that was slippery enough to slide right out of your fingers. One crazy was all it took, just one. The thought made Triesman's flesh crawl.

Racer was the latest code name for the vice president, chosen for the man's penchant for fast cars. As Pit Crew Leader, Triesman had a hundred men at his disposal; they were with the motorcade, scattered along the route, and perched strategically on rooftops. They couldn't cover everything, but when a fifteen-year Secret Service vet was running things, you came as close as you could.

The service had cost Arnold Triesman one marriage and had kept him from considering another until his tour was up. Except he hadn't been able to walk away when it finally was, and another two years had come and gone much the same way as the first thirteen had. Even if he wanted to get out, it was questionable whether the service would let him. As far as running security details in the most impossible of situations, Triesman had no peer. It wasn't so bad, after all. Impressed the hell out of his sons six months back when he had finally relented and let them come along on a detail for the president. Kids even got to meet Top Guy himself and couldn't sleep that night from the excitement. Triesman felt as if they were really his kids again for the first time since the divorce. It seemed ironic that the very thing that had broken the family up was now the only bond he had with his children. Damn strange, it was.

A helicopter soared overhead, drawing the stares of the thousands crowded together behind the blue sawhorse barricades along Chestnut Street. Triesman lifted the walkie-talkie to his lips again.

"Fly Boy, this is Pit Crew Leader. How's the sky looking?"

"No movement on rooftops except for our boys, Pit Crew Leader."

"Can you see Racer?"

"That's a roger. Estimate city outskirts reached in five minutes. Fifteen to your position at the hall."

"Stay frosty, Fly Boy."

"Roger that, Pit Crew Leader."

Triesman continued his walk. A number of his men were scattered throughout the crowd gathered on the motorcade route that ran the length of Chestnut Street. The heaviest complement was concentrated in the area of Independence Hall itself, both inside and out. The vice president would be making his speech inside the courtyard, near the statue of Commodore John Barry, founder of the U.S. Navy. The logistics from a security standpoint were tenuous at best. A nest of tall buildings forming the Penn Mutual complex overlooked the courtyard from across Walnut Street. The twin Public Ledger and Curtis Publishing buildings afforded an equally clear view across Sixth Street, which was adjacent. Triesman had men posted throughout all the buildings as well as sharpshooters on the roofs, but he still wasn't happy. And he wouldn't be until Racer was safely back in his limo after giving his speech. It would be Triesman standing by Racer's side at the podium, and Triesman who would play pin cushion to bullets, if it came to that.

"Pit Crew Leader, this is Pit Crew Fifteen," a voice squawked through his walkie-talkie.

"Read you, Pit Crew Fifteen."

"I think I may have something here."

"Report your twenty."

"Corner Chestnut and Seventh."

"What have you got?"

"Suspicious party moving in the crowd."

"Description."

"Male. Tall and broad, very tall. Beige pants and worn leather vest. Black hair tied in ponytail."

"*What?*"

"Pit Crew Leader, I believe he's an Indian. I believe—"

"Come in, Pit Crew Fifteen. Fifteen, are you there?"

More silence filled the air, broken finally by Pit Crew Fifteen's voice.

"I'm here, Pit Crew Leader, but subject isn't."

"Say again!"

"I lost the Indian, sir. He just isn't there anymore."

"Hold your position, Fifteen. I'm coming your way."

Weetz did not raise his eyes to the helicopter when it soared over the Curtis Publishing Building. Instead he kept his head down and right eye pressed against the scope of his sniper's rifle— Well, not really *his* rifle. Actually it belonged to the Secret Service sharpshooter now lying dead in the stairwell. The agent's clothes had made a decent enough fit, and the rifle was fortunately one Weetz was well versed in using.

In spite of this, though, the problem was no two rifles fired exactly alike. From this distance, miscalculation by a micro-inch could send the shot hurtling hopelessly off course, and one shot was all he could realistically depend on. The tree cover in the courtyard was a bitch, but he had chosen a spot on the roof that allowed a clear vantage. Wind could pick up and fuck things up royally. Good thing the forecast was holding up so far. In fact, all his intelligence was holding up. He shifted his rifle slightly and sighted two feet over the podium.

The very spot the vice president's head would be occupying in a matter of minutes.

Johnny knew he had been seen. He could feel the eyes burn into him as clearly as a blue laser piercing his skin. Instantly he dropped into a crouch and stayed there until he was certain the eyes had lost him.

The spirits had spoken, and Johnny knew why he had been guided here. There was going to be an attempt made on the vice president's life. It was Wareagle's fate to face the bullet fired by the enemy. His *Hanbelachia* was upon him. His enemy was in range. Johnny rose from a crouch to a stoop; reaching out, probing. Just as he had known it in the Amazon, he knew it now.

One of the *Wakinyan* was here!

He recognized the thing's spiritual scent, but the precise take on it was denied him. Johnny felt the unfamiliar grasp of impatience. He distracted himself with thoughts of the area itself. Security was tight and very well orchestrated. Secret Service agents, like the one who had picked him out, were scattered in large numbers throughout the crowd and stationed on various rooftops. It was impossible for even the best sharpshooter to move about unseen. Unless, unless . . .

What would I do if the assassination was mine to accomplish?

The answer led him toward the tight crowds packed along Chestnut Street. His eyes swept across the buildings until they locked on a pair of brick structures rimmed at the top by white granite rails. He counted fifteen stories. A perfect number.

A strange calm possessed him then. The spirits were there guiding him, showing him the way.

To the twin brick buildings, one of which held the *Wakinyan* upon it.

"Seven-foot-tall Indians don't ordinarily disappear," an exasperated Arnold Triesman said to Pit Crew Fifteen at Seventh Street.

His subordinate looked dumbfounded. "Has anyone else reported seeing—"

"Not a thing!" Triesman cut him off. "No sign, no sighting."

"I could have been wrong."

"You don't believe that, and neither do I."

"Oh, he was there, all right, but I can't honestly say he was dangerous. It was just that he . . . stood out. And it was more than the fact that he was so big, too. Something just didn't feel right, chief.''

"Yeah," acknowledged Triesman, walkie-talkie back in its accustomed spot near his lips. Triesman figured a few more like this and he'd wear a groove into his jaw. "Come in, Pit Crew One."

"Read you, Pit Crew Leader."

"How goes it back there?"

"Coming up on the route now. I can see the people. Nice crowd by the look of it."

"I wish it had rained."

"Ditto, chief."

"Look, One, be ready for an immediate cover and evac from the area. Clear?"

"Sure, chief. What have you got?"

Arnold Triesman gazed at the befuddled agent by his side before responding. "A feeling, One. Just a feeling."

Weetz watched the motorcade slide by along Chestnut Street, urging it to go faster. The crowds cheered and applauded, American flags waving everywhere. He wanted this to be done with. Normally it was unheard of for a man in his position to remain in the open for so long. The circumstances, in this case, had dictated his actions, but that didn't make Weetz feel any the easier. He was even tempted to change the strategy, go for the shot while the target was stepping through the arch en route to the Independence Hall courtyard. Too much risk going for a moving target, though.

The motorcade moved to within a hundred yards of Independence Hall, and he returned his attention to the podium.

Johnny could feel eyes searching for him as he moved among the crowd, just precautionary and no more. He reached Sixth Street and prepared to veer left at Congress Hall toward the twin buildings. He could not get a fix on which one of them held the *Wakinyan*. Confused feelings rushed through him. Something was not as he expected it would be, but he could not let that throw him.

* * *

"Pit Crew Leader to entire Pit Crew," said Triesman into his walkie-talkie. "Pit Crew Leader to entire Pit Crew. Racer's car has come into the pit. Let's look sharp."

Ten yards before him, the vice president was stepping out of his limousine, which had stopped directly in front of the entrance to Independence Hall, the tumultuous cheers of the crowd reverberating in Triesman's ears. God, how he hated moments like this. Twenty thousand people jammed into a city block—and all it took was one crazy with a gun. He met the vice president at the arch and glued himself to the man's left side.

"I have Racer," Triesman said into his walkie-talkie. "Keep your eyes open."

Weetz's vantage point on the Curtis Publishing Building precluded him viewing his target's arrival. He saw the vice president for the first time when he stepped through the arch into the courtyard engulfed by a Secret Service detail. His audience rose from the steel chairs that had been arranged in neat fashion and applauded. Weetz eased his eye tighter against the sight and caressed the trigger.

He had the side of the vice president's head locked in briefly, but there was no sense risking a shot yet. Not until he was stationary behind the podium.

"Come on," he urged the vice president, "just a little further now."

Arnold Triesman wanted to call the whole thing off. Right then and there, before Racer pulled out his speech behind the podium, he wanted to shoo him back out through the archway. The nag in his gut had escalated into full-scale cramps, and he had all he could do just to stay upright. He'd learned to trust such feelings over the years.

But this time his fear seemed uncalled for. There were no working threats, no possible perps other than a giant Indian who had disappeared, and his boys had thrown a blanket around the area that was thick enough to keep the sun out.

"On the whole, I'd rather be in Philadelphia . . ."

Racer's opening remarks were greeted by polite laughter and

applause in the courtyard. Triesman hovered by his right side and gazed upward at the skyline through his sunglasses.

"Hold it, mister! I said freeze!"

Johnny knew he had chosen the wrong roof as soon as he emerged through the door on top of the Public Ledger Building. Something had confused his feelings, and all he could do was what he was told.

"Now turn around. Slowly."

He obliged—and found himself facing a Secret Service agent holding a sniper's rifle on him.

"Stay right where you are or I'll shoot! . . . Hey, can you hear me or what?"

Wareagle's eyes had drifted across to the next roof and another figure sighting down through his own rifle. The commotion on this roof should have drawn his attention but hadn't. The coldness that emanated from him wasn't that of a *Wakinyan*, but something was all wrong about the man, nevertheless.

"Now, turn around and kiss the wall. Hands in the air!"

Johnny had no choice but to obey for now.

"Pit Crew Leader, this is Sky View Eight," he heard the agent bark into a walkie-talkie. "I have suspect in custody at my twenty. Repeat, Sky View Eight has suspect in custody."

The man was eight feet away, a safe distance, especially considering that Johnny's back remained turned to him. No way, logic dictated, that a man could both turn and close that gap before you could fire if you had him properly covered. The agent saw the big Indian swing, but never actually recorded the lunge that cut the distance by more than half. He had been lowering his walkie-talkie and, before he could record another thought, he felt himself parted from his gun, which clacked once on the edge of the roof and then dropped over. He was never aware of the blow launched at him until a numbness raced through his head. There was only a flash and then darkness as consciousness fled with his footing.

More relaxed now, Triesman slid away from the vice president in order to more easily issue instructions. The Indian was in custody on the Public Ledger rooftop, so apparently the sighting hadn't been so innocent, after all.

"This is Pit Crew Leader. We have a Code Red on rooftop of Public Ledger. First and second teams converge. Fly boy, you copy that?"

"That's a roger, Pit Crew Leader."

"Let's move!"

Weetz's mouth was parched. He ran his tongue over his lips and adjusted the tip of the rifle one last time. In that final instant, when thoughts of the kill are more real than the kill itself, he pulled out of the real world. He heard nothing—not the crowd, or the helicopter, not even his victim's words. There was only silence, and he gave himself up to it. He knew that when the rifle went off, he would not hear the gunshot. There would be a slight kick against his shoulder, the feeling quickly muted by the sight of his victim's head exploding through his sight.

Weetz relished that. No kill was complete unless he could register the end result himself. Same reason fathers wanted to be in the delivery room, he supposed, in a twisted sense.

Weetz started to ease the trigger backward.

Wareagle knew there was nothing he could do now. He had chosen the wrong roof, and the error had cost him. This wasn't a *Wakinyan* on the adjacent roof, just an ordinary paid assassin readying his shot. That's what had thrown him off. But the *Wakinyan* was about. Somewhere.

The *wop-wop-wop* of the helicopter soaring directly for him distracted Johnny as the second shape appeared on the Curtis Publishing Building roof. A blast of cold thumped into him, his eyes swung to lock on a blur whirling toward the gunman fast enough to deny its own motion. Wareagle knew he was watching the enemy who had drawn him here, knew it even before the *Wakinyan* reached the gunman from behind.

The sudden extra influx of security around the area had almost denied Abraham access to the building. He had finally made it in after incapacitating two Secret Service men, but something remained very wrong. He had never known such a feeling—or the slight tremor of fear that came with it.

He recalled the escape he and the other disciples had made

into the Amazon jungle. The seven soldiers had proven no contest at all, but in their wake two others had come. Different. Much more . . . challenging. Could one of those two be here today?

He had barely been able to get to the roof in time. The gunman pulled the trigger at the precise instant Abraham reached him, and the errant bullet flew harmlessly by. From there it was over very fast. Abraham twisted the man's head in a sudden, violent motion. The head turned all the way around and flopped down between his shoulder blades. It was then that Abraham felt eyes boring into him like hot coals melting through his flesh and swung to find their source.

Arnold Triesman never heard the gunshot. What he did hear was a granite-splitting smack against the statue of John Barry. Instinct took over from there.

Before he could form any thought, Triesman had barreled into the vice president and taken him down. Instantly the other agents enclosing the podium plunged with him to complete a blanket of cover. Long seconds passed before Triesman could separate himself from the pile and free his walkie-talkie. He brought it to his lips, wondering what the hell had gone wrong on the rooftop above.

"We have shots fired from Sector Eight! Repeat: Shots fired! Converge! This is a Code Blue! *Everyone* converge!"

Johnny Wareagle watched the *Wakinyan's* eyes find his from the adjacent rooftop. The chill within him deepened. The *Wakinyan* radiated cold in all directions.

In that instant he knew he was face-to-face with something more machine than man, knew this was the opponent that had been chosen for his *Hanbelachia*. Everything in his life had been a prelude to this.

Their eyes held as the *Wakinyan* leaned over and pulled the rifle from the corpse's grasp. There was plenty of time for Johnny to dive to safety, but he didn't. He watched as the *Wakinyan* brought the rifle level with his chest, holding it out with one hand on the barrel and another on the stock.

Johnny saw the weapon bend, then heard a sharp snap as it broke in two pieces.

The *Wakinyan* might have smiled slightly. It was too far a

distance to tell. Someone from the hovering helicopter shouted something through a bullhorn and Johnny gazed up briefly. When he looked back in the direction of the Curtis Publishing Building, the *Wakinyan* was gone. And before the chopper's sharpshooters could find him in their sights, so was Johnny.

CHAPTER 28

BLAINE knew the Japanese weren't going to kill them when they didn't shoot right away. Instead, the gun-wielding group herded him and Patty toward a trio of waiting cars. Their moves were well processed, almost mechanical, the mark of orders being carried out to the letter.

They drove on to Galeao Airport, through an open security gate, then on to a private hangar, where a Learjet sat waiting. Six of the Japanese led the two of them on board.

"Where are you taking us? What's going on?" Patty demanded.

Blaine had the same questions, but he didn't bother to pose them, he knew no answers would be forthcoming. These men were simply soldiers, dispatched by a party with a vested interest in whatever was going on. On which side, it was impossible to say. The fact that they were still alive was a good sign.

Once inside the plane, Patty was placed down in the front on the right, Blaine in the rear on the left—as far from her as the confines of the cabin would allow. The unspoken intent of the Japanese was clear: If he tried to move against them, success would come at the expense of her life.

"We will not bind you," the man who seemed to be the leader said in English. "It would insult your honor."

"Does that make us allies?"

"It makes us nothing. We have a long flight ahead of us. I would ask you to make yourself comfortable."

"Where are we going?"

"Japan."

"What a shock."

Much to his own surprise, Blaine *did* sleep. It came in fitful bursts that were hardly refreshing, but it did come. Occasionally he tried to make eye contact with Patty, but the distance precluded even that. They endured the flight together, yet alone.

Blaine did not recognize the airport they landed at after eighteen hours, which included a refueling stop. He calculated it to be 4:00 A.M. Japanese time on Wednesday, but he was blindfolded before he could pick up any clues as to exactly where in the country they were. He was shepherded into one car, Patty into another, and then they were driven off into the night. Another hour passed, and Blaine concentrated on charting the exact route they were taking by the motion of the car, just in case he needed it for future reference.

At last the car bounced to a halt and the engine was shut off. The hands of his Japanese escorts yanked at him, dragging him off toward the sounds of running water. He thought he heard a gate first opening, then closing, then was next aware of most of the Japanese leaving. One who remained behind removed his blindfold, and he looked over to see that another had done the same for Patty. He moved toward her, touching her shoulder tenderly.

"Long time, no see," he said as the last two Japanese disappeared from view.

A quick scan of their surroundings revealed them to be in a Japanese garden of such loveliness even the night could not cloak its beauty. The sound of rushing water had been a small waterfall cascading into a brook that wound its way through the perfectly manicured shrubs, trees, and flowers. Everything was perfect, peaceful in its symmetry.

"I love the night," said a voice, and Blaine watched a Japanese man in a white suit emerge from the trees. He stopped just at the point where he couldn't be seen.

"Who are you?" McCracken asked.

"To you—no one. Yet, everyone."

"I've had it with riddles."

"The best ones are yet to come, Mr. McCracken. . . . And we have what remains of the night for me to tell them to you."

The man stepped directly into the spill of the moonlight, and Blaine realized he was an albino. He had never seen an Oriental albino before and the sight was a bit unsettling, worsened perhaps by the fact that the man's white suit blended too well with the tone of his flesh.

"I am Takedo Takahashi. But I don't suppose that holds any meaning to you."

"Not a one."

"By the same token, yours held little meaning to me until just over a week ago."

"I tend to make a quick first impression."

"Your previous stay here was well noted."

"Thanks to the patience of one of the best friends I ever made."

"Hiroshi Sensei," said Takahashi. "I know the story."

"Not all of it."

"More than you think, I'd wager. I make it my business to know precisely who it is I am dealing with."

"And are you dealing with me, Snowman?"

"I prefer the term *Kami-san*."

"Suit yourself."

Takahashi moved closer to McCracken and seemed to squint. On the grass between them a trio of small rattan chairs had been set.

"Sit, please," Takahashi said.

"Just the three of us?"

"I hope the gesture will help you trust me, as I now must trust you."

Blaine took Patty's arm and led her to the chairs. Takahashi waited until they were seated before settling in his own chair directly in front of them. The garden was lit by nothing other than the moon. Occasionally the breeze would lift up some of the whispering water and spray their faces.

"We have an hour until dawn," Takahashi said. His English was perfect. "You will hear my story in that time."

"Gotta crawl back into your coffin with the sunrise, *Kami-san*?"

"It's you who will need to be elsewhere after you've heard what I have to say."

Blaine exchanged glances with Patty. "So talk," he told Takahashi. "What the hell is going on here, and where do you fit in?"

"At the beginning and all the way through, Mr. Mc-Cracken. Everything's related, you see."

"I figured that much. What I don't know is how."

"After you do know, you will come to regret it."

"I'll be the judge of that."

"Passing judgement is what all this began as. Nearly forty-seven years ago, Mr. McCracken."

"The end of World War Two . . ."

"Exactly. Our country was ravaged. The two bombs your President Truman ordered dropped on our cities destroyed our spirits, bankrupted our souls. But we are an infinitely patient people, Mr. McCracken. Our history speaks of this."

"I know your history, Mr. Takahashi."

"Then you also know one of the prime ways of dealing with an enemy is infiltrating his ranks and striking from the inside. It has been that way since the days of the clans and the shogun, when the word of the samurai was spoken with his sword."

"We were speaking of World War Two."

"We still are. Nothing had changed up until that point. . . ." Takahashi's voice trailed off briefly. "Even now, not much has. Your bombs forced us to accept defeat, at least outwardly. In point of fact, it was more than just appearances for many of our leaders. They saw the futility of where our philosophy had taken us. A new order was required, and if working with your occupation forces was the best way to ensure it, they would do so."

"There would have been opposition, though."

"Most of it squelched, the rebels being made outcasts, *ronin*. But there were still others who resorted to the old ways of placating the enemy on the surface while within thirsting for revenge. Patience was the key. You are familiar with the work *The Art of War*, Mr. McCracken?''

"Somewhat.''

"One of the postulates deals with maximizing available weapons instead of seeking new ones.''

"The best defense is a good offense.''

"In a sense, yes, but we are talking of vengeance here. And the key was available weapons. Unbeknownst to your government, our scientists had made great strides in the field of biochemical research. It was along different lines than the Nazis, but we, too, were seeking the creation of supermen.''

"Soldiers?''

"No, that was where we differed. We were seeking the scientific means to imbue characteristics that would virtually guarantee our subjects rising to great heights in their chosen spheres. We are an insular people, Mr. McCracken, and the original intent of the work was to assure the propagation of the ruling class, certain to be severely depleted by the war. But when we lost the war, the focus was altered. A legion of superbeings, yes, but used as agents in important positions in the country of our enemy, so that in the future, they could be destroyed from the inside out.''

"The United States," Blaine said.

"Toward this end, five hundred American newborns were kidnapped from the United States between the years 1945 and 1948. The planning was elaborate. Deals were struck with doctors to arrange the babies' apparent deaths shortly after birth. Since both the doctors and hospitals were carefully selected and well spread out, no pattern was ever detected.''

"That's monstrous," Patty snapped.

"So was what the United States did to my country, Miss Hunsecker.''

"I see you're acquainted with me, too.''

"Quite well. Quite well, indeed.''

"Because of my father. My father was one of these babies, wasn't he? That's why he's dead.''

"Please. We are getting ahead of ourselves. First you must understand our work with the infants. When they reached the age of eighteen months, certain chemical compounds we had discovered that stimulated areas in the brain connected with superachievement and power were injected into their brains. In other words, we altered the chemical balance of the infants' brains to create the types of personalities desired. With proper programming—and early training—loyalty could be assured as well. Of the five hundred infants in the experiment, two hundred either died or were pronounced unfit. With the three hundred still remaining, we were able to accomplish our acceptable margin of error of one complete success in every three—ninety-seven to be exact—all working in concert toward the goal of virtual economic takeover by Japan.'' Takahashi's gaze turned strangely distant. ''They were called the Children of the Black Rain, after the awful force that created the need for their existence in the first place.''

''Which must make you one of the fathers, Takahashi.''

''My mother was pregnant when your bombs fell.'' Takahashi slid a hand across the white skin lining his face. ''And this is what emerged from her womb as a result—a freak, to use your terminology. There were plenty of us, many much worse than I. We would provide guidance. We would direct the actions of the Children of the Black Rain when our time came, when the original aging founders of the operation passed to their destiny. A smooth transition had to be assured. The plan could not suffer the burden of a different generation coordinating it. So it became our lot to extract revenge for the White Flashes your country set upon mine.''

''But something went wrong, didn't it?'' Blaine challenged.

The albino seemed reluctant to speak. ''For some in our number, victory was not enough. They wanted a revenge more fitting the black rain you set falling from our skies. They had been selected for the same good reasons I had been, but all the time they were plotting their own vengeance—without the support or knowledge of the rest of us. Infiltration, yes. Takeover, yes. Virtual enslavement, yes. But accomplished through a much more drastic means, with far more dire results. You see, they knew quite well how the Children of the Black Rain had been created in the first place. And modern technology afforded them the ability to advance the procedure beyond anything the rest of us had ever conceived of.''

''And so the Omicron legion was born? . . .''

Takahashi nodded. ''Their own private army, soldiers who

could fight their battles for them and become the builders who ensured that, long term, their twisted vision would come to pass. The chemicals we had used to create the Children were replaced by incredibly advanced microchips that, once implanted into the brain of subjects deemed fit, would create the ultimate warrior.''

"Ultimate monster, you mean," Patty said. "Which makes you a monster, too, because you let it happen. You were a part of it.''

Takahashi stood up and turned sideways, speaking as much to the night as to Blaine and Patty. "And that is why I have chosen to fight it. The small group of rebels in our midst moved against the rest of us before we had fully grasped their plan. All the others who stood apart from them were wiped out. I alone remained—and was able to ascertain exactly what their plan was by lashing out at the traitors. I killed them all, at least thought I had, but obviously their plan accounted for just that eventuality, because one remained at large—one whose identity I had no idea of and could not uncover. This failure left me with no choice other than to destroy the Children of the Black Rain I had devoted my life to protecting. I retained six professional killers of considerable prowess to accomplish that feat.''

Patty gazed up at him, her eyes showing an uneasy mix of rage and frustration. "And one of them killed my father. Forced his car off the road and made it look like an accident. You *are* a monster, Mr. Takahashi. There could have been other means, other ways.''

"Which wouldn't have worked any better than the ones I chose to employ did, I'm afraid.''

"What are you talking about?''

"Your father isn't dead, Miss Hunsecker.''

"What?''

Patty stared at Takahashi for what seemed like a very long time. She continued to stare at him even as he spoke again.

"General Berlin Hardesty was the first on our list, and several others followed almost immediately. But we underestimated the Children's ability to mount a response. They let me *think* I was succeeding, while all the time I was playing into their hands. The contingency must have been set in place for sometime, a complex communications network made even more complicated by the fact that the very nature of their operation required that the Children not be in contact with one another. But they found a way to spread the word of warning. In the case of your father and many others, we killed doubles, replacements.''

"If my father's alive, where is he?" Patty demanded. "Where can I find him?"

"Undoubtedly at one of the underground bunkers the Children of the Black Rain have constructed all across your country. But he is not the man you knew as your father, Miss Hunsecker. A child of the Black Rain has no love for anything but the ruthless movement that spawned him."

"No more ruthless than a man who would send killers after me and my brothers."

"You were stirring up trouble, casting attention on a pattern of killings we could not afford to have attention drawn to. Please try to understand." Takahashi came closer to her. "Your father is one of them. Your father is part of a plan to destroy your country as you know it today."

"I've heard that before," said McCracken. "From the disciple I killed in Rio. Now I'd like to hear how."

The slightest bit of color seemed to flush into Takahashi's cheeks. "If it was black rain that forced us to remake our country, so it would be black rain that forces you to remake yours."

"Nuclear weapons?"

"Nuclear *power plants*."

Blaine went cold.

"A dozen or so of them sabotaged, forced into a complete meltdown," Takahashi continued. "A dozen or more meltdowns, each three or four times the potency of Chernobyl."

"My God," Patty muttered.

Takahashi looked her way. "He was not there for us when the black rain fell in 1945, and He will not be there for you when it falls so very soon."

"But it makes no sense," she continued. "All these years my father and the others were laying the economic groundwork to take over the country only to *destroy* it?"

"I did not say destroy, Miss Hunsecker. I said destroy as it is known today. The power plants in question are concentrated within the heaviest areas of population. The metropolises of the East Coast, the larger cities of the Midwest, South, and California. Many will die, tens of millions, but far more will survive and be totally uprooted."

"Half the population," Blaine said, considering the potential targets. "Perhaps even more."

"The survivors in the targeted zones will be forced from their homes, forced to resettle their lives away from the cities that will be no more than steel-and-glass graveyards for a thousand years.

"And, of course, those same steel-and-glass graveyards contain the lifeblood of American existence," McCracken added. "Information, data. Government and business."

"Exactly. The United States, especially, is held together by the glue of people pressing keys and switching relays, bringing you your television signals, radio broadcasts, and dial tones. Those major relays and stations happen to be centralized in the very centers that are most at risk. How will your government function? And what of your economic base? Everything will be frozen, suspended."

"Except the people," Patty said indignantly. "The ones who can get out will. Resettle, you called it."

"Yes. Toward the areas of the nation unaffected by the radioactive clouds spreading on the wind. Those areas at present, of course, are the least populated."

"The corn belt," Blaine said, picking up Takahashi's trend of thought. "Areas west of the Mississippi, the mountains and plains."

Takashashi nodded. "A vast population shift will ensue. Millions flooding areas that lack the capacity to handle them. Goods and services will be at a premium, along with the very rudiments of life and the capacity to effectively distribute them. Necessities such as electricity, water, waste disposal, sewers, all forms of fuel will become woefully inadequate. The panic will continue, even escalate." He turned his pink eyes toward Patty. "This is what the Children of the Black Rain have laid the groundwork for, Miss Hunsecker. They will emerge from the bunkers they have fled to, in total control of the goods and services so drastically needed, because that is what we arranged their placement for. They will have taken over.''

"They'll still need the government to do that, Mr. Takahashi.''

"And they'll have it.''

"You're not going to tell me the president is one of them.''

"No—the vice president. The final element of the plan will be the assassination of the president before the nuclear plants are destroyed.''

"One of our six killers was dispatched to kill the vice president,'' Takahashi continued. "He . . . failed.''

But McCracken's mind was elsewhere as he tried to make sense of the pictures Takahashi was painting. The great cities of the United States reduced to skeletons. Massive ghost towns of steel and glass, the raw power of the world's most advanced nation abandoned to the deadly rads. And in the safe zones the survivors living crowded and cluttered; many already dying, others wishing they were.

But that wasn't all, was it? The Children of the Black Rain would emerge from the bunkers prepared to take over the nation they had effectively destroyed with a blueprint for remaking American society and the resources to bring it off. The men who had formulated the original plan nearly a half century before were long dead, their legacy perverted by a single rebel standing over the Children, controlling them. And that single member was about to preside over the nuclear devastation of the United States.

"Which nuclear plants?'' McCracken asked finally.

"That I do not know. Most are centered along the East Coast, where the prevailing wind currents will blow the deadly clouds over the largest clusters of your country's populace.'' Takahashi paused. "But if you can uncover which ones, the operation can still be stopped.''

"How?''

"The Omicron legion. Everything depends on them successfully sabotaging the nuclear plants. You can stop them. You are the only man who can.''

McCracken looked up. "What makes you say that?''

"Because they fear you. You escaped them in the Amazon

and killed one of their number in Rio. You are the one factor the Children's plan did not account for. You are the one factor that can destroy it.''

Something flashed through Blaine's mind. "Can you give me a list of the Children?''

"I've already had one prepared.''

"What about the locations of the bunkers where they're hiding out?''

"Unfortunately, I cannot help you there.''

"But you know when this is all going to happen. I can tell that much.''

A thin smile crossed the albino's milk-white lips and lingered there as he spoke. "When else, Mr. McCracken? December seventh, 1991. The fiftieth anniversary of Pearl Harbor.''

CHAPTER 29

Mira's eighth victim proved the easiest to reach of all. Newton Samuels regularly used an escort service, and it was an easy chore for her to replace the woman scheduled to accompany him tonight. As was the procedure, his limousine swung by an assigned spot at the proper time, and Mira climbed into the back. The limousine pulled off instantly, not a word spoken by the driver. She checked herself in the built-in vanity mirror and then pulled the file from her handbag.

It looked like an ordinary nail file, even felt like one, albeit a bit heavier. The file was formed, though, of a high-grade carbon used in sharpening tools. While the limousine slid through the night, Mira busied herself honing her steel-tipped nails to a razor edge. The sight would have looked harmless had the driver been looking.

The car deposited her in front of the mansion, and another of Samuels's servants led her up the steps and into the study. She counted at least a half-dozen guards present on the grounds now, including two at the front gate. Her options for escape after she dispatched Samuels would be curtailed.

"If you'll be good enough to follow me, miss," said the butler two minutes later. "Mr. Samuels would like to see you upstairs."

The butler brought her to his door and knocked quietly. "You may enter," he said, without waiting for a reply from within.

Mira did, and closed the door behind her. The room was dark, lit only by the thin spill of light coming from a partially open bathroom door.

"Come here," Samuels called.

He was seated in a leather reading chair near the rear wall, reclining comfortably. Mira could see he had his tuxedo shirt and tie already on, but was naked from the waist down. She walked across the room and stood over him.

"Now," he said. "Immediately."

Mira dropped into a crouch and grasped him.

"Hurry," he said, sighing.

He grew in her hand, and she lowered her mouth to him. It was going to be easier than she thought, the easiest yet. Her hands climbed past the studs, marking a neat line up his chest, the throat just inches away from her deadly nails. She had to make sure the initial slice was deep enough this time. She couldn't afford him screaming or crying out before death took him.

The nails scraped against his collar. Mira prepared to flick them.

And realized he had gone limp in her mouth.

She was already into her motion by then and it was too late to correct it, even though she sensed something was terribly wrong. Before her deadly nails could find flesh, she felt her hand being snatched out of the air and twisted violently. She heard her wrist crack an instant before the explosion of pain rocked her. She fought through it and tried to pull away, lashing out with her other hand as she did. But the blow found only air as the figure whirled through the darkness.

What are you?

Mira asked that question in her mind in the instant before her hand was caught between desperate flailing motions. She felt a grasp of steel close on her fingers and wrench them savagely backward.

Crack!

Her scream from the resulting pain would have been even louder than the snap if her face hadn't been shoved into the cushion of the chair. He had broken the fingers cleanly at the joints. They flapped helplessly, like the limbs of a puppet with no strings attached. The thing over her jammed downward with a thrust strong enough to split the chair, then forced her facedown into its innards. She knew she was dying now and just wanted it to come fast, wanted the pain to be gone.

Bartholomew kept her there a very long time. He liked to feel people die, especially the precise moment death claimed them. But he also enjoyed the moments that came after. He imagined life didn't pour from them, it seeped, and he kept at it until he had swallowed in all there was to take.

It had been over much too fast this time.

Much too fast.

All things considered, the thing Berg liked most about America was french fries. He ate them by the dozens, liking best the fast-food variety the magazines said were loaded with fat and cholesterol. Berg wasn't worried. He figured he'd never live long enough for cholesterol to kill him.

He'd purchased three extra-large servings at the McDonald's across the street after sliding the bomb into place beneath the target's car. It was parked in the lot of the plant the target owned and operated. Getting to the car posed only a minor difficulty. Berg had pretended to be doing some filler work on the asphalt parking lot to permit him access underneath its chassis.

"About time they got these potholes fixed," someone said to him right after he had slid back out.

Berg smiled in the man's direction, wondering if he had noticed anything. But the man sauntered off without another word, and Berg was safely off to stow his equipment in the trunk. Then he headed for his fries.

By the time his target emerged two hours later, Berg was ravenous again. He'd blow the sucker as soon as he was inside and then pick up another four orders before pulling off. Guy said good-bye to everyone he passed, by name, Berg could tell, smiling a lot. Berg had never liked killing nice people, but he didn't get to choose very often. Arabs were the best to kill, and he'd done that plenty of times—they were seldom nice.

And they made lousy french fries.

Berg smiled at his own joke as he activated the detonator. He saw the target climb into his car and close the door behind him. Berg noticed a stray fry on the floor of his car and stuffed it into his mouth as he was pushing the button.

He was still chewing when the blast blew him into oblivion. He had no awareness of anything other than a sudden flash and maybe, just maybe, a realization that he had become the victim here; he hadn't noticed the switch because he was out buying the damn french fries.

In fact, the bomb worked better than Berg had even hoped for. So well that it took fire and rescue authorities nearly thirty minutes to ascertain there had actually been someone inside his car.

Berg's target was among the first on the scene to see if he could lend any assistance.

The thing was, Khan liked to kill. He wasn't sure exactly how that had happened, but what little Chinese philosophy he knew attributed it to birth. He was Mongolian, actually, and by any standards a huge man. He had practiced his trade first as an enforcer on the docks of Shanghai and later as an assassin for the Tong. Knives, guns, hatchets—the weapon mattered not at all. Khan liked his sticks best. He loved his sticks.

The sensation of twirling the galvanized steel, making it whistle through the air en route to its target was the most fulfilling thing he could imagine. Yes, the sticks—combined with his incredible quickness—made for deadly effectiveness. He could follow a man without the man ever knowing. If he stopped to gaze back, Khan would be gone, the action undertaken in the same instant it took the target to swing round. He had shaved his head for as long as he could remember, because hair was something a foe could grasp if the kill had to be made in close. He allowed himself a thick Manchurian-style mustache—he wasn't worried that anyone would grab that.

But tonight he had plenty more to worry about. The last two men on his kill list had disappeared before he could get to them. He had planned on going for a third today, only to find that he, too, had vanished. Khan did not know who to blame. Could the white-faced man have betrayed him somehow, sent others to do his job for him? Perhaps the brutality of his earlier kills had disturbed the whiteface.

He always stayed in rundown, seedy hotels when on the job, and cover was only part of the reason. Khan actually liked the feeling they brought with them, full of the mad, the failed, and the helpless. He fed off their thoughts and the stink of their souls. He could kill them all, not a single room spared, if he chose.

Not tonight, though. He was a half block from the shabby hotel where he was currently staying in downtown Chicago, on the outskirts of Wrigleyville, when he veered away. Something was wrong. Someone was watching for him. He could see nothing, and that bothered Khan. The enemy always, *always*, revealed itself somehow—if not by sight or sound, then at least by feeling.

Khan kept walking and jumped on the L the first chance he got. He rode it for over an hour, switching trains regularly. Then, judging he was safe, he jumped off and hailed a cab after a short walk. The meter had rung up close to thirty dollars before Khan was satisfied no one was following him. He got out and took to the alleys and back streets that had been his home since his early years in Shanghai. He could sleep without giving up his senses, use garbage for cover, if necessary.

Khan had embraced the thick darkness of a garbage-strewn alley when he realized someone was behind him. Certain he had not been followed, Khan assumed it was just some hopeless bum whose turf he had invaded. He would kill him fast and be done with it, then give himself up to the blessed night for refuge.

The sound of a misplaced step froze his thinking.

He wants me to know he's back there.

Khan wasn't sure where that thought originated because it made no sense. He dismissed it and ducked into hiding, melting into the scenery so he might see his adversary pass by.

No one passed. No one came. There was only the night before him.

Khan stayed as he was, rooted in place, one with the garbage cans about him. Someone was out there all right, someone who was very skilled in his own right, which was just fine.

Because Khan had his sticks.

He drew them fast and twirled them nimbly into gripping position. Held them low by the hips, ready to whisk in any direction in the shadow of an instant.

He was just turning to check behind him when the hand closed over his throat from the rear. The pressure against his windpipe would have snapped off his Adam's apple if instinct hadn't made him twist his head enough for his powerful neck muscles to save his life. Sucking in what breath he could, he spun away and lashed at his attacker with his sticks.

The blows struck nothing. The attacker was gone.

He came up behind me, and I never even heard him. . . .

Khan swung around suddenly, and a savage kick pounded the back of his head from the direction he had been facing until a second before. The blow thrust him back against the garbage cans, and he whirled to be met with a blow that split two of his ribs on impact. Another blow was aimed for his face; Khan deflected it with one of his sticks and countered with a strike for his opponent's solar plexus. It drew a grunt when it should have resulted in a kill! No man could still be standing, no man!

But this one was—he countered with a combination series of fists that pounded Khan's right cheek and jaw. Khan realized the awful splintering sounds in his ears were his own bones breaking. Yet he was able to jump back to make time and distance his allies. The figure before him was considerably smaller than he was, which perhaps accounted for why he hadn't been able to finish Khan off when the advantage was his. Well, he'd had his chance and missed it. Khan bellowed and unleashed the fury of his sticks in a blurred frenzy.

The disciple named Thaddeus elected to hold his position. He had been expecting more of the giant Mongol than this. There had to be some sport, some enjoyment. He would bait him, let him have his chance to use the killing sticks.

Thaddeus stood his ground as Khan charged. The Mongol's half-swollen face held no expression; the sticks twirled nimbly in his hands as he made his charge.

Khan lunged in with sticks crisscrossing the air in a vortex of death. Thaddeus caught the hands blurring through the night in midmotion. He twisted the Mongol's arms together at the elbow and jerked them mightily. A snap as loud as a gunshot sounded, and one of the arms hung limply by the Mongol's side.

Khan still had one stick left, which he sent into motion a breath before he saw the stick he had lost was in the hand of his opponent. The last thing he remembered was switching his motion to a blocking form—too late—as the enemy's stick slid under the defense and bashed into his nose, driving the bone backward through his brain.

Khan stood there briefly before he crumpled, and Thaddeus wondered how it could have been so easy to kill a man of such reputation.

Fox was finished with the whole damn business. His first few kills had come smooth and sweet and then everything had fallen apart. Targets impossible to reach, or even to find. The wrong man killed on the most recent occasion. Messy, very messy, and Fox hated mess above everything else.

Well, fuck the albino Japper and his mother, too.

Fox hit his home turf of Boston running, making straight for the bank that held his safe-deposit box. He'd clean out the cash and jewels and disappear for a while. The Jap fuck wouldn't know the difference, and his whole plan was gonzo anyway.

Fox had just finished emptying the contents of his safe-deposit box into his black leather briefcase when the lights in the cubicle died. The silenced Beretta was in his hand a second later, while the other hand found the doorknob and twisted it open. The whole damn, windowless box area was pitch-black. A power failure now. If that didn't beat fuck all . . .

Fox heard the sound just before he started to head in the general direction of the exit door. Someone else was with him in the darkness. Not another customer, obviously; he was alone when he came in, and no one had entered since. The guard, then, perhaps . . .

The sound came again, not made by a guard at all, because a guard would have spoken and wouldn't have tried to conceal his presence.

Fox fired a silenced round in its direction.

Another sound sprang from the opposite side of the twenty-foot square room filled wall to wall with safe-deposit boxes. Fox fired again, and this time the bullet ricocheted madly.

I know you're in here, fucker.

The sound of rushing footsteps sounded to his right, and Fox shot that way. More footsteps came from the left, and he wasted two more bullets.

There's more than one of them, he thought. There's gotta be. Well, that suits me just fine!

Fox slid away from the door to the cubicle and pressed his back against the middle row of safe-deposit boxes against the far wall. Muzzle flashes would give him away sure as shit. He'd keep his ass calm and make sure he had something to fire at next time before he shot. Better yet, better yet . . .

Fox holstered the Beretta and pulled out a killing knife courtesy of cool, blue Vietnam. The separation of sounds told him three figures were in the darkness with him. Just like the good ol' days as a tunnel rat, squeezing his big frame into the passageways dug by gooks and slitting their throats as he passed them along the way. Yup, darkness suited him just fine.

Fox moved away from the boxes and joined the darkness. He owned the fuckin' night in Nam, and he would own the asses of the men who had invaded this darkness. If he couldn't shoot them, they weren't about to shoot him, which placed the odds in his favor.

I'm gonna get you, motherfucka!

Fox figured the enemy was shittin' their pants trying to find him in the pitch-black, when he walked straight into a gun barrel. Nothing behind it he could feel, just cold steel touching his forehead.

"Hey!"

Fox had time to scream that as he whipped his blade out at a target as untouchable as gas. Funny thing was he heard the gun go off, actually heard the shot that blew the brains out the back of his head.

The disciple named Peter did not need the light to see. Yes, the darkness kept him from seeing shapes, but auras showed up plain as day, and he decided to taunt this one before finishing the job. All in all, it was boring, disappointing.

There had to be someone out there who could provide a bit of a challenge.

Somewhere.

PART FIVE

Vision Quest

The bunker:
Thursday, December 5, 1991; 7:00 A.M.

CHAPTER 30

Even though the bunker's conference hall was huge, those seated at the table felt cramped and uneasy. Only the shape seated in the shadows at the front of the room remained immobile as always, apparently unfazed by the exchange of words that had been going on for some minutes now.

"I'm telling you, it's out of control!"

The voice of Virginia Maxwell, droning into the hall through an unseen speaker from Gap headquarters in Newport News, had a desperate ring to it.

"Nothing is ever out of control." These words emerged from the shape at the front of the room.

"This is an exception, and I am not the one to blame for it," the head of the Gap said. "I did not lose McCracken in Brazil."

"But you were the one who insisted we involve him in the first place."

"I had nothing to do with the series of failures that followed. Using him for our own best interests was the best track to take. If everything had gone as planned, he would have eliminated the six killers and led us to Takahashi himself."

"But it didn't go as planned, did it?" said Pierce. "Your Mr. McCracken—and the people working with him—ended up dangerously close to the truth, and now all of them have vanished."

"I'm doing my best to correct that," Virginia Maxwell said.

"How?"

"McCracken, Belamo, and the Indian have been red-flagged, marked for immediate execution. Shoot on sight, is the old terminology. Every intelligence agency in the book has gotten the word."

"Your voice is not exactly brimming with confidence, Miss Maxwell."

"I've done what I can."

"But it isn't enough, is it?" Pierce challenged her. "McCracken's been red-flagged before and all it did was make him madder, more determined. I don't like having him as an enemy."

"That's why I came to you with the problem."

"You came to us because you are no longer capable of handling it!"

"What is it that you want?" the darkened shape asked from the front of the hall.

"He's going to come after me," droned the voice of Virginia Maxwell. "I want to let him."

"Fine with me," muttered Pierce.

"To set a trap," the head of the Gap continued.

"Have you come for our blessing?" This question came from the shape.

"No. For your help."

"You have the resources of an entire organization, an entire intelligence community, behind you."

"They're no match for McCracken. I want to draw him out, but once he surfaces I've got to be sure he can be taken."

"Yet by your own admission . . ." The shape broke off his own words. "Yes, I see what you're getting at."

"They alone can stop McCracken and his Indian friend."

Pierce got to his feet. "They? Are you suggesting we use the disciples against a *pair of men*?"

"The security of this operation may well depend on it," Virginia Maxwell insisted.

"I can't believe I'm hearing this. Think of the risk involved if we do this!"

"Think of the risk involved if we don't."

Pierce's eyes fell proudly on the huge wall map dotted with

red lights to denote the targeted nuclear power plants. "Our operation is less than two days from activation."

"There may not be an operation if McCracken remains at large. I submit to you, gentlemen, that he disappeared in Brazil because Takahashi reached him before we could. That means he knows everything—and knowledge in the hands of a man like this is the most dangerous weapon of all. Don't you see? If he met with Takahashi, he has the list! He knows our names, our identities, all of us. Even if our operation is successful, he will hunt us down."

"He could not know the location of these bunkers," the shape told her.

"He'll find them. He'll find us. It's what he does. We'd be playing right into his hands."

"You sound very certain of all this, Miss Maxwell."

A sigh preceded Virginia Maxwell's next words. "I've been in the intelligence game for over two decades now. The operatives I haven't worked with I've read about, and McCracken stands apart from all of them. He's not the best in any single facet of the game, but he's the best by a long shot when you consider all of them together. Goddammit, he killed a disciple. He killed someone we made to be unkillable."

"You're sure he'll go after you and not one of the others on the list?" asked the shape.

"Absolutely."

"Why?"

"Because he knows I'm still available, and he's already familiar with the logistics involved."

"That being the case," said Pierce, "it's conceivable even the disciples won't be able to help you."

"Just give them to me and let me worry about the rest."

"We'd be risking the entire operation if we did."

"You'd be risking it even more if McCracken is left at large."

The shadow projected behind the shape showed the semblance of a nod. "I want to hear your plan first, Miss Maxwell. If I approve of it, we'll do as you say."

The car was an ancient Yellow Cab pockmarked with rust.

"Ain't much, but she runs," said Sal Belamo, slamming the driver's door with a creak.

"Always nice to travel in style."

"Good to see you, too, McCracken," Belamo said, and scooted around to open the door for Patty. " 'Scuse my manners, but being red-flagged tends to stress me out. You ask me, I'd be better off taking up boxing again and hoping Carlos Monzon comes outta retirement to finish the job."

After leaving Takahashi, Patty and Blaine had left Japan on a commercial airliner. No way, McCracken figured, could every flight coming into the country be watched. As a further precaution, on the chance the enemy knew of their brief stay in Japan, they changed planes at Heathrow and boarded a flight bound for Chicago. The last leg was a nonstop to Boston's Logan Airport, where Sal Belamo was waiting. With the hours lost to plane changes and time zones, they arrived late in the morning on Thursday, forty-eight hours before the disciples would begin their deadly work.

"You get ahold of Johnny?" Blaine asked Sal.

"We're on our way to pick him up now, boss. Things ain't been great for him, either. Had a bad experience in Philadelphia, where one of the six killers got himself dead in a bad way."

"Aren't many good ones."

"Even fewer worse than this. Somebody twisted his head like a bottle cap. Johnny said it was one of those Thunder whatevers."

"I'm not surprised."

"Then check this out. Four of the other killers are toast, too, and the last one is probably floating in some river. That surprise ya?"

"Not in the least."

Sal honked the horn in frustration. "When you plan on telling me what the fuck went down in Jap land?"

"After we pick up Johnny."

Wareagle met them in a rest area just north of Boston, as planned. As soon as he got into the back of the cab, Blaine could feel something wasn't right. He couldn't explain exactly what; the big Indian simply felt, well, *different*. In all the years they had known each other, Johnny had been unflappably measured, existing on a keel so even it was maddening. But today an uneasy edge hung about him, something sharp and new.

"Hey," Sal Belamo broke in as their stares held, "you ask me, this tub doesn't make for our best route of travel south. Not exactly inconspicuous, if you get my drift."

"We'll find the nearest shopping center and make a change."

"Big Lincoln if I can spot one?"

"Sounds good," Blaine replied. "Give me a chance to tell you boys about our unscheduled trip to the Orient. . . ."

"You gotta be fuckin' kidding me," Sal Belamo muttered after Blaine had finished detailing the incredible story of the Children of the Black Rain. "This goddamn albino hires six icemen to whack a bunch of people the Japs planted as *babies*?"

"All grown up now and holding the fate of this country in the balance."

"Not them alone, though, is it? Shit, *that* we could handle. They got your Omicron legion in their corner, and that changes the odds."

"In our favor, maybe."

"You got an idea, chief?"

"The makings of one, anyway."

"What comes next?"

"We ride south."

"Washington?"

"Not quite."

"I'm not afraid of you. I want you to know that."

Abraham looked up from the fire he was kneeling in front of in Virginia Maxwell's study that night. The flames lent their color to his straw-colored hair and glistened off his ice-blue eyes.

"Nice of you to say so," he replied.

"The others will be arriving at the rendezvous point shortly. You, of course, will be there. I leave it to you to brief them on what they will be facing tomorrow."

"You're that sure you can predict McCracken's actions?"

"He has no choice," Virginia Maxwell insisted. "This is

the only course of action available to him, under the circumstances.''

''Yes,'' Abraham said, with a smile Maxwell did not understand. He rose and stood there in front of the fireplace. ''Is this the way you treat all your people?''

''I don't know what you mean.''

''You haven't come within eight feet of me since I arrived, Ms. Maxwell. I had hoped our first meeting would have been more pleasant.''

''This is business.''

''Everything is business to me.'' He shook his head as if disappointed. ''I can understand it coming from the others, but I expected more from you.''

''We have a task before us and nothing more.''

''No, Ms. Maxwell. You are scared of me, because you don't understand me. And what you don't understand, you can't control. Would you like me to tell you about myself? Would you like to hear about the feeling that rushes through me when I kill? I live for those opportunities, Ms. Maxwell, and when they are not provided, I create them. This bother you?''

''Er . . . no.''

''The Indian understood me. I saw it in his eyes. He understood me because we're the same. It's the same with McCracken. I can feel it. That is not good.''

''They'll be there together.''

''I know.''

''You'll have your chance.''

Abraham glided close enough to Virginia Maxwell for her to see his lean face clearly for the first time. ''And perhaps then you'll understand me and the others. Without McCracken and the Indian, we'll be all that is left.''

They checked into the Days Inn–Oyster Point in the center of Newport News; they would be using it as a base. Patty Hunsecker retired to her room for a bath, and Sal Belamo went out for supplies, leaving Blaine and Johnny alone.

''What gives, Indian?'' Blaine asked Wareagle, who was staring into the mirror suspended over the room's dresser. It was too small, of course, to accommodate him, and he had to bend slightly at the knees to look into his own eyes.

Wareagle said nothing.

McCracken spoke again. "When you got into the car, you felt different, Indian, like I never felt you before."

Wareagle turned his gaze toward McCracken. "Look in the mirror, Blainey, and tell me what you see."

"Let me open the blinds and turn the lights on first."

"Without the light."

"A pair of outlines without much detail, Indian. Yours is bigger than mine."

"Before facing his *Hanbelachia*, such is the true warrior. A figure from a child's coloring book before any shades have been added between the lines." Wareagle turned slowly from the mirror and looked at Blaine. "Facing Abraham across the sky in Philadelphia should have faced me with the *Hanbelachia* that is my fate, but instead it faced me with something else." Johnny turned back to the mirror. "I looked into his eyes and I saw a looking glass, I saw myself. I realized that my shape had been filled in by the will of others." Wareagle turned his gaze hard into McCracken's "The *Wakinyan* are what the country made us into first."

"Or tried to."

"No, Blainey, succeeded. We were trained and tempered, and then the hellfire forged our souls in an image that has held us hostage ever since. We hide behind the illusion we are doing right, but that is only from the perspective they gave us."

"What about justification?"

"Each act finds its own. The doing provides the context, but in the end the act is the same."

"You're saying we're no better than the disciples are?"

"I'm saying we're no different."

Blaine came a little closer; his reflection sharpened next to Wareagle's in the mirror. "No, Indian, you've got it wrong this time, and you said how yourself. Nam—the hellfire— forged our souls because we had souls to forge. The disciples had their souls stripped away. That's what made them. That's what *makes* them."

A slight smile from Johnny flickered in the mirror. "It seems, Blainey, that you have forgotten the first lesson we learned in the hellfire: Never judge the enemy by your own values. The Black Hearts did not consider themselves soulless, and in another way neither do the *Wakinyan*.''

''This is more than just us against them.''

Wareagle's bear claw of a right hand flattened out against the mirror and seemed ready to tear through the glass. ''It is our vision quest to face them. Passing the rites successfully means smashing the mirror. We trap their reflections inside, at the same time we free our own from what others have made us.''

''Eleven of them left. Plus Abraham.''

''Yes, Blainey.''

''We can do it, Indian, but only if we meet them on our terms.''

''Not an easy task.''

''But you said it yourself, Johnny: *I* know how they think, and I know how the Children of the Black Rain think, too.''

''Your plan is to outguess them, Blainey?''

''My plan is to do exactly what they expect me to do, and take it from there.''

Wareagle's head tilted slightly. ''There's something else, isn't there?''

''I never said we could reasonably expect to be able to handle the *Wakinyan* alone.''

''It appears we have no choice.''

''Appearances, Indian, can be deceiving.''

CHAPTER 31

VIRGINIA Maxwell's limousine rolled into the underground garage constructed beneath the Oyster Point office building housing the Gap at 9:00 Friday morning. Access to the organization's floors could be gained only through a single entrance at the garage level. The entrance had a single door that looked utterly innocuous except for the small electronic slot that accepted identification cards to permit access. The doorknob was just for show. It opened and closed mechanically and was formed of eight-inch plate steel.

Maxwell's limousine slid through the serpentine garage structure and parked in its accustomed spot. Seconds later, surrounded by four guards, the head of Gap was ushered to the door and led through it. Two more armed guards were waiting in the claustrophobic entry, one already pushing the button that opened the elevator doors. Seconds later, the compartment was whizzing straight to the eighteenth floor, where Virginia Maxwell's office was located.

The guards were still enclosing her when the compartment doors slid open on Maxwell's floor.

McCracken and Wareagle had watched the limousine arrive through binoculars from the top floor of one of the soon-to-be completed buildings adjacent to the one housing the Gap. It had taken all of the previous afternoon and evening to get the

257

logistics of the operation in place and, even now, too much remained unsure.

"How many, Indian?" Blaine asked Johnny, who still had not taken the binoculars from his eyes.

"Four men with her in the backseat, Blainey."

"Can you make any outside the building or on the roof?"

"Two shooters on the roof. Five scattered about the garage entrance in various guises."

"Makes eleven in all."

"None of them *Wakinyan*, Blainey."

"What else is bothering you, Indian?"

"She knew we'd see all her guards."

"Of course."

"And she knew we'd be able to get by them."

"Equally true, Johnny."

"Too much show, Blainey. She is making this too easy."

"Then what do you say we take her up on her invitation?"

At ten-thirty, with the building residents settled in for the morning, Patty Hunsecker drove the van up to the main entrance of the underground parking garage.

"Go right on through," the guard told her, and just like that she was in.

The van belonged to the Virginia Air Filtration and Conditioning Company and had been appropriated by Sal Belamo the previous night. The building containing the Gap had permanently closed windows, relying totally on its internal system for proper air flow. Accordingly, the Virginia Company's vans were common enough sights on the premises and, of course, anyone wearing the proper overalls would have easy access to just what Blaine needed.

Sal had obtained the overalls, too, although Johnny's fit only as well as could be expected.

Blaine and Johnny leaped out of the back of the van as soon as Patty had put her foot on the brake.

"Wait five minutes and then drive the hell out of here," he said when he had come around to the driver's side window. Wareagle unloaded a pair of tanks from the van as Blaine gave Patty her instructions.

"Explaining to the guard—"

"That you left a tank back at your base. Just like we went over."

"I'd rather wait for you."

McCracken shook his head. "You know where you've got to be."

"You sure you've got all this figured that perfectly, Mc-Cracken?"

"Close enough. Wish us luck."

Before she could, Blaine and Johnny moved off, a walkie-talkie up against Blaine's lips.

"Yo, Sal."

"Got ya, McCrackenballs."

"We're in."

"Okay, my watch is on. Eight minutes and counting, boss."

"You'll have my signal in three."

"Ain't we punctual."

"Comes with the territory."

Blaine accepted the tanks from Wareagle and stowed one under each armpit. They were about half the size and weight of a full scuba tank. He made his way to a door marked AU-THORIZED PERSONNEL ONLY, which was ten yards to the right, while Johnny moved to the door beyond which lay the Gap's private entrance. McCracken picked the lock in twenty seconds, then stepped into a brightly lit, tiled corridor that wound its way to the air systems control bay that linked up with the central core.

"Who the fuck are you?" A thick voice assailed his ears when he was halfway there.

"Who does it look like?" Blaine shot back. The voice's owner was a beefy man with olive skin who was chomping on a cigar.

"Some asshole in coveralls with a pair of tanks that don't belong here."

"Says who?"

"Building plant manager."

"Oh."

McCracken let the tanks drop. The resulting clamor took the building plant manager by surprise, and Blaine lunged at him. His first blow caught the man in the solar plexus and doubled him over. Blaine's second cracked into the rear of his

skull and the cigar went flying. The man crumpled, and Mc-
Cracken caught him before he hit the ground. He dragged the
unconscious form to the entrance of the air systems control
room. He was returning to retrieve the tanks when he ran into
Johnny Wareagle.

"That was fast, Indian."

"Simple work, Blainey. The Gap entrance is sealed—the
elevator leading to it rendered inoperative."

"I ran into some complications."

"No plan can account for everything, even when drawn by
the spirits."

"Well, this might turn out to be a blessing. . . ."

Sure enough, Blaine found a set of keys in the manager's
pocket, which saved him the trouble of picking the lock to the
much more secure door of the air systems room. He brought
the tanks in with him while Johnny dragged the manager into
the room.

McCracken had done plenty of work for the Gap over the
years, but he'd never once been in this room. Somehow he was
expecting it to be like the boiler room of an elementary school,
yet he found himself looking at something that looked like it
had come off of the starship *Enterprise*. Shiny silver and plain
plastic tubing ran in neat rows from the walls and ceiling,
linking up with a series of boxlike chrome devices that looked
like home heating units.

"The main exchangers and pumps are built into the ground
beneath us," he said, remembering Sal's words and starting
to move toward one of those Belamo had indicated. "These
are the filters that recirculate the building's air. Highly effi-
cient. Totally new air every thirty-seven minutes. Particles going out now will reach the whole building in two and a half."

"We have under six left."

McCracken found the first of the two filters and squeezed
the walkie-talkie between his shoulder and ear while he went
to work with his tank. Johnny looked his way to confirm he
had found the second filter.

"The Indian and I are hooked in, Sal. Get ready to do your
thing."

"Tell the fuck-wads upstairs pleasant dreams for me."

Blaine and Johnny turned their valves at the same time;

instantly a potent form of knockout gas flew into the air pumps servicing floors ten through twenty. Though the Gap occupied only five floors within those ten, it was impossible to isolate them, so some innocent people had to be knocked out as well. McCracken checked his watch.

"Let's go!"

They bolted from the room and rushed to the service elevator. The Gap could not be reached through any of the regular building elevators, but the single service elevator provided access to the fourteenth and lowest floor. Blaine and Johnny had already donned their gas masks by the time the elevator doors had slid closed again. Even though the effects of the gas were instantaneous, it would continue to pump for several minutes. Both masks had communicators built in, tuned to the same channel Sal Belamo was on. The service elevator reached the fourteenth floor, and Johnny squeezed his thumb against the Close Door button.

"We're in position, Sal," said McCracken. "Do your thing."

Blaine knew he needed a final diversion to assure against unwanted entry or discovery of the sleeping workers on ten of the building's floors. That diversion had been set through the empty building the preceding evening. Sal Belamo's special smoke bombs would activate the fire alarms and a number of sprinkler systems. The elevators would automatically shut off, forcing the people inside the building to use the stairwells to reach the street. Even more importantly, no one would be permitted to enter.

When the alarms sounded, Johnny pulled his thumb from the button; the compartment doors slid open.

The Gap could have been a law or accounting office by the first look of it. Individual offices lined the corridor they stepped into, many with desks perched before them personed by now-sleeping secretaries. The five floors containing the Gap were entirely self-contained, linked together by open staircases joining one level to the next.

"Conference room's three floors up," Blaine announced as he started up the first staircase. "Maxie will be at the morning briefing."

He and Johnny had to hurdle bodies several times during

their rush upward. The Gap seemed to have simply frozen in place. Blaine saw spilled coffee in several places, imagined he could smell it in spite of his gas mask. The sound of his hard breathing echoed through his eardrums and added to the chaos generated by the constant wail of the activated fire alarm.

"In here," Blaine said to Johnny finally, and they stepped into the conference room where the morning briefing would have been proceeding had its members not been gassed to sleep.

All the heads slumped over the table belonged to men.

"I don't like this, Indian. She should have been here."

"Late, perhaps."

"Maxie's never late. Let's check her office. Next floor up."

"I do not feel the *Wakinyan*, Blainey," Johnny said on the way there.

"Good sign maybe."

"I don't think so."

"Yo, boss," Belamo called, and his voice reverberated through Blaine's mask. "Fire trucks coming fast, lots of 'em. Time's a-wasting."

"We'll pick up Maxie and follow the plan."

The fifth floor up belonged entirely to her and the Gap's senior staff. It was more isolated than any of the other floors to start with—and even more so now since several of its occupants were asleep in the conference room Blaine and Johnny had just left. McCracken stopped briefly at the door to Virginia Maxwell's office.

"Morning, Maxie," Blaine said to her shape, which was slumped over the big desk asleep. "Aren't we looking chipper this morning!"

McCracken moved behind the desk and eased her head back. "We've got problems, Sal," he reported over the walkie-talkie.

The woman behind the desk wasn't Virginia Maxwell.

"We've been duped!"

"Come again, boss," Belamo said.

"The real Maxie didn't make it in this morning. What we got ourselves is a double."

"A fucking trap!" Sal squawked into the walkie-talkie.

"Could be."

"But nobody went inside after you, I tell ya! None of *them* went inside!"

"They might have been in already."

"Jesus Christ, boss! Jesus Christ! You ask me, you boys better make time gettin' out."

"Plan B, Sal."

"I read ya, boss."

A sound reached McCracken and Wareagle at the same time, barely rising above the continuous screech of the fire alarm. Little more than a door opening, perhaps some furniture being disturbed as someone approached from the floors below. They looked at each other.

"We got company, Sal," Blaine said hurriedly into the walkie-talkie.

"Oh, fuck."

"Get away from here!"

"Hey, I'm—"

"I said get the fuck away! *Now!*" Blaine ordered.

Blaine looked at Johnny, who stood as rigid as a guard dog sniffing an intruder's scent.

"They're here, Blainey."

McCracken drew his pistol an instant ahead of Wareagle. They carried identical 9-mms loaded with Splat exploding bullets. No sense bothering with anything else today. Johnny started for the door.

"No, Indian. I've got a better idea," Blaine said. He looked up and pointed his pistol at the ceiling.

The first Splat he fired shook the entire room and showered him with rubble from what had been the center of the ceiling. The second Splat blew a hole straight through the crawl space containing the wiring and filtration ducts into the floor above.

"Going up, Indian?"

They slid Virginia Maxwell's desk over so it was directly beneath the hole in the ceiling. Blaine jumped, grabbing hold of some ruined corrugated piping for purchase. Wareagle pushed him the rest of the way into a smoke-filled office on the nineteenth floor, which was directly above the Gap. McCracken was helping Johnny up when gunfire erupted in Virginia Maxwell's office, just missing the Indian's legs as Blaine hoisted him the rest of the way up. With Wareagle safe, Blaine dived to a portion of the floor that was still intact and tried to get off a shot through the hole. He caught a glimpse of a large figure garbed in a gas mask almost identical to his own and fired at it as it whirled.

The sons of bitches were ready for us, goddammit!

An explosion followed, but no scream. Blaine rolled again, and now it was Johnny who fired down through the jagged hole in the floor, his target Virginia Maxwell's desk. The desk ruptured into a thousand pieces, effectively turning it into a massive grenade of wood fragments. McCracken was on his feet by then, and they moved out into the corridor together. McCracken looked in the direction of the elevator bank outside the glass entry doors.

"Switched off, Blainey, because of the fire alarm."

"Thanks for reminding me."

McCracken led the way through the glass doors and back-pedaled down the short hall as if expecting some of the disciples to charge at them at any second.

"You take the left, I'll take the right," he told Johnny.

Wareagle knew instantly what he meant. Not hesitating at all, the two of them pried open the doors to the shut-down elevators. The car on Johnny's side had stopped eight floors down. The one on Blaine's was in the lobby or possibly the garage. A straight twenty-story drop.

"Put your gloves on, Indian."

"Not the shorter drop, Blainey?"

"With another door to pry open once we get down there? Not on your life. This'll give us the head start we need."

If Johnny had any doubts as to the necessity of that strategy, they vanished when a pair of dark, gas-masked figures—with machine guns firing—came at them from the direction of the glass doors. Blaine and Wareagle fired a pair of Splats each; the result was a chaotic symphony of exploding glass as the entrance blew inward. Flames blew back toward the retreating figures, then quickly gave way to black smoke. McCracken reached across the threshold of the elevator shaft and grabbed hold of the cable.

"Ready or not," he said to the void beneath him, "here I come!"

The instant he dropped downward, Johnny leaped over the

threshold after him, thick gloves digging hard against the cable as his slide began. The cable was well greased, which added to the blinding pace of their descent. To keep reasonably under control, Blaine found himself turning around the cable as he moved. He grew dizzy, and the shaft spun about him crazily. He closed his eyes, but the fear of dropping blind gripped him tighter than the dizziness, so he opened them again.

It couldn't have been more than four seconds in all before the stalled elevator compartment itself drew dangerously close. Instinctively he wrapped his feet around the cable and twisted it tight between his calves and ankles. The impetus stopped his spin and drove him into a straight downward slide, the greased cable flying through his hands. He fought to slow himself at the end, but still hit the roof of the elevator with a thud. He went down hard, watching Wareagle land a foot from him with a mere flex of his knees. In unison they stripped off their gas masks.

"Uh-oh," McCracken muttered as he came to grips with his one miscalculation.

The compartment doors would still be centered directly before the garage level. And they couldn't simply drop into the elevator through its roof and open those doors to safety, because Johnny had sealed them minutes before. The only option left was the lobby-level floor just beyond their reach.

Blaine was about to relay his conclusions to Johnny when the gunfire erupted from above. It slammed off the shaft walls, ricocheting madly, and Blaine had to cover his ears.

"We've got to stop them, Indian!" McCracken shouted as he hugged the wall for cover.

Wareagle was directly across from him. "Your gun, Blainey!"

"Splats aren't much good at this range!"

"No, shoot at the—"

The rest of Johnny's words were drowned out by a fresh barrage of bullets, but McCracken had already realized the intent of his words. He aimed his pistol directly in front of him, at the elevator cable attached to the car they were standing on. The Splat thumped out and shredded it with a burst that took out a portion of the wall across the shaft. Instantly the counterweight fell and the cable shot up the shaft in a steel-weighted blur that would sever any flesh it came into contact with.

"Give me a boost, Indian," McCracken asked Johnny, listening for a scream to pour down the shaft from the nineteenth floor. Even though none came, at least the disciples had been prevented from following the same route down.

He was on Wareagle's shoulders a blink later, working the doors with all his strength. He ended up splitting them six inches apart, which was enough to force his shoulders through, and leveraged them the rest of the way. He pushed himself out of the shaft and onto the lobby floor, then grabbed hold of Johnny's arms to hoist him up. It took all his strength, but he managed it just ahead of another battery of automatic fire aimed down the shaft from the nineteenth floor.

Together they moved out of the alcove housing the elevator bank and eased in among the crowds still pouring out through the lobby from the building's highest floors. They used the hubbub to change their clips of exploding bullets for normal ones. If the disciples confronted them down here, the Splats would unquestionably kill innocent people. The bullets chambered now were Glazer safety slugs, composed of dozens of small pellets suspended in liquid Teflon and finished in a blue tip. Guaranteed one-shot stop for a normal man. With the disciples, who could tell?

Johnny and Blaine continued through the lobby. They made no effort to disguise themselves, staying wary as they moved.

"You think we finished any upstairs, Indian?"

"Doubtful, Blainey—and several would have started down the stairs as soon as our plunge down the elevator shaft became known."

On the street fronting the building's entrance in Oyster Park, police and fire and rescue officials continued to arrive in droves. The first team was already moving through the lobby en route to the floors that had set off the alarm. They moved quickly, but were not panicked. The safety of the building did not seem at stake, plus the sensor board was still reading problems only in those select areas.

"The *Wakinyan* will fire indiscriminately into the crowd once they have spotted us," Johnny said when they stepped outside. "Innocent lives mean nothing to them."

Just then McCracken spotted two ladder and engine trucks that had pulled into a fire lane directly against the curb. "And since we have to make sure they see us . . . You'll know the disciples when you see them, right, Indian?"

"I'll know them when I feel them, Blainey."

"Once they reach the lobby, I mean."

Wareagle nodded.

Blaine gestured toward the nearer of the two trucks. "I assume you can drive one of those things?. . ."

Johnny smiled.

"They've reached the lobby, Blainey," Wareagle told him less than thirty seconds later as they lingered on the other side of the nearer truck.

"Then we'd better let them know we're here."

The truck's powerful engine was humming. Only a few of the arriving firemen were anywhere near it. One was sitting behind the wheel, but before he knew what was happening, Johnny had tossed him out. McCracken started to work the control panel on the near side. He pulled a pair of levers labeled DECK GUN and TANK TO PUMP and then located the red throttle control and drew it out as well. At the same time, Johnny, who was now in the cab, switched the truck's engine to power the five-hundred-gallon main pump.

"Ready, Indian?" Blaine asked as he climbed on the truck.

Wareagle flashed him the thumbs-up sign, and McCracken positioned himself behind the deck gun. He adjusted the nozzle for a narrow stream, then rotated the control wheel for the angle he wanted. At first McCracken couldn't distinguish the disciples moving among the crowd; then he noticed a number of figures that seemed to cause the throng to buckle as they surged forward. Blaine spun one last knob, and the water exploded from the deck gun in a narrow stream that was directed toward the crowd. The people who were trying to leave the building from the lobby entrance were shoved harshly backward. Those already outside were blistered by the powerful jets and thrust in all directions.

McCracken first made sure the deck gun was aimed straight for the main entrance, then he retraced his steps from it to the control panel.

"Get ready, Indian!" he shouted into the cab on his way.

At the panel, he shoved the throttle inward. Instantly the deck gun's flow slowed to a trickle and then stopped altogether.

"Go!" Blaine screamed, and Johnny shoved the engine into drive without disengaging the power takeoff. The gears screeched in protest, but the truck lurched away from the curb.

McCracken was working his way through the cab's rear window; over the jump seat, when the truck bashed into a pair of police cars that had been parked in their path. Several police officers had their guns out, but none fired, frozen in what must have been a moment of total confusion.

Wareagle crashed through three more parked squad cars and a rescue wagon as he picked up speed down the street, where a path was clearing for him right down the middle. Wareagle kept the ear-wrenching siren going and used the loud horn regularly to continue clearing the street ahead. The top speed of the fire truck wasn't much over fifty, which meant they'd have to rely almost purely on the head start for escape.

"The police, Blainey," Johnny said, looking in the rearview mirror as they continued down Thimble Shoals.

"Yeah," McCracken said, starting to ease himself back over the jump seat.

He gazed over the truck bed in search of a plan, then one made itself available in the form of a hose—over a thousand feet long—that was twisted into neat layers before him. He crawled over it to the back of the truck, grabbed its end, which featured a heavily weighted coupling made to be fitted into fire hydrants, and dropped it out of the truck. The hose began to unravel instantly, flying from the truck bed like spilled milk. It hit the street wildly, an uncoiling snake snapping for a victim. Cars swerved to avoid the hose, or lost control when they climbed over it, catching the pursuing police cars in the snarl.

Once again McCracken joined Wareagle in the cab, almost banging his head on the air tank bolted to the seat between them.

"A brief stretch on Route 17, then we pick up 64, Indian. Straight ride from there."

Johnny checked the large sideview mirror. "Nothing, Blainey."

"They'll be coming, Indian. They'll be coming."

"Where are the vans?" Abraham had screamed as soon as he and the others were at last able to make their way through the lobby—just in time to see the fire engine screech away.

He had joined the other disciples, some of them drenched far more than he, on the curb, where they were all gathering now. Everything was so chaotic no one noticed them or, a few minutes later, the dark vans that screeched around the corner and pulled into the spot vacated by McCracken's stolen truck several minutes before. Abraham and the eleven other disciples piled into the vans, taking off in the same direction as McCracken and the Indian.

The men the disciples had been before Omicron would have felt at least some apprehension over the sudden turn of events in the building. But the members of the legion felt something akin to excitement. There seemed little doubt that McCracken and the Indian could match their skills and abilities. Everything else up until now had been too easy. McCracken and the Indian made for a challenge. They looked forward to the final confrontation that was now coming, their only fear being that their foes would escape before it could happen.

Then, as the vans weaved through the clutter of cars bottlenecked by the freed water hose, which was now being cleared from the street, Abraham gazed up and saw signs for Route 17 and Route 64 dead ahead. "That's the way they went," he said, and the two vans headed that way.

"I've got them, Blainey," Wareagle reported, spotting them in the sideview mirror.

They had been traveling on Route 64 West for eight minutes now.

McCracken leaned his head out the window to see for himself. "How fast are we going?"

"Fifty."

"Not fast enough."

Johnny kept the siren going and leaned on the horn to clear

a path for them down the freeway, but the vans were simply able to go faster than the fire engine.

"Guess we'd better slow them up a little, Indian," Blaine said, and once again he was slithering his way through the cab window.

The truck bed was almost empty now, the water hose having taken up an enormous amount of room, and Blaine's eyes almost immediately locked on a half-dozen white plastic drums.

"Foam," he said to himself, with a smile.

Well, not foam so much as a heavy, thick white ooze used in fighting oil and gas fires. Very, *very* slippery. In other words, perfect . . .

McCracken had to lean clear across the bed to reach the drums, and the *Wakinyan* chose that moment to open fire from their vans, now closing in from a hundred and fifty yards back at most. He ducked lower and grasped the first of the heavy drums as bullets bounced off steel, ricocheting around him. He sent the drum rolling down the vacant truck bed and heard a *splat!* as it shattered on impact with the road. The second was already in motion, with the third and fourth fast behind. By then he could see the foam spreading in wide splotchy waves across the highway, the first van's tires just reaching it.

From there Blaine could barely believe his eyes. As he slid the final two drums off to further widen the pool, the lead van spun wildly out of control. It was slammed into by a tractor trailer whose driver had made the unfortunate mistake of applying his brakes, sending his vehicle jackknifing across the road. The lead van bounced off the truck and careened from left to right, narrowly missing the trailing one, which had ended up doing a full-circle turn to avoid it.

Behind the vans, a massive pileup resulted as dozens and dozens of cars crashed into one another as soon as their tires met the white ooze covering the highway like a blanket now. By the time Blaine had rejoined Johnny in the cab once again, the *Wakinyan* were gone from sight in the chaos taking place behind the engine truck. They would regroup, yes, but not before McCracken and Wareagle took full advantage of the final cushion.

"Here we are, Indian," McCracken said ten minutes later.

Wareagle's eyes were on the mirror. "I can see them behind us, Blainey. A half mile back, but coming."

"Right on schedule," Blaine said as the road sign he had been waiting for appeared on the right of Route 64:

EXIT 56
COLONIAL WILLIAMSBURG HISTORIC AREA

CHAPTER 32

"EVERYTHING'S set," Sal Belamo reported as Wareagle and then McCracken jumped down from the fire engine. They had stopped at the intersection of Jamestown and Richmond roads. Even at the edge of the expertly reconstructed eighteenth-century town, their truck seemed utterly out of place.

" 'Bout time you get some historical culture, Sal," Blaine commented, gazing down Williamsburg's main artery, Duke of Gloucester Street.

"Guess we didn't need Maxie to draw your Frankensteins here, and ain't they in for a surprise now." Belamo gazed around him. "You know, I kinda miss the people in their outfits."

"I'm sure they don't mind getting the day off."

"Yeah, well, the evac order didn't give them much choice. It looked so real, I almost believed the story myself."

Johnny Wareagle's shoulders tensed. "They're coming, Blainey."

"Then I guess we'd better get ready."

* * *

The single van squeezed to a halt next to the fire engine. The disciples of the Omicron legion showed no expression whatsoever as they emerged. They had packed into this van following the loss of the second one back on Route 64. Their number was complete, but several were injured. Of the injuries, a pair of separated shoulders appeared the worst, along with one disciple's limp, and several nasty lacerations. They were not immune to pain, but they were quite adept at controlling it, and even making it work for them. They definitely wanted to do that now.

The disciples stopped to check the weapons they had brought with them from the van. There were mostly machine guns, high caliber and otherwise. Three of these were M203s, M16s with grenade launchers attached to their undersides. There were two shotguns, as well, and grenades were affixed to the belts of three of the legion. Three more carried pistols and if everything fell short, they would use their hands.

Abraham hefted one of the M203s and advanced ahead of the others.

"It's a trap," he said, as much to himself as the others.

"What is this place?" one of them asked.

"Reproduction of a colonial town," Abraham answered. "Complete with authentic props and workmen."

"There's no one here," another member of the legion said.

"Because that's the way McCracken wanted it. He drew us here. It was his plan all along."

"Do we go in?" a third asked matter-of-factly.

Abraham flipped off his weapon's safety and nodded.

There were twelve of them in all; they split into three pairs and two groups of three. They fanned out toward grids of Williamsburg assigned by Abraham. Their mission was search and destroy. If McCracken wanted to make his stand in a confined environment with plenty of areas for concealment and cover, then so be it. It was not their turf yet, but it would be soon.

The scene seemed placid, even to them. Late fall was in the air; the trees lining the Williamsburg streets shifted in their near nakedness, the remaining leaves brown and dry. The main streets were formed of hard-packed gravel. The unpaved walk-ways lined the streets in landscaped symmetry in front of the rows of colonial buildings. The numerous benches were unsat on. A few horseless carriages stood abandoned down Duke of Gloucester Street. The brick and brown wood of the buildings drank in the sun and gave some of it back. The air smelled of chestnuts and crackling leaves.

Abraham started warily down Duke of Gloucester Street, flanked by John and the wounded Judas. He felt certain Mc-Cracken had made a strategic error in choosing this site to make his final stand. No matter how large it was, Williamsburg was still contained. Sooner or later, this would allow the disciples to flush McCracken and the Indian out. It was only a matter of time.

As he came up even with the red brick courthouse on the left-hand side of the street, Abraham reached into his pocket and came out with a motion detector that was a smaller version of the one the Green Berets had brought with them to the jungle. He switched it on and watched the sweep the arrow made through a grid directly before him. He could approximate the positions of the other disciples and thus identify any signals that might come as a result of their motion.

The red line swept the screen, disappeared into the machine's side, and then swept again.

Abraham knew McCracken's strategy would be to take them out slowly. It was the best ploy to use and was one he had always excelled in. If he and the Indian were lurking about, preparing their first lunge, the motion detector would betray their strategy and position.

Abraham turned to the right and eyed a section of Williamsburg's Market Square, which contained a clutter of buildings surrounded by rolling green lawns and well-tended gardens. The motion detector caught a splotch in the lower left of the screen. Abraham quickly superimposed the grid over the area before them and felt his eyes lock on the magazine, an octagonal building used in colonial times to store arms and gunpowder. A high brick wall had been erected around the building to protect the townspeople against a possible explosion. Something was moving inside that wall.

Maybe this is going to be easier than I thought. . . .

"This way," Abraham said.

The disciples on either side of him, actually, did not need to be told a thing. Perhaps they had seen the indication on the motion detector. Perhaps the slight change in Abraham's footsteps and the tightening of the rifle in his hands was enough. Either way they had already leveled their weapons when Abraham spoke, and now they cut across the grassy square with him toward the magazine.

The next sweep the arrow made through the grid showed no movement at all in the vicinity. McCracken, or the Indian, was still again, but it was too late. The damage had been done. Abraham was onto him.

Thirty yards from the magazine, he signaled John and Judas to spread out. He figured surprise was on his side, but didn't want to take any chances. Up ahead, he could see the gate leading through the magazine wall was open. It was not like McCracken or the Indian to commit such an error.

Abraham directed the wounded Judas to move through first from the right flank. John was holding to the left, while Abraham himself was behind a tree, his rifle ready to fire, twenty yards in front of the magazine. Once Judas was through, he would follow, with John bringing up the rear. Abraham watched Judas slide along the brick toward the open gate.

The detector began registering motion inside the fence again, coming straight for the gate, straight for Judas. Abraham signaled Judas to hold his position and steadied his own rifle behind the tree. The blotch on the detector's small screen continued to move in the gate's direction.

Abraham gave Judas the signal at the perfect time. Judas spun around the corner and opened fire, a clip emptied in the time it took Abraham to finally realize something was very wrong about all this. He had begun to ease out from his own position of cover when Judas's body was blown outward through the gate from the force of a fusillade of bullets. Abraham tried to focus, but the sun caught something metallic and blinded him for the instant it would have taken him to aim.

Rat-tat-tat . . .

The automatic spray was undoubtedly from John's M16, and Abraham's vision at last sharpened to see his target. Whatever had emerged from the magazine had reflected sun like metal because it *was* metal. And not a man in a protective suit, either.

It was a robot!

All of a sudden Abraham realized Blaine McCracken hadn't played into his hands at all; he had played into *McCracken's* and now he was facing a madman's version of backup.

Obie One seemed to be smiling as he aimed the gun attached to his right hand and opened fire.

"Did you see that? Did you see it?" Professor Ainsley beamed as Obie One fired a hail of bullets into the second disciple his sensors had locked onto.

"I'll buy him a beer when he comes back in," said Mc-Cracken.

"You mean a lube job," Belamo quipped.

The picture of a second disciple being torn apart by Obie One's bullets was transmitted by the snakelike Obie Four to the main board in Professor Reston Ainsley's control truck. They had parked it back near Williamsburg's eastern border, behind the cover provided by the Capitol Building. Blaine had known that defeating the disciples under normal conditions was not possible. He knew they would be waiting for him when he came for Virginia Maxwell at Gap headquarters and used this to set a trap—with Wareagle and himself as bait the disciples could not possibly resist.

The problem from the start had been how to snare them and where. Utilizing Professor Ainsley's *original* Omicron legion for reinforcements had actually occurred to him as far back as his meeting with Takahashi; the logistics followed from there. What was needed, Ainsley had explained the previous day, was a confined space whose layout could be programmed into his robots, who would then be controlled from a short distance away. McCracken had originally feared Ainsley would laugh off his idea and send him packing. But the old man had embraced the plot with excitement and enthusiasm. Perhaps he just wanted to prove to the world that his creations could perform as no one ever believed they could.

The Gap's location limited their options for the site of the final battle, Williamsburg by far the most advantageous given its proximity to Newport News. Yet there were problems. Yes, the Operational Ballistic Droids would still learn as they moved, but having to negotiate around so many structures could cause significant problems as the battle progressed. Another equally pressing problem was that the Obie series had been constructed purely with counterinsurgency in mind. No thought had been given to how the droids would perform when placed in the field with friendlies. Essentially, how would they distinguish the good guys from the bad? What was there to stop them from shooting anything that moved, including McCracken and Wareagle, if circumstances forced them out into the battle as well?

Ainsley had provided the solution to this in the truck—just minutes before—in the form of twin necklaces for Wareagle and McCracken. A small medallion around their necks would jam sensor mechanisms and thus exclude the two men as targets. The professor, meanwhile, had spent the better part of Sunday night programming the layout of Williamsburg into his Obies. He had managed to get all four operational, and of these the boxlike Obie Three, along with One and Four, were already in the field. The hulking shape of Obie Seven stood outside the truck, between the Capitol's central pillars, waiting to be dispatched. The red LED lights that flashed across his eyeless head and chest made him look impatient to McCracken.

Right now, though, Blaine's eyes were glued to the main monitor screen as Obie Four scanned the area.

"Where's Abraham?"

Reston Ainsley punched some commands into his keyboard. "Obie One is still locked on to him. I'll put him in pursuit mode." And his fingers flew over the keys once more.

"Can you tell him to be cunning?"

"It's built into his programming."

"That's good, because it's built into Abraham's, too."

Even if Abraham had realized earlier he was facing a gray silver robot, there was nothing he could have done. The impossibility of its existence reached him an instant before the gun that was an extension of its right forearm began firing into John. John was blown backward, his Kevlar vest shredded by the robot's powerful bullets, his head almost torn from his shoulders. Judas lay across from him, his corpse a mirror image.

Two of the disciples had been killed! By a robot, goddammit, a robot!

And he would end up the third unless he fled now, before the thing's firing sensors locked on to him. Yes, a few well-placed grenades could splatter his steel guts as easily as flesh and blood ones. But the fact was, a single miscalculation in aim would cost Abraham his life—because the robot *couldn't* miss.

Abraham bolted from the tree, back in the direction of Duke of Gloucester Street, his small, hand-held communicator raised to his lips.

"This is Abraham," he said, and then did his best to explain to the remaining nine disciples what they were up against.

In the control truck behind the Capitol Building, Reston Ainsley punched another series of buttons. "I'm sending Obie Four to scout out the next group."

"Make it fast. The disciples know what they're up against now," advised Blaine.

"They know only of Obie One."

"Won't be hard to figure out he didn't come alone any more than we did."

Ainsley looked almost pleased. "Then I suppose I should get to it."

The disciples now moved in five pairs. On Abraham's orders Thaddeus, the second of those badly injured, had joined him in the hunt for the killer robot at the Prentis Store at the intersection of Duke of Gloucester and Colonial streets. Abraham, the store giving him cover, held fast to the motion detector, but no sign of the robot appeared. The tight cluster of buildings was working in the robot's favor here, offering a layer of confusing cover for the detector. Abraham had realized what had to be done even before Thaddeus came up alongside him.

"How is it?" Abraham asked him.

"It hurts," Thaddeus replied, grimacing slightly. "But I can move."

Abraham nodded in apparent satisfaction and raised his communicator to his lips. "Continue your sweeps," he ordered. "Check all buildings and shops. Find their headquarters. Keep me informed."

Abraham clicked off his communicator and looked back at Thaddeus. "Take the rear. Stay ten yards behind me."

Thaddeus nodded, then asked, "Where are we going?"

"Where else? After the robot. . . . "

"What now?" Blaine asked Reston Ainsley.

He had barely completed the question when a series of red lights began flashing on the main console. The professor slid himself over to it.

"Obie Four has locked on to another pair of the monsters. Let's have a look, shall we?"

Ainsley punched a button on his console and the view from the snakelike reconnaissance droid filled the screen. Obie Four had the ability to plow under and then come back up through solid asphalt if necessary. Ainsley explained that its entire length was essentially a drill that spun at blinding speed, enabling it to burrow inside virtually any substance. Only the very base of its head had to rise back to the surface to provide them with a picture, much like a submarine's periscope.

The screen sharpened to reveal a pair of the disciples veering off Palace Street toward the Brush-Everard House. Directly behind them now was the wide, grassy expanse of the Palace Green Obie Four had burrowed up through. The disciples made their way warily down the walk, then kicked open the door without testing the knob.

"No respect for property," Blaine quipped.

"Neither does Obie Three, I'm afraid—and fortunately he's in the area," said Ainsley.

With that he keyed in Obie Three's access code and swept his fingers across the control keyboard. A slight adjustment of Obie Four's camera allowed the occupants of the truck to see the boxlike figure of Obie Three emerge from the cover of the shell of a reconstructed colonial theater three buildings to the right of the Brush-Everard House. Ainsley brought Obie Three up the house's front walk, in essence following in the footsteps of the two disciples who had entered.

Then another series of commands from Ainsley had the droid's top sliding open to allow its multiple extremities to ease upward and out. One of them held a powerful explosive that looked like two Frisbees squeezed against each other. It placed the charge upon the front steps and then affixed a detonator to it with a second and more adroit extremity. What might have been a steel finger flipped a switch.

On Professor Ainsley's control board, a light on the lower panel switched from green to red.

"It's armed," he said, and returned his attention to Obie Four's monitor screen.

Professor Ainsley kept his eyes on the monitor while his fingers flew across the keyboard to issue Obie Three instructions, which moved it to a safe distance. His finger then eased to a button beneath the light that had been flashing red for ten seconds now.

"We wait until we see them emerge," he explained. "That way we're sure." Ainsley looked back at McCracken. "You want to do the honors?"

"The pleasure's all yours, Professor."

"Yes," Ainsley acknowledged. "It certainly is."

At that point the two disciples appeared on Obie Four's screen, approaching the door they had kicked open. Reston Ainsley waited one last second and then pressed the button.

For some reason, Blaine had been expecting a smaller, more contained explosion. What followed was a blinding, horrific blast as the better part of the Brush-Everard House's front half fragmented into wood shards and splinters that blew out from the fireball. He never saw the disciples; they simply vanished into the oblivion of the blast, consumed by it. The screen cleared to reveal flames picking at the ruined shell of a building, charred portions still falling from the sky.

"That makes four down, Professor," Blaine said.

"Still eight to go, chief," Belamo reminded him.

Nonetheless, McCracken was about to give Ainsley a celebratory slap on the shoulder when a new explosion sounded from another area of the park. He barely had time to wonder what it was when Obie One's control board flickered once and then went dead.

* * *

Abraham respected the prowess of the foe he was facing here. The robot's programming made it a virtually indestructible and independently acting machine. In a confined area, the layout of which was certain to have been programmed into its microchip circuitry, it would inevitably track him down before he could possibly track it. His only hope lay in using that knowledge to his advantage.

That was why he had summoned Thaddeus, why he had the wounded disciple watch his rear. As bait, a sacrifice. He knew the robot would close from the rear, and, in the instant its sensors and firing mechanism were locked on to Thaddeus, Abraham would take his shots. If he missed, the robot would have him, too, but he didn't plan on missing. As an added precaution, he was careful to keep himself as much in line with Thaddeus as possible, hoping this would confuse the robot into believing the motion it detected was that of a single man, not two.

Abraham knew his M16 by itself was useless against the robot's steel composition. But the grenade launcher built into its bottom was something else again. He hadn't had time to get in the shots he needed when the thing had killed John and Judas. Now he would.

This, of course, was just the preliminaries. McCracken and the Indian might be content to let the robot fight their battles for them, but once that robot was neutralized they would have no choice other than to show themselves.

He was passing behind the William Waters House when the blast reached his ears; he turned in time to see a cloud of debris hurtling into the sky from the Palace Street area. No screams followed, but he knew all the same he'd lost another pair of his number. Could there be more robots than the one he was after? Yes, there had to be. He felt an unfamiliar chill of anxiety, perhaps a flutter of fear. McCracken was even better than he had expected.

"Abraham!"

Thaddeus's scream reached him a breath ahead of the non-stop clacking of the robot's built-in gun. He turned to see Thaddeus's body being pulverized by bullets, literally torn apart before he was even able to fire a shot. Abraham leveled his grenade launcher toward the robot and fired. The charge *whoooooosh*ed out dead on line with the thing. Impact tore away the entire right side of the robot's midsection and part of its head. The thing staggered, listing, but incredibly turned on Abraham to fire just as he sighted in with another grenade.

This time the explosive impact blew off the rest of the thing's midsection to below the torso. Its leg extremities continued waddling about briefly before keeling over.

Abraham charged on in the direction of the plume of black smoke still rising over Palace Street. More of the machines were about; if he were going to draw McCracken and Wareagle from their hiding place, he would have to take out the machines first. The rest of the disciples meant nothing to him now. Whether they survived or not was meaningless, as were their parts in the remainder of the plan. McCracken mattered, and beyond him the Indian.

Abraham was heading toward a ruined building across the Palace Green when a strange impression carved into the ground caught his eye. It was perfectly cylindrical and deep, like a gopher hole made in dirt. Abraham suddenly had a very clear idea about what it was he was looking for.

As well as how to find it.

"They killed Obie One," was all the transfixed Ainsley could say. "They killed him."

Ainsley wheeled himself to the console controlling the monstrous Obie Seven and flipped on the control switch. Outside, near the Capitol's pillars, a red light locked on in the center of the huge robot's head. The arms that housed the specially modified Vulcan 7.62-mm miniguns snapped up to forty-five degree angles from locked positions at his side.

Blaine grabbed Ainsley's hands before he could press any more switches.

"Not now, Professor!"

"What are you saying?"

"That they're not concentrated enough for Seven to do us any good yet. He'll get a few of them, and then they'll get him." Blaine paused. "Just like Obie One."

Ainsley stiffened. "We can't have that."

"No, we can't. Stick with the plan. Bunch them up, force them together, and then sic Obie Seven on them."

McCracken, Belamo, Patty Hunsecker, even Johnny let their eyes wander in the direction of the professor's—out the rear of the truck, toward the menacing shape of Obie Seven.

"You'll tell me when," Ainsley said to Blaine.

"I'll tell you, all right."

Reluctantly the professor wheeled himself back to the main control console, where a flashing yellow light alerted him that Obie Four had locked on to the position of another pair of disciples.

"We've got scores to settle now," he said to the two machines still active in the park.

Having completed their assigned sweep, Thomas and James moved down Duke of Gloucester Street with twin automatic rifles leveled before them. They saw none of the other disciples and knew, as the rest of the survivors did, that their number had been cut by at least a third. They were on the defensive now, searching for machines as well as men, the hunted as much as the hunters.

Against his better judgment, Thomas raised the communicator to his lips.

"Abraham," he called. "Abraham . . ."

No response came. Could the best of their number have been killed in one of the two blasts that had come just minutes before? No. Much more likely, he was merely keeping radio silence. The reasons didn't matter. Thomas and James would keep it as well.

The sweeps of the disciple team were concentric in nature, designed to bring them together near the end of Duke of Gloucester Street. If McCracken and the Indian had not been found by then, there would be precious few places left they could be, and these few could be better covered in larger groups. Thomas and James walked toward the rendezvous point uncertain and uneasy, the scent of smoldering wood still thick in the air.

Obie Four surfaced twenty yards behind the pair of disciples as they proceeded along Duke of Gloucester Street between Colonial and Botetourt. Reston Ainsley checked Obie Three's position and nodded happily.

"Got you, you bastards," he said out loud.

"Where's Obie Three, Professor?" McCracken asked.

Ainsley had the snakelike head of Obie Four pan to the right and asked for a close-up. An old-fashioned picket fence sharpened into view between a pair of buildings just across Botetourt Street.

"Coming up on this spot," Ainsley announced. And, as if on cue, the boxy shape of the demolitions droid rolled onto the scene.

The professor pulled the picture back to capture the approaching disciples once more.

"Perfect," Ainsley muttered. "We'll get them here."

Ainsley repeated the series of instructions he had issued in front of Brush-Everard House, telling Obie Three to plant another of his charges. A sudden beeping filled the cramped confines of the truck's rear.

"Oh, no!"

"What is it, Professor?" McCracken asked from behind his shoulder.

"His top doors are jammed. Must have been damaged by debris from the last blast."

"Check out the screen, Doc," Sal Belamo urged.

Obie Four's picture now showed the pair of disciples to be twenty yards from Obie Three's position.

"Pull Obie Three out of there, Professor," said McCracken.

"No, I can't. . . ,"

"We'll get another shot."

The old man's hair flew wildly about his face as he swung around in his wheelchair. "You don't understand. I really *can't*. One of its wheels is jammed on something. The advisors were worried about this sort of thing. It was one of the reasons the project was—"

"Yo, boys," Belamo chimed in. "I see two Frankensteins almost to the corner."

Professor Ainsley hesitated no longer. He turned his attention back to the console and hit a single button set apart from the rest at arm's length. A large red bulb began to flash. The computer screen showed a countdown beginning at fifteen in huge LCD figures.

"I've just ordered Obie Three to self-destruct." A strange smile crossed his lips. "A suicide mission, that's what this has become. My God, he would understand. I know he would."

The countdown had reached seven.

"Professor—"

Before McCracken could speak further, a large figure charged into the picture being broadcast by Obie Four. He came from the side of the picture, rushing in from behind the pair of disciples five seconds before their deaths. The pair swung, weapons ready, as the figure leveled an M203 behind the fence where Obie Three was perched. A charge thumped out with a trail of smoke. When it cleared, a large section of the picket fence was gone—along with whatever had been behind it. The LCD countdown on the computer monitor was locked at two.

"Fuck me," Belamo moaned.

"The explosives wouldn't have been armed until the sequence was complete," Ainsley said distantly. "He died for nothing."

"Uh-oh," moaned McCracken, his eyes back on the screen.

The group in the truck watched as the same large figure that had destroyed Obie Three grew in size, charging straight toward Obie Four in its exposed position on the other side of the street.

"No!" Ainsley screamed, working his keyboard feverishly.

He succeeded in turning Obie Four around, the screen's picture spinning with him. But suddenly the picture filled with tremors, shapes rushing past in a blur as the snakelike reconnaissance droid was grabbed and pulled upward.

A face with a twisted half-smile, straw-colored hair, and the coldest eyes McCracken had ever seen filled the screen.

"Abraham," Wareagle said. The big Indian's stare searched out the deadliest disciple, certain Abraham could see him as well.

The face stayed centered for an elongated moment, as if Abraham could indeed see through and beyond the screen. Then everything turned to fuzz, and the signal was lost.

"*Goddammit!*" Ainsley shrieked.

He propelled himself across the truck's cab, over to the console controlling Obie Seven. Blaine caught his trembling hand before it could reach the keyboard.

"Not yet, Professor."

"Get your hand off me!"

"No. You're playing into their hands!" he said, looking at the screen which had become staticy. "You're playing into *his* hands."

"I can't just sit here!"

McCracken tapped the old man's wheelchair. "Yes, you can. You've got to." His eyes turned to Wareagle, who had hoisted a crossbow he had made for himself years ago out of a duffel bag stowed in the corner. "Leave this to me and the Indian."

"I've got a stake in this, too," Ainsley said more quietly. "They were like my . . ."

"I know. The thing is the two of us specialize in settling scores." His eyes turned in Obie Seven's direction. "When the time's right, he'll get his chance."

"What exactly are you planning to do?"

"Give Abraham exactly what he wants." Blaine looked at Johnny. "Us."

CHAPTER 33

ABRAHAM had smashed the snakelike robot's camera eye with his fist, then had twisted its steel frame into a monstrous knot. Still not satisfied, he proceeded to tear it apart with fingers that were steellike themselves. The ease of it amazed him. Somehow moments like these inevitably brought back memories of just how inadequate he had been before the jungle. Mere scraps of memory now, as distant from him as a normal man's recollections of the limitations of early child-hood. He turned back to Thomas and James.

"We've killed their toys. They'll be coming now."

Just then, the remaining two pairs of disciples charged into the scene from opposite directions. They had been converging on the rendezvous point just as the latest explosion sounded. Abraham's smile told them everything as they ground to a halt.

In silence, the seven surviving disciples fanned out in a spread across the width of Duke of Gloucester Street.

McCracken checked his 9-mm pistols—each loaded with a fresh clip of Sal Belamo's Splats—one last time before sliding out from the cover of the Capitol.

"You knew this was coming," he said to Wareagle.

"I knew something was. *Hanbelachia*, Blainey, for both of us."

"Sorry to disappoint you, Indian, but once we draw them out, we give Obie Seven back there a ring."

"Yes, Blainey," Wareagle said in the tone he always used when the spirits had his other ear.

"Let's move, Indian."

They approached Duke of Gloucester Street the long way around, from the back of the Capitol Building. They walked side by side, steps in perfect unison. McCracken handled his pair of pistols loaded with Splats. Wareagle grasped one in his right hand, while his left held fast to a crossbow. Both had donned bulletproof vests, but neither expected them to do much good against the kind of firepower the disciples were wielding, not to mention the aim they were capable of.

"We're almost to Duke of Gloucester Street, Professor," Blaine said into the microphone concealed beneath the lapel of his jacket.

"Obie Seven's ready on your signal."

"Make sure he doesn't roll until I give the word."

"As you wish."

They reached the eastern edge of Duke of Gloucester Street and stopped dead. There, spread across the street two hundred yards before them, were the seven remaining disciples; Abraham was in the very center.

"Just like an old-fashioned gunfight, Indian."

"That's what they were hoping for, Blainey."

"Well, let's give it to them."

They started walking.

"How far before they start firing, Johnny?"

"Seventy-five yards."

"We'll walk fifty—then call for Obie Seven. He takes out four or five more of them, we clean up the rest."

Wareagle said nothing.

"Steady," ordered Abraham, just loud enough for the three disciples flanking him on either side to hear. "No one fires until I say so."

Several of the others shifted uneasily, and he sensed their impatience.

"We've got what we want," he offered as explanation. "But we've got to be sure this time."

James spoke with his eye glued to the long-range sight on his rifle. "I can hit them from here. Head shots. Neat and clean."

"Wait," Abraham said suddenly. "They wouldn't be doing this if they didn't want us to respond precisely as we are. We've . . . missed something."

"We couldn't have. There's nothing," another voice shot back.

"We should open fire now!" a third insisted.

"Not until we're sure. Not until we've all got shots."

"You know what they're doing, don't you?" Patty Hunsecker said accusingly to Sal Belamo as he struggled for a view of what was transpiring on Duke of Gloucester Street.

"Lady, I don't know—"

"You do! I know you do! They're sacrificing themselves, using themselves as bait. To draw those . . . things out, so Ainsley's monstrosity can finish them off."

Belamo tilted his head toward the area beyond. "The real monstrosities are those Frankensteins out there. And MacBalls knows the key is makin' sure they don't get outta here."

"He didn't take you with him," Patty said abruptly.

"Huh?"

"If he really thought he had a chance, he'd have taken you."

There was a brief crackle of static before the soft echo of McCracken's voice rose from Sal's walkie-talkie.

"It's show time, boys," Blaine called. "Send the big fella in."

"With pleasure," Ainsley said.

The professor's attempted activation of Obie Seven, though, brought the most feared phrase possible flashing across his monitor: NOT PROCESSING.

"Yo, Professor," Sal Belamo yelled to him, "he's not going anywhere."

"No," Ainsley said, mostly to himself, as he worked the keyboard desperately, "he isn't."

"MacBalls!" Blaine heard Sal Belamo yell into his ear. "You guys got to pull out. The big guy ain't ready for his walk."

"What the fuck's going on?"

"I can't get him on line!" Ainsley screeched. "His programming won't accept the sequence!"

"Get outta there, boss."

The flurry of fire from the disciples began just as Blaine and Johnny dived toward opposite sides of Duke of Gloucester Street.

"After them!" Abraham screamed above the booming reports from their weapons.

The disciples took off in seven separate directions, certain to catch their quarries in the spread. They could smell victory now, the taste of it as welcome as blood.

They liked the taste.

McCracken and Wareagle's only chance for survival was to separate, splinter the opposing forces, and buy themselves the time it took for Ainsley to get Obie Seven working.

Fucking thing must have blown a fuse! McCracken thought to himself, going for a little humor.

But the humor swiftly vanished as something else occurred to him. This unexpected breakdown not only forced Johnny and him into flight, it also left Patty, Sal, and Ainsley exposed back at the Capitol. If the disciples chose to concentrate their efforts toward that end, three corpses would greet Blaine . . . if he managed to stay alive and get back there. No, he told himself, the disciples would only be thinking in terms of Wareagle and himself for the moment. Their vision was sharp but narrow. With Blaine and Johnny in their sights now, they would sweep the rest of Williamsburg only after their two primary targets had been dispatched.

All the more reason to stay alive.

Blaine headed south briefly, hit Francis Street and swung west, keeping to the cover of buildings as best he could.

"You read me, Sal?"

"Still fucked at this end, boss."

"Don't break radio silence, no matter what. Let me have the first word. Talk to you soon."

"Roger."

Blaine kept moving. He knew the disciples would be circling in an attempt to enclose him. His two major priorities were to draw them away from the Capitol on Williamsburg's eastern perimeter and find safe haven for himself until Ainsley got Obie Seven back on line. He moved quickly, using the buildings for cover and darting between them only after being certain none of the disciples were about. He heard their footsteps on several occasions, but was fortunate enough to be near heavy concentrations of bushes or a hefty porch that provided concealment each time.

He ended up amid a thick nest of buildings between Colonial and Botetourt streets. Plenty of places to find cover that would make the disciples spend extra time trying to locate him. He would hold off using his pistols for as long as he could, since using them would alert them to his location, and Blaine was not in the self-sacrificing mood.

McCracken stayed to the rear of the James Anderson House, moving among the seven reconstructed forges that dominated the Blacksmith Shop. His hand strayed to one of the brick forges and came away singed. The damn coals were still hot; a quick gaze inside showed Blaine hot pokers of steel, their edges glowing reddish-orange.

He was thinking about how the occupants of Williamsburg must have truly dropped everything and run, thanks to Sal

Belamo, when a flash of gun metal appeared just ahead of the figure; one of the disciples about to round the corner.

Johnny Wareagle stuck to the area of Nicholson Street, heading northwest. He could feel the eyes of three of the *Wakinyan* searching for him and sensed none of them belonged to Abraham. This comforted him, for, above all, he knew that it was his *Hanbelachia* to face the most fearsome of these monsters. He had known this since they had seen each other briefly in Philadelphia. The confrontation might come here in Williamsburg, or it might come later, but it would come.

Johnny's communicator had stayed silent since his split from McCracken back on Duke of Gloucester Street. He knew the call would come when Ainsley got his final and most impressive droid on line. He only needed to keep himself hidden from the *Wakinyan* until then.

Johnny passed near North England Street, hugging the rear white-frame expanse of the Peyton-Randolph House. Fields and brush lay before him in this more rustic section of Williamsburg. Set in a clearing, detached and by itself, lay a fenced-in windmill. The sailcloth wheel spun quickly in the stiff breeze. Johnny remembered how it had helped grind the corn when he was young and still living on the reservation. It looked and smelled of home, and he took this as a sign from the spirits.

Crouching low, he made a quick dash for the steep steps leading into the building the wheel was attached to. The structure supporting the windmill was propped up on a base of logs, the reconstruction perfect in all respects. Wareagle thought he might find refuge inside.

He felt the presence just as he passed through the entrance, felt it in time to dive for the floor just as the muzzle flashes erupted and bullets split the air above him.

The disciple's angle of approach had prevented him from firing when McCracken lunged. He managed to squeeze the trigger, but Blaine had already locked a hand on the stock and shoved the M16 away. Equal to the task, the disciple had responded by shoving Blaine in the direction his momentum had already taken him, launching out with a kick. McCracken took the impact in his bent knee and felt it buckle. The leg went numb and rubbery, but he kept himself from falling. He'd learned his lesson from facing another disciple down in Rio. He could not let things be drawn out, especially not with reinforcements as close as a scream away.

Still holding tight to the rifle, McCracken faked falling. The disciple released his right hand from the grip and formed it into a fist; he would try for a killing strike to Blaine's throat or face. McCracken was ready. He avoided the blow with a deft twist and lowering of his head. In the same motion he tore the rifle from the disciple's remaining hand and heard it smack into the brick forge behind him. Blaine whipped one of the pistols from his belt, only to have the disciple kick it into the air, where it landed in a nest of hot coals.

The disciple reached into one of the forges for a red-hot poker, which was glowing at the tip. McCracken probed desperately behind him and found its twin, burning his hand in the process.

The disciple came in first with an overhead blow. Blaine deflected it and tried to use his poker with a backlash motion. The disciple simply ducked and brought his weapon hard into Blaine's ribs in roundhouse fashion. McCracken lost his breath in a throaty gasp. The blow had stunned him, but he recovered his senses in time to see the disciple lunging at him, aiming the poker's glowing tip straight for him. McCracken turned at the last instant, knocking the blow aside and ramming his own poker into the side of the disciple's face.

Now it was his opponent who gasped. A hiss sounded as flesh burned and blackened and a bulging welt swelled across the disciple's right cheek and jaw. But the disciple came back at him as if he hadn't felt anything. A damaging blow was headed for Blaine's collarbone, but he deflected it enough to turn the impact into a mere graze. He tried to retaliate, but the disciple had launched a furious flurry of blows with both the poker and his free hand. McCracken barely managed to ward him off as he was forced backward against a forge that was still burning with a white-hot coal fire. The poker slid from his hand, his injured leg giving way as he stooped to retrieve it.

Seeing the opening, the disciple reared back and launched a savage overhead strike with the poker. At the last moment,

McCracken threw up both hands in an X-block that caught his opponent's wrist between his forearms. The poker flirted with the top of his skull and, as the disciple drew it overhead once more, Blaine rammed a foot up into his groin.

The disciple's eyes bulged. As he doubled over, Blaine grabbed him by the bulk of his Kevlar vest and brought him forward, facefirst, toward the white-hot flames. Blaine felt his own hands paying part of the price as he jammed the disciple's face and chest against the sizzling coals. McCracken heard the *sssssssssss* and was assaulted by the sickening aroma of frying flesh and hair. He waited until it had all but subsided before releasing the pressure on the twitching frame. He regained his feet and dashed away, the scent still fresh in his nostrils.

Wareagle kicked out at blinding speed toward the source of the muzzle flashes. It was like a cartwheel—with his hands down, his legs spun around like a propeller. His feet struck the rifle square in the stock and separated it from the *Wakinyan's* hands. The *Wakinyan* whipped out a pistol, but as Johnny lunged back to his feet he locked his hand on the wrist holding the gun before it could fire. The disciple was at least eight inches shorter than Johnny, but he looked up into the Indian's eyes and smiled at him. The test of strength was going his way. The gun was coming back up almost in line with Johnny's face, the disciple's finger still on the trigger. Their free arms had locked, and they were grappling with each other like wrestlers.

The *Wakinyan* smiled again. He was winning.

Because Johnny wanted him to.

The wind-driven grinding stones on the *Wakinyan's* right side squeezed against each other like a huge mouthful of chomping teeth. The process was continuous: lower, grind, separate, rise . . . lower, grind, separate, rise . . .

Johnny knew the disciple would wait until his shot was sure, wait until Johnny had a long moment to contemplate his own death. Wareagle let that moment start with his eyes staring down the pistol's bore for a microsecond. Then he jerked the disciple's gun hand across his body, back and to the side. He timed the move for the exact moment the stones were separated enough to allow for the hand and arm to pass between them, in the instant before they began to lower again.

Flesh tore, and Wareagle's ears were burned by the sound of bones being ground to pulp. The *Wakinyan's* eyes bulged in agony. Wareagle's free hand clamped down over his mouth to muffle his screams, then drew the head toward him before jamming it backward against the grinding mechanism.

The skull shattered with a *pop!* Blood and brains splattered the walls. The *Wakinyan's* eyes locked unseeingly with Johnny's. Blood streamed from his nostrils. Wareagle left him there and headed back for the door.

"What the fuck, Professor?" Sal Belamo shouted back into the truck from his post near Obie Seven.

"I'm trying! I'm trying!"

"Ain't good enough, chief."

Patty Hunsecker emerged from the truck with machine gun in hand. "We've got to go out there, Sal. We've got to help them."

"What you gotta do is stay here. Like you were told."

"Screw what I was told!"

She made a motion to leave on her own, and Belamo restrained her. "MacBalls wants you safe, and that's the way you're gonna stay," he said quite calmly.

"You read me, Sal?" jabbered Belamo's communicator almost on cue.

"Got ya, boss."

"Any luck?"

"Professor says he's almost got it licked."

"Almost ain't good enough. Case you didn't notice, we got a situation here."

"Just stay out of sight a little longer, boss."

"No can do, Sal. No can do at all."

McCracken ended up back in the center of Duke of Gloucester Street, pursuit having forced him that way. He whipped his remaining pistol out just as Johnny Wareagle emerged between a pair of buildings directly in front of him, crossbow in hand. They had barely met each other's gaze when the remaining disciples appeared, three from the west end of the street led by Abraham and two others from the east end, effectively enclosing them.

"No more running, Indian."

"Indeed, Blainey."

A hundred and fifty yards separated them from the disciples at either end of the street. The Splats in Blaine's pistol were effective from only fifty yards and less, giving the disciples even more of an advantage.

"Good idea to bring the crossbow, Johnny."

"I'll take west, Blainey."

"East sounds fine to me."

As he spoke the disciples began to move forward.

"We've got to do *something*!" Patty yelled at Sal Belamo as he sprinted back for the truck.

"Just what I had in my mind, lady."

While Professor Ainsley continued working feverishly on his keyboard, Belamo grabbed an automatic chambering shotgun and rushed back for the front of the Capitol Building.

Patty blocked his path. "You stopped me from leaving, and now I'm stopping you! You go out there and you'll get killed. We'll *all* get killed! You've got to get that damn thing working!"

"Right," Sal snapped as he raised the butt of his shotgun in front of Obie Seven's chest, "I'll just give him a smack and the reception will turn crystal clear."

In frustration Belamo did just that and, suddenly, lights flashed everywhere inside of Obie Seven's oblong head. Its cylindrical hand openings returned to their ready position, 7.62-mm miniguns locked and loaded. Its tread began to roll through the arches of the Capitol toward Duke of Gloucester Street.

"Well, I'll be damned," muttered Sal.

Johnny tightened his grip on the crossbow as the *Wakinyan* slid closer. It was suspended near his midsection, held in both hands so he could load it with a fresh arrow; less than two seconds after firing. But that wasn't good enough, Blaine knew. He had to figure out a way to use the Splats to at least slow them down.

A hundred and twenty-five yards . . .

Blaine suddenly thought about the many buildings the disciples had to pass between on their way to the kill. The colonial structures were constructed of heavy wood and brick with lots of windows dotting their exteriors.

Lots of glass.

Fire an exploding bullet into a few and that glass might, *might*, shatter into deadly flying projectiles. It would buy Johnny some time for his crossbow, if nothing else. But none of that would work until the disciples were dangerously close.

He felt Johnny's hand coming for him before the blow lashed hard against his side. Impact from the big Indian's shove pitched him airborne off the street, behind the cover of a huge chestnut tree.

"Johnny!"

His scream reached Wareagle as his first arrow shot outward from his bow, another following in its place as the bullets punched into the big Indian and drove him backward. He saw blood leap out as Wareagle went down.

"Johnny!"

McCracken lunged out from behind the tree and threw his body over Johnny's. He grabbed the Indian's pistol from his belt and fired it, along with his own, at the buildings as planned. But the Splats's limited range merely created a path of debris and destruction through which the disciples continued to converge on them. Blaine had grasped Johnny's crossbow when they opened fire on him from Abraham's side of Duke of Gloucester Street. A trio of hits into his Kevlar chest protector blew him backward, and he groped desperately for one of the pistols again.

So this is how it ends.

He remembered forming that thought, when his eyes locked on the most wonderful sight ever. Rolling fast down Duke of Gloucester Street, from the area of the Capitol, came Obie Seven. Massive and ominous, the last of Professor Ainsley's droids tore forward toward the disciples, approaching from the east. They swung, and one of them fired a grenade that exploded just in front of the droid, but Obie Seven rotated his torso slightly and kept on coming.

If the sight of him had been the greatest ever, then the sound that came next rivaled it. A metallic clanging burned through Blaine's ears as the dual miniguns blasted an incessant hail of fire toward the two disciples closest to him. Obie Seven might have appeared to be the most advanced of the OBD series, but in essence he was the most simple. In design he was powered by a tanklike tread. His torso could spin in a full 360-degree turn on top of a four-and-a-half-foot-high square base. His oblong head contained his visual sensors, which were programmed to find—and fire—at motion.

Any motion.

Blaine saw his dual cannons fix on the first pair of disciples and literally tear them apart with targeted fire. Obie Seven never even stopped through it all, just rolled right past their ravaged bodies as a hail of bullets from the west end of the street greeted him. When even a pair of direct grenade strikes didn't slow him in the least, Abraham and the two other remaining disciples abandoned the battle and attempted to flee. Obie Seven traced their motions and rotated his arm extremities accordingly. The resulting paths of gunfire stitched lines of total destruction through colonial Williamsburg as Seven sought out his prey. Windows exploded. Huge segments of structures blew apart and showered into the air. A few of the smaller buildings collapsed under the onslaught. Some of the larger ones had been peppered with enough gunfire to look as if they had been through the Civil War for real this time.

Blaine had to cover his ears from the clamor when the droid moved between Johnny and him, safe in the knowledge that the medallion flopping near his chest would keep the robot from firing on them. McCracken saw one disciple literally blown to pieces by the robot's fire and a second perish when its fire obliterated a small stand he had taken refuge behind. In all, Obie Seven's fire raged for just over a minute. That period saw him expend sixteen hundred rounds of ammunition, which filled the air with the smell of sulphur and cordite. Smoke rose from the debris created in the paths the disciples had used trying to escape. There was nothing still standing in that grid that did not show the effects of the droid's powerful bullets.

"Johnny," Blaine muttered, moving his way. "Johnny . . ."

He reached him expecting the worst. What greeted him was the slightest of smiles from the Indian.

"It seems we have found an able partner at last, Blainey."

"You're alive! You son of a bitch, you're alive! Why the fuck didn't you say something?"

Wareagle raised himself gingerly to a sitting position. The front of his Kevlar vest showed a dozen splotches where hits had been recorded. The blood had sprouted from a flesh wound just above his collarbone. Blaine knew Johnny wouldn't bother to feel it until he was ready.

"I didn't come around until our friend made his appearance. You wouldn't have heard me at that point."

"I'll say."

With that Obie Seven's torso suddenly whirled. Its empty miniguns traced a diagonal path across to the northwest of Williamsburg and the Governor's Palace. A continuous beeping sound was its way of pleading for more ammunition.

"Abraham," Johnny said.

"No way, Indian No way."

"He's out there, Blainey."

"He couldn't have survived all that. No one could."

"I feel him," Wareagle insisted, trying unsuccessfully to get up.

"Take it easy, Johnny," Blaine said. "This one's on me."

He palmed one of the pistols loaded with Splats and rushed off to the northwest.

The Governor's Palace was a stately baked red brick building enclosed by the most elaborate landscaping Williamsburg had to offer. McCracken approached warily. Mazelike in construction, the exterior offered an infinite number of hiding places. But Blaine knew Abraham would be after escape, not concealment, and tuned his thoughts accordingly. The disciple would not have entered the building itself because it would give Blaine the advantage of a confined space to work in. A faint hope that Johnny was wrong, that Abraham had perished with the others, flickered inside McCracken. Only Johnny wouldn't—*couldn't*—be wrong about something like that. If he felt Abraham was still alive, then Abraham was still alive.

Blaine passed through the tall iron gate and looked quickly around the grounds. It was a sound, though, that grabbed his attention, from somewhere on the right. Familiar somehow, but what?

The sound came again, a deep chortling.

It was a horse, a goddamn horse!

McCracken bolted for the stables on the eastern side of the grounds, sure now of how Abraham intended to make his escape. Blaine had reached the closed double doors out of breath and was raising his pistol when the doors blew outward. A team of horses, latched to a carriage Abraham rode from a standing position, charged straight for him. The pounding hooves made the ground tremble. Blaine tried to keep his balance to steady his shot, but one of the horses' hindquarters slammed into him, knocking him senseless. The pistol went flying. Abraham snapped the reins and tore off across the fields.

By the time Blaine recovered both his pistol and his bearings, the final disciple had passed out of range on Lafayette Street, en route to the main roads away from Williamsburg.

Halfway back to Duke of Gloucester Street, McCracken met up with Sal Belamo and Johnny Wareagle. Patty Hunsecker was pushing Professor Ainsley's wheelchair in an attempt to keep up. Wareagle was walking gingerly, a makeshift bandage already tied around his bleeding shoulder wound. His eyes asked the question for him. Blaine's answered.

"Can you believe what Obie Seven did?" Ainsley said after Patty and he had caught up to them. "Can you believe it? Amazing! Truly amazing!"

"He missed one, Professor."

The professor looked disappointed. "Oh."

"I missed him, too."

"We will find him, Blainey," Wareagle said.

"For sure, Indian. But it won't be here. Time to haul ass."

"Where to, boss?" Belamo asked.

"Tell you once we're on our way."

CHAPTER 34

VIRGINIA Maxwell's summer home in Hampton Roads, Virginia, was a sprawling estate that had been in the family for generations, long before the town had become a popular spot for vacationers. The guards who had surrounded the area since late in the afternoon did so openly, their show of force obvious. Gossip would result, though not a great deal. Plenty of important Washington types kept homes in the area. Security guards, both uniformed and otherwise, were not an unusual sight.

By the time darkness fell, there were twenty patrolling the three-acre grounds. Virginia Maxwell spent the evening alone, and allowed herself a pair of brandies in anticipation of retiring early. Guards had been stationed both inside and outside her bedroom all evening, and Maxwell felt safe in locking the door behind her. Two guards would spend the night in chairs by her door, a shout away. Relaxed in her bedclothes, she sat down in her favorite chair to read for a bit.

The hand closed over her mouth as she opened to her place in the book.

"Hello, Maxie."

The book fell to the rug. At first Virginia Maxwell's bulging eyes swam wildly, then they were drawn to the cold stare of Blaine McCracken.

"You would do well to keep quiet. Screaming won't end pleasantly for either of us."

McCracken took his hand away. Virginia Maxwell did not scream.

"How?" she managed.

"Did I get in or remain undetected? Neither was all that difficult. You really should hire better people next time. I've been in this room for hours."

McCracken came around to the front of the chair and loomed over her.

"It's over, Maxie."

"And that's why you're here?"

"Not quite. I meant it's over for you. I've still got some unfinished business. You heard about Williamsburg."

"Some. Enough."

"I hoped to use you as bait to lure the disciples there. Neat trick with the double. Almost worked. But you wanted me so badly, your legion walked right into the trap and now they're finished. Your project is finished."

"Then you're here to kill me."

Blaine shook his head. "Not my style."

She regarded him questioningly.

"Abraham got away, Maxie. I want him, and I want you to deliver."

"Abraham's . . . alive?" Her surprise looked genuine.

"The sole survivor."

So there was still a slight ray of hope for the operation. Virginia Maxwell's eyes darted briefly to the door. If she screamed now, what chance was there the guards could burst in and kill McCracken before he killed her? None at all, reason told her and, more than that, without the rest of the disciples the project could not go forward. Another time, perhaps, but not now, not effectively.

"You want me to *help* you?" she asked incredulously.

"We can help each other."

"How?"

"It's all finished. You know that as well as I do. Takahashi gave me the list. I know the identities of you and the other Children of the Black Rain. I know about your plan to kill the president and your operation to destroy those nuclear power plants. Finally, without the disciples, I know the means to accomplish all this has been lost."

"And how does that help me?"

"I'm going after the Children, Maxie, and I'll find them no matter where they run. You know I will."

"There's still Abraham to consider."

"My point exactly. You're going to tell me where I can find him—and also the bunker where the Children have gone."

"And in return . . ."

"I'll let you live."

"If I run away and disappear, of course."

"Not at all. Just quit as director of the Gap. You can keep your money and your houses."

"How benevolent."

"I try."

"I could scream for the guards now," Virginia Maxwell snarled. "They'd kill you."

"No, they wouldn't, and then you'd die for nothing. Let's talk, Maxie. It's the best thing. Really."

"And, of course, I trust you because you would never go back on your word."

"You're right; I wouldn't."

"Bastard!"

"You drew me into this. You've got no one to blame but yourself."

She sighed. "What do you want?"

"For starters, where's Abraham?"

"Listen to me, McCracken. If he hasn't called in, it can only mean he's going on with his part in the operation. He's like a computer following its programming. You can't stop him. No one can."

"Try me."

"He had two major roles in the operation, a second added after you killed one of the disciples in Rio— That was sabotaging one of the power plants: Pennsylvania Yankee."

"A weather system's distance from New York City, Boston, the whole upper East Coast . . ."

"Precisely. But his primary role was to assassinate the president."

"Do you know how?"

"Only where and when. It's tomorrow, as the presidential motorcade makes its way through Boston. But I can deal with that. A few well-placed phone calls and the president doesn't leave Washington.''

"Which means we don't get a shot at Abraham, risk him disappearing underground. No, Maxie. You'll have to convince 1600 Pennsylvania Avenue to go through with at least the facade of the motorcade. Leave the chief out of the limo, but make sure the limo rolls on schedule. Tell them it's our only chance to catch a determined assassin. That's language they can relate to.''

"Maybe.''

McCracken nodded. "Okay, so that leaves us with the Pennsylvania Yankee Nuclear Power Plant. I catch him there, and he doesn't even make it to Boston.''

"He's probably already *been* to the plant,'' Virginia Maxwell said. "He's had twelve hours since Williamsburg. Plenty of time.''

"And the timetable?''

"Everything was set to key off the assassination. Anytime after tomorrow morning and evening. It was left to the disciples' discretion.''

Blaine looked at her very closely. "And now you've cost the operation these disciples. It doesn't take a genius to figure out that their presence at Gap headquarters was your doing. You knew they made for the only chance you'd have against the Indian and me so you took it. Now I'd say you're an outcast in your own right. Otherwise, you would have gone to the bunker with the others.''

Virginia Maxwell's first response was the slightest of smiles. Then she said, "A year from now we could still have an army of disciples in place. The power plant operation could be reactivated.''

"Toward what end?''

"Toward creating chaos—out of which a new order will be born. We would preside over that order, my dear. The nation would be ours to do with as we please.''

"What's left of it, you mean.''

"All the better. We were Children born out of the worst chaos man has ever wrought. We were born to thrive in chaos, to want to make it happen simply because the remnants would belong to us.''

"A nuclear-ravaged wasteland."

"But a land, all the same. *Our* land. A different America, one that would prosper on different terms. You have the list. You know the positions we have reached—positions from which centralized power can be wielded. The areas were hand-picked for us."

"Too bad you can't be a part of it anymore, Maxie. You know that. Your only hope to be *anything* is to help me. I'll hunt them down with or without your help. Without means your name stays on the list. What'll it be?"

"Damn you, McCracken!"

"Where's the bunker, Maxie? Where can I find the rest of the Children?"

"Got it, Indian," Blaine reported. He was back in the passenger seat of the car Wareagle had parked a quarter of a mile from Virginia Maxwell's house. "Old Maxie decided to play ball."

"Her route was chosen long ago, as ours was."

"Well, thanks to that route, she's going to alert the president for us. The motorcade will be staged to draw Abraham out, but the Secret Service will be ready to drop a net on him as soon as he shows."

"I don't think so, Blainey."

"Let it go, Indian. We've got other—"

McCracken's words were cut off by the explosion that shattered the night. The sudden brightness of the fireball forced him to shield his eyes even from a quarter of a mile away as the Hampton Roads home of Virginia Maxwell gave itself up to the flames.

"Abraham," he said.

"A step ahead of us, Blainey. Abraham got to her. Abraham knew."

"Which means he could have set the explosives for earlier, but he didn't. He let Maxie talk to me. He wanted her to."

"He wants to beat us."

"Because of Williamsburg?"

"And something more. He wanted me to know where to find him. He wishes to face me."

McCracken realized Johnny didn't sound sorry. He looked

back at the flames. "No help from the Secret Service now, Indian."

"Just him and me."

"Vision quest?"

"At last, Blainey."

"And that's where my father is?" Patty asked as the four of them gathered around the map placed over the coffee table. The area of the Utah Salt Flats was highlighted in red, a small *x* denoting the bunker's position.

"According to Virginia Maxwell, yes," Blaine confirmed.

"And what are you going to do? . . . Oh, go on with your planning. I didn't mean to stop you."

McCracken looked at Sal Belamo. "How many men did you say you can get?"

"A dozen I can trust. Another six I can kill if they fuck up."

"You'll need a plane to get there."

"What are you going to do?" Patty angrily asked again. "My father's in there! Do you hear me? *My father!*"

Blaine heard, and wished he hadn't. He should have stuck with his instincts and not included Patty in this part of the plan. She had a stake in this, though. She deserved to know, and she deserved an opportunity to make her own decision.

"He's one of them, Patty. There's nothing I can do."

"Yes, there is. Let me come with Sal. Let me talk to him."

"You'd never get that far."

"You don't know that."

"I do, Patty."

Patty Hunsecker backed away, as if repulsed. "Listen to you. Listen to *all* of you. It's over. You've won. These people don't have to die."

Blaine moved next to her, easing her further away from the table. "I warned you about what letting yourself become a part of this meant. Welcome to my world. It's not much, but I call it home."

"You're not a murderer. I know you're not."

"That depends on your perspective. I wasn't a murderer when I helped save your life at the circus in Rio, and Sal wasn't a murderer when he saved the lives of you and your brothers ten days ago.''

Patty realized Johnny Wareagle had crept up silent as a cat behind her. ''Each deed demands its own definition,'' the Indian said. ''We become prisoners of those definitions, each as unique as the person who seeks it.''

''What the two of you are saying is that I won't sanction what you want to do, even if it's necessary, because my family's involved. I won't deny that. I started all this to find out what happened to my father, and I'm not about to give up now that I've found out where he is!''

''He gave up on you first, kid.''

She shook her head. ''Shit, McCracken! Stop trying to make everything sound so simple! Things just don't work that way. There are repercussions, accounts to be settled.''

''Yes, the proverbial moral balance sheet. I've been there and back a hundred times, Hunsecker, and the picture's always the same. There is no right or wrong, only cloudy levels of both. Through the muck, though, lines have to be drawn somewhere. Your father is part of something that meant to destroy much of the United States. We haven't won as long as the Children are still out there—as long as *he's* still out there.''

''So you kill him.''

''We do what we have to.''

''Say it!''

''Oh, I've got no problem with killing, Patty, not insofar as it means millions of lives are going to be saved.''

Patty Hunsecker wouldn't back off. ''You once told me one innocent life was as important to you as a million. You were talking about a young boy who'd been kidnapped, remember?''

''Your father isn't innocent. Neither are the rest of the Children. I'm sorry.''

''So am I,'' Patty shouted, and stormed out of the motel room.

Johnny Wareagle touched Blaine's shoulder. ''You know where she will go if we don't stop her, Blainey.''

''She's got that much coming to her, Indian—if that's what she wants.''

"Still, she is entering the crossfire, where bullets kill without aim or discretion."

"She knows."

"Does she?"

A thinly veiled smile crossed Blaine's lips. "It's what she has to do. That's all."

Sal Belamo cleared his throat. "And what I got to do is round up my team and head West. That rich bitch'll probably beat me there, at this rate."

"That's my hope, Sal."

McCracken reached the Pennsylvania Yankee Nuclear Power Plant at 10:00 the next morning. Maxie's death confirmed that Abraham remained committed to fulfilling his role in the operation. A roundabout route to reach the site was thus mandated, and Blaine squeezed from it all the time he could.

"Look," the guard at the front gate repeated, "I can't let you in unless your name's on this list." He tapped his clipboard. "And it ain't."

"Call the shift supervisor."

"Need a pretty good reason to do that."

"How's this?" Blaine asked the guard, pressing the pistol against his temple.

Every guard on duty at Pennsylvania Yankee had Mc-Cracken in their gun sights as Blaine and his hostage moved for the front of the complex. The main entrance was built in the shadow of the massive white tower that housed the nuclear reactor itself. He kept the steel barrel hard enough against the guard's head to push the blood from the area, no doubt left as to the sincerity of his intentions. A man wearing a white shirt and tie met him on the front steps, his hands raised in the air.

"Let's try and stay calm, shall we?" he said to Blaine.

"I've never been calmer. Who are you?"

"Jack Tunnel."

"Supervisor?"

"Plant manager. Let that man go. We'll talk. I promise."

"I'm not here to talk, Mr. Tunnel."

"Sir, you don't realize what you're doing. The penalty for unlawful entry into a nuclear facility qualifies—"

"Fuck penalties, Mr. Tunnel. An hour from now you're not going to give a good goddamn about penalties unless you listen to me."

"Let the man go. Then I'll listen."

McCracken drew his hostage closer and drew back the pistol's hammer. "You'll listen now, you son of a bitch. Your plant's been sabotaged. Do you hear me? We've got maybe an hour to find out how and where or there's gonna be one major hole in the ground come dinner."

"You're a *terrorist*? Is that what this is about?"

"Not me and not terrorism. Something much worse, Mr. Manager, and we've got no time to waste talking about it."

Jack Tunnel's eyes met McCracken's and his expression changed. "Who *are* you?"

"Who I am doesn't matter. You want to arrest me—fine. You want to call the FBI—fine. Just do it after you've shut down your reactors to check for explosives, to check for anything out of the ordinary."

"Our security precautions make what you're suggesting impossible."

"I got through, didn't I?"

"Not to the central core. You could shoot us all and still not get there."

"But somebody else did late yesterday. Somebody no one here had reason to suspect." The words came with his thoughts, as Blaine put it all together. "A surprise inspection by the NRC or Atomic Energy Commission. Noteworthy only for the fact that only a single man came out. Big. Straw-colored hair and deep blue eyes," Blaine finished.

"Hey, chief," said another shirt-and-tie man to Tunnel softly, "a guy from the AEC did show up around six. . . ."

"How did you know?" Tunnel asked McCracken.

"Because it's the way I would have done it."

"And what else would you have done?"

Before Blaine could answer, the repetitive beep of a shrill alarm buzzed in their ears.

"All personnel to safe areas!" blared a mechanical, prerecorded voice. *"All personnel to safe areas! We have a Code Red. Repeat: We have a Code Red."*

"Oh my God," Tunnel muttered.

"The control room, Tunnel!" McCracken shouted over the alarm. "Now!"

CHAPTER 35

AIR FORCE ONE had come in on schedule to Logan Airport, and Arnold Triesman was counting his blessings. All things considered, the time Top Guy was in the air was the time he felt the most helpless. Couldn't save Mr. Pres from a blown engine, a midair collision, or a missile. Nope, not even the Secret Service could do a damn thing until he was ground locked, which was when Triesman felt at least some measure of control.

Today's agenda was simple, routine all the way. Top Guy lands at Boston's Logan Airport, and then from the Callahan Tunnel takes the scenic route down Boylston Street to give as many locals as possible a gander en route to the Ritz Carlton Hotel for a luncheon with the governors from all the New England states. Airport time included, he'd be outside for no more than forty seconds and that was the name of the game. Rule number one: Ninety-nine point nine percent of all problems arose while Top Guy was *outside*. In a containable area or the safety of his rocketproof limo, no one was bothering.

Of course, that didn't mean they wouldn't try someday, and Triesman had a full complement of agents and police personnel scattered along the route—two hundred in all—as insurance. The agents didn't bother camouflaging themselves. Indeed, they made sure everyone about could see their well-known earpieces just to create a presence. A presence made for the best prevention of all. Rule number two.

Triesman waited outside the Ritz Carlton and drank in the routine of it all. A trio of police helicopters buzzed the sky in a continuous sweep, the rooftop perimeter clear as could be. Triesman breathed easy. The mundane made for his lifeblood. The extraordinary he savored not at all.

Which was why the sudden squawk of his walkie-talkie shook him alert, making him fumble it as he raised it to his lips.

"Alley Cat, this is Stray Seven!" one of his field men called over the emergency channel.

"Come in, Stray Seven."

"Alley Cat, you're not going to believe this, but I think I saw him *again*."

"Saw *who* again, Stray Seven?"

"The Indian, Alley Cat. The same damn giant Indian from Philadelphia."

"Oh, fuck," was all Arnold Triesman could say.

McCracken tossed his hostage aside on the way to the control room, and a number of guards converged on him immediately.

"Leave him alone!" Tunnel ordered. "He's on our side."

Inside the control center, which filled an oblong room at least fifteen hundred square feet, everything was chaos. Red lights flashed in so many places that a dull haze seemed painted over the white fluorescents.

"What's going on?" Tunnel demanded of a man behind a central console who was feverishly pushing buttons.

"We lost the main pump to the cooling system."

"What do you mean lost?"

"Valve blew. We're losing a hundred gallons of flow a second."

"A hundred gallons? How the fuck did we end up at Code Red so soon?"

The man at the console swallowed hard. "Because it's been spilling for hours, even though all warning systems are running green."

"Sabotage," Jack Tunnel muttered, looking at McCracken. "Okay, seal the pipe and run a bypass."

"I can't, sir. The whole circuit board in the shaft must be down. Nothing's responding."

"Twenty minutes to critical stage," blared the mechanical voice.

"What's that mean?" Blaine asked Tunnel.

"It's like this, friend. The secondary loop sends water to the primary—to cool the core and prevent the whole mess from going critical. Take away the cooling and the core superheats its way down until it hits ground water, which then blasts upward as a steam cloud. With the early warning system malfunctioning, we're coming up on that now."

"Meltdown," Blaine concluded.

"The China Syndrome, to be precise." Tunnel turned back to the console operator. "Okay, trigger the emergency core coolant and take us off line. Frank," he called behind him, "order immediate evac of all nonessential personnel, and I do mean everyone."

"Roger," Frank said as he rushed away.

"Nineteen minutes to critical stage. . . . "

"Sir," blared the console operator, "emergency coolant release not responding!"

Jack Tunnel leaned over the monitor board in disbelief. He swung back to McCracken with sweat pouring down his face.

"What the hell's going on here?"

"You know better than I do."

"But you knew before I did. What else? Tell me what else!"

"I don't know. The saboteur could have anticipated every one of your possible responses and planned accordingly."

"Oh, yeah? We'll just see about that. . . . " Tunnel grabbed a headset and pressed it to his ear and mouth. "Come in, Purdy."

Yankee's chief engineer came on the line, the sounds of men charging from the scene providing backdrop for his words.

"Read you, Jack."

"We're flat busted on this end. We been fucked and good. Valve circuits are down. Gonna have to run a bypass manually."

"Oh, shit."

"Got any volunteers?"

"Just one asshole down here stupid enough to even consider the job. I'm going remote. Give me forty seconds—then talk to me about what's gotta be done."

All of the forty seconds passed before the chief engineer's voice came back over Tunnel's headset. "Okay, Jack."

Tunnel consulted the computer screen again. "It's Valve 1275 that's been blown. You gotta close it down and open 1374 in its place."

"I'm almost suited up. Sounds simple enough."

"Seventeen minutes to critical stage. . . . "

"It ain't," Tunnel said, his eyes on McCracken.

Thirty seconds elapsed before Purdy spoke again. His voice came into the control room over the main speaker now, accentuated by a slight echo.

"Okay, Jack. I'm opening Hatch 8B of the secondary loop. Got three other volunteers with me to provide backup if I need it. I'm leaving them up top for the time being. . . . Okay, I'm on the ladder and descending. I can see the water spewing from way up here. It's already getting god-awful hot. Jesus Christ, I'm scared."

"You're doing fine, Purdy."

"Okay, I'm down fifteen rungs, another twenty to the catwalk above your blown valve. Piece of—"

A roaring blast cut off the rest of his words.

"Purdy!" Jack Tunnel yelled.

"Ahhhhhhhhhhhhhhhhh!"

The chief engineer's scream was all Tunnel heard.

"What the hell's happening down there? That sounded like a gun—"

"The chief was shot!" replied one of Purdy's assistants. "Somebody down there shot the chief!"

"Jesus Christ! Can you see who did it?"

"Negative, but we will. Descending now."

"Stay where you are, goddammit!"

"The chief may still be alive. We're going down. Son of a bitch can't get all three of us before we reach those valves."

"Fifteen minutes to critical stage. . . . "

"Ten rungs covered," the chief engineer's assistant reported.

And then Blaine cursed himself for not seeing it from the start. "Tunnel, pull them back! Get them the hell out of there!"

Tunnel didn't bother to question McCracken's order. "Hold your position! Do you hear me? Stay where you are. That's a goddamn order! Hold up and climb back the hell out of there!"

"Fifteen rungs," the climber closest to the bottom called out.

A series of blasts sounded this time, rapid thumps sifting through the hiss of static. Screams and shouts followed, then a drawn-out wail.

"Benny's hit!"

"He's going down. Jesus Christ! *I'm hit!* Oh, god, I'm hit!"

"Get the hell out of there! Can anybody still hear me? *Get the hell out of there!*"

"This is Burt, Mr. Tunnel," came a panicked voice trying desperately to compose itself. "Lost Benny, lost Sims. I'm hit in the leg. Climbing back up now."

"Did you see anyone? Did you see who was doing the shooting?"

The only reply came from McCracken. "No one's down there, Mr. Tunnel."

"What the hell are you saying?"

"Our saboteur rigged a motion sensor to the trigger of an automatic weapon."

"Christ! *Who* did all this?"

"Thirteen minutes to critical stage. . . . "

"Bypass that blown valve and we can still avert meltdown, though, right?"

"Sure, if there was a way to reach it in time."

"Any other approach we can use?"

"Nothing direct, and direct's all we've got time for."

"Then that's the way it'll have to be."

"I'm fresh out of volunteers, in case you didn't notice."

Blaine shook his head. "No, you're not."

The skeletal steel superstructure of the unfinished skyscraper made for perfect cover for Abraham. The high steelworkers normally manning its top floors, which were five hundred feet off the ground, were down on the sidewalk waiting for the presidential motorcade to pass along Boylston Street. This gave him freedom of movement in an area the sweep of helicopter surveillance would never think to investigate. The girders were all he had to move on, but they were enough, the shell providing his camouflage.

Abraham had chosen this viewpoint for effect more than anything. His sole weapon was the black transistorized detonator in his pocket. He had known from the outset that routine clearing of the streets would make a car bomb unfeasible. He also knew that blasting upward from the sewers below was dramatic but unreliable. Options eliminated, though, are often options gained, and out of what remained, he found the best one of all.

The yellow line painted down the center of the street, the one marking the lanes, was too good to be true, in his estimation. He had retrieved the C-12 plastic explosives, twenty times more potent than the common C-4, from the drop point and melted them down into a liquid form. Then, while the city slept the previous night, dressed in the garb of a public works official, he had gone over a twenty yard section of the line. Affixing the six ultrathin detonators, disguised in the same colored paint, into position was the only part Abraham had hurried through. He did not even have to inspect his handiwork to know it was perfect. Upon detonation, the *plastique* would reduce the road within its sphere to rubble, in the process blowing apart anyone and anything riding above. Even the president's tank of a car would be reduced to shrapnel.

That car would be approaching any minute now.

Abraham had not slept in a very long time now. Since his rebirth, time had held a different meaning for him. It passed not in terms of days and hours, but in tasks and accomplishments. Behind him was the visit to the nuclear plant yesterday. Ahead of him was the murder of the president. Beyond that there was nothing.

He had gone to Pennsylvania Yankee in a disguise prepared for another disciple long before. He had descended into the bowels of the reactor's secondary loop on a surprise inspection, watched only cursorily from the hatch above. He had reached the valve in question and affixed C-4 plastic explosive fully confident it would not be removed, even if discovered. Then he tacked on a sign: DO NOT REMOVE! ATOMIC ENERGY COMMISSION.

Anybody who got close enough to see the charge would read that sign. From there, he quickly located the main conduit that linked the computers to the thousands of valves and controls in the labyrinth of multicolored pipes. He placed another, smaller charge across it to cut off computer control as well as the early warning system. The valve charge would blow, and it would be well over an hour before anyone knew; by then the plant would be at the critical stage.

If that wasn't enough, Abraham had taken precautions against manual interference as well. Besides the explosive charges, his tool satchel had held a 9-mm submachine gun complete with extended sixty-shot clip. Rigging it to fire upward—in the direction of the nearest access ladder—was no problem at all. Neither was affixing a motion sensor to its trigger mechanism. The device was no bigger than a small tape recorder and was nothing more than a sophisticated version of the one used on home security alarms. The final fail-safe element of his plan: Abraham had left the power plant confident in the knowledge that it would blow at the very instant he detonated the explosives beneath the president's car.

His outfit, typical of a high steelworker, had helped him gain access to one of the elevators when no one had been paying much attention. He crouched now on a horizontal steel support beam halfway to the front of the structure, in clear view of the road below. He found this setting to be slightly ironic in that he had a lot in common with the steel shell. After all, that was what his entire existence had been reduced to in the Amazon. All the covering conscience and sensibility had been stripped away. What remained had been hardened into tungsten and rendered impenetrable.

Abraham rose to his feet and pulled off his helmet. He had not brought binoculars along, but he could see the motorcade making its way through the downtown Boston streets well off in the distance. He fingered the detonator through the fabric of his pocket and counted the minutes before the time would come to use it.

* * *

Money might not be everything, Patty Hunsecker reckoned, but it sure helped. It was money that had allowed her to hire a private Learjet to fly her across the country to the Utah Salt Flats the previous night. She could only hope to arrive at the bunker ahead of Sal Belamo and his killers, yet knew that hope had nothing to do with it. Blaine McCracken had let her go, which meant he was giving her time. Why, she could not say. His code of honor was a constant enigma. She hated him for some parts of it, loved him for others. She supposed she couldn't blame him for what he had to do, but that didn't mean she couldn't try to save her father first.

She rented a helicopter at the airport where she had landed and asked the pilot to fly her over the flats, where she hastily reconstructed the bunker's location in her mind. She had trouble with her bearings, was almost ready to give up, in fact, when a narrow one-story building appeared out of nowhere.

"What the hell? . . ."

"This is where I get off," she told the pilot.

There should have been security. They should have been met along the perimeter and warned off. Patty feared that Belamo and his men had gotten here ahead of her after all, but that seemed impossible. No, something else was to blame, and she could not possibly say what.

A hefty bonus convinced the pilot to wait for her, and Patty entered the building through its single unlocked door. The inside was lined with counters and shelves, an outpost abandoned to the elements, complete with layers of dust. It took her a few minutes before she found the false door in the wall that led into a closetlike cubicle. It was dark and she fumbled for a light switch; a fluorescent came on and illuminated a simple control panel, a single arrow pointing up and another down.

Patty pressed the down one.

Instantly the elevator began its whirling descent. With speed impossible to judge, she had no way of telling how deeply she was descending into the bowels of the earth. Several seconds passed before the compartment ground to a halt and the single door slid open.

Before her was a long corridor, the white floors indistinguishable from the walls and ceiling of the same shade. The sudden brightness stung her eyes and it took them a few seconds to adjust. She started down the rounded hall with the *clip-clop* of her boot heels the only sound.

Where was everyone?

Perhaps the Children of the Black Rain had abandoned the bunker when the scope of their failure became known. It seemed logical. Return to the surface and disappear until another day dawned down the road in the future. After nearly a half century of waiting, surely the makers of the plan could wait a little longer. Video surveillance cameras dotted the hallway at regularly spaced intervals, but she could not tell if they were on or not.

Her heart was starting to sink. If her father wasn't here, she would never see him again. And, yet, if she did find him, she had no idea what she would say. He was still her father; whatever else he was made him no less than that. But she knew she wasn't doing this for him. She was doing it for herself. She had to know, had to understand, wanted to prove Blaine and the others wrong.

An open doorway beckoned her, the first she had seen so far. Stepping through it brought her into a sprawling meeting hall. A huge conference table was centered on the floor. One of the walls was dominated by a map of the United States showing a dozen glowing red lights. And set before that wall was a darkened figure facing her. Although the figure's face was cloaked in shadows and half-light, she could still see he was an Oriental. He sat there immobile and expressionless, as if waiting for her to approach.

Patty recalled Takahashi's story of how he was the only overseer of the Children of the Black Rain to survive the onslaught of an unknown militant in their midst. It was this militant who had so drastically changed the rules, opting to expand Japanese revenge into the deadly nuclear scenario. And she knew that this must be that man. He regarded her with inexplicable indifference as she approached him.

"Where's my father?" she demanded, fighting to sound strong and fearless. "Where's Phillip Hunsecker?"

The Japanese just stared at her. Patty stopped, then came closer.

"I want to see my father. I want to—"

Patty froze when she was close enough to see why the figure was so silent, so still.

The figure was an elaborate mannequin!

She had started to back dazedly away when a voice echoed through the hall's gaping expanse.

"I'm here, Patty."

And she turned to see a figure emerging from another section of the room into the light. The figure was her father.

"Eight minutes to critical stage. . . ."

Along the green, flourescent-lighted corridor directly above the Pennsylvania Yankee reactor complex, the temperature was already in excess of a hundred degrees. Sweat poured from Jack Tunnel's face as he helped Blaine fasten himself into the layered radiation suit.

"Gonna be close to a hundred and fifty at the bottom of the ladder—if you make it that far."

"I'll make it, all right."

"Temperature's rising a degree every five seconds—that's gonna increase as we get closer to critical stage. Even in the suit you can take maybe three minutes down there. Probably less."

"It's all I'll need."

"The valves are clearly marked. I'll stay up here and direct you to them."

"That ring on your finger tells me you've got a family, Jack. Might be a better idea for you to hightail it out like everyone else."

"And let you take all the credit for saving the greater Northeast? Not on your life, McCracken."

Back near the hatch that led onto the ladder, two volunteers from the control room had finished stuffing towels and padding into another radiation suit. They were tying the rope under the filled-out suit's arms when Blaine approached.

"Show time," McCracken said as he eased the makeshift dummy through the opening. "You boys better stand back and cover your ears."

And with that he began to lower the thing down, giving slack on the rope to match the pace of a man's descent down the ladder.

"Seven minutes to critical stage. . . ."

Just after the fifteenth rung, the firing began, the motion sensor having picked up the dummy's descent. Bullets ripped through its suit and stuffed innards and clanged off pipes and ladder rungs, ricocheting off walls in all directions. The metallic echoing burned Blaine's ears, and several times he flinched when bullets flew maddeningly close to the open hatch. Through it all, he continued to lower the dummy at a pace designed to draw continuous fire from the rifle Abraham had planted until its ammo was exhausted.

At last he heard a repetitive clicking sound that told him the firing pin was striking an empty chamber. McCracken let the dummy drop the rest of the way down the ladder and reached back for his helmet.

Jack Tunnel touched his arm. "With the coast clear, I can get the job done better than you, friend."

"Coast might not be clear, Jack. Might be more surprises waiting for anyone who goes down there. It's got to be me."

"Sounds like a song."

"Hopefully a happy one."

Tunnel tightened Blaine's helmet into its slot, but didn't clamp the faceplate down. "Look, if she goes to critical stage the rest of us will still be able to get out with limited contamination. But you, friend, are gonna get zapped by enough rads to make your skin glow."

"Get to save on my electric bills then, won't I?" Blaine said, flipping his faceplate down before disappearing into the rancid heat of the loop below.

"Six minutes to critical stage. . . ."

To Johnny Wareagle, this all had a shade of familiarity cast over it, as if he'd already been through it before. Perhaps he had. In the many dreams the spirits had sent to prepare him for his *Hanbelachia*, a battle with the greatest enemy he had ever faced, they had shown him all.

Abraham could have chosen anywhere along the motorcade's route to strike at the president, but Johnny knew the spirits would guide him in the right direction. Suddenly Wareagle gazed up at a nest of buildings squeezed claustrophobically against one another on Boylston Street, five blocks away from the Ritz Carlton. The entire city seemed to be choking on its own progress. The beginning structure of yet another skyscraper was piercing the sky where a parking lot had been just months before. Gazing that high up from ground level, there was nothing that could be seen clearly.

But Johnny didn't have to see. He felt a sudden chill pass through him. The high steelworkers were clustered on Boylston Street, where everyone was waiting for the motorcade to pass by. The steel skeleton was deserted.

Not quite.

Johnny could feel the presence quite clearly now, could feel it as clearly as if it were a yard away. It was something cold and vile, with a manitou as dark as the night itself. The stink of its spiritless soul reached him, assailing his senses.

The motorcade was coming.

Johnny jumped the fence enclosing the structure and rushed to one of the scaffold construction elevators.

"Stray Seven to Alley Cat! I've lost him! Goddammit, I've lost him!"

"Not again!" Arnold Triesman shouted, rushing down Boylston Street toward Stray Seven's last reported position. In the streets around him a number of agents were doing the same on his orders. A nag had suddenly hit Triesman's gut about this one. He probably should have ordered the motorcade back to the airport; it was in his power. But everything he had been taught advised against panic, and, if this proved to be a false alarm, he'd be finished.

"Wait a minute!" Stray Seven's voice echoed in his ear. "I think I just caught a glimpse of him!"

"What's the twenty?"

"Near the Commonwealth Insurance Building."

Right along the motorcade route, Triesman thought. But he couldn't reroute without taking the president into an unsecured area. And a slowdown or outright stoppage would subject Top Guy to more danger than letting him go on. The situation, in any case, was under control. They had their man sighted.

"Did he enter any building, Seven?"

"No way to be sure, Alley Cat."

"Get sure! Do you hear me? Get sure by the time I get over

there!'' Triesman switched his communicator to all bands. ''All Stray teams, converge on the area of the Commonwealth Insurance Building shell. Choppers, do you copy that?''

''Roger,'' the three pilots replied in virtual unison.

''All buildings considered compromised. Let's move! *Everyone* move!''

''Dad?'' Patty asked tentatively, tremors rising through her stomach and chest.

''I'm sorry,'' Phillip Hunsecker said.

''You should be,'' Patty blurted out.

''Not for what I've done. Sorry that you came here. You should leave.''

''Not unless you leave with me.''

He kept approaching, shaking his head. ''I can't do that.''

Patty's eyes flicked about the room. ''This is more important to you than your family, your life?''

''This is my family, my life. Always has been.''

The man who had come to a halt a yard from her did not look like her father. Oh, it was him all right, but she barely recognized him. Part of her had envisioned herself running into his arms; now those arms might as well have been a stranger's. Patty shivered.

''I can get you out of this,'' she made herself say. ''McCracken will help me. He can fix things.''

''It's too late for that, Patty.''

''It's never too late.''

''This time it is. We've failed. Our identities are known. Our plan is known. For our honor to be preserved, we must disappear, become the past.''

''What are you saying?''

Patty heard a second set of steps behind her just before the voice reached her.

''She must leave, Pierce. She must leave now.''

Patty turned and watched as a second figure emerged from the shadows in the front of the room, stopping next to the Japanese mannequin. It was a woman's figure, a woman she had known almost all her life and loved like a mother: Shimada!

* * *

McCracken felt the incredible heat building in the loop as soon as he began his descent. Even through his radiation suit, his skin seemed to be burning. Sweat ran from his forehead into his eyes, steam misting across his faceplate. He had spent his share of time in steam rooms, and that was the only comparison that came to mind—a steam room still pumping heat long after the cycle should have ended.

Blaine passed the fifteenth rung, his breathing labored. He had considered the possibility that Abraham had set up a second firing apparatus to thwart precisely the strategy he had employed. At this point, though, dying from a bullet seemed preferable to radiation poisoning or being boiled alive, both of which were equally real possibilities.

"Can you hear me, Blaine?" came the garbled voice of Jack Tunnel.

McCracken adjusted the communicator built into his helmet. "Loud. Not so clear."

"Okay. If you look down, you'll see you're coming to the first catwalk. You don't want that one or the next one. It's the third one you've got to reach."

"How much time?"

"Just over five minutes now."

Blaine quickened his descent. The rungs of the ladder passed swiftly, his drop falling into a symphonic rhythm of hands and feet moving together. The second catwalk was gone before he knew it, then the third was upon him. He stepped off from the ladder and onto the catwalk.

"Okay, Jack. I'm on it."

"You should be able to see the water gushing out . . . thirty yards down on the right."

"Yup, there it is."

"The valve you've got to close is above the pipe, say about eye level."

McCracken started for it. He took each step on the thin catwalk cautiously, wondering if Abraham had left more surprises for anyone who managed to get this far. The water rushing out of the burst pipe was superheated now, boiling hot and getting hotter. Approaching it, Blaine realized his flesh seemed to be baking. He was breathing hard and the sweat continued pouring into his eyes from his brow. He felt light-headed and wanted desperately to have something to catch hold of, but nothing was available. He reached the blown valve, choosing his steps carefully to avoid the plume of steam he could already feel through his radiation suit.

"I'm at the valve, Jack," he said when he was behind the steam's flow. The valve was circular, six inches in diameter, colored in the same almond shade as the rest of the pipes and valves in this section.

"Reach up and turn it to the left, counterclockwise. Your gloves will insulate you from the heat briefly, but when your fingers start to burn, pull your hands off and let them cool."

"Hey, this isn't a pie we're talking about here!"

"Just go to work. Four and a half minutes left now."

Blaine ran his fingers cautiously around the circumference of the valve. Along its squat neck, he felt a small attachment no bigger than a matchbox. Abraham's final precaution would have done the job just fine if the man who had come down here hadn't known what to look and feel for. Blaine closed his fingers on the small but potent charge and pried it away.

"Son of a bitch," he said, letting it drop harmlessly to the catwalk and returning his attention to the valve.

"My hands feel hot already, Jack," he said an instant after his gloved fingers tightened around it. "God, this thing's tight!"

"Is it moving? If it's been jammed we'll have to go to a backup."

"I can get it. . . . There, it's starting to go now. . . ."

McCracken twisted with all his strength. Progress came slowly. Finally he detected a marked slowing in the water sprouting from the pipe. When at last the valve was turned tight against the other side, it slowed to a trickle.

"That's it, Jack."

"Halfway there, Blaine. All we gotta do now is reroute the cooling water by opening up a backup valve and bringing it back into the central core. You've got to go down to the next catwalk."

"Four minutes to critical stage. . . ."

"That bitch has been known to be wrong before," said

Tunnel, venting his tension on the mechanical female voice that sounded through the core area.

"How many times?"

"Twice in simulations."

"I'm back at the ladder, Jack, and going down."

"Okay. The valve you've got to open is in the same spot as the other, just along the next catwalk. How you holding up?"

"Dizzy. I can't catch my breath."

"No wonder. The temperature down there just topped the hundred-and-fifty-degree mark."

"And I'm not even getting a tan to show for it."

Blaine reached the fourth sublevel catwalk; the piping was colored blue instead of white. He proceeded down it as quickly as he could through the intense heat and located the valve just where Tunnel said it would be.

"I'm here," he said.

"Okay, Blaine. This one you want to turn to the right. You've got to open it all the way or there won't be enough pressure to cool the reactor in time."

"Just how much time is that?"

"Thirty seconds to a minute—or we go to the critical stage."

"That means we've only got something over two left."

"Turn the valve now and you'll have time to spare."

Blaine reached up for it, his hands burning with the intensity of fire. "It won't give, Jack."

"Ease off a little. No pressure inward. Just twist."

"That's what I'm doing," Blaine said, the strain of exertion telling in his voice. "It feels like somebody's—"

He felt it all go at once and realized the valve had come off in his hand.

"Jack, I think I've got a problem down here. . . ."

CHAPTER 36

THROUGH his binoculars, Abraham could see the motorcade edging down Boylston Street. A pair of motorcycle cops, sirens screaming, led the way. There were three more squad cars both in front and in back of the president's limo. The helicopters were hovering above the steel structure of the building where he was hidden, but they couldn't possibly spot him. Two to three minutes more and the limo would have reached the stripe lined with his deadly explosives. Abraham felt no excitement, only anticipation.

He had started to reach into his pocket for the detonator when he felt the hairs on the back of his neck rise. Something alerted his senses enough to make him swing. He never actually heard the elevator coming, but as soon as he turned he saw the steel coil sliding through the pulleys, unaccompanied by any engine sounds.

Someone was coming up!

Abraham only distantly registered that whoever it was had taken precautions so he wouldn't be heard. He sprinted across the steel skeleton of the building, strides bringing him from one girder to another. He already knew who it was, did not have to see the big Indian he had glimpsed across rooftops in Philadelphia to know that their fated meeting was about to take place.

He reached the edge of the skeleton just as the exposed elevator had cleared the floor immediately beneath his. He gazed down and locked stares with the Indian once again. Still staring into the Indian's eyes, Abraham grabbed hold of the cable pulley. The Indian was barely a floor from him when Abraham tore the steel cable from the left slot harnessing it, instantly sending the elevator platform careening downward.

Wareagle had stopped the elevator two floors down. The automated pulley system shut down, he had hoisted himself up the rest of the way manually to keep Abraham from hearing his approach. He had watched helplessly as the *Wakinyan* yanked the steel cable free of the pulley on the platform's left side and lunged to grab hold of it at the last moment to keep from falling himself.

The move met his expectations. The results exceeded them.

The burden of the platform's entire weight forced the attached right cable into a grinding downward slide, the momentum of which drove the loosened left cable straight upward. Johnny felt himself launched like a rocket and drew his legs inward. As soon as Abraham's frame flashed before him, he kicked out, throwing himself forward through the air. The move carried him over the edge and head-on into Abraham.

Impact between the two giants was stunning. Equally stunning was the fact that both gave only slightly. Abraham grabbed hold of a support beam to steady himself; Wareagle lowered himself to a crouch to lock home his balance. Then he rose to the full breadth of his seven feet and squared off against his foe. Johnny knew a gun might have finished the job quicker, but a gun was not a weapon his ancestors knew; if they were to help him here today, he would have to fight on terms they would understand. Against Abraham, he'd choose his ancestors over a clip of shells any day.

The steel girders that created a checkerboard effect of open air fifty stories high severely limited mobility. They were on the same girder briefly; then Wareagle leaped to the adjacent one and faced Abraham on a diagonal. Abraham's eyes darted sideways and he leapfrogged away from Johnny. At first it looked as if he were retreating, but then he stooped to pick up a six foot steel rod used to fasten the girders together.

He had barely grasped it when he was airborne again, this time skipping a girder entirely and landing on the one next to

Wareagle's, the rod already coming overhead. Wareagle dodged the blow and lashed out with a dangerous kick for Abraham's left wrist. But the *Wakinyan* let go of the steel rod with his left hand, so Johnny's foot struck only steel. Abraham took advantage of the moment by swinging the rod sideways, aiming for Johnny's planted leg, but the big Indian jumped deftly into the air, the rod passing harmlessly beneath him.

Abraham kept the heavy steel's momentum going in the same direction by rerouting its force into a baseball-like swing directed higher, for the ribs. Wareagle ducked under this blow and jumped backward, to the next girder, as yet another swing whistled for him. The *Wakinyan* came after him, but Johnny's eyes had spotted a stray piece of chain generally used to fasten the girders together. He gambled and dipped to grasp it; the gamble paid off when he managed to bring the chain upward in time to deflect the blow.

Abraham went for a straight thrust with the steel rod next, reaching across the open space separating the girders. Johnny whipped the chain in a downward snapping motion and forced it aside. Abraham came around fast for another overhead blow, and this Wareagle blocked by stretching the upraised chain taut between his hands. The *Wakinyan* responded by switching his strike to an uppercut, but again Johnny was equal to the task. He used the chain to parry the thrust, then forced the steel rod downward. This latest strike left the right side of Abraham's head exposed, and Johnny used the opening to lash his chain against the *Wakinyan's* face.

The blow mashed Abraham's flesh. He grunted in pain as blood spurted upward, some spraying into his right eye. He sensed the next blow coming in time to snap his steel rod upward, in a diagonal line in front of him. The chain clanged home, and Abraham used the higher end of the rod to jab at the Indian's ribs. He felt a bone crack under the blow and brought the rod around for what should have been a killing strike to the head.

Instead, Johnny locked his hands on the steel bar that the *Wakinyan* controlled. Using it as a pivot point, he hurdled across the space between girders and joined Abraham on his. They grappled, each trying to shove the other over the edge with brute force, neither about to relinquish their hold on the rod. But Johnny still held on to the chain with two fingers, a fact that was clear to him, though not necessarily Abraham. The next time the *Wakinyan* thrust forward against the steel they jointly held, Johnny let him complete the move, ducking down and coming up behind him. Before Abraham could respond, Johnny had wrapped the chain around his throat from the rear. He pulled his hands across each other, fighting against the incredible strength of the *Wakinyan's* neck muscles.

Abraham pummeled Johnny's broken rib with a series of elbow blows. The Indian winced and bit his lip, but did not release his death grip. Abraham flailed desperately with the steel rod, his blows finding nothing. His eyes dipped downward and saw Johnny's boot next to his shoe. With the last effort of strength he could manage, the *Wakinyan* slammed the rod down toward the boot, then let go of it.

Johnny howled in agony at the impact. His grip on the chain slackened enough for Abraham to pry his hands up between his flesh and the chain. He yanked powerfully and dipped his shoulder at the same time. Wareagle flew up and over him, coming down hard enough to shake the steel girder they shared. They both had hold of the chain now, and the *Wakinyan* leaned over to yank it from Johnny's hand. Wareagle's response was to launch a kick behind him that caught Abraham square in the chin. He reeled backward and slammed against a steel support beam.

Johnny turned around and tried to get up again. By the time he had started to rise, though, the steel rod was back in Abraham's hands and whipping around. The blow caught Wareagle in the hip and buttocks and pitched him sideways off the girder. The force of the blow was potent enough to drive Johnny all the way to the next girder over; he managed to grab a desperate hold of the steel rim, saving himself from falling all the way down. Abraham leaped on the girder after him and began slamming the rod down in the direction of the Indian's hands. Johnny jammed his fingers into a precariously small groove cut in the girder and began to shimmy across it.

"Ahhhhhhhhhhhhhhhh!"

Abraham's blows were preceded by wails now, as Johnny swayed back and forth fifty stories up. He had only one chance left. Abraham had dropped to his knees, one hand holding the girder for support while he used the other to lash Johnny with the steel rod. Wareagle let go with his right hand and relied only on his left to hold him there dangling, while his right slid into his belt and withdrew the hunting knife that had been passed down through his family for generations. It was bulky and poorly weighted compared to the Gerber MKII he was used to, but it had worked for his ancestors, and that was good enough for him. The palm Abraham was using to support himself was visible through a slight crack in the girder, and Johnny jammed the blade upward.

Abraham's wail turned into a scream of utter agony as the blade cut all the way through his palm and hand and emerged coated with blood and gristle. The incredible force of the blow had actually wedged the sides of the knife into the steel of the girder. Abraham yanked his mutilated hand up off the blade with a cry that bubbled in Johnny's ears and heaved himself backward.

Wareagle seized the moment to swing himself back up on the girder. When he regained it, ready to spring, Abraham, leaning uneasily against a support beam, grasped something black in his hand.

"You've failed," the *Wakinyan* said calmly, the presidential motorcade moving ever closer to his mark. "You've failed."

Johnny froze. He could see that Abraham was holding a detonator in his hand, and that if he lunged for him it would activate. The *Wakinyan* was smiling, his eyes on the approaching motorcade.

Johnny stood there helpless. What was the *Wakinyan* waiting for? Why wasn't he pushing the button?

The motorcade snailed a little closer.

Of course! Johnny realized. *Of course!*

Suddenly, as if somehow reading the Indian's thoughts, the president's limousine took off. It shot forward, police cars suddenly rushing up alongside it.

"No!" Abraham screeched. "Noooooooooooo!"

And with Wareagle halfway into his lunge, the *Wakinyan* pressed the detonator's button.

* * *

"I've got them, Alley Cat!" one of the choppers had reported seconds before. "High steel building. Three floors from the top."

"What do you mean *them*?" Triesman demanded.

"Two guys, big as houses. Looks like they're fighting, Alley Cat."

"What? Say that again."

"I said they're fighting."

"Do you have a clear shot?"

The pilot checked again with his on-board marksman. "Negative, Alley Cat. We've got open air between us and the next office building if we miss."

"I'll take the responsibility."

"This is Boston, sir. It's my call."

"Dammit!" Triesman yelled, and pressed the button linking him to all his men in the field. "This is an evac order. Let's get Top Guy the hell out of here!"

Triesman was already into a sprint, heading toward the high steel shell the limo had been passing in front of, when the explosion came. The force of it staggered him; his ears filled with a terrible ringing. His vision never betrayed him, but all he could see was a gray-black cloud of rubble encompassing the entire street before him.

"Top Guy, come in! Top Guy, do you read me?"

When no response came, Triesman ran still faster.

"Okay," Jack Tunnel said, "I've got one."

"How much time have I got?"

"Under a minute before the core gets too hot for the cooling mechanism to touch it at all." Blaine heard Tunnel take in a thick gush of air. "But if she goes critical, you'll never get out in time, no matter what."

"Last thing on my mind right now."

What was first on McCracken's mind was the pliers Jack Tunnel was dangling seventy feet above him in the open shaft. Because Abraham had taken steps to sabotage the second valve, the only chance he had now of rerouting the cooling water through the backup pipe was to open the line with pliers. Tough work under the best of conditions, and these were anything but.

"Okay," Blaine said when he reached the ladder directly beneath the open hatch. "Can you see me?"

"Just barely."

"Well, I can't see you at all. I'm gonna have to take my helmet off."

"It's approaching a hundred and seventy-five degrees on your level."

"Call it a free face peel. Might take years off my life. When I give you the word, count to ten and then drop the pliers down. I catch them, we got a shot. I don't, get the fuck outta here." McCracken unhinged the locks on his helmet and made sure it was ready to come free. "Okay," he told Tunnel. "Start counting."

He had the helmet placed beneath him and was gazing upward by the count of four. The heat tore into his face and burned his eyeballs. He wanted so damn much to close his eyes, to stop the pain, but he didn't. And then they started filling with tears, blurring his vision. Dammit! How was he going to catch the damn pliers?

Blaine risked a second and dabbed them with the sleeve of his radiation suit. When he looked up again, a silver blur was dropping toward him.

Too fast to catch, he had time to think. *Too fast to catch.* . . .

McCracken managed to get his chest under the falling pliers, but it was a wasted motion. He caught them in his gloves with the dexterity of an all-pro receiver and stooped to retrieve his helmet. He jammed it gratefully over his head again, locking it down as he rushed back toward the bolt the valve had broken away from.

"You hear me, Jack?"

"Barely."

"Nice toss. I'm back to the spot. What's the time?"

"Forty seconds till we pass the point of no return. Another forty or so to get back up here. If she goes to critical stage, getting back up won't matter."

Blaine had trouble gripping the pliers through his gloves and pulled them off. The wet heat of the secondary loop complex burned into his hands, but his improved hold on the pliers made it worth it. The bolt began to turn.

"She's moving, Jack."

"Hurry!"

McCracken kept twisting. His eyes followed the bolt's grad-ual clockwise turn through his faceplate. His fingers were on fire, total agony encompassing them. He could feel his flesh puckering, the top layer starting to blister. Still he worked the pliers as the last seconds ticked away, worked them until the bolt would turn no more.

"That's it," he told Jack Tunnel.

The pipe near him vibrated ever so slightly as the powerful jets of water found their way into it, charging through. Mc-Cracken shoved his gloves back on and rushed down the cat-walk toward the ladder. His hands were so swollen that he could barely squeeze them over his fingers.

"One minute to critical stage. . . . "

"What the fuck, Jack?"

"I told you, the process doesn't work instantaneously. That water's got plenty to cool. Just get your ass up here!"

McCracken reached the ladder and began to climb. The rungs themselves were boiling now. Bubbles of steam rose off them, and he could feel the intensity of the heat even through his gloves. It was like climbing out of a furnace, the conditions made all the worse by his already damaged fingers. They were raw now, and he had trouble closing them around the rungs to supply him the rapid lift he needed. The agony deepened by the instant, making it impossible to place him-self beyond it.

"Come on, Blaine. You've got it!" Jack Tunnel said. "Get your ass the fuck up here!"

Blaine gazed up at the hatch through his faceplate and tried to smile. The additional two catwalks had been left behind, leaving him barely another fifteen rungs to scale. Unless the cooling water was too late to stop the core from melting down, he was going to make it.

And then the eighth rung from the top gave way under his grasp. McCracken wasn't sure whether it had melted from its casing or simply snapped. Whatever the case, he felt himself falling, falling into a superheated hellhole from which there could be no return.

* * *

The explosion shook the steel structure. Johnny felt himself totter on the edge and grabbed for the nearest support beam for balance. Abraham was wavering badly, the girder becoming a tightrope for him. Wareagle seized the opportunity to lunge out sideways with both legs leading, holding fast to the beam as he did. The heavy blow connected with Abraham's side and staggered him further. The *Wakinyan* twisted to grab Johnny's legs, but Wareagle kicked out again and then locked Abraham's neck in between the knees.

Abraham managed to tear free of the grasp, his momentum forcing him forward. Johnny kicked back at him in the same direction, and the blow caught the *Wakinyan* square in the head and pitched him over.

He headed straight for the huge hunting blade, which still protruded bloodily through the slat in the girder.

Abraham's scream was awful as his midsection was impaled upon the knife. He spasmed and writhed there as Johnny leaped two girders over, closer to the street side and the hovering helicopter, to gaze downward.

A huge irregular crater lay where a large portion of the street had been just seconds before. Bodies lay everywhere, some moving, some not. Sirens wailed. Johnny's eyes searched for and found the president's limousine. Rubble had compressed much of its top and carved huge dents in as many places as not. It had escaped the major brunt of the blast, though, and Johnny could tell from the congestion of Secret Service agents around its perimeter that the president was safe inside.

Johnny might have let himself feel triumphant if the scent of blood hadn't burned into his nostrils. It caused him to swing around even before he heard the wheezing sound Abraham made as he regained his feet on the nearby girder, his insides spilling out. The warning gave Wareagle the instant he needed to grasp the steel support rod that was now beneath him and swing it around, trying to knock the raging *Wakinyan* aside.

Abraham's lunge had brought him too close to Johnny for the Indian to reach him with a sweeping blow, so he changed the motion to a savage jab. The collective force drove the heavy steel through the *Wakinyan's* already gaping wound, shredding more flesh and bones before emerging through Abraham's back. His wail became a gurgle. Johnny let go of the rod and shrank back from the bitter stink of blood and oozing innards.

Abraham dropped downward off the girder, the steel rod looking like a spike driven through his body. The rod caught on a pair of neighboring girders, halting his fall and driving the steel straight up against his sternum. His feet twitched and spasmed and Johnny watched death take him at last.

The Indian heard the approach of another elevator coming up from the building's rear and took one last look at the glaze-eyed Abraham.

"We're up!" announced the head of the Secret Service unit that poured tentatively onto the high steel girders.

"Shoot to kill!" ordered Arnold Triesman from his position next to the battered limousine, a deep ringing still cursing his ears.

"Nothing to shoot at," the team leader replied after a pause.

"What?"

"I got one target already big-time dead and nothing else."

"Say again?"

"No Indian, Alley Cat. He gave us the slip again."

McCracken saw the rope at the beginning of his drop. By the time he could grasp it, he was already even with what remained of the shot-to-hell dummy that had preceded him down the shaft.

"Blaine!" he heard Tunnel yell through the communicator in his helmet.

McCracken felt his shoulders strain and pull from the sudden pressure. His neck snapped backward in whiplash effect. He slammed forward and struck the ladder with enough force to jiggle it and crack his faceplate. But he had managed to hold fast to the rope supporting the radiation suit that was leaking stuffing through the dozens of bullet holes pierced through it.

"Hold on, you son of a bitch!" Tunnel shouted.

"Get the fuck out of here!"

"Not until we pull you up. We fry, friend, we fry together."

McCracken felt himself being hoisted upward, powerless now to help in the slightest. All he could do was keep squeezing the rope that had become his lifeline. The rungs of the ladder passed by him in slow, surreal fashion, in an almost dreamlike way. And a dream it might well have been, based on the words that reached him as he came within a grasp of the hatch:

"Critical stage warning is canceled. Critical stage warning is canceled."

Patty gawked disbelievingly at Shimada, the loving Hunsecker house servant for twenty years. "You're the leader! You're the one Takahashi couldn't identify!"

Shimada stared around her. "My legacy to inherit and now to lose, *Hana-shan.*"

"Don't call me that. Don't ever call me that."

"It is what you still are, just as I am what I have always been."

Patty gazed back briefly at the front of the conference room. "You spoke through that mannequin so no one would know it was you."

"Traditionally, women are not highly regarded in our culture. Accordingly, the illusion was necessary."

"Dad—"

"You've got to leave, Patty," Phillip Hunsecker interrupted.

"Not without you."

He shook his head serenely. "No."

"The boys! Think of the boys!"

"I am." He looked toward Shimada. "That's why we're letting you leave. You must go. Your friends are drawing closer."

"They're not my friends! I came alone! For you!"

"Would you have joined us, Patty? Is that what you came for?"

"I . . . don't know."

"Our vision was pure, direct. No one will ever understand."

"You were going to destroy the country, murder millions!"

Shimada stepped forward. "The deaths would occur, yes, because fitting revenge could be achieved only by reducing America's great cities to what Nagasaki and Hiroshima had been reduced to. But enough of America would have been left to serve as foundation for a new America, *Hana-shan.* Our America . . . *Japan's* America. A new society would have been chartered, rebuilt, and controlled by us. A new and different order that would look to the Rising Sun for direction.''

"Madness!"

"Truth, Patty," said her father. "We were placed here for a purpose, and now that purpose has failed. Our lives were dedicated to the secrecy of our existence. Without that secrecy we cannot live."

"Stop it!"

Shimada drew close enough to touch her but didn't. "The decisions are irreversible now. Our fate was chosen for us long ago. Leave now or you join us in it."

"For the boys," her father said. "You're all they've got."

"No!" Patty wailed. "There's got to be another answer!"

Shimada and her father backed away, toward the mannequin. She made no motion to follow.

"Please," she pleaded.

"Go, Patty," her father said just before the shadows swallowed him. "This is your last chance."

Patty turned and ran, heart thundering in her chest, eyes clouded with tears. She lost her bearings briefly, then recovered them, finding her way back to the elevator that had brought her down.

The elevator her father had left operational for her, she realized now.

Her tears spilled over and ran down her cheeks as the compartment hurtled upward. Her body felt heavy and used up. When the elevator stopped, she had to drag herself out into the shell of the cover building.

Outside, a rumbling in the ground underfoot shook her senses alert. She bolted into a run toward her waiting helicopter, realizing it had been joined by several others, all packed with armed men.

Patty spotted Sal Belamo standing twenty yards in front of his eager troops, rifle slung over his shoulder. As she ran into his arms, another rumble shook the ground. A blast followed, muffled by the blanket of covering earth. She turned back long enough to see the wooden shack crumble into the ground that had become a mass grave for the Children of the Black Rain.

EPILOGUE

"**W**HY did they do it?" Patty asked Blaine as she sat by his hospital bed.

"Honor," he replied. "They were following the samurai code. That was what this whole mission was about—and once they failed, there was only one recourse."

"They could have waited, could have tried again another time."

Blaine shook his head. "Samurai thinking doesn't work that way."

"It makes no sense." She sighed. "They're willing to wait almost fifty years for revenge, but not try it a second time."

Blaine propped himself up as best he could. His hands were wrapped in thick bandages, and his face and neck looked as if he had a severe sunburn.

"You're talking about a society that has never been able to grasp the 'live to fight another day' credo," he explained. "Plenty of our POWs learned that the hard way in the war. Maybe this is poetic justice, or karma. The Children of the Black Rain got fucked by the very principles that led us to drop the bombs in the first place."

"They didn't miss by much. If those nuclear plants had gone up, the country could only have rebuilt itself by depending on the Japanese-owned stockpiles the Children controlled."

Blaine smiled. "Sound familiar?"

"My God," Patty realized. "Japan in the aftermath of World War Two."

"Yup, except with the roles reversed. Again, they didn't heed their own lessons. They rebuild our world and sometime down the road everything's set right again, maybe even more so."

Patty suddenly looked sad. "Not for everyone."

"How are your brothers?"

"I . . . haven't told them yet."

"Want me there when you do?"

"That depends."

"On what?"

"Whether you plan on staying."

"I didn't think that was your style."

"Well, things change."

"I don't."

"Is that a warning?"

"Just an assurance, kid. You know me well enough to count on that much."

"Better than ever," Patty acknowledged. "I never really understood you until I faced my father in that bunker. That someone I loved could have fooled me that much . . ." Her eyes gazed into his knowingly. "It's why you exist alone, isn't it? It's why the only people you let into your life are the same as you. Like Johnny and Sal."

"And you, Hunsecker?"

"Before—no. Now, yeah, I think so."

"Uh-uh."

"What?"

"I said no, kid. I can never remember being anything but the way I am now. If you can remember something different, then forget it. You'll slip back. My world's a dark one, where it's okay to hide for a while. As soon as you start feeling for the light switch, it's time to go."

"I won't."

"You *will*. We are what we are, Hunsecker, and it's crazy to try to pretend otherwise."

Tears filled Patty's eyes. "So—so what do I do?"

"You go back to your brothers. Maybe you take them out on the ocean for a while. That's *your* world—the best place for you to make them understand and accept. Then you ease them back into theirs.''

"Like you've done for me . . .''

He looked at her proudly. "You're learning, Hunsecker.''

"I had a good teacher.''

"You look restless, Blainey,'' Wareagle told him two days later.

"The doctors won't even let me go outside until I heal up. I miss the sun.''

"There are other places to seek light than beyond the window. Look inside yourself.''

"Plenty of blown bulbs.''

"And plenty that aren't. New ones burn as old ones are extinguished.''

"Your vision is better than mine, Indian.''

"Because I know the right places to look. Your focus is elsewhere.''

McCracken held Wareagle's stare for a long moment. "We didn't get all the *Wakinyan*, did we, Indian?''

"We killed all of those whose inward view finds only the dark.''

"Which we were able to do because we're no different than they are. Better maybe, but not different.''

Johnny's stare grew reflective. "In the old ways of my people, Blainey, a young warrior must drink the blood of his first kill. My first kill was a wolf that attacked our livestock. But I was not allowed to drink its blood because the blackness of its murderous heart was not worthy to taste. Its death gave nothing to the world because it had nothing to give.'' Wareagle's huge hand touched McCracken's shoulder. "That is the difference, Blainey.''

"Why do we do it, Indian?''

"Hanbelachia.''

"But now that Abraham's history, you've finally passed yours.''

"No. I was wrong, Blainey. The vision quest is not one event, but a continuous series. We keep growing and changing. And each phase we pass into requires its own *Hanbelachia*. The shaman had tried to tell me as much when I was a boy, but I did not realize the truth until my slaying of Abraham left me feeling no different than killing the wolf had. A means to something that has no end.''

''So we keep going.''

Wareagle moved to the window and turned opened the slats on the venetian blind. The sun streamed through and made McCracken raise a hand in front of his face. Wareagle adjusted the slats so the light aimed harmlessly downward.

''The light can be controlled, but not the sun that brings it, Blainey.''

McCracken smiled. ''That says it all, doesn't it?''

''It says enough.''

''No more Omicron legions, Indian. We've got to make sure of that.''

''Before your flesh feels the sun again, Blainey.''

The explosions occurred over the next two days, a dozen in all. They created no publicity and were felt only as tremors deep in the earth's underbelly by the few bystanders who strayed too close. Nature would cover any signs before long, the secret bunkers entombed by rubble and the final fall of the Black Rain lost forever.

About the Author

Jon Land is the author of *The Doomsday Spiral*, *The Lucifer Directive*, *Vortex*, *Labyrinth*, *The Omega Command*, *The Council of Ten*, *The Alpha Deception*, *The Eighth Trumpet*, *The Gamma Option*, and *The Valhalla Testament*. He is thirty-four years old and lives in Providence, Rhode Island, where he is currently at work on *The Ninth Dominion*, a sequel to his bestselling *The Eighth Trumpet*. It will be published in early 1992.

JON LAND

**Look for these Fawcett paperbacks
in your local bookstore.**

To order by phone, call 1-800-733-3000 and use your
major credit card. To expedite your order please mention
interest code LM-7. Or use this coupon to order by mail.